THE SKI JUMPERS

THE SKI JUMPERS

A NOVEL

PETER GEYE

University of Minnesota Press

MINNEAPOLIS

Published by the University of Minnesota Press
111 Third Avenue South, Suite 290
Minneapolis, MN 55401-2520
http://www.upress.umn.edu

ISBN 978-1-5179-1349-6 (hc)
ISBN 978-1-5179-1350-2 (pb)

LC record available at https://lccn.loc.gov/2022015169

Printed in the United States of America on acid-free paper

The University of Minnesota is an equal-opportunity educator and employer.

30 29 28 27 26 25 24 23 22   10 9 8 7 6 5 4 3 2 1

For my brother, the best ski jumper I've ever known

&

Pops, who gave us those winter days

&

Emily, whose love is like an endless flight

Contents

I

Dream, Memory,
the Thing Itself

E VEN NOW, almost four decades since your last jump, you're
ecstatic in flight. The memory is as indelible in your mind as it is
in your old and softening body, which still, all these years later, will
tremor you from sleep and dreams and go taut as though into the
cold winter air above some steep, snow-covered landing hill. There
in bed, under the soft down, you cock your ankles and lift your chin
and rudder your hands as you close your eyes and pull back into the
dream. And though of course there's no rush of air, no danger, the
thrill remains. So does the peace.

And it's into that peace you alight. Most mornings you'll coax a
minute or two in the air. First, you find the hollowing sensation that
comes with the leap itself. It was then, as it remains now, the surest sign of a good jump. You're lighter. You're empty of inhibitions.
And it compels you forward, your hips following the emptiness and
grace. A twitch of one shoulder, then the other, as you accelerate, as
the world simplifies. Just you and the air and the landing hill below.
There's no concentrating now. Only divination. Only weightlessness
and yearning, and, for as fast as it always happened, timelessness.

3

The *stall,* your Pops called it. That moment when you reached the perfect position, when control and calmness met and the speed vanished and you were no longer flying but only suspended there. Almost inanimate. Like a bird on a gyre. The moment of reckoning. If the air was friendly, if you'd executed your jump properly, if you'd aligned yourself well, then you pulled and pressed and cajoled. Not consciously, but by reflex and instinct.

If you were lucky, the second act of flight was exultant. It was easiness, even as you accelerated, shredding the atmosphere and racing back to consciousness and the Earth. It was your reward. Then your wings unfolded slowly, and slowly you breathed again. Your Pops always said that landing was like shattering glass, but for all you learned from him, for all you believed in him, this was not your experience. Landing, for you, was an insult. And even now, in your warm bed forty miles and forty years from any ski jump, it remains so. You open your eyes to the dark. You reach behind to touch your wife's hand. Ingrid's hand. But she's not there and you roll over and not only is the sweetness of the memory gone but so is she. The house is alive. She's beaten you awake. She's in the kitchen.

You swing your legs out from under the covers. You put them on the ground. You have landed on another day. Dream, memory, the thing itself? What's the difference? You had your dose of rapture, and now it's time to be him again. Me again.

My eyes are gaining on the dark. I hear Ingrid running water to fill the coffee maker. I hear the cabinet door creak and the rattle of a spoon being lifted from the cutlery drawer. The clock on the bedside table tells me it's five minutes after five o'clock.

I walk out into the hallway and follow the path of light to the kitchen sink and put my arms around Ingrid and settle into her backside, looking at us in the reflection of the window. She doesn't say anything. She appears about to cry.

"You're up too early, sweetheart," I say.

"I couldn't sleep."

I nod, and kiss her cheek and close my eyes and decide on another short detour from waking all the way. I hold her. We warm.

"How many mornings have I hugged you like this?" I say.

She doesn't answer, but I can feel her loosening. As quick as I can, I do the math.

"Ten thousand, it must be. More even. Fifteen?"

"And each one as sweet as the first," she says, the look of sadness blanching her face in the window again.

I turn her around in my arms. "We've plenty of these mornings left."

Now she nods, and kisses my cheek, then feigns one of her sweet smiles. These gestures we echo? They're the work of a thirty-five-year marriage.

"Let me finish the coffee," I say.

"Nonsense. I haven't made the coffee in I can't even remember how long. Here," and she takes my elbow and urges me toward the kitchen table. She turns on the lamp hanging above the fruit bowl. She even pulls out a chair, as though I were feeble.

"What else do you want for breakfast?" She's already back at the counter and spooning the grounds into the filter. "Oatmeal, toast?"

"Just coffee, love."

"You've got to eat something."

"I will. But not yet."

She presses the button to brew the coffee and returns to the table, but before she sits down she raises a finger and hurries into the mudroom off the kitchen and is back before she's even left. She has a bag from the bookstore in her hand and she gives it to me and says, "I stopped at Zenith yesterday while you were resting." She nods at the bag.

Inside are three of the notebooks I favor.

"Oh, Ingrid—"

"You stop that. You heard what Doctor Zheng said yesterday."

"That I should take up a foreign language."

"She suggested that merely as one option," she says.

I resist the impulse to admit that I'm already sometimes unable to conjure words or phrases in my own language, and instead take out one of the notebooks and peel the cellophane wrapper off.

"You should be working, Jon. Now there will be more than one benefit. You'll be tolerable *and* you'll be taking care of yourself." She lifts my hand and kisses it, then holds it for a long moment. When she sets it down, she rises and goes to the counter and pours two cups full, adds a dram of cream to each, stirs them, and brings them back to the table.

"Is it still okay to tease you?" she asks, sitting back down.

"I'd never take that away from you."

"Thank goodness," she says, and takes a sip of her coffee. "And you still want to go up to see Clara this weekend?"

"Of course."

"She's looking forward to the company."

Our younger daughter and her wife live in Gunflint now. They're artists—Clara a potter and Delia a painter—and they bought a small house just off the Burnt Wood Trail. In winter, the lake view through the bare aspen and birch surrounding them settles below in black and white layers, depending on the ice and snow. They both work multiple jobs. Clara at Hivernants Brewing, where she tends bar on weekends, and at the ski area in Misquah, where she's on the sales and marketing team. Delia works for the arts colony and at the Burnt Wood Tavern. They're happy and young and Clara describes their five-year plan as one long working honeymoon in the most beautiful place on earth.

"Clara has a surprise for you."

"Is that right?"

"Yep." She takes my hand and kisses it again. "What time should we leave?"

I look at my watch. Habit more than necessity. I can tell what time it is the way I imagine owls can. And anyway, it doesn't matter what time it is. "I had a thought to call Noah and see if we can stop by the lake." Noah Torr is my best and oldest friend.

"Wouldn't that be nice? Are you wanting to talk to him about yesterday?"

I rearrange the notebooks one, two, three across the kitchen table. "I don't know, but I've been waking up in those ski jumping dreams again. He tells me he has a trove of memorabilia I ought to see."

"Memorabilia?"

"Ski jumping stuff. Photographs and what not."

She gives me another sad smile. "Another woman might be jealous. You go to bed thinking about it. You dream about it. You wake up thinking about it."

"It's in there deep. But you know that." I do more math. "I reckon it's the only other thing I've done as often as kissing you good morning."

Now she smiles more simply. "Or kissing me good night." She takes a long drink of her coffee and sets the cup down. "If you and Noah are going to spend all morning talking about the good old days, I'll bring a book to read." She stands up and kisses the top of my head. "I'm going to shower. And I'll make us something for breakfast when I'm done." She steps over to the junk drawer and fishes a pen out of the mess and sets it down in front of me. She tilts my chin up to meet her face. "I'll take another, please."

I kiss her again, and watch her walk down the hallway. I listen to her in the bathroom, turning on the water, revving her electric tooth-brush, her wedding band tumbling onto the pottery ring holder. All the sounds of my mornings.

*

Ingrid, with all her sweet knowing and patience, is the one who's really going to suffer. My first thoughts sitting in Doctor Zheng's office yesterday went to sparing my wife. Don't get me wrong, she's up for the challenge. I'm certain of that. Our devotion to each other, I've always believed, is as sure as the morning coffee. It's one of the reasons we've been so happy together. And frankly it's the reason we have this diagnosis now. At Christmastime, she noticed I was ill-tempered and forgetful of our traditions. *We've never made krumkake,* I'd said. *We've never hung mistletoe.* These things I know we have done required reminding from her. And we bickered about it. Like she was unreasonable for wanting Christmas the way it's been done for the past three and a half decades. There were other signs, too. She'd send me to the grocery store for pancetta and eggs and I'd come home with a box of cereal and a bunch of bananas. I'd walk around the house wondering where my satchel was while it was slung over my shoulder. These are just a few of the examples—and in truth, for the better part of twenty years I've been forgetful and absentminded. I teased myself about being old before my time, jokes she never found amusing. It was when I stopped them, though, that she finally said we should go see someone.

So we did. And after two months of tests and examinations, Doctor Zheng told us what we had already come to expect: younger-onset Alzheimer's. The litany of information and instruction that followed was overwhelming. *The road ahead would be hard to predict; it was a disease that took many different routes; likely I could still work for a year or two; make a financial plan; talk to your employer; tell your friends and family; do everything you can to keep your mind active.* To Ingrid,

8

Doctor Zheng advised patience. To me, a whole gamut of stimulating activities. And if, after suggesting writing as one of those activities and meeting Ingrid's rebuke that I *was* a writer, and a fine and notable one at that, the good doctor was embarrassed or surprised, she didn't let on. Instead, she walked us through the next steps and answered Ingrid's many questions.

Me? Well, I guess my thoughts took a pretty frantic tour of my life and loved ones. I thought of my kids, naturally. Annika and Clara and Ben. They're all grown and making their own way. Annika lives in Minneapolis with her husband. Ben out in Boston where he goes to grad school. Clara, as I've mentioned, up in Gunflint. They're all three smart and healthy and well loved. And though I'm very close with each of them, and though they'll no doubt be worried for me and sad for themselves and Ingrid, they'll also be fine.

I thought of work, too. I teach English at the liberal arts college here on the hillside and had been planning to retire soon anyway. Teaching has been a satisfying part of my life, but after thirty years of it I've stopped being useful to my students. I don't know them anymore, and they certainly don't know the likes of me. Which is not a complaint. Over the years we've had a lot to teach each other, and as careers go it was a good one. But there's also the question of my other work, these books I write. Or, anyway, have written. Not least the one Ingrid thinks I should get working on with these new notebooks.

It was too much to think of her in Doctor Zheng's office, so as we drove home I practiced thinking of nothing. We held hands over the console and listened to public radio and I wanted to ask her to take me away, as she so often has. But she just wound up the city hillside, and when we got home said she had a few errands to run. I took our dog for a walk around campus. Only then did I think of my brother and my father and our long estrangement. It rules a part of my life as if I'm merely a character in some Norse saga, not a mortal man from north Minneapolis living now on the shore of Lake Superior. I love my brother ferociously, but I'm not sure he'd say the same about me. It's been five years since we reconciled, since I saw his daughter, since we had dinner with Bett, since I saw his life, since our father died. We've seen each other often during the intervening years. He's come up here, Ingrid and I go down to Minneapolis. I should tell him about the diagnosis. Despite our checkered past and all the complicated feelings, I think he'd want to know.

Ingrid comes back into the kitchen, dressed now in a sweater and wool skirt, brushing her still-blonde hair, the sweet smell of her shampoo filling the room.

"You haven't moved," she says, taking my coffee cup and filling it again. "Do you know what day it is, Jon?"

I shake my head.

"February twenty-eighth."

"So?"

"So it's five years to the day since your father died."

"Is it really?"

"Well, he passed on the twenty-eighth, in 2014, right?"

She knows I'm terrible with dates, and the answer to her question would elude me in the best of circumstances. Still, I say, "That's right."

She points at the calendar. "And today's the twenty-eighth." She tops her own cup of coffee and joins me at the table. She gathers my hands in hers and sighs. "Have you forgiven him yet?"

"Forgiven who, Pops?"

She looks at me, patiently, and says, "Now would be a good time if you haven't."

"Of course I have. A long time ago, I did." I take a sip of coffee and feel stumped. I've always been stumped on the matter of him.

"Who the hell am I to have forgiven him? *I'm* the one needed forgiveness."

This is well-trod ground for Ingrid and me. When Annika was born, I spent as much time laboring over what sort of father I wanted to be as I did simply relishing my baby girl. Ingrid of course knew that my relationship with my family was difficult. But she didn't know—couldn't possibly have known—the depth of our breach.

After a couple months of watching me with Annika, our first-born, she finally said, "You need to call your Mom and Dad. And your brother. Everyone is fine now, it's time for you to be, too."

And I did call. I can still remember Pops answering the phone and acting like we'd talked the day before—not ten years since. I remember how I fell in love with him all over again—and like a little boy—in the span of an hour's conversation. It was the first of hundreds we'd then have over the years.

My mother I didn't talk to. And Anton didn't return my call. Not back then.

"Are you hungry yet?" Ingrid asks.

"Sweetheart, I won't forget to eat. And I can still make my own coffee. You don't have to get up to take care of me."

"That's not—"

"You'll know when we get there. But don't let me be a burden already."

"You're no burden, Johannes. I'm only talking about breakfast. I like making you breakfast. Just like you like making me breakfast. And if you don't want it, I guess I'll go to the grocery store. What else is there to do at this unholy hour?"

She kisses me on top of my head, runs her hand through what's left of my hair. I'm still sitting at the kitchen table when her headlights shine through the window. The darkness they leave behind serves as a cruel reminder that in a year or two Ingrid won't be able to drive off alone. Even for something so simple as a trip to the gro-cery store.

*

Unholy. It's not how I think of these hours before dawn. In fact, they're the closest my life has come to religion since I was a boy and had my ski jumps to play on. For twenty years I've been getting up this early to commune with my better selves, these lives more righ-teous and curious than mine. I've loved and worshipped my char-acters in much the same way I've loved and worshipped my own children and wife, and I count their companionship as one of fate's great kindnesses.

Not only does Ingrid know all this, she as much as taught me to observe it. Each morning, as I awake and sit up, as I put on my watch and rub the sleep from my eyes, she reaches over and scratches the small of my back. It's love, simply, and I know that. But it's also, I think, a kind of encouragement. And hardly a day goes by without it. This is just one of the reasons my fumbling mind this past year has been so hard. I've been unable to write the final book I thought I had in me. A story I've been calling *The Ski Jumpers*. These note-books on the kitchen table, what are they for? The answer, it's plain to me, is a story I can't write. One that Ingrid has gently been push-ing me toward. If I haven't admitted that until now, it's because the only thing I've ever wanted to do was impress her. In this respect, at least, I know I can't, and the recognition of this truth is in its own way as brutal as yesterday's diagnosis.

Last night, after dinner and a nip, while Ingrid sat on the couch reading the newspaper, I went into my office and pulled from the back of the file cabinet those pages that have bedeviled me for five years. I meant to write a thinly veiled story about my mother and fa-ther and brother, about the unlikeliness of us all, of the crimes and wrongdoing, and of the years that drove us away from each other.

12

And it would be about ski jumping, the only thing that held us to-gether. During the past half-decade the story *has* found its way to the page. Hundreds of pages, actually.

As I sat there last night, marveling at the mess of them, I tried—for the umpteenth time—to understand why I've never been able to submit to this one. Part of the failure, no doubt, has to do with a fear of confronting what went so wrong in our lives. The time Pops spent in prison. The way his incarceration poleaxed my mother. Her time in the state hospital, which coincided with Pops's time in the clink. The way Anton was left with only his teenaged brother to take care of him—well, a teenaged kid and Magnus Skjebne, or Sheb, Pops's cousin and the root cause of so much of our grief. And of course it's meant confronting my own remorse and culpability—indeed, my guilt—which is the provenance of all the wreckage. I remain as fear-ful of it now as I did my lifetime ago. Who would relish the thought of dredging that past to life? Not me, apparently.

But there's at least one other reason this novel has always ended up back in the drawer, and it came clear to me only last night: the story of our unraveling is bound in so many ways to our ski jumping together. And *those* memories—outside of the ones I have with my own wife and children—are the best I've got. No wonder I've never been able to reconcile the two threads, or been able to see this book through.

Nothing's changed this morning except that I'm perhaps more dubious. A superstitious man might blame his diagnosis on the viru-lence of his memories. Might see his own life as the root of the sick-ness. But I'm not superstitious, and for every moment of misfortune from my childhood, I've been, in the years since, ten times charmed. Which only makes my prospects crueler, and the fact that the story in this particular redrope will never be finished as bleak as the dim-ming years I have to look forward to.

*

Our lives. My mother and father and brother and me. Or, more often, just the three of us: Pops and Anton and me. When my brother and I were kids, we used to sit around our kitchen table, and while Pops stirred up a batch of his cream of cod and corn soup or made us grilled cheese sandwiches with slices of government cheese, he'd regale us with stories of his own ski jumping past. He was not braggadocious, Pops, though he had rights to be, given his accomplishments. I think he was trying to steward in his boys the kind of confidence a religious man finds when faced with a doubting crowd. He told us there were all sorts of families in America—rich and poor, lucky and unlucky, self-made and silver-spooned—and that we were like the Rockefellers of ski jumping. He meant Anton and me. He meant that we were of the self-made and lucky class, and that it was our job to believe in the righteousness of our endeavor. He used to say that we had to believe in it like others believed in God: with reverence and solemnity and the conviction that it alone might save us. I spent my childhood imagining it could, and the rest of my life since trying to understand why it didn't.

It also occurs to me that those evenings around the table were in some ways a stay against our poverty, which is not a word I use frivolously. Because Pops was like a preacher on the subject of ski jumping, and since Anton and I were such devout young believers, and since we couldn't afford other entertainments, those dinners were as much our trips to the movies as they were our time for prayer and contemplation. Even now I see how those nights shaped us in ways as profound as our mornings on the jumping hills did.

I certainly miss Pops and Anton and how we used to be, but what I miss more than anything are the stories we told each other. I've never thought of it like that until now. Even when Pops was sent to the Stillwater penitentiary, I missed the retelling of our lives as much as I missed him. Is such a thing possible? Or am I already falling victim to my nostalgia?

The surest cure for my nostalgia has always been Magnus Skjebne. Sheb, as everyone called him, and the root, as I've already suggested, of our undoing. He became, for part of one fateful year, our guardian, a responsibility so unlikely and corrupt as to seem unimaginable now. Yet it happened as surely as any of this. It was a year marked not only by the devastation of the absence of our parents but also by the splintering of the love between my brother and me. I don't know that I've ever articulated this to myself quite so simply, but for a long time—decades—Anton chose Sheb and his way of life over me and ours.

You'd know him if you saw him, old Magnus Skjebne, all six-foot-five and two hundred fifty pounds of him. Handsome and sly and quick-eyed even as a gaffer. The last time I saw him was the night of Pops's wake. This is five years ago now, down in Minneapolis. I was sitting in the visitation room at the funeral parlor and watched him walk in. He wore a fine worsted suit and a pinpoint shirt and Italian leather brogues covered with black rubbers. He looked, I thought, like he could have been anything. A farmer or pastor, a banker or private eye, a hit man or a pimp.

He had aged, of course, in the years since I'd seen him, but still had a youthful extravagance. He didn't carry a paunch like so many men his age; his eyes were wide and bright and as menacing as ever. But he also looked more kindly than he had remained in my memory. I wondered how many among those gathered knew that beneath his handsome suit he was tattooed and scarred. The words VARMT and KALD were stamped on either collarbone, and an elaborate ouroboros wound around his body in blue and black ink parallel to a scar as old as his time in Chicago.

In the funeral parlor, he moved from person to person, shaking hands and squeezing shoulders, leaning down to whisper in ears or kiss cheeks. I'd been there for half an hour before Sheb arrived, and I hadn't yet said a word to anyone. After five minutes, he'd greeted everyone, saving me for last.

"Do my eyes deceive me? Is that you, Johannes?" he said, offering his enormous hand.

We shook. "Hey, Sheb."

He smiled then, his teeth flashing, and put his hand on my shoulder. Even at arm's length I could smell the anise on his breath. I knew it could be either the licorice candies he sucked or the aquavit he drank like water. Without looking back, he gestured at the assembled guests. "A bunch of old ski jumpers here tonight, aren't there?"

"I guess there are."

"Where's your brother?"

"You'd know better than I."

"Probably he's tipping a few."

"Probably he is."

He let go of my shoulder and motioned to the casket at the front of the room. "Have you been to see Pops?"

I looked up there. All I could see was his forehead and the wisps of gray hair that couldn't be tamed even in death. "Trying to work up the courage," I said.

Sheb nodded. "The reaper does make cowards of us all."

"And fools," I said.

"And fools." He smiled again, this time close-lipped, and nodded his head. "When your brother gets here, tell him I need a word?"

It was my turn to nod.

"Good to see you, Jon."

I nodded again.

In truth, it was not good to see Sheb, and not merely because of the occasion. The years between our meetings were coldly and exactly planned by me, and as I watched him join a circle of mourners, I felt the tightening in my gut that any encounter with him brought.

It occurred to me that I should have stayed away. That I should not have come home even for Pops's funeral.

I took a mint from the candy dish on the table behind me, unwrapped it, and looked again toward my father in his casket. My mind went wandering and I couldn't tell you how long it was before Anton walked in, but I had about half a dozen candy wrappers in my fist when he did.

He stood in the entryway, his knit hat dusted with snow, and he stomped his boots before searching me out. We locked eyes and I raised my chin and he ambled over. We looked at each other for a moment before he spread his arms. We hugged a long time. When finally we separated, he said, "Big brother," and peeled off the black leather gloves he was wearing.

"Hey, Anton."

A drop of snowmelt fell from his hat onto his hand. He looked at it, then back up at me. "That should be our tears," he said.

"There's still time for all that," I said. "It's good to see you. You're fit. You look good."

"You're not. You don't." He smacked my gut with the back of his hand and laughed. "Someone's feeding you well." I could see he was trying to summon Ingrid's name.

"Ingrid," I reminded him.

"That's right. How's Ingrid."

"Very good."

"And the kids?"

"They're all moved away. I miss them."

"Ben?" he said.

"And Annika and Clara."

He nodded, and scanned the room, hardly interested that his brother was standing in front of him. We might as well have been classmates at a thirty-year reunion.

He wasn't embarrassed, nor should he have been. I'd distanced myself a long time ago, not just from Minneapolis but from Anton and Bett and Pops, too. I met Ingrid at college in Duluth, where she was born and raised, and we settled down just a few blocks from her childhood home. On that night in Minneapolis, I hadn't seen Anton in years.

"This room is rotten with jumpers."

"Ski jumpers and Sheb. He's looking for you."

"He always is."

I didn't know what he meant, though I had my suspicions. In order to change the subject, I said, "I imagine Bett is, too."

He looked at me, mean in the old way, and then stole another glance around the room, looking for Bett. "There's Ma, sitting up by Pops." He ducked his chin under his shoulder, took a flask from his coat pocket, uncapped it, and took a swill. I guess it steadied him, because when he lifted his face, his expression and tone had changed. "You been up to see him yet?"

"I can't."

"I'm gonna. Before Sheb tracks me down." He stole another drink. "You better fucking say hi to Ma."

"I will. I'm bringing her home after this. I talked to her this morning."

Now he looked at me in the hurt way, and we were five and ten years old again. He took a few seconds and then put his hand on my shoulder. "Well, then, we'll all be there together. It'll be just like old times, eh? Dinner at the kitchen table." With that, he slunk into the crowd, and I was left alone with the bowl of mints.

Standing under that wall sconce in the funeral parlor, watching so many ghosts move around, the newcomers covered in snow from the blizzard outside, I might have died from remembering. But it was a funeral, after all, and a gathering of old ski jumpers, too, which meant no end to the flickers of recognition and the old folks coming up to say hi to me—one of the Bargaard boys. My own

Bargaard cousins, Tim and Ted, paused for a moment to offer their condolences. After a while, Noah arrived and for the rest of the service stood guard beside me. Otherwise it was a parade of vaguely familiar faces.

A dozen times some wizened man I should have known would stop and say, "You're one of Jake's boys."

"I'm Jon."

"The older or younger one?"

"I'm the older."

"The one who left town?"

"That one," I'd admit.

These men, they were all jowly and slim and had still piercing eyes, eyes that had spent some fair amount of time up in the sky, flying. We had that in common. They'd say things like, "I knew your old man from way back," and then look into the light of the sconce as though they could get back there, or as if they could see themselves still in the air, their skis neat beneath them. After a moment of fond remembrance, they'd look back at me. "I jumped with him down at Norge." Or, "We skied together at Wirth." They'd get lost in some story, sometimes for a split second, sometimes for a full minute. Then: "You were both jumpers. You and your brother. One of you was good."

"Anton was."

"Anton. That's right. I remember watching him."

"So do I," I'd say, surprised to feel the pride that always crept in.

Most of those old men would stare off for another moment, on their way back from the memory of my brother in flight. Some, when they returned, would give me a knowing nod. Others, the ones with better memories or more of the story, would take half a step closer and ask, "Did he turn out all right? Anton?"

I'd look across the room at my brother. He lingered near Pops's casket but hadn't yet stood next to it. Instead he spoke with people in that easy way of his. "Ask him yourself," I'd say, and point at him. He always seemed to be smiling back.

Eventually, Anton did move over to Pops. He stood right above him. I imagined he was holding Pops's hand, looking down on his closed eyes. Anton's own face turned, in the short distance of those few steps, back to the innocent boy he used to be. He appeared, for a minute or two, very much as he had the first time Pops went away. Like he'd had his voice ripped out. Like he was going to have to subsist on the memory of something he didn't know the whole truth about. I thought, just then, about the nights we used to sit around the kitchen table and how Anton held on to Pops's words as if they were the only thing in the world that made sense.

Of course, there were lots of those stories that night. The first person to speak at the service was Pops's best friend, a man named Selmer Dahlson. He was a ski jumper himself, and surely the oldest person in the parlor. Next up was Sheb, who commanded that room as if he were the mayor of the northside, and who spoke of my father as if he were a saint.

Last to the lectern was Anton, who took a long pause before he began. He thanked Pops's friends—more than two hundred of them had filtered through over the course of the wake. He thanked the folks at the funeral parlor. He thanked Selmer, not only for his kind words about Pops but for giving so many of us our start at ski jumping over on the golf course at Wirth Park. When it came time to talk to Bett, Anton's tone changed, and he went from garrulous and almost backslappy to earnest, if not downright melancholy. He told her how much Pops loved her and what their life together had meant to him. He told her what a fine mother she was. He told her that he loved her, which I know was true. And then, before he commemorated Pops, he looked around the room until he found my face at the back. He paused again and collected himself and then he said, "Ma worked a lot of overnight shifts at the hospital, which left

Pops in charge of us. He was a good dad. He did the best he could. My brother, Jon? He was a good son. And a good brother. One of us turned out all right." He smiled at me—or maybe it was a smirk—and then told a few stories about our beloved father.

Even now, five years since, I can still hear the crack in his voice. He was replaying abridged versions of some of the classics. I closed my eyes to listen, and to quell my tears, and when I opened them a few minutes later Sheb was standing beside me in the amber light of the wall sconce. He winked at me, and I turned away. That old bastard had been there from the beginning, when he and Pops and Mom and her sister Lena escaped Chicago in 1954. It was our family origin story. The flames from which we rose.

Like Shattering Glass

THE SOLDIER FIELD COLONNADES cast long shadows on the street below, where a canvas circus tent had been erected. A dozen trucks from the Gilco Scaffolding Company had parked along the waterfront. Ten men had been ten days in the building of it, and now the ski jump stood 184 feet above the street. From where they stood, it seemed to rise much higher than that.

"Only Patollo would drum up something this big," Sheb said.

"This ain't big," Pops said. "Just high."

Sheb crossed his arms. Even cloaked in his leather overcoat, his brawniness was plain to see. He wore size thirteen boots, the bulldog toes of which had been used on a dozen unlucky chumps. "What's the difference?"

Pops craned his neck to look up at the scaffolding rising above the colonnades. "Big is what happens when there's air between you and the ground. This is a goddamned bunny ears." He looked back at Sheb. "I'm about to teach Andrus Patollo the difference."

"Andy ain't in the business of learning new things."

Pops cleared his throat and spit over the railing. Boats were still docked in the harbor, and when the wind gusted they could hear their hulls gently slapping against the water. "Fuck him. He's unglued."

"It's his livelihood you're after. He's just protecting what's his."

"What's his?" Pops said. "As if she's a fancy red car?"

"Just leave her alone, would you? Forget you ever laid eyes on her, and consider yourself lucky."

"Lucky my ass."

Sheb uncrossed his arms and laid one of them over Pops's shoulder. "No disrespect, but she's a goddamned showgirl. A cabaret singer."

Pops shook Sheb's arm from his shoulder. "She's a beautiful singer." He took a cigarette from the pack in his shirt pocket and put it to his lips and lit it. He blew out a long stream of smoke, and watched it catch on the wind. A smile came to his eyes. "To hell with him. Let's go see this thing from the top."

Pops hurried up the scaffold. Sheb kept pace, taking two steps at a time. The whole structure swayed under his lumbering gait. When they reached the top, Sheb crouched down and clutched the railing.

"Come over here, pansy. Nothing's gonna happen to you." Jake had gone right to the starting gate. He stood with his feet on the precipice of the inrun—the slide or ramp—and when he looked down he could see the snow soon to be on it. The shaved ice they'd haul up in gunnysacks. He could feel his skis waxed and smooth under his feet. Could feel the twitch in his legs, the urge to jump. His breath caught, just as it would when, in three days, he'd hear his name over the PA system and pull himself over the edge. Even now, he could hear the silence of the roaring crowd; could feel his breath come back to him as he crouched and gained speed on the inrun. And even as he accelerated, everything would slow, not least his pulse, which would practically stop. He'd be as weightless in those three seconds on the slide as he was in flight, a body remade into one taut and effervescent muscle. And when he got to the end of the slide, he'd use that memory to launch himself. That single muscle would uncoil with such quickness that the moment he thought it, it would be done and he'd be in flight and he'd no longer be himself but a pane of glass flying high above the Soldier Field crowd, invisible to all thirty thousand people, if the reports were true. And he'd be perfectly alone. There were *years* in those seconds. Whole lifetimes. When he'd land, the crowd would cheer him back into himself and he'd come to a stop before the platform at the end of the Soldier Field turf. He'd look at Patollo there in a fur coat, and Pops . . . Pops would own Patollo in a way Patollo had never owned her.

Sheb said, "What kind of lunatic does this?"

Pops, dizzied, looked up at the city spread before him in shrieks of glass. The early autumn sky reflected off the buildings. Pops loved the sky. His arrogance laid claim to it. He turned to look at Sheb again, who still clutched the railing, his face revealing that maybe he wasn't the tough guy he thought he was.

"If all the sorry assholes you've beaten senseless could see you now," Pops said.

"They can't."

"You'll have to pay me to keep quiet. That's for damn sure."

"You keep quiet all by yourself, cuz."

It was true. About town, in the saloons and eateries he frequented, Pops blended in with hardly a peep. He was diminutive with hard, transparent eyes. He wore dungarees and canvas workshirts—the shirts tucked in—and a leather belt cinching his pants. He had a shock of hair so blond it appeared white at noonday. It was the loudest thing about him. He wasn't much. There was little denying that. But the poverty of his constitution served him well in at least one respect: he was light as a bird and could damn well fly.

Sure, he swept between the pews at Minnekirken. He shoveled snow there on winter mornings. He cleaned the kitchen in the church basement after the Friday night lutefisk dinners, taking his paycheck each Monday. And he did it all without complaint. In fact, he did it all with humble pride. He listened to Cubs games afternoons he was free. He went to the library or for walks through Lincoln Park. But these things he did by rote. It was on Saturdays in winter, when he climbed into his jalopy and drove an hour out to Fox River Grove to ski, that he felt loud and alive and like a person of this world. There were days he might have admitted he felt above it.

He had a room on West Altgeld where he kept almost nothing. A chair and a table. A Murphy bed. A chest of drawers that held his meager wardrobe. A pan for warming soup and a bowl to eat it from. A kettle for coffee. It would have been easy to mistake it as abandoned, his room. But on the floor beside his bed he kept a stack of books, including the electrician manuals he studied and a collection of crime novels that were his guilty pleasures. And against one wall—like proof he was alive—next to his gabardine keilhosen and stocking hat hanging from the old coat rack, his wooden skis leaned in the glow from the streetlight outside. He kept a block of paraffin and an electric iron in a shoeshine box and each Friday night, after mopping the church basement floor, he'd walk home, crack a bottle of suds, and spend an hour waxing his skis.

First, he'd melt the paraffin into the grooves with the iron. Then, after it cooled, he'd rub it out with a tuft of steel wool so that in the morning his skis would sizzle down the inrun. He used to hear the devout old men in the Minnekirken basement talking about pressing their shirts and pants on the night before church, and he imagined for them something like the solemn devotion he felt waxing those skis. Preparation for communion. Prayerful fidelity.

In the air, he found peace with the unkindness and loneliness of life. All of his wonder was validated in the exultation of those few seconds aloft. How many people had asked him what it was like to be up there, with nothing but two wooden planks under your feet?

His answer was always the same: it was like being invisible. Landing, he'd say, was like shattering back to life. The rush and the cold and the thrill. The danger. The serenity. These things he thought, but only abstractly and only to himself.

It was hard to believe those Saturday mornings could entirely sustain someone, but they did Pops. Had until now.

"Well?" Sheb said.

Pops flinched and took a last drag off his cigarette and flicked it over the edge of the scaffolding. "Is Patollo really flying Erling Erlandsson and Arnfinn Bergmann in for the competition?"

"Along with half the Norwegian national team and some Finnish boys said to rival them all."

Pops took one last look down the inrun. "And I'm supposed to have a chance?"

"Let me tell you about your chances, Jake. Win or lose, Patollo's not letting Lena go."

"That ain't what we agreed."

"You think you're the first guy Patollo ever stiffed?"

"What about Lena? It's her damn life. She's got a say."

Sheb laughed. "Sure she does. But tell me, what makes you think she *wants* to leave? She's damn near famous and you, you're what to her? You've been out a dozen times. You think she's in love? No offense, but you're a goddamned janitor. You're built like a ten-year-old schoolgirl." He shook his head as though these two qualities said everything there was about him. He unlatched his arms from the railing and scooted over to Pops's side. "Christ, man. You know my hands are tied."

"It's strange to see you fear a man."

"It ain't fear. Patollo's livelihood is my livelihood."

"That's a hell of a cart to fix your horse to."

Now Sheb stood, his knees knocking. "It's a crazy sonofabitch who'd hurl his ass over this edge."

"Yes, it is."

"Just because you got the sand for this"—he pointed down the jump—"doesn't mean you should tempt Patollo into making an example of you, which, sure as the day is long, he will."

"I ain't afraid of him."

"I don't care if you are or not. But I'm telling you, he won't forget you. That fancy meal you shared? I hope you enjoyed it. You'll be paying for it for a long time. I warned you before we went in there."

Pops waved him off.

"I told you to leave it alone."

"I can't."

"You can't."

Jake lit another cigarette. "Lena's in the family way, Sheb."

"And you're the author?"

"Of course I am."

"Hells bells," Sheb said.

"It's a mess, I'll grant you that."

"A mess? I guess it's a little more than that."

Pops took a long drag on his cigarette. "Whatever it is, there's nothing to be done about it. Me and Lena are leaving on Friday night, right after I stomp Erlandsson and Bergmann and the rest of Patollo's blue ribbon boys."

"And where do you plan to go?"

"Minnesota. Minneapolis. I got a job lined up. And there's jumps up there. Plus, I got an aunt and uncle living north of the city."

"Minnesota ain't that far away. You think Andy won't sic one of his gorillas after you?"

"I think the one he'd send for the job will already be with me."

Something happened then. Sheb unbuttoned his leather coat and it flapped in the wind. He looked at Pops and Pops saw something shift, slow and significant. Then Pops looked out over the city once more, and it too was altered. Pops saw it in the wind and in the towers of now dull glass. He turned and saw it in the weight of Lake Michigan, as hard and tempered as the skyscrapers before them. Later, when he told the story, he'd say it was Sheb coming alive for the first time in his enormous life. The simple suggestion that there was more to Sheb than being one of Patollo's grunts emboldened him. It filled him with purpose. And it did so with all the urgency of a Windy City gust off the lake.

Sheb said nothing. He just looked over the city, his eyes growing darker and wider with the setting sun. He lit a cigarette. Sheb was facing north now, his face in profile, and Pops could see the muscles of his jaw flexing. He could see the smile rising on his cheek like a snake coming out of a hole. For a long moment his cousin just stared up the shore, the smile growing a whisker at a time, until together he and Pops heard a distant drone above the other noises of the city. They listened, ears cocked, as a plane banked from the east, heading, no doubt, for the now-lighted landing strip at Meigs Field. A light on the wing blinked as it leveled. The silver-plated fuselage caught a glimmer of the setting sun before it flew into the city's shadow.

"That could be him," Sheb finally said.

"Who?"

"Andrus."

"Patollo has a plane?"

"He pilots it himself."

Pops turned, wide-eyed, back to the incoming aircraft.

"The freak can fly a little himself," Sheb said.

*

The agreement had been made in the private dining room of Patollo's club, a debauched nitery on the near north side called The Valhalla. One metal door under a red lamp opened to two flights of descending concrete stairs where another door—this one three inches thick with a barred peephole—opened into what Patollo called the reception. Here, under an enormous chandelier, Sheb or another of Patollo's toughs collected admission and sized up the guests.

They might be schoolteachers or college boys, executives or stevedores, aldermen or "L" conductors. They might be clergymen already sauced on communion wine or housewives stoned out of their eyes. The entire first line of the Chicago Blackhawks came in after home games, and that lumbering short-timer at first base—the Bilko of the Bingo-to-Bango-to-Bilko double-play call—was known to come in for steak tartar and four or five steins of beer on Friday nights. Whoever came in—and they did, in droves—entered through the reception. A dollar cover charge and approving nod from Sheb was all it took to get past the black curtain that let into the action.

A massive subterranean hall unfurled beyond that curtain. There was a circular zinc bar in the center of the room, backed by a fountain that poured from the ceilings into a tank filled with exotic fish. Two stages bordered by brass railings sat in the far corners of the room with an orchestra pit between them. There were perhaps a hundred tables and a bank of leather-backed booths between the bar and the pit, and for two or three more dollars you could as easily order a plate of pickled herring and a soft-boiled egg as you could five minutes of company from one of the dozen peelers sashaying by. On any given night thirty or forty women worked the room, each according to her rank. Cigarette girls and taxi dancers and B-girls. Teasers and tossers, chippies and hip-flippers. Someone for everyone, as Sheb liked to say.

Behind the stages, countless doorways led into a warren of poker rooms and private dining rooms and opium dens, and behind all this was the Rabbit Hole, where another entry waited. It cost twenty dollars just to knock on the door of the Rabbit Hole, and instead of being greeted by a black curtain and some galoot like Sheb, Madame

Ehaema, dressed in a tuxedo jacket and not much more, sat on a velvet cabriole smoking her cigarettes from a foot-long holder. The curtains behind her were sheer, and she could tell from the look on a man's face which of the women, women she called hares, would best suit his needs.

A wealthy enough man might enter The Valhalla on a Friday at nine and not leave until it was time for church on Sunday. Usually those men left through a back door. The streets of Chicago were lined with clubs like Patollo's back then. Places like The Tavern Club, Mister Kelly's, and The Gaslight Club, where people flocked for the music and merrymaking. But for all the devilry at The Valhalla, there was one thing pure and right: each Friday night Lena Lyng took the main stage.

She wore sequined gowns and feathers in her hair and she occupied the pink glow of the spotlight like stardom was made for her. She sang Kitty Kallen and Patti Page and Rosemary Clooney songs, and when she sang she seemed to use all the breath she stole. The entire hall would fill with her voice the way it clouded with cigarette smoke. The patrons would squint to watch her on stage, confirming with their sight what seemed hard to believe with their ears: that something so lovely could come from just one singer. For a year she'd been up on that stage and in all that time Andrus Patollo had never so much as looked at her with impure thoughts. This man who wouldn't think twice about killing another man for doing the same.

He drove a blood red Kaiser Manhattan, the idea of a chauffeur being an affront to the simple bounds of masculinity. Most noontimes he'd wake in the penthouse apartment he kept overlooking Lincoln Park. He'd dress, drink a tomato juice and eat two raw eggs, then get in his car and roll down the window and light a cigar.

Each day at two, after he'd arrived at The Valhalla and after his personal barber had shaved his head and chin and massaged his hulking shoulders, Patollo briefed his crew over lunch. He'd stand before them bare-chested, a plate of the afternoon's fare in one hand and a sterling silver fork in the other, and go over the order of the day. No detail was too small. He knew the names of the day's expected dignitaries as if they were close relatives. He knew what the mayor and the Outfit were up to. He knew his staff down to the cigarette girls.

Patollo wore mutton chops on his round face and, from a chain around his neck, a human skull carved from a chunk of white gold the size of a golf ball. His tattoos were legend, his entire chest and stomach covered with a giant trudging through knee-deep water and carrying a sack of stones, the word KALEVIPOEG writ from collarbone to collarbone. A word from his native Estonian that he never translated for anyone. He spoke four languages and could as readily discuss a Ford Motor engine as the military strategy of Sun Tzu. By any definition he was a funny man, one quick with a joke at his own expense. He loved the opera and the picture shows and you might find him at the slaughterhouses watching the executions like he was taking in a ballgame.

Aside from the bartenders and bouncers, the girls and the card dealers and the aforementioned barber, Patollo also employed lawyers and accountants and press agents, to say nothing of a pocketful of Chicago's finest quick on the graft. He was as likely to invite the governor to dinner as he was Tony Accardo, and both accepted without reservation. The night before Pops feasted with him, Ralph Kiner sat at the same table, swilling beer and making eyes at one of Madame Ehaema's hares.

Pops was there against Lena's wishes and despite Sheb's warnings. He sat at a table covered with white linens in Patollo's personal dining room. Candles guttered in a golden candelabrum, casting a doleful light onto the fare: rare roast beef soaking in its own blood, fingerling potatoes, a salad of warm beets and roasted onions, ramekins of horseradish all around. Sheb had joined them at Patol-lo's behest, and he sat at one end of the table with an old man introduced as Vaclav Hruby while Patollo sat beside Pops.

"Your cousin tells me you're a ski jumper," Patollo said. He spoke with a mouthful of roast beef, mixing his manners to suit his company.

"I get out there some," Pops said.

Patollo picked at his teeth with a tine from his fork. He nodded. He raised his hand and a waiter brought the decanter of bourbon around again.

Sheb interrupted. "No kidding, Andy, Jake here's the best I've ever seen."

Patollo shifted his gaze onto Sheb. "And you've seen many ski jumpers? You're some sort of expert?"

"Christ, Andy, I'm just saying he's tops."

Patollo took another bite of his roast beef and leaned toward Pops. "And you've heard about this tournament at Soldier Field on Friday night?"

"Everyone has," Pops said.

Patollo sawed another strip of beef from his shank and put it into his already full mouth. "Bargaard, that must be a French name."

Pops smiled. "Some of my people have been known to eat mayonnaise. That's about as close as we get to old France."

Now Patollo smiled. "A wit. I admire that. Especially of a man in your position."

"Speaking of my position," Pops ventured.

Patollo raised a hand—the hand with his fork in it—and pointed at Pops's plate, which was untouched. "You prefer whitefish, no? Whitefish and lingonberries and whatever the hell else?"

Pops looked down on his supper. He speared a fingerling potato and put it in his mouth.

"You're a toilet scrubber, yes? A floor mopper?"

Pops took his napkin from his lap and spit the potato into it. "I'm a hard worker. And I'm a ski jumper."

"We've established that you're a ski jumper. But to make ends meet, you scrub toilets and mop floors. Is that not true?"

Sheb bristled. He scooted forward in his chair, and as soon as he did Vaclav Hruby reached out with his wrinkled hand and held Sheb in place.

Pops looked down the table at his cousin. He took a deep breath. "Mister Patollo—"

"Andy. Call me Andy."

Pops looked him dead in the eye. "Mister Patollo, about Lena."

Again Patollo raised his hand. This time he met and held Pops's gaze. A smile crept up from Patollo's heavy face. "Tell me, what's it like?"

"Excuse me?" Pops said.

"Ski jumping. I've seen it many times and always wondered."

Pops stared across the table, unblinking.

"Surely it's thrilling? Tell me more." Patollo stabbed his fork in the air as if to extract an answer from it. His voice had taken on the quality of a ringmaster's.

"I always tell people it's like being made of glass."

"Ho-ho! Now we're talking." Patollo speared the last piece of meat on his plate, swirled it in the ramekin of horseradish, and shoved it into his mouth. "So, you're made of glass!"

Now Pops closed his eyes. "Those first moments in flight, at least. It's like you're invisible. Still and invisible, even for all the commotion. There's no sound. There's almost nothing to see. Just the landing hill. It's only you and the air in the sky. It's the most peaceful place on earth."

"Well, not exactly *on earth.*"

Pops lifted his head and opened his eyes but kept them on the memory of flight. "Right. But peaceful all the same."

Patollo turned and looked at Vaclav Hruby and Sheb, shrugged his shoulders, and finally put his fork down beside his empty plate. His smile fell back into his jowls, and he picked up his bourbon and took a tight-lipped drink, turning his attention back to Pops, staring at him over the rim of his crystal cocktail glass. "You were stuck in flight, my friend."

"I was."

"Tell me what it's like when you land. When you come back to earth."

"It's like glass shattering. All the silence and stillness go away. The roar of life, of the crowd, it comes back like a passing L train."

Patollo's smile rose in increments. He rotated the cut crystal in the light of the candelabrum, and a hundred colors spread across the white linen and dirty dishes. Many years later, Pops would say that he could see something alight in Patollo's eyes just then. Anger or doubt or maybe even admiration. But also a sort of possession, and certainly a scheme for the moment. Patollo's whole vast empire was built on schemes of the moment. Some simply lasted longer than others. In that particular instant, he quaffed the last of his bourbon and then held his empty glass back to the candlelight. A new spectrum of colors danced across the table. The only sound in the dining room was the faraway tinkle of The Valhalla's orchestra so many doors down.

Patollo stood and pivoted and threw the cocktail glass against a stone wall. The concussion in that dimly lit room was enormous. He straightened his dinner jacket, lowered his fists to the table, and stared at Pops. "Like that?" he said.

Pops held Patollo's gaze. "That was more of a thud than a shattering." Now Pops smiled. It was a smile he wore for most of the rest of his life. "But sure, something like that."

Patollo looked calmly at the waiter standing in the corner, his waxed mustache quivering, who understood he was to clean up the glass.

Patollo sat up and took from his breast pocket a fat cigar. He clipped its end and leaned heavily back in his seat. Before the cigar was between his lips, another waiter was beside him with a lit match. He puffed three, four, five times and then waved the waiter away.

"And during this entire courageous feat, are you ever afraid?"

"Afraid?"

"Yes, man! Does fear ever enter the equation?"

"I wouldn't say fear."

"What would you say?"

Pops thought for a moment. "I suppose if the wind is all wrong, or if it's snowing too much or if the snow's for shit, then I might get a creepy feeling."

"Describe that creepy feeling."

"Oh, it's like a knot in your gut."

"But not one that causes fear." This Patollo said more to himself than to Pops. He took a series of puffs on his cigar and blew the smoke through the candlelight. "What do you fear, Jakob Bargaard?"

Pops lifted the napkin from his lap and laid it across his plate. He unbuttoned the collar of his canvas shirt and removed his pack of cigarettes from the breast pocket and lit one and looked around the room as if he had just arrived. The stately wainscoting. The gilded mirrors. The candle sconces on the stone walls. He thought of his reason for being there, and looked back at Patollo and said, "This," gesturing with his hands at the room he'd just taken stock of.

It was an answer that satisfied Patollo, who called a waiter. "Bring another round of drinks," he said, "and cigars if they want them." He sat back then, and unbuttoned his pants.

"What scares you?" Pops asked.

Patollo raised an eyebrow and smoothed his bald head. He smiled. "Rats," he said. "Rats and Vaclav Hruby down there." He gave Hruby a two-fingered salute. "Fear the man who made you, isn't that right, sir?"

Hruby hadn't said a word all night. Pops remembered he was as old a man as he'd ever seen. His eyes set in the folds of his face caught none of the candlelight despite peering down the table to meet Patollo's smile. He wore a necktie and a brown coat that might have fit a child but was altogether hanging from his sloped shoulders. His food had been brought to the table cut into small pieces.

"He isn't much to look at anymore, but once upon a time Vaclav consorted with the toughest men this country has ever known," Patollo said.

Hruby almost smiled. He ran his thin and bent fingers under his nose.

"Yes, sir. Old Hruby knows where the bodies are buried. And he knows who dug the graves."

The waiter brought cigars and a tray of fresh drinks. Patollo slid the cigar cutter down the table. When Hruby picked it up and clipped his cigar, a waiter hurried to his side and offered to light it. But he was brushed away, and Vaclav removed a gold-plated Zippo from his pocket and flipped it open. A flame as tall and orange as a carrot blazed, and he sucked the cigar to burning.

Patollo held his stogie at arm's length. "I'd rather smoke a good cigar than get my ashes hauled."

Sheb, his own cigar clenched in his teeth, said, "That's plain crazy."

A peevish, scolding look came across Patollo's face. He blinked hard and took a puff and said, "You're a workhorse, Magnus. A hard-working grunt without much of a mind. I understand all of this and I like you no less for it. But please, don't sully our evening with your spirited asides."

Pops looked down the table in time to see a small smile appear from the fleshy folds of Vaclav Hruby's face.

When Pops laid eyes back on Sheb, he was already stammering a reply. "I was only making a joke."

"A contrary workhorse." Patollo regarded the end of his cigar. "The fields do need plowing from time to time. Magnus, why don't you escort Vaclav out front. Let him hear the orchestra before they take their break."

Patollo stood and buttoned his trousers. He took a few steps around the table and lent his arm for Vaclav Hruby, who took it and pulled himself up. The top of his head barely reached Patollo's waist. Sheb held his unlit cigar in one hand, his drink in the other. Patollo took the cigar from Sheb's hand, bit the end of it, spit, and handed it back. When Sheb took it, Patollo lifted Vaclav's lighter from his shirt pocket and offered Sheb the flame.

"Thanks for having dinner with me, Magnus. Listen to whatever Vaclav has to teach you, yes? Forget the strumpets for a night?" He handed Hruby to Sheb, then put his hairless paw on the back of Sheb's neck and leaned in to kiss him on the cheek. "Good night, Magnus." He bent and kissed Hruby's cheek. "Vaclav, *dobrou noc,* my friend."

After he closed the door, Patollo stood with his hands in his trouser pockets and his back to Pops. For a long moment he waited, his head turned toward the ceiling, only the glowing tip of his cigar visible from where Pops stood at the other end of the table. Alone in the room with Andrus Patollo, Pops felt smaller and more alert and as though there might come a time in the next few minutes when he'd be required to decide the story of the rest of his life.

"Is he really your cousin?" Patollo said, his head still turned to the ceiling, his back still to Pops. There was a new quality to his voice. An accent that brought with it a softness. Pops felt some of the tension run from his shoulders.

"He is. My mother was his mother's sister."

Patollo finally turned around. "Your aunt must have married a colossus."

"She never married anyone. Sheb wouldn't know his father if he walked in here now."

Patollo smiled.

"Likely my aunt didn't even know who his father was. My mother never had much nice to say about her own sister."

Patollo stepped back across the room and sat again in his chair at the head of the table. He motioned for Pops to sit down as well. "And the rest of your family?"

"Don't really have one anymore, except Sheb and some cousins way the hell up in northern Minnesota. A town on Lake Superior. Dad's brother and his clan. I never knew them much. I've hardly left Chicago."

"Your mother is passed away?"

"Last year."

"And your father?"

"Died when I was a kid."

Patollo shook his head. "My own father was a drunk and a thief and worse, and I hope he's still rotting in Patarei Prison. I hope he lives forever in his stinking cell."

"Patarei Prison?"

"In Tallinn. Where I'm from."

"Tallinn, that near here?"

"On the Baltic Sea, my friend. Thousands of miles from here."

Pops blushed. "It's been a while since I was to school."

Patollo smiled. "Family," he said, and took a puff of his cigar.

"It ain't much."

"It's everything."

Pops met Patollo's gaze and held it. The two men put their smokes to lips simultaneously.

"We seem to be of like minds," Patollo said.

"I hope so," Pops said, still not looking away.

Patollo balked first, dropped first his cigar and then his eyes to regard its glowing tip. "I think having a local boy to challenge the Scandinavians will increase the gate on Friday night."

"Every club skier out at Norge is planning on jumping."

"And only one of them has a chance to win. This is what I've been told."

"A chance to win."

"Have you ever seen this Swede jump? Erlandsson is his name."

"Nope. But I've heard about him."

"And?"

"He's good. That's what they say. The best in the world right now, according to anyone with an opinion."

"Magnus says you might give him a run for his money."

"Only because it's a small enough jump. On a real hill, I couldn't carry his skis."

"Even through all this smoke I can see the shine in your eyes."

"I'd be lying if I said I didn't want to give it my best shot."

"Well then!" Patollo put his cigar in his mouth and clapped his hands in mock finality. "You'll jump in the tournament at Soldier Field. I'll have my man call the *Trib*. We'll write it up in the paper." He rose and snapped his suspenders. "Thank you for dining with me." He extended his hand toward the door.

Pops stood now, too, crushing out his cigar as he did. "What about Lena Lyng?"

"Of course. We were going to talk about La La." Patollo stepped around the corner of the table and put his thumbs back beneath his suspenders and stood above Pops.

For the first time that night, Pops shrank before Andrus Patollo. He lowered his eyes to Patollo's shoes. He could hear and feel

Patollo's breath around the cigar burnt now to a nub in his mouth. They stood like that for too long.

Eventually Patollo lifted his arm and checked his wristwatch in the space between them. "Say it, man!"

Pops took a step back, kept his eyes fixed on Patollo's shoes. "Lena wants out of here."

"Impossible."

Pops tried to stand taller. In any case, he looked up. "It's not impossible. She doesn't want to sing here anymore."

"She was made to sing."

"She can sing anywhere."

"Have you seen her on that stage? Have you seen the way she stuns the room?"

"I have seen it. More than once."

Patollo's heavy smile spread across his face. He clapped Pops on the shoulder. "Then you know!"

Pops stood there dumb.

"You see? It's impossible. That spotlight *requires* her."

Pops looked back up at him. He nodded as though agreeing but then said, "You got enough women working here. Find another one to sing some songs."

Patollo cocked his head, as though seeing this little nit from a new angle might help him understand his moxie. It had been some time since a man had taken Patollo past his first answer, but he responded calmly. "Let me tell you about the morning Lena first came to see me. I remember it very well. She answered a call for cabaret dancers, you see. Lena and a hundred other girls. Each one, they did a dance. They sang a song. I alone judged them. I alone decided whether or not to bring them into my club. When Lena came onstage, do you know what she said to me?" He didn't wait for Pops to answer. "She said, 'I've never sung outside of church.' Can you imagine? That voice and she'd never used it."

"I've heard her sing in church, too."

Patollo held up his hand and closed his eyes. "She stared humbly at the floor and sang, at first barely above a whisper. But so uncommonly graceful. I asked her what song it was and she told me it was a church hymn called 'Beautiful Savior' and do you know what I thought?" He opened his eyes and held Pops steady with them. "I thought, here is *my* beautiful savior. Here is someone to help me rise above. Had it been any other voice, I would have thought, Girlie, I'm *your* savior. But not with her. Not with La La."

"She sings like an angel. Everyone knows that."

"Do you think you're talking to a fool?" Patollo turned and walked around the table and stubbed his cigar out, then walked back to Pops. "You might as well say she sings like a mermaid or a gorgon." He raised a hand as though to slap Pops but only held it there. "Or a goddamned siren. Some fucking sphinx. Christ, man! She sings like more than any of that."

"Why are we talking around this?"

Patollo reached for Pops, cupped the back of his neck with his giant hand. "You don't know anything, do you?"

Pops was paralyzed in Patollo's grip.

Patollo leaned in, his face only inches from Pops. "What about Lena's sister?"

"Sister? Lena doesn't have a sister."

Now Patollo loosened his grip. He brought his face back inch by inch until he was standing at arm's length again. He took his hand from Pops's neck and slapped him on the shoulder. "You poor fool. I suppose you've fallen in love with Lena? I suppose the two of you are going to live happily ever after?" He snickered. He shook his head. "Jakob Bargaard, Lena is here because she wants to be. She needs to be. She's here because her sister needs to be cared for. Because *I* care for her. Without me, the two of them would be living under some southside viaduct. Without me, Lena would be digging through my dumpsters in the alley, looking for something to bring home for her sister to eat."

Pops looked at the floor, which seemed to be rising toward him, as though it were water around a sinking ship.

"I pardon your ignorance. Christ, I might even pity you. And frankly, I don't care if you and your gal live long and prosper. Just don't dream of it at any cost to me. La La's the main attraction. She's Friday night. And she's not going anywhere." Patollo turned to leave but paused a last time. "She went to that tabernacle you work at. She asked them for help. A good Norwegian girl. And so young. And her sister, the poor girl, daffy and simple and who knows what else." He shook his head as though a great sadness had seized him. "And do you know what the pastor told her? He told her she was a sinner. He told her she must repent. That she had to earn the right to their charity. Cold comfort to a girl with no roof over her head and no bite to eat. That's when she came here and sang for me." Patollo gave Pops a good long stare and turned to leave.

"All the same," Pops said.

Patollo spun around, his eyes widened to twice their usual size.

"I mean no disrespect. But you got no rights to her. Not like that. She ain't a piece of chattel."

The rage on Patollo's face was mixed with a kind of twisted pleasure.

Pops was afraid. "I came here honorably," he tried.

"Honorably? You don't mean that, do you? You wouldn't know honor any sooner than I'd know failure. And for fucksakes you *certainly* don't know manners. Someone should have taught you some."

"I guess no one taught me much of anything."

"Then allow me, you fucking noodge. The next time someone invites you to dinner, come bearing gifts, not offering to rob him blind. And for God's sake, scrape the mud from the bottom of your boots. Put a dose of Brylcreem in your hair and press your trousers."

42

Patollo ran his hand across his bald dome again. "Why do I persist in these reclamation projects? What is it about you shovelers of shit?"

"I ain't—"

"Be quiet!" Patollo boomed. "I know *you*. We've had to deal with rats in the basement before." He cracked his neck by touching his ears to his shoulders one at a time. He appeared again almost to smile. "I haven't met a man with your persistence in a long time. You're a goddamn badger. I can see you won't let those teeth out of my pant cuffs until this is resolved." He looked at his watch. "How about a wager, Jakob? You win the tournament at Soldier Field, Lena is free to go. The five-hundred-dollar prize? I keep that, as payment for all I've done for La La and her sister."

"All due respect, it ain't up to us if she stays or leaves."

As if Pops hadn't said anything at all, Patollo continued. "You don't win, you bring your trade here. You sweep my floors. You plunger my toilets. You take out the trash. You even scrub the head-boards in the warren. And you do it all as a courtesy for me. For one year. Without pay."

"If Lena—"

Patollo put his finger to his lips. Then he lowered that same finger to point at the door.

When Jake found Sheb sitting with Vaclav Hruby and three women in one of the booths behind the zinc bar, Sheb jumped up and stepped to his side. "I was afraid I was gonna have to scrape your guts off that dining room floor. What the hell's the matter with you? What did I tell you about him?"

"Fuck him."

Sheb grabbed Pops's arm and hissed into his ear. "Goddamnit, don't talk like that here. You're tempting the wrong man, I promise you."

Pops looked at Vaclav Hruby, sitting in the booth with the women. Two of them had their arms over his diminutive shoulders.

The third was looking into the crowd, her expression tragic. "What the hell's wrong with these guys," Pops said, too loud again so that Sheb jerked him away.

"Don't even look at him, all right? Just fucking knock it off."

Pops tried again to peer around Sheb, but this time Sheb kept Hruby blocked. "That man owns a stake of this place. He owns a stake in the hide of every one of these girls. He's the oldest crooked money in all Chicago, and if he thinks you're looking at him sideways he'll supervise the worst beating you'll ever get." Sheb finally loosened his grip on Jake's arm. "Do you understand? Have I made it clear who these people are?" Now he dropped Pops's arm with gusto. "God*damnit*, Jake."

Pops stepped to the bar. He held up a finger and ordered a beer and when the barkeep said, "That'll be a quarter," Sheb waved the man away.

"Drink those suds and beat it. You understand? Don't even look back."

Pops took a long pull on the stein of beer and nodded in agreement. He took another drink and then turned to Sheb. "La La?"

"La La Lyng. The Norwegian Nightingale," Sheb said. "Or just La La. Or whatever the hell Andy says."

An Accumulation

Pops had somehow managed to live not only through that night at The Valhalla but through all the years since. What's more, the man he thought might kill him had done much less than that: he'd died himself, years later, in Pops's disbelieving company.

It was a long way from that night in Chicago to Pops's wake, and maybe longer still from La La Lyng to Bett Bargaard, but there she was. Spending her final moments by his open casket. Her head tilted heavenward, her black shawl like something from central casting, her fingers laced at her chest, she appeared in much the same way I imagined Pops would have, had his ghost walked in to comfort her. The funeral director waited in the otherwise empty funeral parlor, his finger swiping an iPad, his tie still knotted. I'd not worn a tie, or even a jacket, and suddenly that felt shameful. As I buried my hands in the pocket of my khaki trousers, Bett unlaced hers and turned to offer wordless permission to the director, who stepped to the casket and lowered the lid. He shook Bett's hand and bowed his head and, though I could not hear him, I suspected from the look on his face that his condolences were sincere. While he whispered, she turned to face me for the first time since I'd arrived. She didn't smile. But then, she rarely did.

When the director turned to leave her side, he signaled me to join them.

"I beg your pardon," he said. "I didn't know there were two sons." He gestured toward the casket. "Would you like to see your father? I can open it again."

"No. Thank you. I'd rather keep the memory I have."

"Not uncommon," he said, then held up the iPad as though to say he had details to attend to. With that he hurried off, leaving Bett and me alone and face-to-face for the first time in years. It occurs to me now how instructive it is that the first thing I said to her, there beside Pops's cold casket, was "Can I help pay for this?" I meant all of it—the casket, the service, the burial plot wherever that would be. I hadn't meant to be businesslike, hadn't meant to replace the director's tone with one no doubt similar. I simply didn't know how to talk to her.

"It's okay, Jon. Your father had all this accounted for." She took my hand with both of hers and held it between us. "You didn't want to see him?"

Her touch was like a dizzying spell, and I can remember well the sensation of weakness in my legs. I looked over at the casket, then back at her. The softness of her hands holding mine, Pops there beside me, cocooned in white silk and his only suit: it was as if I finally realized why I was back in the first place. I can also remember those few tears sliding down my face. And Bett reaching into her purse to retrieve a handkerchief.

"I guess not," I finally answered, wiping my cheeks.

"I understand."

"I don't," I said, and hiccupped a laugh. "Anton did a nice job."

"He did."

"Where is he?"

"He went to pick Angelica up at the airport. Her flight was delayed because of the snow."

"Of course," I said, as though I hadn't forgotten about his daughter. A new wave of shame rose in me.

"I need to sit down," she said, and did, in the same chair she had occupied during the service. "Here," she patted the one next to her. "Angel is almost fifteen now, can you believe that?"

"I can't."

"How are your kids?"

"They're good. Great."

"And Ingrid?"

"She's terrific."

"She's not here," Bett said.

I might have bristled or been embarrassed again, but the best I could do was admit she wasn't. How could I explain to Bett that Ingrid's grievances shared no resemblance to mine? How could I describe Ingrid's fierce loyalty to our children to a woman who had no loyalty to me, much less to Annika and Clara and Ben? Did I dare say that if it had been she who had passed away, I might not have been there? Did my expression betray any of this?

I didn't know the answers to these questions, but when Bett said, "Should we go have dinner?" it was a relief to escape from the pall of resentment.

"Sure," I said.

We sat silently for a moment, each of us looking at Pops's casket, before I returned the handkerchief. She put it back in her purse and snapped it closed and then held it tight on her lap. "He'd be very happy you're here, Jon. It would be a great relief for him to see the two of us sitting together." Now she took my hand once more. "It's a relief to me, too."

This calmed me, and we looked at each other and smiled before she said, "Let's go home."

*

Home. For Bett that meant the house Pops built on Fifth and Russell in north Minneapolis when she found out she was pregnant with me. This would have been the summer of '59, the same year he shelved his competitive jumping skis after finishing in third place at the national championships in Leavenworth, Washington. He always told us the house took him three months from the concrete foundation to drapes in the windows, and all that without a power tool in his arsenal.

Here was the house I grew up in but also a place that seemed almost never to have existed at all, and when I followed Bett's old Ford Taurus into the driveway it felt not like a homecoming but as though I were visiting the home of a character in one of my novels. As she parked in the garage and her taillights flicked off, I killed my engine, too. The headlights dimmed and the falling snow disappeared in the darkness. I got out and walked over to her, and offered my arm as we walked to the door on the side of the house.

"Anton will shovel this blasted snow when he gets here," she said, searching for the keyhole in the dark. "Sixty winters I've lived in Minneapolis. Never missed one of them."

"How many in this house?" I said.

As she unlocked the door, she spoke over her shoulder. "Fifty-five."

Bett removed her coat and hung it carefully behind the door. She untied her boots and slid them off and stepped into a pair of house slippers before going to the kitchen sink and turning on the light above it. I recognized the choreographed arrival, one practiced since I was a teenager. Next would come the transistor radio on the windowsill, and the voice of some WCCO news anchor announcing headlines and weather on the 8s. I told myself I'd remove my own coat and shoes if the radio came to life, which it did only a second later.

When I reached behind the door to place my coat on another of the hooks, I saw Pops's mackinaw hanging there, the green wool worn smooth by so many Minneapolis winters. His hat was there as well, one of those Elmer Fudd numbers with the ear flaps. His boots sat on the floor next to Bett's. It was not the last time I'd experience his ghost that night.

"Come in. Sit down," she said, tying an apron behind her back and gesturing at the kitchen table. As soon as I saw it, the tears welled up again. I pressed them back.

"Can I make you some coffee?" she said.

"Do you still keep a bottle of brandy up there?" I pointed at the cabinet above the stove.

"It was your father's brandy," she said, standing on her tiptoes and opening the cupboard. The bottle was still there. She nudged a footstool over and stepped up to retrieve it. She uncapped the bottle and poured a finger into a snifter brought down from the same cupboard as the booze. "Jon," she said. "Please sit down."

I took the glass to the kitchen table and sat facing the window onto the backyard. The light above the garage door showed the swirling snow and it occurred to me that driving home to Duluth wouldn't be a good idea. I took my phone out and looked at the weather app. It was snowing at home, too, with several inches forecast before midnight.

"Honestly," Bett said. "You kids can't go five minutes without looking at your gizmos."

"Just checking the weather. I was planning to drive home tonight."

"Oh, nonsense. We're supposed to get ten inches of snow. That's what they said on the radio."

As if to take her side, the radio trumpeted its news alert, then a familiar voice crackled over the airwaves. "This is Tom Allworth with your WCCO news update. Snow continues to fall over most of Minnesota tonight . . ." he droned, filing a weather report three entire minutes and chock full of details. As a Minnesotan, I hear those reports like I hear old, almost-forgotten songs. Which is to say I practically hummed along with Mr. Allworth, right up until he concluded: "A travel advisory is in effect for all of Minnesota through noon tomorrow."

"See?" Bett said, nodding at the radio and sitting across from me.

"I wasn't planning on this," I said, checking the time on my phone. It was a few minutes after seven o'clock. "I better call Ingrid."

"Ingrid can wait a minute, yes? Sit here with me. Before Anton gets home. Enjoy your brandy."

I unwrapped the scarf still around my neck and took a sip.

"It's been a long time since you and I sat together, Jon."

"It sure has." I took another sip and set the snifter on the table. Bett reached across and lifted the glass and took a sip herself.

"Not much has changed around here," she said.

"I noticed." It even smelled familiar, like the furniture polish she used and of coffee left too long in the pot.

"And what about you?" she asked.

"Not much is changed with me either. Still teaching at St. Scholastica. Still wondering how the kids grew up so fast. Still doing my best to impress Ingrid."

"And still writing those books. I read the last one. About the lighthouse keeper and his wife." Her eyebrows arched. "I wonder where you come up with those stories."

"I couldn't say, to tell you the truth."

"A woman who pretends to be a man? An upstanding man who has to keep his true self hidden? All that shame and lying, it's interesting to you?"

"They're more than interesting," I said, and took another long sip of brandy. "What time will Anton and Angel be here?"

"Are you hungry? You must be hungry," she said as she stood. "I can find you something to nibble on before dinner."

"You don't need to do that. I'm fine."

"How rude of me—"

"Bett," I said, "it's okay."

She stopped where she stood, reached for the bottle of brandy on the counter, then came back to the table. She sat down and poured another ounce in the glass and took another sip before sliding it across the table. "I'm sorry, Jon. I just don't know how to act around you."

"Like you said, let's just sit here. Tell me about Pops. What happened?"

She folded her hands atop the table, sighed, and looked at the ceiling, her long, thin neck whitening in the light from above. "He was out in the garage. Had just shoveled the driveway and he was changing the wiper blades on the car. Anton found him. He was coming over for Sunday dinner. I was just in here making pork chops. I didn't even know."

"I'm sorry," I said.

She lowered her chin and looked at me. "I'm sorry, too. They say when things like this happen, you're supposed to *know*. You're supposed to sense it. Feel it in your heart. I had no idea." She sighed. "They say he probably had a heart attack. They say he probably died quickly." Her voice was emotionless, but the expression on her face betrayed something. A vulnerability I don't think I'd ever seen before.

"Will you be okay here?" I asked.

"I hope so. Anton will help."

"Where's he living now?"

"He's got an apartment up on Broadway and Washington. Right

by the bar," she said, and whatever vulnerability had briefly touched her was gone as quickly as it had come.

"It's okay for Angelica to stay there?"

"She'll stay here, of course. She has your old room."

"Anton's running the show there at Boff's?"

"Well, it's still Sheb's place, but yes. Anton's the manager."

It was with Sheb's godforsaken name reverberating in the space between us that Anton's headlights appeared muted in the snow. The light shone through the window beside the kitchen table and stalled there, almost throbbing, the snow outside lit again. Bett pulled the curtain aside and nodded and said, "I told him to put new tires on that truck."

I looked outside, too, and could see his pickup stuck on the slight incline of the driveway. My car, even with its snow tires and front-wheel drive, had slipped as I pulled up. I watched him back the truck out of the driveway and park it on the street. A moment later Anton and Angelica stepped out, their silhouettes moving swiftly toward the house. They burst in behind a gale of laughter. Bett hurried to meet them.

"Angel," she said, her voice more alive than I ever remember hearing it. "You're here, sweetheart."

"Hi, Nana. I'm sorry the plane was late. I'm sorry I missed Pops's funeral."

I watched them hug, saw Anton kiss Bett's cheek as he dropped his daughter's bag and smile as he looked at me. "This guy's every-where I go all of a sudden." He turned to his daughter. "Hey Angel, you remember your uncle Jon?"

She pushed the fur-lined hood of her parka back and offered her outstretched hand. "Hi," she said.

"It's been such a long time, Angelica. You're not a kid anymore."

"I guess it's what happens," Anton said. "They change when it's a decade between seeing them." Next he spoke to Bett. "Almost dinner time? I could eat a goddamned horse."

"I'll get it ready."

"Thanks, Ma. Angel, want to help Nana?"

She followed Bett into the kitchen while Anton took off his coat and boots. Angelica was already helping Bett unload dinner from the fridge and was cutting cheddar cheese and folding slices of roast beef onto a small platter before Anton sat down and looked out the window. He motioned for me to join him.

"If it keeps snowing like this," he said, grinning, "we could have an accumulation." And then he sprang up like he'd forgotten the most important thing, weaving between his mother and daughter and into the fridge, where he grabbed two bottles of High Life and a can of Coke. The soda he cracked and set on the counter by Angel, the beers he uncapped, handing one to me and tipping the other in my direction as he sat down again.

"That was a very nice remembrance you gave tonight, Anton," Bett said.

He finished a long pull from his beer. "It's what you're supposed to say at something like this, right?" He took another drink of beer. "You have something to snack on, Ma?"

She stopped what she was doing and reached into a cupboard and retrieved a bag of potato chips, which Anton tore open and grabbed a handful. His phone pinged, and he removed it from his pocket and read the message.

"You driving back to Duluth tonight?" he asked.

"I don't think so."

He finished the last third of his beer. I hadn't even sipped mine yet. "Then enjoy your beer. You can crash at my place."

His phone pinged again. He looked at it, said "Fuck you" under his breath, and then turned to Bett. "Let's get this grub on the table. Jon needs something to wash down his beer."

As quickly as that, the fixings were spread across the counter. Roast beef and cheese and mustard and pickles and onions. A bowl of macaroni salad. The bag of chips. A loaf of bakery bread, which Bett cut in slices as we made our plates. We all gathered around the kitchen table again, the three of them conversing easily and happily, almost as if we hadn't just said goodbye to Pops for the last time. Only once was he mentioned. Angel asked what he looked like in the casket and Anton said, "Like he was dressed for church."

"How's your mom?" I said.

Angel looked up at Anton in what I understood was a request for permission to speak. He nodded, and she said, "Fine."

"What's she up to?" I asked.

"I don't know. She waitresses at this place called Pequod's. And she takes classes at City Colleges."

"Always trying to improve her circumstances, that one," Bett said.

"Hey," Anton snapped.

"I miss you is all," she told Angel.

"I miss you too, Nana."

"But you're here now—right, girl?" Anton said. "Tomorrow we'll go out to the mall. I bet that sounds pretty good."

"Thanks, daddy."

"What kind of classes is she taking?" I asked, not oblivious to the tension Esme, Angel's mother and Anton's ex-wife, aroused as a topic of conversation, but also genuinely curious. I'd seen her only six or eight times, but she had impressed me from the first minute as the best thing that had ever happened to Anton. At least until Angel came along.

"She's taking phlebotomy classes."

"Like, how to take blood?" Anton said, smirking.

"She's gonna get a certificate, then she'll work at a clinic or blood bank."

Bett sat up to say something, but before she could, Anton shot her a warning stare. They both might have been thinking the same thing—that Esme was already a bloodsucker—but Anton didn't want Angel to hear them badmouth her mother.

"Good for her," I said.

"She'll be done in May."

"Tell her hello from me," I said.

"Yeah, me, too," Anton said, taking a bite from his sandwich.

"Don't be an asshole, daddy."

"Never." He reached for her hand and held it for a moment. "Angel's gonna be a senior next year. Straight As for this one. Just like Uncle Jon."

"You misremember," I said. "I hardly ever got *any* As, much less straight." To Angel I said, "What're your favorite subjects?"

"Math and science."

"Maybe you could go to college for phlebotomy, too," Anton said, the tone of his voice shifting. "You and your mom can open a business togeth—"

The chime of his phone interrupted his meanness. He read the message, closed his eyes against it, then looked at me. "Well, big brother, we have to end this fête a little early." Then he turned to Angel. "I've got some work to do tonight, kiddo. Uncle Jon's gonna come with me. But I'll be back first thing tomorrow morning. We'll be at the mall when the doors open."

"But what about the cake?" Bett said. "I made Angel's favorite."

"Save me and Jon a piece for breakfast tomorrow."

Bett put her fork down. She got up and walked through the kitchen and into the living room.

"What's up?" I asked, meaning with Bett.

"I suppose she's upset we're leaving." He took Angel's hand again. "Why don't you finish your sandwich and then clean up this mess for Nana. Maybe you can talk her into a game of cribbage."

"Do you really have to go?" she asked.

"Sheb's an asshole."

The look on her face changed immediately. Resigned and disappointed and understanding. I wondered if it was the look of a child used to moving between her parents. Used to wishing things were different.

"I'm sorry, sweetheart."

"It's okay, daddy. Tomorrow will be fun. Can we go to Vescio's for dinner?"

"Anything you want," Anton said. "I'm gonna say goodbye to Nana."

He walked into the living room, leaving Angel and me alone in the kitchen. "It was a nice funeral," I told her. "Your dad's eulogy was terrific."

"Well, he loved him."

"Did he?"

She ignored my question and finished eating.

"What did you think about Pops?" I asked.

"I thought he was the nicest man in the world." She got up and brought her plate to the counter. "Do you want anything more to eat, Uncle Jon?"

"No, thanks," I said. When Angel started putting things away, I got up and helped her. We worked without speaking and it wasn't until we were wiping the bread crumbs off the cutting board that Anton came back to the kitchen and clapped his hands.

"All right, sweetheart. Grandma wants to play some cribbage. Don't keep her up too late. You too. Hit the sack early. We've got a big day tomorrow."

"Okay, daddy."

He took his leather coat from the hook and gave her a big hug. "I love you, Angel my angel."

She smiled. "I love you, too." To me she said, "It was nice to see you, Uncle Jon."

"Yeah. It was. I hope it won't be so long before it happens again."

I stepped to the door and kicked my boots on and donned my coat and stepped out into the night. Anton was right behind me.

"We can take my truck," he said, clicking the remote key so the lights beamed on the unrelenting snow.

As he drove off, I looked up at the house. The curtains were half-open in the big front window and Bett was standing there, watching us go. I hated myself for the relief I felt at leaving her. I hated myself again when I took a pull off Anton's offered flask, but the wash of hot bourbon shook me from my self-incrimination.

"Life's just never gonna be easy for her," Anton said, his truck fishtailing in the snow. He took a drink, too.

"Will she be all right?"

"She was never all right," he said.

"So it's not just me?"

He looked over at me, his face glowing in the light of the dashboard. "Never has been, brother."

It was a good reminder. "Where are we going, anyway? What's the rush?"

"First stop's the barge office. After that, let's see where the night takes us."

As he turned north onto Penn, I dialed Ingrid's number. When the call went to voicemail, I told her I was staying the night in Minneapolis and asked her to call me back when she could. I put my phone back in my pocket, and Anton turned the radio on. It was tuned to a classical music station, and he started playing an imaginary violin. Outside the snow swirled in the streetlights like it would never land. When we got to Plymouth Avenue, he made a right and turned down the volume on the radio.

"There's something you should know about Sheb. He's old as fuck and looks like half the man he used to be, but what he lacks in youth and size he makes up for with meanness."

"Why would I care about Sheb?"

With his right hand slung over the steering wheel, he turned to look at me. "Because you're going to want to tell him to go fuck himself, and I'd advise against it."

"Tell him to go fuck himself?"

Now he looked back out at the street. There were no cars in front of us. Any time he slowed or accelerated the truck fishtailed. At times, it seemed almost to be floating off the street. "Not all of us are out from under him."

It was my turn to look sideways at Anton. He glanced back at me and raised his arms as though he were an orchestra conductor focusing on the oboes, whose sound suddenly filled the truck. "Not out from under him?" I said.

"Fucksakes, Jon, quit repeating me. You know what I mean. You know Sheb's got us by the balls. That hasn't changed just because you drove down from Duluth to say goodbye to Pops."

I didn't respond.

"Listen, just don't be a prick. To Sheb especially. But don't give me any shit either, right?"

"Yep."

He knocked back another drink of whiskey and dropped the flask on the center console. "I can't believe the son-of-a-bitch called me out in this." He gestured at the blizzard. "Of course, Sheb's got a driver, and brand new snow tires."

A question occurred to me, and I asked it before I thought better. "Did he pay for Pops's funeral?"

Anton glanced at me again. He reached inside his coat and fished from the pocket not his booze but a wad of cash. "I paid for the fucking funeral," he said, holding up the bills as we passed under a streetlight. "Feel free to kick in."

I might have pleaded my case—that I'd already offered Bett money, that I was willing—but I only nodded and told him I would. I was beginning to see myself in a way that felt unfamiliar. And despite the fact that by that hour in our lives Anton and I were as removed as we had ever been, he seemed to know me better than I knew myself. It was almost as if he possessed my own sixth sense. And it wouldn't be the last time that was true on that night.

You'll Make a Girl Jealous

T HE HEADLINE READ *Local Flyer Expected to Challenge World, Olympic Champions at Lakefront.* Pops sat on a bench at the Diversey Harbor lagoon, waiting for Lena. The air was swampy and close and he was sweating under his canvas shirt. Every few minutes he'd remove his newsboy cap and wipe his brow with the heel of his palm. The dull ache in his head would not pass, not even after a second cup of coffee, this one bought in a diner on Fullerton and carried out in a paper cup. The bourbon and beef of the previous night were a far cry from his usual supper, onions and liverwurst on rye or a bowl of chicken soup and a glass of milk.

He'd never read his name in the paper before, but there it was. *Jakob Bargaard, a 25-year-old janitor from Chicago, is expected to compete with a large international field at the Lakefront Ski Jumping Festival at Soldier Field this Friday night. Among the other competitors will be Erling Erlandsson, the Swedish national and world champion, and Arnfinn Bergmann, the former Olympic champion. The event is organized by local financier and impresario Andrus Patollo and will feature two days of festivities, culminating with Friday's one-round, out-of-season ski jumping exposition. Fireworks will follow.*

"Goddamn right there'll be fireworks," Pops whispered. He folded the paper and took a sip of his coffee and watched the lake brume settling over the park. He knew Lena would be late but didn't mind. The waiting only made the seeing sweeter.

He'd met her two months earlier, at a July Fourth picnic here in the park after church. Mutual friends from Minnekirken and a basket of sandwiches, bottles of beer, and a badminton net. He'd seen her, of course, at church and up on the choir risers. She had about her, always, a lightness. A frivolity, or so he imagined. And on the day of the picnic she laughed and flirted and chased butterflies like a child. But when they talked, which they did for an hour, he found her curious and her gaze like a lance. He felt like he was being inspected. But sitting on the blanket in the park, he could hardly look at her for being so smitten. When he asked her questions, she turned them away with the skill of a city alderman. He couldn't believe it when she asked him to walk her home, and found it still harder to believe when, on their way, she insisted on an ice cream sundae. After they stopped, they stood outside the creamery and she thanked him for the company and said she would walk herself the rest of the way. She pointed up the street and said it was just up there. He'd insisted on escorting her, but she declined, and told him to come see her at The Valhalla on Friday night.

Instead, he waited until church the following Sunday. They walked around Logan Square after service, went to the same place for ice cream, and found their second date as pleasing as the first. In the months since, they'd seen each other often (though not enough as far as he was concerned) and never at her place. He didn't even know where she lived. He knew simple things about her—that she liked root beer and read the funny pages and could watch flitting birds for an hour at a time without saying a single word—but he could not tell you her middle name, did not know if her parents were alive or dead or where they came from, did not know how she spent her time except for Friday nights, when she shone under the spotlight at The Valhalla. He wondered if she spent their hours apart like he did, remembering everything they had said to each other, every kiss, every damn soft part of her. He was certain he would never forget, not as long as he lived, the way her hair smelled of lilacs. And he was certainer still that he'd never misplace the memory of the way she looked crossing the few steps from his Murphy bed to his kitchen, or how her lips puckered when she lit a cigarette. He often thought, watching her from across the room, that he would happily trade however many years the good Lord had allotted him if it meant he could have just one with her. Not that she ever asked, but he swore to her that he'd do right by her, whatever she thought that meant. Her wish, he told her every chance he got, was his command.

So why was it that whenever he tried to know her better, whenever he asked her about something more than her pretty dress or the hymns she sang at church, she turned sullen or pouted or kissed him to change the subject? Why had she never mentioned a sister?

He finished his coffee and walked over to the trash can and tossed the empty cup, then returned to the bench and fanned himself with the newspaper before opening it and reading his name again.

When, finally, she did arrive, it was as if she'd materialized from the lagoon. One moment he was lost in his wondering, the next she was stepping from the overgrown shallows with an offering of water lilies. She wore a seersucker skirt the color of the flower stems and a billowy white blouse. There were other flowers in her hat. Her lips were painted pink. And despite the stillness of the air, she moved as if pushed by a warm breeze.

"I ought to be cross with you, Lena," Pops said.

She unleashed her smile. "Never mind *that*."

He took the offered lilies, set them on the bench beside the folded newspaper, then took her in his arms as if to prove her being there at all. Petite as she was, she sat shoulder to shoulder with him. Hers were covered with tresses so blonde and fine that in the light and fog of that morning one might have overlooked them altogether. Sheb, one Friday night at The Valhalla, standing at the zinc bar with Pops, watching her on stage, said she had the chassis of a movie star. Pops had told him to shut the hell up, but it was true she was voluptuous, and in his hands that morning at the lagoon she pressed against him. When he sat back, he studied her eyes. The palest beryl blue, transparent as glassine, unblinking.

"You might have told me about your sister."

"So you could run away?"

She took his hand and removed his hat and put her head on his shoulder as she sat down beside him.

"Well? What about her?" he said.

"I hardly even know where to begin."

"What's her name?"

"Elisabet. We call her Bett."

"And you take care of her?"

She didn't say anything.

"Andrus Patollo says she's simple."

Lena sat up straight. "She's no such thing."

He pulled her back to him, tucked a strand of hair behind her ear.

"She's nervous. That's what some would say."

"What does that mean? Nervous?"

"Oh, I don't know. It means she's afraid of men. It means this godawful town scares her. It means she'd rather bake a loaf of bread or batch of cookies than sip champagne and sing songs in a nightclub." She shook her head. "But she also has episodes. Nervous breaks."

"Why are you the one taking care of her?"

"Who else would? And besides, she helps me as much as I help her."

Pops knew better than to press. He'd seen how quick Lena was to change the subject to easy things. How quick to sulk. But he also knew the question of her sister was urgent, and not only because of their plan to leave Chicago. His mind was reeling that morning, much faster and with more complicated questions than it was used to answering. So he waited for her again. This time for a version of a story he could not have imagined only twelve hours before.

When finally Lena spoke, she said, "Bett is three years older than me. She's shy, but not around me. And Jake, she's very pretty. Much prettier than I could ever be. The problem is she dresses like a pastor's wife and keeps her hair in a bun on top of her head. She doesn't go out much and she doesn't do much at home besides read and cook. She's a wonderful cook. Once in a while we'll go to the picture shows, but she's happiest with a cake in the oven and a book on her lap." She paused, Lena did, like she'd said too much. But Pops just waited.

"She believes in going to church, too. Works part-time in the office at Minnekirken and she prays each night before bed."

"You say that like it's a character flaw."

"She can go to church and pray all she wants."

"You go to church."

"I take my sister to church. And I sing in the choir."

"Okay," Pops said. He shook his head. "Okay."

Lena leaned up and kissed him.

"I still don't understand about her. What'll she do when we go to Minneapolis?"

"She'll come with us, of course."

"Have you told her? About leaving?"

"Don't be silly."

He didn't know what that meant. "Why haven't you told me about her before now?" he said.

"She's never come up."

"Well, you've never mentioned her. How else would she come up?"

She put her hand on the bench between them and leaned away from him. "I knew she would spoil things. I can see what's happening. She's ruining this whole day."

"She's not ruining anything, Lena. She can come along to Minneapolis. Of course she can." He tried to bring her back into his arms but she resisted, her chin still tilted down to the space between them.

"I'm happy she's coming with," he said, feeling suddenly desperate to please her. "The more the merrier."

"Oh, Jakob."

He could hear her breath catching, and when she finally looked up tears were rolling down her cheeks. "Hey now," he said, this time successfully taking her back into his arms. "What's this all about?"

"It's Andy. He talked to me last night."

"Last night? When? I was with him last night."

"He came to my place."

Pops jumped up. "The hell you say?"

She wiped the tears from her cheeks with the back of her hand. "You shouldn't have gone to him."

"Patollo was at your apartment?"

"I told you not to. I told you to let me talk to him."

"How does he even know where you live?"

"You shouldn't have made that deal, Jakob."

He turned away from her. "Well, I did."

"He doesn't make deals. You should know better than that."

"I'm not afraid of him, Lena. Andrus Patollo can kiss my sweet ass."

Now she spoke barely above a whisper. "Because you're not afraid of him, I'm afraid of you."

He turned back to face her again. "What did he say to you?"

"He told me he loves me. He loves the way I sing. He loves to see the looks on the faces in the crowd while they watch me. He said he thinks of me like a daughter. That he'd do anything to help me and Bett. He helps us an awful lot."

Pops sat again, put his elbows on his knees and hung his head.

"He said it wouldn't be good for anyone if I quit The Valhalla. He said he didn't think it would be good for me to go anywhere. He said..."—her voice broke, and she cleared her throat—"that he was sure bad luck would follow us anywhere we went."

"Sonofabitch." Pops reached for her hand. "He's threatening us. You see that?"

"Andy would never hurt me."

"You can't stay here. No matter what. You think he's some up-standing man? You think he cares about you?" He shook his head. "You're a full house on Friday night. That's all he cares about. He takes care of you and your sister because it keeps you loyal. When he finds out you're pregnant he'll get someone else to sing on Friday nights. He'll toss you aside like he never knew you."

She looked at him as if he had just slapped her.

"That's the kind of man he is, Lena. When he hears you're preg-nant, he'll send you somewhere to take care of it. You say no, and he'll force you. By hook or by crook." Pops was furious. "You might as well be one of his racehorses, don't you see that?"

"That's an awful thing to say."

"But it's true, and it's another reason we have to leave. No matter what happens on Friday night."

"Why are you being so cruel?"

"You should know I'll never lie to you. Not for any reason. And you should know that you don't need Andrus goddamn Patollo. Not

66

anymore. You've got me. I'll take care of you. We're going to be a family. You and me and the baby. And your sister."

She appeared lost in thought. Pops couldn't imagine what there was to ponder.

After a long moment, she said, "I'm not a racehorse. I'm a singer."

"You've got the prettiest voice I ever heard."

Again, she drifted off.

"And soon you'll be a mother. Soon we'll be out of this place and starting a life of our own and to hell with Patollo and this rotten city."

She wiped her cheeks again, looked up at him almost eager now.

"The only reason we're not leaving right this minute is because I aim to teach Andrus Patollo a lesson."

*

Pops insisted on meeting Bett straightaway. If Lena had misgivings, she was also in deep water now, and Pops was her buoy. So they hailed a cab and were at her place in five minutes. She lived in a street-level flat on Halsted, not far from the Biograph Theater, where he'd met her more than once. When Lena unlocked the door and went in ahead of Pops, she seemed almost to disintegrate into the shadows. Rather than opening the window drapes to the sidewalk, she turned on a floor lamp in the corner.

"Home sweet home," she said, her luster suddenly gone. She looked tired in the dim lamplight. Tired and afraid and as though she were a miner, not a nightingale. "Can I make you some coffee?" She walked back toward Pops and pulled his jacket from his back and hung it on a rack by the door. "I'll make some coffee. Come sit down."

Pops sat on her sofa and watched her in the kitchen. One bare lightbulb hung above the sink, another above a Formica table pressed under the window. Lena stepped from cupboard to counter to stovetop, filling the teakettle and setting it to boil and filling the filter with coffee. She moved now not like the carefree woman he'd known until just that moment, but rather like his mother had on the mornings when her arthritis was worst. The memory of her brought Pops to his feet and into the kitchen.

"Let me help," he said.

"No," she said, trying to brighten, stepping on his feet as she reached for the icebox door. "I want to make it." She pulled out a bottle of cream and set it on the table next to the sugar bowl. "Sit down," she said, sliding out a chair.

There was a fruit bowl on the table with one overripe apple in it. There was a butter dish and salt and pepper shakers. She moved all this aside with a single sweep of her hand, leaving only the cream and sugar in the center. She took three coffee cups from the cupboard and set them on the table, then stepped back to the stove to wait for the kettle to start boiling.

From his seat Pops took in the rest of the small apartment. In the open cupboard, besides the coffee, there was a box of Corn Flakes and a few cans of soup and canisters of flour and sugar. On the windowsill above the sink, a fern gone brown veiled the alleyway light. In a hallway off the kitchen he saw two doors and against the wall across the living room there was a sliding door and bed. Lena's room, he guessed, judging by the mess of feathers and sequins adorning the cocktail dresses lying around. He walked over to a piano near the entry and saw that better than half the keys were missing.

Lena spoke from the kitchen. "That was here when we moved in." She stepped to the edge of the kitchen floor and crossed her arms. She held a dishtowel and used a corner of it to dab her cheeks.

"This is a real nice apartment," he said.

She raised a hand as though to shush him. "It's terrible. There are mice in the walls. It gets cold in winter. Might as well not have any windows for how drafty these are." She snapped the towel in the direction of the window above the sink as though there were some question as to where the windows were. "And it's dim. Dark. We live in a tomb. Worst of all, the landlord is a creep. He lives across the hall."

"We'll find a nice place in Minneapolis. An apartment at first, but then I'll build you a proper house. We'll raise our children there, with a fence around the backyard and an apple tree in front. I'll see to all that."

"Will you?"

He hurried to her, held her by the elbows. "You bet I will. We'll have windows in every room. We'll get a piano with all the keys. You can sing us all awake each morning."

"That sounds nice, Jakob."

The teakettle whistled, and she kissed him before turning off the burner.

"Your sister, is she here?"

"You'll make a girl jealous, asking around like that." There flashed across her face one of her encore smiles. The sort he'd never be able to understand. She took the kettle from the stove and poured it over the filter. "Maybe she's out for groceries. Maybe she's still in bed. She sleeps late." She watched the water filter into the coffee and then drip into the carafe.

"I see." Pops lit a smoke and watched her. When it was done brewing, she poured them each a cup and put cream and sugar in hers.

She moved to the sofa. There was a newspaper spread across one of the cushions and she gathered and folded it and set it on the floor. "Come over here." Finally, she pushed aside the curtains on another window. He heard her singing softly as she reached for another lamp switch, and whether it was the glow from that lamp or the sound of her voice he could not say, but the room lightened. It lightened and it sweetened and the weight of all that had recently passed became less a thing to fret about. He might even have forgotten about Patollo for a minute or two, as long as it took her to step back into the kitchen to wipe the counter and stovetop and then come back to face him. Her singing had brought some color back to her cheeks and they too seemed to brighten the room.

He tapped the ash into his cupped hand and thought, *We'll be happy. We'll have a simple, happy life.*

No sooner did he think those modest thoughts than they became obsolete. Standing there in the dusky light was Lena's sister. Pops startled. He forgot her name for a moment, but he sat up as though to introduce himself and then couldn't. He stood, his smoke in one hand and ashes in the other. Bett, he remembered. She hadn't looked up, only stood there in her bathrobe, her hair wet and brushed and hanging down her back. She smelled clean and of flowers and though her robe was threadbare at the cuffs and lapels, it was also pretty. She was tall, he saw now that he was standing. With long arms and long slender fingers. She pointed one of them at his hand and said, "Please put out that cigarette."

Pops looked at the smoke in his hand and then quickly around the room; finding no ashtray, he dropped the cigarette and ashes into the half-drunk coffee on the table between them. He wiped his hands on his trousers. "I'm Jakob Bargaard," he said. "Maybe Lena mentioned me?"

Bett looked at Lena now. "Who is this?" she said.

"I believe he's just introduced himself. It's Jake Bargaard. My fiancé."

"You must be Bett? Lena's told me all about you. It's nice to put a face to the name."

Lena walked over to her sister. She took one of her hands and said, "Look at me, would you?" Her voice was soothing and patient. Bett did as she was asked and Pops could see Bett's faraway green eyes, faint and lovely and suspect. He could hardly look away.

"Jake works at church."

"I've seen him before."

"It's a beautiful place, eh? Minnekirken. Your church."

"It's not your church?" Bett asked.

He looked to Lena, like a child imploring his teacher for the answer. But Lena only smiled, so he turned back to Bett. "Well, I work there, see?"

"Lena said that." She looked down. "What's he doing here? Why do men keep coming here?"

"I wanted you to meet him," Lena said. "How would you like to move away? To another city?"

"Fiancé?" Bett said. "You're getting married?"

"Isn't it wonderful news?"

"Why?" Bett risked a glance at Pops, who stood there dumb as a mule.

"Well, because he's a good man and we're in love."

Bett glanced at him again. Longer this time. Her eyes like scoops. He felt dizzy and embarrassed for who he was. Embarrassed for Lena's pregnancy. And, what was worse, he felt like a liar. Like a con-man.

"Move where?" Bett asked.

"To Minneapolis," Lena said. "Up in Minnesota. Jakob and I are going to get married and have a family and you'll come and live with us, too."

Bett braved one more look at Pops, then turned and walked down the dark hallway. He stood there, flummoxed, watching her go, trying to blink her back, the faint smell of flowers trailing Bett away. After some time, he turned to Lena. Before he could say anything, she started singing. Softly at first, almost whispering. *"We were waltzing together . . . to a dreamy melody . . ."* She walked toward him as she sang, reached into his shirt pocket and took his cigarettes and shook one loose. *"When they called out change partners . . . and you waltzed away from me . . . now my arms feel so empty . . . as I gaze around the floor . . ."* Her voice trailed off and she put the cigarette to her lips

71

and lifted her head without looking at him. Pops lit her cigarette. She took a drag and then did meet his eyes. "I told you she's beautiful. I saw how you looked at her."

As though he hadn't heard her, he said, "There's nothing wrong with her."

"She'll trick you, that one. She acts like she doesn't know her chin from her elbow, but she does. I know what looks like that mean. Fifty nights at The Valhalla will teach you all you need to know about looks like that."

"Lena, sweetheart, what are you talking about?"

"I'm a simple girl. I've been trading on that fact my whole life. I know how to swap a wink or a smile for a quarter in my tip bowl. Every night I make that trade. Bett, she sits in this awful apartment every day. She reads her novels and knits her scarves and who knows what she cooks up in that head of hers. She acts like she can't cope, but she's a woman all the same. I saw the way she looked at you. It's like how the men at The Valhalla look at me."

Pops had no idea what she was saying, a fact the blank expression on his face clearly conveyed.

"I'm saying she has ideas of her own. I'm saying she stole a glance at you and me, and now she has *other* ideas." She took a long drag of her cigarette and then dropped it in the same coffee cup Pops had doused his in. "I used to think she didn't know much. For most of my life, I've bought it. But now I'm not so sure."

Pops sat down again. He looked at Lena's slim waistline. It was hard to imagine so much possibility taking root in there. When he looked up to her face, her eyes were glassy and she appeared ready to cry. He put his hands on her hips and was about to say something but stopped. Bett had come back down the hallway. She wore a peach-colored dress and a white cardigan sweater and had a purse hanging from one arm and a suitcase in her other hand. She'd braided her hair and when she set the suitcase down, the braid fell over her shoulder.

"Okay," she said.

"Okay what?" Lena said.

"I'm ready to go now."

Lena smiled then. Pops could see the softness coming back into her eyes. He could see that for this moment, at least, she saw Bett as the girl who needed to be taken care of. She rested her hand on Bett's arm. "It's not time to go yet. Not until Friday night."

"But I'm ready now."

Lena cupped her sister's cheeks in her hands. "We can't leave yet. Jake has business to settle first."

Every Old Ski Jumper's
a Liar

AND WHAT A LONG BUSINESS IT'S BEEN. Almost sixty years had passed between that morning in the apartment on Halsted and the night Anton and I pulled up to Sheb's office under the lighted arch of the Lowry Avenue bridge. Among his many enterprises was a Mississippi River barge and recycling racket, and buried beneath mountains of scrap metal a single-story cinderblock building with two barred windows, lit by a trio of towering lights, served as his headquarters. As Anton parked beside the Suburban and three other cars, my phone rang.

"It's Ingrid," I said. "I'll wait out here. Leave this running?" I patted the dashboard.

He stepped out, and I answered the call as I watched him head toward the door. A motion sensor light flickered as he reached it, and he disappeared into the shop.

"Hello, my love. Are you all right?" Ingrid said.

"I'm just fine."

"How was dinner with Bett? How was the funeral?"

"Everything's fine. There were lots of folks at the visitation. Lots of people I haven't seen in decades. He was well loved. Dinner at Bett's? What can I say? Anton was there. So was his daughter. She flew in from Chicago. I haven't seen her in, how many years? She seems like a great kid."

"Well, you always liked her mother."

"Better than Anton did, I'm afraid."

"Are you at his place? That's where you'll stay the night?"

"We're headed there soon. And what about you? How're things at home?"

"You should see the snow! It's coming down in curtains."

"I wish I were there. There's nothing I like more than a winter's night with you. Especially a cold and snowy one."

"We could share a bottle of wine in front of the fireplace."

"For starters," I said.

"You flirt," she said. "Tell me, what are you boys doing tonight? Don't say you'll go to that bar he runs. What's it called?"

"Boff's. God, I hope not, though I guess he lives in an apartment right next door. I can't imagine what it'll be like."

"Is it good to see him?"

For a long moment, I stared at the squat building in front of me, thinking it looked like a munitions shelter, and that inside my brother was as likely rigging a bomb as disabling one. I had no idea what kind of business he was in with Sheb, and no idea about the sort of person Anton had become.

"It is," I said. "Truly. I can't believe I'm about to say this, but I forgot how much I love him."

"Oh, Jon."

"He seems adrift, though. I've only been with him for three hours and he's already had half a dozen drinks. He gets a text message every fifteen minutes, and talks back at his phone. He got a text from Sheb

75

and we left Bett's house like it was on fire. You should've seen the way he looked at Angel when we left. Christ, you should have seen how she looked at him."

"I suppose your father's passing is hard for him."

"I wonder."

Until then only one of the two small windows set in the cinderblock had been lit, but there was suddenly a bright light in the other. The silhouette of someone's head and shoulders passed, filling the small space, then passed by a second time a moment later before that window went dark again.

"You should have seen all the old ski jumpers there tonight. Most everyone I ever knew. My cousins. All the old guys. Noah came down."

"I can imagine the hum in that funeral parlor, what with all the stories going around."

"There was lots of lying, that's for sure. But not from Noah. And not from Anton. He gave a nice eulogy. I wish it hadn't surprised me." In the background, I heard the doorbell chime.

"Oh, honey, Clara and her new girlfriend are here."

"In the middle of a blizzard?"

"They made us a loaf of pumpkin bread and rode their new fat tire bikes over in the snow to drop it off."

"Tell me again this new friend's name?"

"It's Delia. She seems nice. And I don't mind at all that she's got Clara bringing treats over. In the middle of a storm or otherwise."

I heard Clara shout, "Mom, we're here!" and Ingrid holler back, "Just a minute!" Her voice came back to me. "Now listen, Jon. I hope you and Anton have a nice evening. Don't worry about us. We're all safe and sound."

"Give Clara a hug for me?"

"Of course I will. And call me in the morning? Let me know when you're on the way home?"

"I'll talk to you then, love. Goodnight."

"Goodnight."

The absence of her voice seemed to intensify the storm outside. I switched off the wipers and turned the radio back on and reclined in the big bucket seat. The snowflakes melted as soon as they hit the windshield, so after only a few seconds the view went bleary. The clock on the dash read 8:59. My bedtime most nights, though surely not this one. I knew Anton would keep me up. He'd keep drinking. We'd talk. I was looking forward to it, actually. With the thought of the long night before me coupled with the brandy and beer, I closed my eyes to the voice on the radio announcing Debussy's "The Snow Is Dancing" performed by Noriko Ogawa.

When I opened them, it was 9:30 and Anton still hadn't come out of Sheb's office. I turned the wipers on and sat for a moment rubbing the sleep from my eyes and then killed the engine, put the keys in my pocket, and stepped out of the truck. The footprints Anton had made were drifted over. Eight or ten inches of snow must have fallen by then, and the wind was funneling up the river. The motion light turned on as I stepped to the door. A series of three deadbolt locks descending from eye level to the knob greeted me. I didn't knock.

I don't know what I was expecting to find, but it wasn't the posh space in front of me. Less an office than well-appointed apartment, there was a pool table and high-tops and chairs on a red rug, a bar along the wall to my left beneath the window that had momentarily flickered on before, and to my right another closed door. I opened it, and walked into what was clearly Sheb's office. The cigar smoke overwhelmed, and through it I saw him sitting there, still in his suit from the funeral. Anton relaxed on a couch with his feet resting on a glass-topped coffee table. Across from him, on another couch, two young women reclined with their bare legs and short skirts in a tangle. They looked younger even than Clara, who was finishing college that year.

"Goddamn, if it isn't the prodigal son. In my own office," Sheb said, blowing another mouthful of smoke across his desk. "Your old lady must've had quite an agenda for you, as long as she kept you on the phone. We've been in here raising a toast to Pops."

I saw then a bottle on the coffee table, surrounded by three shot glasses. When I looked back at Sheb, he had another glass raised in his fat hand.

"You *should* remember him," I said.

His face lifted in one of his slow, twisted smiles. "Now that we're alone, the real Johannes shows up. I'm happy to see him."

"You ready to go?" I asked Anton.

"When Anton told me you were coming to grace us with your presence, I thought about how I might welcome you home," Sheb said. "Let me introduce you to Chloe." He stood, and lumbered to a cabinet in the shadows behind his desk. When he reemerged, he held another glass. He came around to the coffee table, and filled the glasses all around. "Chloe," he said, "this is Anton's big brother. He's a famous guy, though you'd not know it to look at his shirt." He offered me a glass. "You couldn't bother to get dressed for your father's funeral?"

Chloe leaned forward and shot her drink. "What kind of famous are you, baby?"

"I'm not famous," I said. "Not by any stretch of the imagination."

"He's a famous author," Anton said.

"I'm not famous," I said again. "And no thanks," I added to Sheb, who shrugged and drank from the glass he'd just offered me.

"Your dad was proud of you. Whenever one of your stories came out, he'd bring me a copy. I liked the last one best, about that nance lighthouse keeper and his bitch wife."

"I didn't know you could read, Sheb," I said.

He smiled again, drank another drink. "I can read everything. Books and otherwise." He went back to his desk and sat heavily. "For example, I can read the look on Chloe's face. She wants to party with you."

"Anton," I said, "let's go." To the women I said, "I'm sorry."

"There's nothing to be sorry about, Jon," Sheb said. "And don't be in such a hurry. The night is young."

"I'm not," I said. "And my brother and I have some things to talk about in private."

"You don't see him much, do you? Why is that?"

"Because I'm an asshole."

"No argument here," Anton said.

I looked at him, sitting back on that leather couch in his black leather jacket, his boots up on the table, his hands behind his head. He winked at me, like this was all a game among fraternity brothers.

"Sit down, Jon," Sheb said. "Please. I want to visit. I haven't seen you in years."

"Yeah, stay," the woman who'd spoken before said. "We *do* want to party." She held up a small vial, asking Sheb's permission. When he nodded, she uncapped it and tapped a small mound of coke onto the tabletop. She divided it into five lines with a credit card and rolled a twenty-dollar bill and snorted one. She handed the twenty to the other woman, who bent and snorted. Anton put his feet on the floor and leaned across the table, his leather jacket creaking. He did a line, and offered me the bill.

I took my phone out of my pocket.

"You calling your wife to see if it's okay to take a little sleigh ride?" Sheb said.

"I'm getting an Uber."

"Jesus Christ," Anton said. "You're such a buzzkill." He stood up, wiped his nose. "You don't need a goddamn Uber."

Sheb laid his palms flat on the blotter centered on his desk. His fingers spread wide, his thumbs drummed some off-rhythm beat.

"I wish I had a brother. Someone to talk to like that. I guess Jake fit that description when we were kids, but even that was different." He cleared an imaginary layer of dust from the blotter. "Chloe, I don't think Jon wants a date tonight." He opened the middle drawer behind his desk, removed and counted out five hundred-dollar bills, and waved them at her. "Why don't you and Kristi go over to the bar and have a night on me?"

Chloe got up and took the money. She crammed it into her purse and pulled a fur coat over her shoulders. And then she looked at me and said, "I never met anyone famous before. Well, except for pro athletes, but they don't count." She took a pack of cigarettes from her pocket and lit one. She handed it to the other woman, and lit a second. To Anton she said, "You guys gonna go to the bar?"

"We'll stop in," Anton said.

"Good," Chloe said before leaning down to kiss Anton on the mouth. When she stood up, she cupped her hand between her legs and pretended to swoon.

Kristi hadn't said a word since I'd come in, but before they went to the door she turned to me and said, "I read your book. The one called *A Lesser Light*. I thought it was so strange. Good strange." She glanced at Sheb, weary, but risked a final thought. "And I didn't think the wife was a bitch. I thought she was bad ass." She walked out of the office. Chloe followed.

When the outside door closed behind them, a whoosh of cold air swallowing up their absence, Sheb said, "I never knew a stripper to read a book, but I guess the world is full of surprises."

"You're just learning this now?" I said.

"I knew another Bargaard with a smart mouth," Sheb said. "Rest his soul."

"We'll all end up like him some day," I said.

"Tell me, Johannes, is that some of your hard-learned professorial wisdom?"

I shook my head. "No. It's the first day of class in every subject, Sheb."

"No wonder I didn't know, never having gone to school much."

"There's no use starting now. Anton?"

I walked to the door. Anton got up and followed me. "Later, Sheb," he said.

"Anton?"

My brother turned back. So did I. Sheb was holding a Nike shoe-box. Anton went and took it from him and together we walked back out into the snow.

When we got into the truck, he stashed the shoebox under a blanket on the floor of the passenger cab.

"What's that?" I asked.

"Business," he said, putting the key in the ignition, starting the truck and blowing on his hands.

"Why don't you hate him?"

"Sheb? I do," Anton said.

"Then why do you still work for him?"

"Because I don't have a PhD, dumb ass. No one's going to hire me to teach English at some tony college. I barely graduated from high school." He flipped the wipers on, backed out of the parking lot, and drove to Washington Avenue, where the truck spun in a snow-drift for a moment before he turned left. "We gotta stop at my place so I can change."

"Change? For what?"

"It's Friday night, man. I've got to get the cuts to market."

"What are you talking about?"

He slowed through an intersection and looked both ways. No cars were coming from either direction. He turned the volume down on the radio and said, "Listen, this is where I live. This is what I do."

"What do you do?"

He looked at me. "I'm a fucking butcher, okay?" He took a pack of cigarettes from inside his coat and lit one, offered me the pack, and pocketed them again after I declined. He cracked the window and blew a stream of smoke out. "I have some work to do is all. Close your eyes if you want. But don't hassle me."

He took another drag from his cigarette and flipped it out the window as we pulled up to the stoplight at Broadway. Boff's was kitty-corner now, and he didn't even glance at it.

I wish I could say that I was free of judgment, that I knew my brother's life was his to live as he wished. But as we sat in the silence of the snow-shrouded streets, I felt only what I perceived to be the unhappiness of his existence, and I took some responsibility for it. Like I might have done more to protect him. Like I should've somehow stopped the decades from passing us by. I felt all this even as I knew I was wrong. I was certain, as he fishtailed through the intersection and we drove by Boff's, that if he could read my thoughts he'd tell me to go fuck myself. And so I said, "How much does a rig like this cost?"

"It's a company car, man."

He turned left on Eighteenth, then took another left into an alleyway and parked beside a twelve-foot cinderblock wall. "Home again, home again." He shifted the truck into park and turned it off. From behind the center console he grabbed the shoebox and got out. He opened the back hatch of the topper and lowered the rear gate and set the shoebox atop another box, this one the size of a treasure chest, and lifted them both out. I closed the truck's gate and the topper hatch. We climbed three flights of stairs and I waited while he set the boxes down and unlocked the door. Below us, and across another alleyway, the neon sign for Boff's throbbed in the blizzard. I scanned the parking lot. Thirty or forty cars covered with snow. It was Friday night, after all.

I wouldn't have been more surprised if the inside of his place was a cathedral nave. It must have been a couple thousand square feet, almost all of them open. Floor-to-ceiling windows of the faux industrial kind were equal size to the brick walls between them. The ceilings were twenty feet high, the floor concrete. In the center of the apartment was a sleek kitchen, all stainless steel and black granite, with four posts towering from the corners of the massive counters, half of which sat above a bank of leather barstools. All of it glowed from the street and interstate lights that filtered through the snow and those many-paned windows.

"Nice place," I said.

"I built it out myself," he said, carrying the boxes to the kitchen and setting them on the counter. He hit a light switch on the wall and a row of recessed lights blinked on one after another. "Have a look around. Want a beer?"

"I'm good." I wandered to what might have passed for the living room in the corner of the apartment overlooking downtown. Where the skyline should have been only a quaver of amber light pulsed, like the beating heart of the blizzard. An L-shaped couch and a table cluttered with car magazines and video game controllers sat on a huge rug. There was a television in the corner. The bedroom and bathroom were the only walled-off rooms of the apartment, and a movie screen hung from a mount in the ceiling above the bedroom wall. Sitting on a table ten paces from the screen was an old reel-to-reel movie projector.

"What's this?" I called across to him.

Anton was unpacking the larger of the boxes into a refrigerator under the counter. "You're going to love that. Give me a second."

I poked my head into the bedroom, which was disheveled, then walked around the kitchen to the other side of the apartment. The windows on this side were covered with vertical blinds, and next to the windows was a dining table that would have accommodated a dozen guests on the benches along either side of it. Between two of the shuttered windows were three five-by-five-foot framed posters of my brother ski jumping (the first in his inrun position, the second in midflight, and the final in a deep telemark landing) and, lined up like a bar chart, his collection of jumping skis were also mounted on the wall. Ten or twelve pairs of them, as close to anything the timeline of his younger life.

"Cool as shit, right?" He was standing on the other side of the dining table, the light above now casting a spotlight on his skis.

"How did you manage to keep them all?"

"I didn't. Pops did. There's a stash of yours over at Mom's. I'm sure she'd be happy if you got them out of the garage rafters."

I went over to the shortest pair. Splitkeins without bindings. Maybe 200 centimeters long. There were Sokols and Kongsbergs and Fischers. But the last six pairs were all Elans, the Bargaard brand of choice. I walked along the wall, my fingertips grazing the skis. When I got to the end, I turned to him. "This is amazing."

He nodded.

I pointed at the posters.

"Harrachov," he said.

"1983?"

He nodded again.

"Which skis?" I asked.

He pointed at the pair of blue Elans.

"Fucksakes, that's more than thirty years ago."

"Believe me, I've done the math many times. The answer never gets better."

I took another survey of the apartment and pointed around him at the box on the counter. "Tell me what's in them?" I said.

"Honest to God, it's pork chops and steaks."

"Why do you need fifty pounds of meat?"

"Sustenance." He opened a different fridge and pulled out a can of beer. "You sure you don't want one?"

"I'm sure."

He switched off the dining table light, and the kitchen light, so that only a floor lamp next to the couch shone. "Come here," he said, closing the blinds on the windows overlooking the skyline and the interstate. "Sit down." He bent to the projector, turned a lever, and it wheeled to motion. "I'm gonna change. Watch this."

From the corner of my eye, I saw him step back to the kitchen counter and lift the shoebox. He walked to his bedroom door and paused. "That's Pops. 1954. I've watched it a hundred times. The projector belonged to the ski club. I found it over in the basement of the bingo hall before it was torn down."

Then I was alone in Anton's living room, with only the whir of the antique movie projector and the film leader counting down from eight. The voice of Jack Brickhouse, the famous Chicago sportscaster, joined me.

"Welcome to Soldier Field, sports fans. What stands before me is one hundred and fifty feet of towering thrills. It's been seventeen years since the city has seen something like this: more than one hundred daredevil ski jumpers from all over the world competing in an out-of-season competition in front of thousands of spectators. Fifteen thousand dollars of crushed ice, and a cool Lake Michigan breeze to keep it fresh, means it'll be just like the middle of winter."

The footage panned the crowd, thousands and thousands of people in the stands. Men in fedoras and trench coats, the women in dresses and matching hats and scarves. The jump was towering indeed, rising from the colonnades like a ramp to heaven. The camera zoomed to the top of it, where four American flags whipped in the wind.

"Will it be world champion Erling Erlandsson, here from Sweden, who takes home the victory?" The camera cut away to a fresh-faced kid, signing autographs on the field. *"Or the Olympic champion, Norwegian*

Arnfinn Bergmann?" Again, the camera cut away to Bergmann, mugging for a throng of adoring young women. *"Or will it be America's hope, Chicago's own Jakob Bargaard, who sets the standard?"*

The camera caught Pops in silhouette, his skis on his shoulder, a cigarette pinched between his lips, his V-neck sweater across his slight shoulders. He glanced at the camera, winked, and disappeared into the parade of jumpers. The film spliced, and when it came back on it was to a stage at the end of the hay-strewn Soldier Field turf, which served as the outrun. It spliced again and picked up in the middle of Lena Lyng's rendition of the national anthem. Her voice cut in and out, but her lips kept singing, her hand stayed on her heart, and, for all I tried to blink him away, the man standing at the bottom of the staircase remained a young Magnus Skjebne. He wore a long leather duster, was damn near the size of the car parked beside him. Still again the film cut out, and for a while only single images would flit across the screen. A shot of the crowd. The announcer on the stage. A ski jumper crashing through the hay bales on the field turf. Occasionally a jumper in midflight, or landing, or standing at the top of the scaffold ready to kick himself onto the inrun. It was like listening to someone talk and only hearing every tenth word.

But then, for twenty or thirty seconds, the film and the announcer's voice would steady and come out together. A sequence of four jumpers in a row, with exclamations of their daring and courage. *"Here's the Finnish jumper, Matti Rantannen, ready to make his first leap. Can he best the 112-footer of the last flyer? He's in the air—"* Brickhouse's voice gave way to the clicking of the film, but the image of the Finnish ski jumper flying down the scaffolded landing hill did not. He was the picture of elegance, his feet locked together, his skis like a single plank, his body purposeful, following his outthrust chin, his hands locked and leading the way. Even through the choppy footage he appeared to not even twitch. Not even blink. And when he landed, his skis still ramrod straight and locked together, his arms thrown wide now, fingertips up, he had about him a stoic and emotionless perfection. *"110 feet for the flying Finn,"* Brickhouse's voice singsonged as Matti Rantannen slid into the hay bales on the outrun. He popped up and dusted the chaff from his sweater and raised a hand to the cheering crowd.

Another half-dozen jumpers came and went without commentary. Two of them crashing, one quite spectacularly. When Brickhouse's voice reemerged, he said, *"And now we're down to the final three jumpers in our competition. First up, wearing number 101, a fellow who could have taken the L to the stadium today, the local favorite Jakob 'The Bird' Bargaard."* Only the roar of the crowd accompanied Pops as he kicked out of the start. He threw his hands in front of him and crouched impossibly low. So low his ass seemed almost to rest on the tails of his skis.

Did the film go to slow motion? Did the absence of Brickhouse's voice intone admiration and hopefulness and respect? Could I actually recognize, in the grainy image of Pops's face, the aspect of a man I knew to be utterly and unfailingly determined on this, his favorite subject, in this, his most important moment? Did the concentration that attended that look give way to bliss, plain and simple, as he sprang from the take off, as he settled his hands not out beyond his face like nearly all the jumpers who had come before him, but at his sides? Did he pause, there at the top of his flight, and ride on the exhalations of thirty thousand Chicagoans? Did a thought of Lena Lyng cross his mind? Did the sound of her voice, singing *"Blow me a kiss, from across the room"* lift his hopes? Or was it the hand of his redeemer, lifting him by the back of his sweater? Surely there was something more than the zephyr off Lake Michigan, because where all the other hundred jumpers had reached their zenith somewhere over the makeshift knoll, Pops kept rising. It looked like he would never land. It looked—and I recall now that this is what he always said about that jump—that he wouldn't land until he was in

Minneapolis with Lena and her sister, his wife, my mother, Bett. Had he seen himself up there? In the Soldier Field troposphere? Is that how he knew what he looked like?

Though of course he did land. At 133 feet. In an immaculate telemark and with a look of ecstasy on his face. 133 feet was altogether too far, nearly on the playing field itself. It was as much a surprise that he didn't fall as that he went so far in the first place. The camera followed him to the hay bales where he came to a sliding stop. He did not wave at the raucous crowd. Did not raise his arms in triumph. Did not wink or grandstand or gloat. He merely removed his skis and stepped out of the hay and waited for the world and Olympic champions to take their turns.

Arnfinn Bergmann went first and, though his jump was stylish, he landed at 118 feet. The world champion Swede went 109 feet, and dragged his hands on landing, skidding into the hay. The last frames of the movie show another hulking man in a fur coat, his hat raised in one hand and a cigar in the other, standing in front of the same microphone that Lena Lyng had used to sing the national anthem. She was still there beside him, in a fur stole, looking like a Hollywood starlet. The woman who might have been my mother. The man who would later die at my feet.

The receiving wheel on the projector sped up, sending the loose end of film flapping. When I looked back into the kitchen, there was my brother standing over the counter, talking to another man I'd not even notice come in. Anton had changed into jeans and a black Adidas track jacket. The man standing next to him was half his size, a wizened seventy-year-old whose shirt collar was four sizes too big. Still, he wore a tie and jacket and a herringbone flat cap. His gold-rimmed glasses covered half his face.

"You don't recognize me, do you, Jon?"

His voice sounded familiar, like something I'd known my life long but couldn't quite place. "You were at Pops's funeral tonight?"

"Sure I was."

We walked toward each other. "I'm Phil Johnson. Tom Johnson's old man."

"Of course," I said. Tom learned to jump with me at Wirth Park under the watchful eye of Selmer Dahlson. "How are you?"

"I'm sorry about your father. He was a friend of mine. A damn good one."

I nodded, and then looked at Anton, who was watching us, one hand on the box on the counter. "Phil helps on Friday nights," he said, divining my question even before I knew what it was.

Phil shrugged his shoulders and arched his eyebrows. "What can I say, my public works pension ain't what it needs to be."

It was my turn to shrug.

"Got a bag each of steaks and chops, Phil." Anton held up two canvas grocery bags. "You got the produce?"

"In my car."

"There's a full house next door."

"In and out, then," Phil Johnson said. "Gimme a hand with this down to the car?" He turned to me. "I'll say hi to Tom for you."

"Please do. Good to see you, Mr. Johnson."

He turned to Anton. "Mr. Johnson, you hear that? Maybe you should take a page from your brother's playbook. Show a little respect now and again."

"Sure thing, Mr. Johnson," Anton said, grabbing the two shopping bags from the counter.

When they were both out the door, I went to the refrigerator and lifted the lid and opened the box sitting inside. There were dozens of cuts of meat and a stack of pre-cut butcher paper and nothing else. I closed the lid on the box, then the refrigerator, and went back to the projector.

I lifted the receiving reel, fed the film back through the front reel, and switched the knob to rewind. The movie wheeled from back to front, and before Anton returned from helping Phil Johnson I was threading the film back through the projector.

The door opened. Anton stomped the snow from his boots. "It's still dumping," he said.

I stood upright. "Phil Johnson?"

He walked into the kitchen and grabbed another bar stool and brought it over to where I was standing by the projector. "I didn't hire him." He finished the job of threading the projector.

"How does it even work? The meat?"

"I wrap it in butcher paper. Phil brings it next door and sells meat from one hand and eight balls from the other. People think he's fundraising for the Boys and Girls Club. Who'd ever suspect an old fucker like him of dealing?"

"Who buys it?"

"Everyone."

"How much does Phil Johnson get paid?"

"I have no idea."

"This is how Sheb makes his money?"

He smirked. "With me and Phil? Fuck no." When the film was ready to roll again, Anton looked up and said, "Want to watch it again?"

"How then?"

He sat heavily on the barstool. "He runs that shit all up and down the Mississippi. Winona to La Crosse to Davenport and Dubuque. All the fucking way down to St. Louis and Memphis and the Gulf of Mexico. A dozen other stops along the way. Hundreds of pounds at a time."

"Hence the barge office."

"Hence the barge office."

"And you, you're just the Minneapolis guy?"

"I run Boff's, man. I run Boff's and I package the meat and I deliver it to the eastside of the northside. When Sheb dies, I get the bar.

When I get the bar, I quit packing the meat. I sell the bar. I open a ski shop in Edina or Wayzata."

"That's your retirement plan?"

"Fuck it. I don't know. That old bastard's never gonna die anyway."

"Don't you worry about getting caught? What would happen?"

"Of course I worry. But what else am I gonna do?"

I didn't know the answer to that.

"We'll go next door for a drink later. After Phil's done."

"Okay," I said.

"And now we'll watch Pops one more time, yeah?"

"Hey," I said, and he swiveled to look at me. "Is all that Sheb business why Esme left?"

"Esme left because I don't know how to make omelets."

He turned the projector on, and the film clipped through again.

*

Most of Pops's stories changed over the years. A perfect jump first described on Big Nansen out in New Hampshire might eventually have taken place in Steamboat Springs, Colorado, instead. Tournaments narrowly won or lost were lost or won. The hairiest winds at Pine Mountain would become gales in Ishpeming. Even if he wasn't keeping track of these discrepancies, I was. His stories went into a diary I kept, and on nights when I had trouble falling asleep or mornings when I woke up before dawn, I lived my boyhood through the lens of his old yarns as told through my own pen, learning those stories over and over the way other kids learned Bible verses or American history or baseball box scores from the morning paper. His inconsistencies I understood to be part of a larger truth the whole sum of which was the story of his life. And, so, my own life, too.

Two things, though, were never confused or conflated: his abiding friendships and rivalries, and what he called "The Great Chicago

Heist," the story that began in the private dining room at The Valhalla nightclub and ended with an eight-hour drive in a Chevy delivery truck with the words PATOLLO VENTURES painted on the side panels. I suppose in most ways it's a story that's not over. I suppose it's a story that never will be.

But for Pops's purposes, or rather for Anton's and mine, the story of the Great Chicago Heist had always unfurled as the old newsreel told it. Lena Lyng singing the national anthem. The throngs of spectators. The towering scaffold. The procession of jumpers. The strong wind off Lake Michigan and the hay bales and the Swedes and Norwegians and Finns. We already knew about the venal Patollo and the shattering glass and the specter of a man named Vaclav Hruby. We knew about the surprise of Bett. And of course we knew about Pops's perfect jump, not only the most perfect jump of his life but the most perfect jump *ever*. He claimed he had proof.

Oh, we were spellbound. At five and ten years old, we gulped his stories as fast as the chocolate milk he mixed for us. "What proof, Pops?" we asked.

He'd raise his hands, spread them like a priest calling down the Holy Spirit. "It's all around us, boys. Just look!"

He was a master of the dramatic pause, and at a moment like this he'd take a sip of his coffee and brandy and study us over the rim of his cup. It occurs to me now to wonder whether those caesuras were part of some calculation, one meant to arouse us, or if his thoughts were only then arising in him. Whatever the case, he'd loll with them, watching us. Smiling. Remembering. Weighing what to say next.

"You boys must remember that the only two jumpers behind me were a couple of crackerjacks?"

"But you beat them, Pops! You beat the best. Is *that* the proof?"

Another, more devilish grin turned up his lips. "You know what it's like, Johannes. To kick your boots into your bindings, pull those cables up over the heels, push the front throws down. You stand up and slide your skis front and back a few times. You double check your bindings, and while you're looking at the cables on your heels, you glance at the guy behind you. He's supposed to be better than you. That's why he's behind you. The best for last, right?"

Anton kept a list of the jumpers who were better than I was, and he'd trot them out one at a time, taunting me. But then he'd sober up, recognizing that his own teasing logic meant that the two men who jumped behind Pops were meant to best him. At this he'd grow lachrymose.

"I always liked having those guys behind me. I especially liked it when I knew they *were* better than me. And let me tell you, boyos, Arnfinn and Erling were a hundred times the jumpers I was. The difference was, they were there for fun. For a free trip to Chicago. I was there to get out of that stinking city. In other words, they were goofing off. I wasn't. I was ready to *assassinate* them."

"That means kill them," I told Anton, at which he sprang from his chair, spraying the room with a hellstorm of machine gun sounds.

"And you did," I said. "You killed 'em!"

Pops put his finger up to his lips. *Shhh*, he meant to say. He meant to say he killed them with beauty and perfection. He meant to say that he was getting to it, that he needed to tell us again. So he did.

He heard Brickhouse call him "The Bird," a nickname never before ascribed to him but one that made him smile. After checking his bindings a third time, he stood and flattened the front of his keilhosen, straightened his necktie and sweater, and closed his eyes for five seconds. All of this, he told us, was ritual. What he did before every jump. The only thing different? When he opened his eyes and saw the upturned faces of thirty thousand witnesses, he smiled at them (though surely they could not see his face so far above) and whispered they should keep watching.

He told us how Arnfinn Bergmann, standing beside him, ready to go next, nodded, and said, "Have one, eh?" and how he nodded back and said, "You, too, champ" before he pulled out into the track. He didn't care about the grandstands or the television cameras. He didn't care about the crushed ice under foot and ski, didn't care about the swirling winds. His only concern was his intended happiness, in the next few seconds and the next fifty years. For him, they were the same thing.

He'd close his eyes here, Pops would. His expression readying for the memory of it. It would have taken him three or four seconds to cover the distance of the inrun, but those seconds were always recalled in slow motion. I swear I could see him conjuring the feeling: his coiled body, his furious energy, waiting and waiting and waiting for the end of the inrun, which was really the beginning. His eyes would pop open and he'd look at us in turn.

"Do you know why I jumped so hard?" he asked every time.

We waited. We never answered.

"Because I knew I had to get all the way to Minneapolis. Do you know how far it is from Chicago to Minneapolis?"

We were mystified, or I was. Probably Anton, even at five or six years old, understood perfectly.

"It would take you seven or eight hours to drive there right now. We could hop in the Ford and be there by sunrise. But," and again he'd drink from his coffee cup, "it's only 133 feet. 133 perfect feet. And I'll tell you what, boyos." He'd get up and go to the fridge and get the carton of milk and the chocolate syrup and bring them over to mix us another cup. He'd serve us another ladle of his cream of cod soup. Sitting back down, he'd say, "It only felt like eight hours up there."

"You said there was *proof,* Pops," Anton would cry. Even at that young age he wanted no ambiguity, while I devoured it.

But Pops wasn't done. He rarely was. In answer to Anton's call for proof, he'd lean across the table. Down on his elbows. He'd say,

"Look in my eyes. Real close. Real hard." And then he'd alternate his gentle gaze from Anton to me and back again. "What do you see?"

"We see your eyes, Pops."

"And your bushy eyebrows."

"And whiskers!"

"Well," he'd say, sitting back, picking up his cup. "I see you, too. But I also see the reflection of myself in *your* eyes. I see my bushy eyebrows and whiskers. That jump got me *you*"—he tousled my hair—"and *you*"—he cupped Anton's little cheeks—"and you knuckleheads are the proof that that was the most perfect jump ever taken. You are proof positive."

How could we not believe? Our father loved us so much that he bested world and Olympic champions to get us. Never mind that the logic of his thinking was corrupted by the five years between that leap in Chicago and my own from Bett's womb. Never mind that the wager made in the secret dining room of The Valhalla nightclub was a vile affront to Lena Lyng and that the depravity of the bet must surely have been the root of our perdition.

Yes, we believed. Because we thought our father was a saint, we did. Because he looked us in the eye and we saw each other's reflection, we did. But mostly we believed because his love was totally uncorrupted. That part proved, over the years, to be true and unmistakable.

After he was handed the trophy and a bouquet of flowers (which he gave immediately to Lena), after he shook hands with Patollo and the runners up, after he shouldered his skis and finally saluted the crowd, before the fireworks, after Andrus Patollo secretly gave Lena the five hundred dollar prize ("To get back home," Pops believed he had whispered in her ear), after he shouldered his skis and brought them to the delivery truck that held the rest of their meager belongings, after he changed into his dungarees and a clean shirt and packed his keilhosen, after he smoked a cigarette on the bumper of the truck, and after Sheb and Lena and Bett came out to meet him, the four of them got in the truck and started driving.

They drove through the night under the Wisconsin sky, crossing the St. Croix River as the sun came up in the rearview. Bett and Lena slept in the back. Sheb and Pops sat up front, each of them conjuring their own plans. Sheb's dreams of that night came true. But did Pops's? He got some of what he wished for. Anton and me, I mean. But after that? To hear Pops speak of his life, which he often did, from the end of a telephone line a hundred fifty miles away, he at least didn't have regrets. And I think that was enough for him. He made his own way, he liked to say.

That night at Anton's apartment, after the second viewing, when he got up and opened the blinds to the still raging snow, and checked his phone, I asked him the only question I could think of. "What do you know about Patollo and Sheb and Pops and all that?" It was a risky question, and from here I can see why I asked it. But that night, I knew I was as much as opening a trap door.

Luckily, he only shook his head sympathetically. "I thought your job was to make shit up." But he looked at me then, seemed to follow the trail of his words across the space between us. I might have interpreted it as a challenge. Or might only have been paranoid. In either case, I felt something open wide in me, and I knew our night would be long and prosperous.

"Did you and Pops ever talk about it?" I pressed.

"Hell no."

"What about Bett?"

He walked to the window and looked down at Washington Avenue in the snow. "What about her?"

"Does she ever talk about it?"

He turned back to me. "You know damn well she ain't much for talking."

I sat there, waiting to see if he'd say more.

His stare was meaningful and measured, and he trained it on me for an interminable length of time. Long enough for me to realize that maybe the biggest difference between us wasn't where our parental allegiance lay, but how we thought of the world. I saw it then, and still do, as something to be reshaped; he saw it as something to be kept secret.

"Come on, man. Let's go raise that glass to Pops." He went over to the door and slipped his feet into a pair of black boots.

I got up and put my shoes on, too. He opened and held the door and we walked out onto the deck. The snow blew horizontal in the parking lot lights next door. Anton zipped up his track jacket and locked the door behind him and we took the stairs down. Along the wall separating the two parking lots, snow had drifted a couple feet deep, and Anton kicked a bunch clear in order to swing open a gate I hadn't noticed. We crossed Boff's parking lot and he put a key in another door and pulled it open. Inside was a concrete vestibule, barely big enough for the two of us to stand in together, and another door that he unlocked. This one let into a small room with an old metal desk and boxes of booze stacked floor to ceiling against one wall, a battered couch against the other. Through still another door I could hear the thumping music. Anton sat behind the desk, lit a cigarette, and opened the center drawer.

"Sit down," he said. "Give me one second."

He took from the drawer a ledger, glanced at a couple pages, and put it back in.

"How's business?" I said.

"Looks like we can keep the lights on for another month."

I crossed his office and stood before a poster of a naked woman with her legs wrapped around a bottle of rum.

"Did you think you were going to find a poster of Tolstoy on the wall?" He took his phone from his pocket and sent a text. His phone pinged back immediately, and he sent another text and then put it back in his pocket and just stared at me for a long minute.

"I've read *War and Peace,* for the record," he said. "Boring ass book."

"I've never read it myself," I said.

He gave me a big smile, shook his head, then planted his hands on the desktop in much the same way Sheb had only an hour before. He kept shaking his head, and looking at me, and I knew what would happen next. I could as much see the words taking shape in his mind. I could see the deliberation. And the hesitation. But the urge to win—the desire to outjump me—overtook him, and he said what I'm sure was more than he intended. "You know, when Pops went away, and we had to go to Sheb's school?"

"Sheb's school, right."

"Shut up for a minute." He shook his head yes and then no and then yes again. "When Ma went to the hospital—"

"When she ran away on us, you mean?"

"You want to hear this or not, dumbass?"

"What?"

"Sheb brought her to the hospital. And after they pumped her stomach and kept her on a respirator for four days, he brought her to the *other* hospital, too."

"Pumped her stomach?"

"She ate a whole fucking jar of sleeping pills. While you were up in Duluth, fucking ski jumping with your buddies. The only reason she wasn't dead that night's because I had to pee in the middle of the night. I called Sheb and he came over and took her to the hospital."

"Fuck you."

He nodded again.

"Where the hell else was he supposed to put me but the School for Boys? For that matter, what else was he supposed to do with Ma?"

"When did you learn this?"

"I've known it my whole life."

"And you never told me?"

He arched his eyebrows, shrugged his shoulders. "I guess every-one thought you'd rather not know."

"Rather not know?"

He only looked at me. In the silence of that moment, the music from inside the bar was louder even than before. I couldn't believe my naïveté. My ignorance.

"Well, shit," I said.

"Listen, she's no saint. Pops wasn't either. And Sheb, well, he's a grade-A son-of-a-bitch. But, Jon, the story you've been telling your-self since you were fifteen? Since I was fucking *ten*? That story's as much a figment of your imagination as the books you write. The sooner you learn that, the sooner we can be friends again."

I sat on the couch, hung my head. I wish I could say that I suffered my shame in that moment, that learning that my lifelong vitriol for Bett was misdirected roused in me some empathy. But I didn't, it didn't. The truth is that though I knew he was right, and I wanted more than anything to be friends with my brother, the thoughts rac-ing through my mind were not about how wrong I'd been about him, or Bett, or how indecently I'd treated them all, but how he'd just told me the next story I'd write.

"I'll give you a minute. Come out and have one with me when you're ready. Drinks are on Sheb."

When I heard the door close behind him, I reached into my back pocket and pulled out my trusty notebook and wrote what I thought would be the first words of this book: *Every old ski jumper's a liar, and my father was one of the best, liar and ski jumper both.*

*

He *was* a liar. Same with Bett. And Sheb, of course. Liars and hoard-ers of secrets, all. But they weren't the only ones. It would be unfair to paint them in a certain light and leave myself in a brighter one. I'm a liar and keeper of secrets, too. And if I'd gone through the years thinking my transgressions were somehow less grievous than theirs, Anton's announcement in the office of that seedy north Minneapolis bar disabused me of that. Or anyway the years since have.

They seem, at once, both incredibly long and like they've passed in less time than the rest of that fateful night did. Ingrid would say that's a consequence of reliving the same regrets without actually confronting them, and I suppose she'd be right. But it's also true that my brother's unvarnished honesty opened portals in my thinking that had—that *still* have—nothing to do with my mother and father and brother and our long-ago life, and everything to do with my wife and children and the truce I've made with my own perfidy. Even if I haven't yet made that same truce with Ingrid.

I suppose this is another reason *The Ski Jumpers* is destined for the redrope and the back of my file cabinet. What wife would want her husband's sorrows and sins and sicknesses brought to bear, even disguised in a novel? Not mine.

And yet, my compulsion to tell her everything that happened those days and nights? It's crushing, especially with the onset of what I can think of only as my eternal dusk.

Ingrid's home now, holding two cups of Starbucks in my office doorway. I didn't hear her come in. Didn't see the headlights sweep back into the garage.

"Look at you," she says. "Showered and shaved and dressed to the nines." She crosses the room and hands me a cup. "What's this?" She picks up my childhood journal from the desk, glances at it and smiles.

I look down at myself, enfolded in my desk chair, but dressed indeed. I touch my face. It's freshly shaven. I take the lid off the coffee—a cappuccino—and have a sip. "You," I say. "Bringing me a treat so early in the day."

"I saw the bowl in the sink, too," she says.

"In what sink?"

"The kitchen sink. Your oatmeal."

Of course. It's morning. Only shortly after seven. I had oatmeal. I left the dishes in the sink. We're going up to Gunflint today, to see our daughter and her wife. To spend some happy time together. Annika, our other daughter, will join us tomorrow. Ingrid will make scones tomorrow morning. We'll have breakfast overlooking the distant lake, and I'll tell my daughters about my mind.

But right now? I look down at the cup of coffee and the papers and that old notebook with all the stories. Ingrid was at the grocery store. I was only thinking about my brother and father and Bett. Remembering us.

"Sure, I had some breakfast," I say. I straighten the papers and notebook and put them back in one of the redropes I use to keep projects organized.

"Here," she says, taking from her sweater pocket a single clementine. "They're perfectly ripe." She sits down on the chair opposite my desk and sips her coffee.

I hold the clementine between my thumb and finger and study it as though it were a rare gem. "Thank you."

"I don't think it has mystical powers," she says, teasing.

"Bett used to treat us with these. She'd buy a bag and let me and Anton take them into the backyard. We'd eat them like candy, one after the next."

She regards me from across the desk. "You've got Bett on your mind?"

"I don't know," I say, and it's the truth. I've been somewhere with them. With Bett and Pops and Anton and Sheb. But as ever, the recall feels less like a memory than it does the shaking of a strange dream, one I'm forgetting as quick as I wake. One I'm not sure I'd want to hold even if I could.

"You look troubled, Jon." She leans forward in the chair, sets her coffee on the edge of my desk. "You're all right?"

"I am. All right, not troubled." I dig my thumbnail into the clementine, begin peeling.

"Did you call Noah?"

The rind is off the fruit, all one strip. "I haven't. It's still so early."

"You think he's not awake?"

As though she's asked an altogether different question, I say, "I owe him and his family so much."

Ingrid nods. She of course knows this story, too. I can see her connecting the dots of my thinking. It's such a comfort to have her here with me. She who'd do anything for me. She who always has.

"I'll call him after I finish my coffee. Why don't you get ready?" I say.

She stands, folds her arms, looks around the office like she's seeing it for the first time. "I always love to see you sitting here. It's where you're happiest."

"I've been happy everywhere."

"You know what I mean."

She's so beautiful, here in the soft winter light, her kindness and patience seem almost to emanate. She's loved me so well and let me love her back. She's made everything simple, without ambiguity, and for this I'll never have enough gratitude. And for the same reason, I hate the trespasses I've committed against her. The big and small ones alike.

"I want to tell you some things today," I say.

"Tell me some things?"

"In the car."

"What sort of things?"

"Confessions."

She says, "*That's* exciting." By which she means to allay the seriousness of my guilt, which she can't believe is real.

"I mean it."

She stops in the doorway. "You think you have secrets, Jon?"

Are these secrets I harbor, or something else? I fumble the last sections of the clementine, wondering. "I think so, yes."

"I wonder if you're confusing our marriage for one you've made up." She points at the work on my desk. She smiles again. "I'll be surprised if secrets are what you have."

I'm suddenly doubtful, and as she leaves I take the file on my lap and untie it and thumb through the pages I put back only a minute ago. They're redolent of futility, and I think for the thousandth time I'd have been wise to have listened to myself five years ago, as that night of reconciliation with Anton ended, when, in the blank spaces of that blizzard, I already knew enough to leave the past alone. I was certain six hours after conception that I had an abortion on my hands.

But the past is hard to annul. Some people keep photo albums, others gather each year for reunions, still others sit on porches—or at kitchen tables—with their kin, with their mothers and fathers and sisters and brothers, and keep the present and past in communion. I fall into a different category of person, one with incomplete photo albums and absent of family reunions or a porch—or kitchen table—to sit by with a mother or father or brother to keep time moving in the right direction. Which I suppose helps explains why I've spent the past five years trying to write *The Ski Jumpers*, and why, finally and resolutely, I'm abandoning it.

I tie the redrope closed, and there's a sensation not unlike *lift*. I can see, suddenly and in a manner of total incorruptibility, the three of us—Pops and Anton and me—on the jump at Theodore Wirth Park. Anton is eight or nine years old and already transcendent on the hill. Pops, for all the pleasure in his expression, all the pride in his bearing, held all his desires in his mittened hand. He was what I have never been: the picture of serenity and contentment and fellowship, his family all around him on the side of a ski jump.

Those mornings, a half-decade of them, I was just a kid. A ski jumper. A boy in his cracked leather boots and wool sweater making leaps of a hundred feet and more. Those rides embodied my childhood. Speed and flight and focus, the sensation of coming back to earth, the elegance of a good landing, the adoring looks of my father and brother afterward. I was in *thrall* of it all. And I was *innocent.* Innocent and uncomplicated and simply happy.

But those days ended. Dramatically and finally, to be sure. And though I can still look back and conjure that quintet of years even now, what I see in the years that followed, in the years before I met Ingrid, is vacancy. And hurt and sorrow and shame, and it seems there are better uses for my remaining cogent thoughts than trying to reassemble the mess of all that happened *after.* It seems, too, that the bounty of peace and love I've experienced ought to get a share of my recollections. And this, I guess, is why I want to come clean with Ingrid. So that I can put the last regrets to bed and get on with what pleasures and happiness remain for us. Will it be the same for her? Or will my admissions leave her as I felt for so long myself: like those who I loved and loved me back best had finally only betrayed me?

I set the redrope back in the drawer and slide it shut. I keep a collection of the editions of my books on the top shelf of the bookcase across the room. The hardcovers and paperbacks, the translations, the galleys. Not from vanity but because they inspire me to keep working. To do better. I pause my gaze on the spine of each hardcover, one at a time, and think—not for the first time—that those stories compelled me to live better, different lives, even if only for a few years at a time. *The Ski Jumpers* will never sit there with the others. I'll have to live better in my own, real life.

I stand up. I scoop the rind from the clementine into my hand and switch off the lamp on my desk. Ingrid and I will take a drive now. Or will soon. We'll head north to see our daughters. I've so much to tell them all.

Telemark Landing

THE SUNRISE AND ITS REFLECTION off the lake has shattered the morning into an infinity of bright shards. Coupled with the new snow on the shoreline and in the trees on the hill, the blinding glare feels as much like a prophecy of my future as it does the natural condition of a northern morning in February. Ingrid's steering our trusty Honda up the highway, and even though we're only five minutes out of Duluth, it already seems like we've crossed into another world. I feel different. Calmer. Entirely less needful.

She's humming along to her favorite Willie Nelson song. Her fingers tap out the beat, her sunglasses keep her eyes from telling me what's on her mind. I can't stop looking at her, and though she knows I'm staring, she's going to wait for me to say something. To divulge my big secret. Her aloofness isn't a taunt. Not by a long shot. Rather, she's being patient. And she'll give me a chance to reconsider all that I think I must tell her.

My silence since we pulled out of our driveway fifteen minutes ago is borne not by reticence, but resolve. I want to tell her my whole and unvarnished story. Finally. But as soon as I think of something to say, a different thought prevails, and I find myself doubtful. As soon as I look back, I feel an urge to look ahead, and neither inclination is right. As a novelist, I've confronted these indecisions often. To solve them, it's always merely been a question of willing them asunder. That's not an option now. Not with Ingrid. She comprehends me better than anyone ever read a book.

"How does he spend his time?" she finally asks. "All day, every day, alone in that small cabin."

"He fishes. He's a serene, almost philosophical fisherman. He's made catching those lakers an art form. Dollars to donuts he sends us packing with a dozen frozen fillets." What I don't say—what I couldn't even if I wanted—is that he goes out on his boat and communes with the loss in his life. It's what Ingrid will be forced to do someday soon, the difference being she'll have our kids to keep her company. "He likes ice fishing best."

"Well, some company will do him good."

"His company will do me good, too."

She nods, knowing my every motivation, understanding what I want before I do myself. Stopping at Noah's isn't just a chance to see my old pal and what memories he's culled for me, but a way to get one more glimpse of an important place in my life.

"How long has it been since we visited?" she asks.

"Must be at least two or three months?"

"More like fourteen or fifteen, I'd bet. Wasn't it the Christmas before last?"

"That can't be." Though of course it can. What passed in an hour in my youth takes only an instant now. When she doesn't reply, I add, "He was happy to hear we're coming by, anyway."

She smiles, and drives through a curve on the highway, and I watch the expression on her face turn into one of conviction. "You know, there's still lots to look forward to. That feels worth saying."

Whether it's her words or the mist in the gorge or the rising, blinding sun, I change the subject by asking something I've been wondering. "Do you think anticipation is the opposite of memory?"

She lowers her sunglasses on the bridge of her nose and regards me for a suspicious second. "Are you thinking about your book or your visit to Doctor Zheng's yesterday?"

I look again out at the lake. "It's the opposite, but it functions the same. Right? I'm only puzzling."

She tilts her head. Another of her best qualities is her intelligence, and her willingness to indulge my ham-fisted notions. She pauses the CD player. Takes off her sunglasses and sets them on the console beneath the clock. "No," she says. "I don't think so. Not quite. Maybe we reflect on them similarly, but to *anticipate* something is abstract. To *remember* something is concrete."

As soon as she says it, I can see she regrets it. Or at least I can see she's worried she's offended me. She hasn't—how could she?—and I reach over to touch her shoulder. "I guess I'm just lost in thought," I say, and press PLAY. Willie starts crooning again.

What I don't say is that it seems I haven't much use for either anymore.

*

My anticipation of ski jumping as a boy is not unlike looking back at it as a man. My prospects began as soon as I could translate thoughts into words. From the time I was three or four years old, most weekends I rode over to Theodore Wirth Park with Pops and Bett in our rusted-out Crestline. Bett and I would go sledding on the fairway of the tenth hole while Pops with a group of thirty or forty guys took their rides on the ski jump that rose from the hill beside the golf course. It was, for him, by then a mere recreation, but I could see in his aspect a reprieve from his daily toil, something akin to what he'd later describe, variously, as his ascension into heaven or his cavorting with angels.

And I knew enough to be venerate, and to desire—indeed *require*—of my own fledgling life a similar devoutness. So, when he asked me, one Friday night in the winter of 1968, as he tucked me into bed, whether I'd like to start ski jumping the next morning, I felt as if I'd received a blessing not from my father but from on high. I felt as I imagine a prince does when he learns of the throne.

I expected we'd drive over to Wirth and that he'd enroll me in Selmer's class, but we didn't do that. Nor would we until half of that winter had passed. Instead, we drove downtown and parked in front of Warner's Hardware on Sixth Street. They had a sporting goods section in the back of the store, basketball hoops and hockey sticks and baseball bats and gloves, of course, but also a rack of skis, against which Pops had me stand, sizing me up against their inventory. He picked a pair of wooden Northlands, and a box of bindings, and we went to check out. To this day I can recall the cost (forty-two dollars), which for us might as well have been a thousand. I can still recall blanching, and worrying that the price would cause Pops to reconsider, and that we'd walk back out to the downtown streets empty-handed, but he only looked at me and pinched the money from his billfold and, in the same motion, rested his hand on my cheek for a moment and said it was time to zip home and get the bindings mounted before the day got away from us.

And we did, finishing in time for lunch, which was cheese sandwiches wrapped in wax paper and stuffed in brown paper bags brought with us as we trekked the few blocks over to Fruen's Mill. Pops carried his skis and I carried mine. I wouldn't have been happier if I had a sack of gold slung over my shoulder. Pops explained, as we walked, that he was going to teach me the basics himself, and then eventually he'd enroll me in Selmer Dahlson's school at Wirth Park. I don't know if it was a point of pride that I should learn from him first, or if there was something associated with the cost of things, or if there was some other reason I've never taken the time to imagine. But whatever the case, those first Saturday mornings with Pops were a time ripe with laughter and wipeouts and the first feel of air under my feet.

He shoveled snow into a pile in the middle of a slope heading down toward Bassett's Creek, formed it into a little bump, packed the snow above and below by sidestepping the hill with his skis, and then set tracks in the makeshift inrun. Before I could go off the jump, I had to learn how to steer and stop on my new Northlands. We did this by riding down the hill starting beneath the bump. I was a quick study, and within an hour on that first Saturday I took my maiden jump.

One late afternoon, after hours on the bump, the cuffs of my trousers soaking wet, my shoulders, too, from carrying the skis back up the hill all day, we sat on the bright side of the creek bank and looked up at the mill, three or four stories high, letting the late-day sun warm our faces. "Someday you'll go off jumps much taller than that building, Johannes," Pops said.

"Taller than the jump at Wirth?" I asked, nervous.

"Five times taller, if you stick with it." He packed a little snowball and lobbed it at me. "How does that sound?"

Of course it sounded frightening, but I'd never let on. "I can do it. I bet I can even go off the jump at Wirth right now."

"You're steady, but I'm not sure about that."

His answer came as an enormous relief, and I remember saying, "Well, I like jumping here with you anyway."

"This is our hill, eh?" He tossed another snowball, and this time I fired back.

As we walked home, each of us with our skis slung over our shoulders, our mittens stuffed into our back pockets, Pops said, "Now that you have the feel for things, I think we should get you started with Selmer. He's eager to get you into the fold."

Selmer was, even then, something like a kindly uncle. I liked him immensely, and the prospect of joining his club, even if it meant I'd soon have to face the big slide just a couple miles up the parkway, was one I cottoned to immediately. "Can we go over there now?" I said.

He put his arm around me. "Next week, boyo."

*

He used to say, Pops did, that a habit in ski jumping, good or bad, took only ten jumps to form. But to correct a fault took a hundred. Whatever faults lie in my memory of that first morning with Selmer are there not by dint of ten tellings, or even a hundred or thousand. But none of those tellings make what I remember less true.

It was the first morning I ever remember waking before my father, and I went to the kitchen thinking that the sooner we ate breakfast, the sooner we could get out to the jumps. I found the bacon and the eggs and I made toast and buttered it and mixed the orange juice and had the fire under the skillet before Pops came ambling in. He looked at his wristwatch and asked me what I was doing.

"Making breakfast," I said.

He looked at his watch again, his eyes adjusting to the light. "It's four o'clock in the morning, bud." He came over and put his arm around me. "When did you learn how to do this?"

"I've seen you do it," I said.

"You're off to a good start."

And so together we finished cooking the bacon and the eggs and we put jam on the toast and a half hour later he was explaining that the job of cooking and eating breakfast wasn't done until the dishes were, so we stood side by side at the kitchen sink and scrubbed and dried the plates and pans. Only after he told me to go brush my teeth and dress in the clothes he'd laid out the night before did he make a pot of coffee and light up his first smoke. I could smell it even down the hall in the room I shared with toddler Anton.

When I came back to the kitchen, ready to go, Pops was still standing over the sink, holding his coffee cup, tipping his ash into the dirty dishwater. "All set?" he asked.

"I put on my long johns and wool socks and my turtleneck, just like you said."

He checked his watch yet again. "Well, I guess we better practice some telemarks before we head over there. We've still got a few hours."

He ushered me into the living room, and asked me to show him my best landing, just like we'd been practicing at Fruen's Mill. I hopped up, and slid my left foot in front of my right, threw my arms up, and bent at the knees, my right nearly touching the carpeted floor. Pops walked around me, gently lifting my arms an inch, nudging my chin up just a hair, straightening my fingers.

"Keep your head up, that's the important thing. Don't look down at your skis but out at the horizon. You drop your head, everything will follow and you'll end up crashed into a knot on the ground."

I lifted my head even more.

"Good. How about another one?"

We repeated this exercise many times, until we'd crossed the living room from the couch to the big wooden television set and back again. Whether those practice landings took five minutes or an hour, I couldn't say. Nor does it matter. But for years, some seven or eight of them, almost all our Saturday winter mornings mimicked this first. At home I learned from the best ski jumper we'd ever know, his patience unending, his commitment to our development the same.

At Wirth Park, though, I'd learn from Selmer Dahlson. What can I say about him that might convey how fine he was? He was the gentlest person I've ever known, and that includes my sweet wife and children. Over sixty years he spent his winters coaching hundreds, if not thousands, of kids. And not just any old recreational skiers (though there were plenty of them, too), but many national champions and Olympians. He never took credit, except to say that he instilled in his pupils a love of the sport and snowy winter days. I know all this not because I learned it then, but because aside from Pops, he taught me more about life than anyone, and before he died, soon after Pops did, I spent a long Saturday afternoon talking with him. When I asked him if he remembered my first day, he said yes, an answer that startled me. But then, he said, he remembered all his jumpers.

We arrived a half-hour before things got started, so Pops left the car idling in the parking lot and uncapped a thermos of hot chocolate. He poured the cap full and handed it to me and sat back and rested his eyes. I can still see the jump across the snow-covered fairway, rising from the trees into a morning shrouded with diamond dust. Because Pops had told me a hundred times about the different jumps in the world, I knew that the one before me was relatively small. What he called a thirty-meter, which made it a third the size of an Olympic jump. I'd come to know jumps like that in the years that followed, but on that morning, despite having seen it countless times and knowing well its true stature, the jump at Wirth looked enormous. Part of the reason must have been its imminence, my knowing that I would someday soon be expected to go off it. But I also like to think that the jump more generally represented what my life was going to look like from now on.

"When do I get to go off the big one?" I asked.

His brows arched, but he didn't open his eyes. "It'll be a little while."

"I want to do it today."

He smiled, sleepily. "You'd be the first seven-year-old kid to go off it on his first day."

I looked up at the jump again. "I can do it."

Now he opened his eyes and let his head loll over to look at me. "Someday, bud. I'm sure of that." He put his head back and closed his eyes again. "But let's take it one step at a time."

After I finished the cocoa, after the half-hour passed and Pops hustled me across the parking lot and into the golf course clubhouse, the first of those steps took place in the locker room. Selmer was there waiting, and though he regularly joshed with me about why I wasn't already in his fold, he treated me on that occasion like an unfamiliar recruit and Pops like someone who'd never seen a ski in his life.

The first exercise, after he explained fundamentals that were already ingrained in me, was to lean my hands against the lockers, jump, and land in a telemark. I remember it seemed strange—and elementary—that I should be asked to participate in such a remedial activity. But I did as instructed. Once, twice, six times, ten times, Selmer said, "Telemark, resume! Telemark, resume!" and with each effort he seemed more and more pleased.

"Good. Yes," he said. "Now Jon, I want you to climb up here." He patted the bench on which I'd sat to lace up my boots. "We're going to practice jumping from here and landing in a telemark."

When I hesitated, he patted the bench again. "The reason we're practicing so many landings is because it's the most important part of the jump. In order to go up and take another, you have to end the last one safe and sound. Understand?"

I nodded.

"Today we'll go to the ravine and practice on a hill back there. The jump is only about a foot high, less even than this bench."

He must have intuited my fear, because he came and stood in front of me and offered both of his hands. For the love of life, I can still see the weather in his eyes. I can still see, beneath the winter wind and snow, the kindness I've already mentioned. But also a resolve I knew I'd have to learn. In that instant I hadn't learned it yet, because Pops had always had it for me. So I turned from Selmer's encouraging gaze to my father, who leaned against a wall of lockers across the room smoking a cigarette, and I said, "I can't do it!"

Pops pinched off his smoke and put it in the pocket of his flannel shirt and said, "What do you mean you can't do it? Of course you can do it." He took a step toward us, but Selmer raised a hand to stop him, then turned to look at me.

"Someday," Selmer said, "you'll be standing atop a big jump. It'll be windy and icy and you can bet your last candy bar you'll be scared. You'll have rights to be. But now's not one of those times." He lowered his hands to his hips, thought for a moment, and continued. "I bet you sleep on a bed, eh?"

I nodded.

"I bet you and your little brother goof off and play together sometimes?"

I nodded again.

"I bet sometimes you climb up on your bed while you're goofing around, and I bet you jump off it, too." Now he didn't even wait for me to nod. "That's all this is. Like jumping off your bed, but with purpose. We'll know more about your balance and courage after you do, so you can see why it's important." He put his hands up. "Grab hold of me if you need to."

It's not too much to say that even still I can feel my feet hitting that concrete floor. I can feel the bend in my knees. I can feel my arms thrown wide and my neck taut as I stuck my chin out. And I can remember my smile as sure as any of it, like it was the first telemark I ever put down, not the thousandth.

Selmer stood back and put his hands on his hips. "You land like that on the hill, and you'll be a champion someday. Try that again."

I count it as my first accomplishment, and remember it like my best jumps—leaps of 350 feet and more. The rest of that first day is blurry. If I thought that being on skis was a birthright, it turns out I was wrong. I remember the sensation when I first clipped my Northlands back in the ravine, and of moving around like a newborn foal, tips crossing, knees knocking, and elbows digging into the packed snow, as if I hadn't been steady as an old Birkebeiner for weeks already. But Selmer was patient, and he helped me up every time. He got me focused on the hill in front of me. He encouraged me to laugh. By the end of that day, I took my first ride off the bump he'd built in the ravine on what I'd later learn was the seventeenth fairway, and though I have little recollection of the leap itself, I know my conversion was then complete.

Anton, a few years later, would require no conversion at all. Nor did he need any pep talks or cajoling. He never hesitated, not under Pops's instruction and not under Selmer's. From the first jump he took, until the last I ever saw, he performed audaciously. Fearless and even sometimes reckless, true, but also as if he were *chosen*. As if he required that sport to fully walk among us. He'd been a quiet, unassuming toddler. Sullen and irascible and envious of me and the time I spent with Pops at the jumps. But as soon as he joined our Saturday morning crew, as soon as his Tuesday and Thursday nights were beholden to the shadowy and ill-tempered lights lining the landing hill, he became a boy reborn. Those days and nights ushered in the golden age of our childhood.

Anton was five years old the first morning Pops brought him to Selmer's class, and as soon as he slid his boots into bindings, his ascendancy was preordained. By then, my rides came on the thirty-meter jump, and Selmer had cleared a lane of trees from the hillside adjacent to the big slide for a new ten-meter, so I got to watch Anton's progress one jump at a time. As quickly as he learned, Pops and Selmer designated him a special case, and when Anton vowed he would be the first five-year-old to ride the big hill, they smirked and shrugged but didn't rule out the possibility.

That season—the winter of 1970–71—began after a Thanksgiving weekend blizzard, and by the end of January Anton's prophecy seemed likely. He was already outclassing kids twice his age on the ten-meter. He was strong and steady and his telemark landing, less than two months into his career, was legendary. Selmer's theory ran that the sooner a kid went off the big hill, the sooner they'd be hooked forever. In this he was rarely mistaken. I'd gone off it as an eight-year-old (only after plenty of convincing) and as soon as I'd felt the rush of it, you'd have had to break my legs or my skis to keep me away. But the thought of Anton flying off the thirty-meter, at three-and-a-half feet tall and thirty-five pounds, gave even the ever-uncautious Selmer pause.

Anton, despite his diminutiveness, would not be overawed. Every Saturday afternoon, once we'd returned home and had our lunch and found ourselves parked around the kitchen table with Pops nursing a beer and Anton and I our chocolate milks, the day would turn to evening while we replayed the morning just passed. Anton insisted on his readiness. He'd perform his nigh-perfect inrun and telemark positions on the kitchen floor, and beseech Pops to let him go off the thirty-meter. When Pops balked, Anton would grow even more emphatic and confident.

For weeks they bantered about it, and for weeks Anton went to bed without the satisfaction of Pops's word. But that changed on the first Tuesday night in February. Every other week, Selmer arranged a club competition on both hills. In those days, thirty jumpers would have showed up for each hill—kids as young as Anton, men older even than Pops—and challenged each other for club rankings. Selmer would set up a registration table in the great room on the second floor of the clubhouse. At six o'clock, we'd show up at Wirth and head for the jumps while Pops went in to sign us up for the competition. That night, when he came back out to the jumps, he handed us our bibs.

Anton took his and slid it over his sweater.

"Uh, oh, doofus," I said. It was snowing—it was always

snowing—and the jumps were haloed in the falling snow glittering in the tower lights.

"What?" he said.

"You're number fifty-one."

"So?"

I checked that Pops's attention had turned to one of the other dads. "That's the first jumper on the big hill, shit for brains," I whispered.

The realization came down on him like snow on the treetops. His face twisted into a wicked smile that wavered between braggadocious and beknighted. "That means—"

"It means it's time to put your money where your mouth is. Come on."

It had been my intention to usher him to the top. To be his wingman. But before he could follow me, Pops asked for a word with him, waving me on ahead.

So I trudged up the jump, nervous for my brother and, if I'm being honest, certain a new dawn was upon our family. By the time I reached the top of the jump, Anton had reached the bottom, and rather than stepping into my bindings I decided to wait for him.

From the top, one could see the downtown Minneapolis skyline lit up. Even on that snowy night, it presided over the horizon, a strobing and distant shine filtered by the snow. I loved that view of the city, felt more akin with where I lived because I got to see it so often. Off the back of the scaffold, the oak and elm trees rose to the height of the jump, cocooning it in the clack of bare branches and stubborn, papery leaves still clinging to the boughs. And us jumpers, we were a bunch of birds up there.

Three, four, five jumpers went as I waited, the snow shooting up behind them like the wake of a speedboat. When I looked down the stairs, I saw Dave Dove, one of the other dads who had been shoveling the steps clear of snow, carrying Anton's skis. When they reached the top, Dave set Anton's skis down and said, "You owe me a six-pack, Anton," to which Anton guffawed and said, "Okay, Mr. Dove!"

Dave pulled a smoke out of his shirt pocket and lit it up and leaned against the railing at the top of the stairs. "I'm going to stay up here and watch," he said. "Get your little ass in line."

"You want to go before me, or after?" I asked.

"Before," he said, setting his skis down as the answer escaped his mouth.

"You want any advice?" I offered.

He only shook his head.

The few jumpers ahead of us took their turns and finally Anton stood ready. By then, Pops and Selmer had both made it to the knoll, peering up through the night and the snow. It would become—that collection and placement of us all—the very definition of my child-hood, but on that night it seemed as much a coronation as a Tuesday night at the jumps. Like now, finally, what had begun in Chicago some sixteen years earlier and been continued that day I was too afraid to jump off the locker room bench without Selmer's encour-agement, like all of that had finally found its purpose.

Anton raised his hand and shouted, "Clear?"

Pops looked down the landing hill, then back up at the top of the jump, and dropped his hand.

Go, I thought, but before the thought was finished Anton kicked into the tracks. Surely what followed him down the inrun was the snow blown up out of the tracks and not some celestial contrail of stardust and heavenly spirit. What attended his leap was not the ringing of bells but only my own lips pierced in a whistle. Dave Dove flicked his cigarette over the railing and winked at me as he slung the shovel over his shoulder. "Hot damn," he said. "Maybe I should buy *him* a six-pack."

If I close my eyes tight enough, I can still see that little boy pierc-ing the air off the takeoff, can still see his hands clutching his sides, not flailing around like most kids on their first rides, can still see the snow kicking up off the top of the landing hill as he stuck his telemark. And I can still see Pops and Selmer, nodding their heads—in what? Admiration? Astonishment? Of course, both of those. But also something more, something special. They believed it then, and they weren't wrong. Anton would become, ten years later, fifteen years later, the very best jumper ever to come out of that program, never mind the Olympians and national champions on the same shortlist of contenders for that honor.

But on that first night, Anton's leap was merely the beginning of five perfect years. Hundreds of days and nights. Thousands of jumps, almost all of them in each other's company, with Pops standing on the knoll, a witness to it all. At the end of each season, in some American Legion or another, the trophies lined a table under the dais, like the heads of so many ski jumpers atop the jump at Wirth. They were our awards for the season past—for the Saturdays and Tuesday night competitions, the Golden Skis and Silver Skis and Evergreen, and the memorial tournaments for the previous club greats—and Anton won more of them than anyone. Pops built shelves in his bedroom, but by the time Anton turned ten, those shelves nearly rent from the wall, so full were they.

We were on our way, Pops always said. And he wasn't wrong. But more than that, the three of us were as happy as we'd ever be together.

*

We were less happy in the few years before Anton began his reign. On the Saturday I began my career at Wirth, a seven-year-old afraid of his own shadow, after we said grace at dinner, Pops replayed for all of us what had transpired that day. He recounted the entire morning and reserved special attention to my crying and insisting I couldn't jump from the bench. But he was teasing and sweet and delighted in a way I'd not seen him before. He'd often tell me, later in life during those nighttime phone calls, that for all he had accomplished in the sport himself, it was the joy and success of his sons that delivered his greatest prize. I still believe him.

If he viewed that night as though I were a prince ascending my throne, as I did myself, Bett must have seen it as a kind of palace coup. Probably I've conflated what happened that season into a single evening, but as sure as I began the day at Selmer's program, she began, that night, what would be a lifelong withdrawal. And as sure as I cried that I couldn't fall off the locker room bench into a telemark landing earlier that morning, she spent that evening around the kitchen table in stoic, befuddling silence, eventually making her way into the darkness of her bedroom with only the quiet and door between us, weeping herself to sleep.

There were plenty of nights like that that season, and to this day I don't understand what happened. Though it's true she'd never been especially kindly or affectionate, we'd always depended on her the way children should. She got us ready for church on Sundays, she made sure I got home from school each afternoon and to bed each night before she left for her shift at North Memorial hospital, where she was an admissions clerk. She'd take me to Glenwood Lake to swim on hot summer days and to see the Christmas show at Dayton's each December. But aside from the kiss she gave my forehead each night as she tucked me into bed, I don't recall a single instance of affection from her, and never once in my childhood did she tell me she loved me. In fact, she never said it at all. If, as Pops always insisted, that love was implied in her devotion, then that season she abandoned even the pretense, at least with me.

How does a child know they're unloved? How might I describe my mother's evanescence? Those tearful nights behind her bedroom door accumulated with shocking speed. By the time ABC started broadcasting the Olympics that February, we hardly ever saw her

except when she came out to refill her coffee cup or from our bedroom window as she backed the car out of the driveway, on her way
to the hospital. Anton, only two years old that winter, was already
asking Pops questions. But with Bett he seemed able to recognize, or
could at least intuit, that she needed his silence to survive the worst
of her spells. While Pops and I watched Peggy Fleming or Jean-
Claude Killy or, on the best night, the local ski jumpers John Balfanz
and Jay Martin in Grenoble, France, on the TV, Anton went into the
maw of our parents' bedroom and somehow consoled Bett enough,
until he fell asleep, that she was able to limp off to work each night.

And each night, before Pops put me to bed, he'd go in and fetch
my sleeping brother. He'd carry Anton down the hallway and lay him
in the bed next to mine and make sure he was tucked in and still
sleeping before coming back to the living room, where we'd watch
the ten o'clock news, just the two of us, me under his arm like I'd
freeze to death without him. He wouldn't talk about Bett, but I knew
his affection was as much an acknowledgment of her lack as it was
his own tenderness. As often as not, he'd carry me to bed next, and
in the morning wake me and feed me oatmeal and orange juice and,
when Bett got home from her shift, her eyes sunken and blank, her
touch the cold my father's embrace protected me from the night before, he'd bundle me up and set me in the Radio Flyer sleigh and
pull me to John Hay Elementary School, where he was a custodian.
When we got there, he'd crank up the furnaces and set me to sleep
on a cot he'd arranged between two asbestos-covered boilers, and
I'd doze for an hour while he made his rounds before the students
arrived.

Those hours were then, as they remain now, dreamlike. The snow
on the walk, the vapors in the boiler room, Bett's lingering rejection,
my own exhaustion—all of it compelled in me a wistfulness that to
this day I can't quite shake.

*

Ingrid would say it's this very quality of heart that has pulled me from the bed early each morning for the past twenty years to write my books. She would say it's the same quality that has made me a fine father. She's no doubt at least partly right. Back in the winter of 1968, I learned not only to ski jump but to care for and worry about my brother, to revere my father and his tenderness, to dread Bett and her dark moods. These lessons were hard won and have reverberated in my life in every way, not least artistically. But more than any of these, the most enduring fact of that year is that I learned to long for something better, something happier.

"It's a far view across the lake. But is it *that* long?"

I look at Ingrid, blink away the cobwebs in my eyes.

"I haven't seen that gaze in a long time. Are you all right?" she asks.

She's taken the scenic route to Two Harbors and we're almost there, tunneling through the dense evergreens on either side of the road.

I blink again. "Was I sleeping?"

"Dreaming, maybe. Working, maybe. But not sleeping."

How is it possible she knows me this well? I smile.

"Well, which was it?"

"What's the difference?" I smile again, and she reaches for my hand and gives it a squeeze.

"Do you think you'll try again, Jon? With *The Ski Jumpers*?"

"Funny you mention it. I was just thinking about it."

"Thinking about the book or about some old trouble you and Noah got into?"

"I must have told you about the day I started? At Wirth Park?"

"How you wouldn't jump off the chair? Only fifty times."

We pass the car dealership and merge with the expressway that also connects Duluth and Two Harbors. There's more snow up here than in the city, and all the gas stations and fast food places have piles of it plowed into mounds surrounding the parking lots. Everything is sharp and dazzling, even under the dull sky. Ingrid pulls up to the stoplight on the west end of town.

"You didn't answer my question," she says.

Now I reach over and take her hand, and as soon as the warmth of her skin courses through my fingers and into my blood I remember something long forgotten. I may even be thinking about it for the first time in my life.

"Do you know that that same year, when I was seven, Bett returned to Chicago for a few days?"

"I thought she hardly left the house, much less the neighborhood, never mind the *city*."

"All of that's true. But I'm certain of it. We took her to the Greyhound station. I can see her waving goodbye from the bus window. I can see the hat she wore." I take my hand from Ingrid's and press my thumbs to my eyes. "In fact, I can see the Christmas wreaths hanging from lampposts on the street. It must have been sometime around the holidays."

"Do you remember why she went?"

I sigh.

"Did it have something to do with her sister?"

"It must have. That was the winter everything changed. I mean *really* changed."

She glances at me and then grips the steering wheel more firmly as she passes through town. "Is this all part of what you wanted to talk to me about?" If she had been teasing about it before we left, I now sense apprehension in her voice.

"No," I say, but then close my eyes and look back again. "Well, not exactly."

"Have you been thinking of Bett?"

"Only sort of. I was thinking about when I started ski jumping. That whole winter. And how she changed. Pops, too. I only just now remembered her going to Chicago." Again I press my thumbs against my eyes. "Do you think I could be mistaken? Is it already happening?"

"No, Jon. Doctor Zheng said it would come on gradually."

"What if she's mistaken?"

"I don't think she is."

"Or maybe I've been wired all wrong my whole goddamned life. Maybe that's the problem."

Ingrid pulls onto the shoulder of the highway just after the last stoplight in town. She puts the car into park and takes her sunglasses off and sets them on the dash. She swivels to face me and takes my hand. "It's okay, sweetheart. We all forget things. Or misremember them. You know that. It's no sign at all. It's just regular life."

It sounds like pleading. Not to me or even for me, but for a sense of normalcy that we won't have much longer.

"You're right," I say, then clear my throat and say it again, my gaze fixed on the lake.

Now she cups my chin and turns my head to face her, demanding my attention. "I'm right here, Jon. And I will be. No matter what."

"I know that."

"I'll help you remember. I'll help you keep track."

I lift my chin from her soft hand and turn back to the lake. "This is why I want to tell you things. In case I forget them. For when I do."

"I'm listening."

"I can't even imagine where to begin. There's so much to say."

"What about Bett? What about that year she went back to Chicago?"

"Bett. Yes. I can start with her." I wipe a tear from my eye. "In order to understand Bett, you need to understand about Lena. And me and Anton the night of Pops's funeral."

She nods. "It's about an hour to Misquah."

"Okay," I say.

She puts her sunglasses back on, shifts the car in gear, looks over her shoulder, and pulls back onto the highway. She drives for another five minutes before she says, "I understand your stories rarely go in a straight line. And I think I understand how whatever's on your mind is gnawing at you. But we've never kept things from each other."

As we speed into the tunnel at Zhooniyaa Cliff, she risks a glance in my direction.

"You're right, love. About my stories. Both the ones I write and the ones we've lived together. I'm not great with chronology. But you're wrong about keeping things from each other. We're both guilty of that."

I've kept my eyes on the road in front of us, but when we get to the end of the tunnel I risk a look at her.

"I guess this is what you meant by secrets?" she says.

Conscience Does Make
Cowards of Us All

Secrets, lies—maybe those are the wrong words. What prevails between Ingrid and me might be better described as faithlessness. Not because we've withheld from or denied each other, but because we've believed our silence protected the other, or our children, or our ideas of ourselves.

Everything that happened with Pops and Anton and Bett and Sheb, though? That was *unfaithfulness*. It was disloyalty. Betrayal. And that night in Anton's office at the bar, after I jotted those words in my notebook—after I jotted that all ski jumpers were liars, and that Pops was the best of them—I felt the shame pass over me like a stiff headwind. And what a complicated shame it was. I felt it because of who we were. And because my first impulse was to use Bett's illness as fodder, and because my own complicity in our family mythology was so depraved, and so grave, I put the notebook back in my pocket and let myself cry. They were the first tears I'd shed for my kin since I was eighteen years old, when I walked out on them and into a city night rotten and without prospects.

What was worse is that even with the truth excoriating me (and

in the shabbiness and tightness of that cinderblock room, no less)
I wanted to get even with my brother. I wanted to punish him for
being wiser than I was. I wanted to abandon Bett all over again, to
hate her with a new and more righteous zeal. Instead of conjuring
Pops's gentle voice urging patience and forgiveness or consoling myself with the memory of my own wife and children, safe and adoring
and loving at home in Duluth, as I should have, I listened instead to
the kick drum and electric guitar of another song pounding through
Boff's and completed that minute's metamorphosis from oppor-
tunist to sad sack to foe. And because I'm being honest, I felt, after
Anton's big reveal about Bett, as I stood and wiped my face with the
sleeve of my shirt, that I had to hold serve against my brother. I had
to match him grievance for grievance, secret for secret, wound for
wound. With my bile churning, I pushed open the door into the bar,
intent on vengeance. Thinking of it even now quickens my heart.

But as soon as I entered the barroom, I recoiled. The music was
quieter than it had seemed coming through the walls. Or perhaps it
was muted by the crowd. There were dozens of customers. Perhaps
fifty people, many of them men as old as Sheb, elbows-up and chins-
down on the bar. Phil Johnson was still there with a table set between
a pull-tab booth and a vending machine across the room. He held a
package of wrapped meat like a carnival barker, his audience of two
younger men and one of the dancers apparently enthralled by his
eccentricity.

The four-sided bar had two keeps. The first sucked on a toothpick
as he limped from one beer cooler to the next. The other was an older
woman with a microphone hung around her neck like an Olympic
medal. A couple of televisions broadcast a west coast Timberwolves
game. Along one side of the bar, two brass poles rose from the dancers' stage. Up on that stage, a woman scrolled through something
on her phone in one hand and held a drink with the other, sucking
it down through a bouquet of straws. Another woman sauntered

down the stairs at the near end of the stage, stuffing dollar bills into a sequined purse and asking the bartender to make her a vodka and soda. The music stopped suddenly at the same moment the bartender put the microphone to her throat and said, "Anton already ordered you one, hon," and she held up a drink sitting on the end of the bar. Those words, spoken through her throat and amplified by the microphone, sounded like an automated voice on the telephone.

"Where is he?" the dancer asked, pulling the straps of a flimsy dress back over her slight shoulders.

Again, the bartender put the microphone to her throat and said, "Playing pool." She nodded with the microphone across the room. I glanced where she pointed and saw a whole new part of the bar through an archway and down a few steps.

It smelled of cleaning solvent and pizza cooking in a toaster oven and perfume, which I soon realized was worn by one of the women from Sheb's barge office, who tapped me on the elbow. "That's Barb. She had her larynx removed a couple years ago. Cancer."

"Barb," I said stupidly.

"She—" Some country music melody came on, and with it the voices in the bar, which had quieted to whispers in the intermission between songs, rose again. The woman standing next to me leaned closer. "She's worked here for more than twenty years."

I nodded, and looked at my informant with a sideways glance.

"You forgot my name," she said matter of factly. "It's Kristi. Well, actually, it's Missy but you have to call me Kristi here." She loosened the fur collar around her neck. "Chloe's not Chloe but Britt. Britney. Same rule though."

Up on the stage, the dancer set down her drink and her phone and started to sashay.

Kristi said, "That's Rose, but really Allison. She plays the worst music."

"I'm getting quite an education."

Now she unbuttoned her jacket altogether. "You're not like your brother, then?"

"Like him how?"

She looked at me seriously for a long moment. "Never mind."

"We're more alike than either of us knows," I said.

"He told us you were coming. Sorry about your dad, by the way. He was a real sweet man."

"My dad? You knew him?"

"He'd come in sometimes during the afternoon and have a pizza with Anton. Just lunch though, nothing pervy. He wouldn't even look at us."

Now I turned to face her. "Really?"

"Really what? Yes, he came in sometimes. No, he was not a perv."

"I'd be surprised to hear otherwise."

"He was an exception. Look around this place."

I did as told. The bar was full of men my age or older, most of their attention flitting between the drink in front of them and the dancer on the stage.

"A bunch of fucking creeps," she said. "Believe me."

"It's not hard to imagine."

"You should write a book about this place. Your brother could tell you stories."

"I'm sure he could. If I got him drunk enough."

"Anton doesn't get drunk," she said.

"Anything else I should know about him?"

She turned and looked toward the pool room. "Your brother's a decent guy. He's fun. He's my boss."

"Gotcha."

"And I can tell you guys are, like, rivals or something."

"Because of what he said about my coming here?"

"Because I can tell when men don't understand each other."

I must have looked surprised.

"You should go play pool with him. I'll order some drinks. What do you want?"

"Sounds like he'd rather not play pool with me."

"Don't be stupid." She stepped to the bar in two graceful strides. "Go. I'll bring drinks."

*

He was sitting on a barstool in the far corner of the room, his face tucked into his shoulder, his hands up at his nose, taking another blow. The other woman from Sheb's barge office had her hand on his knee. There were three pool tables in the room, all spoken for, and another twenty patrons, including a streak of six or eight paunchy men in black leather vests emblazoned with the white tiger-claw patches of their motorcycle gang presiding over a pinball machine outside the men's room. The faint antiseptic stink of the main barroom was more pronounced in here, even with the red door of the main entrance swinging open every few minutes for the smokers to step in or out.

Anton rubbed his nose and watched his opposition aim his cue at the seven ball. Chloe leaned in and whispered something and Anton's gaze and smile rose at the same time, up over the guy taking aim and straight at me instead. That smile was so disarming. Anton had always been able to summon in me a big-brotherly instinct, one that offered help or sympathy or protection without knowing why. In that instant, from across the pool room, Anton shrugged his shoulders as if to say, *What do I need?* Like he was asking for all three.

We met on my side of the table, where he looked at me with yet another expression, one that suggested he'd be patient, maybe even that he understood he'd struck a blow he regretted. Before I said anything, Kristi appeared at my elbow, the waitress trailing her with a tray of drinks.

"Did you order all this?" he asked me.

"I did," Kristi said. "I'll pay."

"Don't be ridiculous," Anton said, pulling from his pocket his roll of cash. He paid with a hundred-dollar bill and told her to keep the change.

He handed Chloe and Kristi a shot, then took one for me and one for himself and raised his glass. "To Pops," he said, "and to my brother, who I love."

"I love him, too!" Chloe slurred.

"For real, Chloe," Anton said, then clinked my glass. To me he said, "Cheers."

We drank our whiskey and set the glasses down.

"It's my shot," he said, cocking his head and examining the pool table. He bent over, aimed for the twelve ball, and missed. The guy playing against him (who I now understood was with the bikers) made three shots in a row, including the eight ball. Anton pulled the wad of cash out again and peeled off another hundred-dollar bill and paid his lost wager. "Easy come, easy go," he said to me.

Kristi and Chloe huddled by the pinball machine, and Anton and I crossed back to the high top, where he picked up his bottle of beer and took a long pull.

"Are you and Chloe together?" I asked.

"Not really. I mean, we hang out, but she's not exactly the kind of girl you'd bring home to Ma."

"Does Angel know her?"

"Fuck no."

"Does Chloe work here?"

"She used to."

"You seeing anyone else?"

"Running this place means I have, like, fifty girlfriends."

"Are you complaining?"

"It also means I have fifty kids. Most of them drive me out of my mind."

Now Chloe walked out the red door, Kristi on her heels, lighting cigarettes before they hit the cold outside.

"You look at her any harder and you're gonna have to confess to Ingrid," Anton said.

"I mean, it's like being in a strange country for me."

"It's your home country, brother. You can't be a tourist here."

"What's that supposed to mean?"

"This is where you grew up. Your people run this place. Sheb runs this whole end of town. I run this bar. That's all I mean."

I glanced toward the door again. "She said Pops used to come in and have lunch with you here."

"Sure."

"I don't know why that surprises me."

"Probably because you're a sanctimonious prick."

I looked around the pool room again. The guy who had just beat Anton was chalking his cue and waiting for the balls to be racked again. Behind him, through the arch into the main room, I thought I could sense the mood rising. People moved about, the general din quavering as the music was getting louder and the lights grew dimmer, even as they flashed more.

"He liked to come in and watch the Twins. Day games," Anton said. "We'd have a pizza and a couple beers. The dancers would play songs he liked. I don't know that he ever even peeked at a woman on stage.

"A lot of the guys who come in here are like that. Lonely. Middle-aged or even older. They just want a finger of whiskey and to sit in a dark bar. Most of the girls, they leave those guys alone. Their radar for who's game and who's not is supernatural. Pops, well, not only was he my old man, but he was the least game of anyone who ever stepped foot in here." He paused, got a faraway look in his eyes, finished his beer, and continued. "This might be hard for you to believe, but he had some pride in me."

I sat up to protest, but Anton put his hand up.

"You don't have to get defensive about it. I'm just remembering him, all right?" He held the empty beer to the light. "He and Sheb have been running together their whole lives. He's seen just about everything Sheb's seen, and I think he kind of liked to be in the muck. For sure he lived vicariously through him. And through me, for that matter. It was hard to do that at the house, or in Sheb's sleazy fucking office. But here?" he gestured at his domain. "Here he got a good dose of it. Like I said, he had some pride in me and this place."

"I was going to say I know that's true."

Anton looked again at his empty beer bottle, set it on the table and took up mine instead. Without asking for permission, he took a drink. "I can't believe he's dead."

The word was like a hammer blow, and we looked at each other, startled.

"Fuck," he said. "When was the last time you talked to him?"

"We actually talked a lot. He'd call me at night, after Bett went to bed. Sometimes the calls would go on for hours."

Anton smiled.

"Is Bett going to be all right?"

"Since when do you give a shit about Bett?"

"Come on, man. Who's being judgmental now?"

"It's a real question."

It was my turn to take a pull off the beer. "I know how he took care of her, that's why I ask. Who's gonna do that now?"

"Ma will be all right. She's as tough as oak bark."

"She can shovel her own walk?"

"I'll shovel her walk."

"Tomorrow you will, but what about the hundred other snowy days?"

"Those, too, Jon."

In a lull between songs, I looked into the main room. There was

135

a shout, and another, and the bouncer sitting on the threshold between the two rooms stood and hurried in the direction of the pull-
tab counter. Anton was quick to follow, leaving me alone at the table
in the corner with the biker gang still shooting pool. I had no instinct
to see what was happening, and the truth is I might have hailed an
Uber and gone to get my car at Bett's if Chloe and Kristi hadn't come
back just then. Chloe went straight for the women's room, and Kristi
sat at our table.

"It's never gonna stop snowing," she said as a shiver rippled
through her shoulders. She loosened her fur collar. "What's going
on in there?"

"I don't even care to know," I said. "I was just about to leave."

"Don't," she said. "I want to talk to you."

"What do you want to talk about?"

She appeared bashful, and picked up one of the empty shot
glasses. "You want another drink?"

"I almost never drink this much," I said.

"Me neither. And I'm not a coke head like Chloe, either. And I
smoke only when I'm here."

Anton ducked back into the pool room and tapped one of the
guys in the biker gang on the shoulder. The two of them left again as
quick as Anton had gotten his attention.

"Is there trouble?" I asked.

"Who knows?"

I leaned across the table and spoke softly. "What's with the biker
guys in the middle of winter?"

"They're not actually bikers," she said, "but some churchy group.
The tiger on the back of their vests and jackets represents the wild
beast that used to be inside them."

"You're joking?"

"Look closely. You can see the crown of thorns on the tiger's
head."

One of the gang ambled around the table and bent over to take a shot, giving me a clear view of the patch on his shoulder. There were the same spread tiger claws but also the crown of thorns she'd mentioned, along with the word INRI woven into the design. After he took his shot, he walked back around the table for a follow-up.

"He's a very strange man," she whispered, so close I could smell the cigarette smoke on her hair. "His name is Lincoln Schmidt. Linc, everyone calls him. He used to be a pro bicycle racer, but he broke his hip and got addicted to something. Thirty years later, he found Jesus, and here he is playing nine-ball at Boff's, drinking soda water and lime."

"You know an awful lot about him," I said.

"I'm a good listener," she said. "And I've heard his story many times."

I watched them take a couple more shots, trading misses and cussing each other out, and turned back to Kristi. "So, you work here? Or . . ."

"Yep."

"And all that bullshit over at Sheb's office?"

"Chloe asked Sheb if she could be one of the girls. I think she wanted to make your brother jealous."

"That's fucked up."

"She's sweet, but she's got her problems."

"What about you?"

"What about me?"

"How'd you end up at Sheb's office?"

She looked away.

"I'm an asshole. Sorry."

"It's a fair question. I wonder myself."

"It's none of my business."

She looked back at me, her expression exuding poise. "You're right about that. But it's no big deal." She caught the waitress's attention and flagged her over. "Hey, Kristen. What's going on over there?"

"Some asshole getting grabby with Laquisha. He was thrown out the back door."

"Was it that prick with the sunglasses?"

"Funny how they're always the same motherfuckers. Anyway, you want a drink, baby?"

"Can I have a Maker's?"

"Rocks? Water back?"

"Yep." She tapped my hand. "What do you want?"

"I'll have the same."

We watched the waitress head back to the bar. When she disappeared around the corner, Kristi said, "I need the money."

"I get it."

"For the record, I'm not some whore. I don't go for that. No way."

"You said Chloe has her problems. What about you?" I said.

"I have a long list of them."

"I'm sorry. I'm just making conversation. It's been a long damn time since I talked to a woman in a bar."

"Now I'm a woman in a bar?"

"See what I mean? I'm just a babbling idiot. You don't have to babysit me."

"My mom, she's the main one. I spend most of my money taking care of her. She lives with me, too, which isn't great. Plus, I'm trying to save for school. I have only three classes left."

"What do you study? Where?"

"It's super geeky. Promise you won't laugh?"

"Why would I laugh?"

"I'm an accounting major. At the U."

"How's that geeky?"

"Credits and debits, profit and loss, ledgers and calculators, insolvency, bankruptcy." She looked at me deadpan. "It's not exactly strippers and cocaine."

I must have blushed, because she was quick to add, "I mean, I actually wear tortoise shell glasses. I spend my free time at the library. *I read your book*, famous author guy."

"I won't hold that against you."

"That I read your book?"

"That you called me famous author guy."

"From Anton's lips to my ears." She glanced at me, then down at the empty shot glasses and beer bottles. "Cheesy. Sorry." She moved all the empties to one side of the table. "What's up with that, though? I mean the deflecting."

"My brother and I don't understand each other very well. He's got an idea about what I do that's far from reality. I guess it embarrasses me. And I guess I wish he respected me more."

"Do you respect him?"

"I hardly even know him."

This was an admission years in the making. But in that corner of his bar, with the religious bikers playing billiards and the naked women in the next room, and the next round of drinks on the way, I couldn't stop talking. "But I definitely respect him. And of course I love him, even if he hates me."

"I thought we covered this. Your brother doesn't hate you."

I wished the waitress would come back with our drinks, or that Anton would reemerge from whatever fracas he was dusting up, anything so we could change the subject. But nothing and no one came to rescue me, and we sat in the silence I couldn't think how to break until Kristi said, "I know how fucked up families can be. My mom, despite the fact she couldn't exist without the help I give her, resents me every day. Like, she relishes it."

"Why?"

"There's no answer to that question. Or at least not an easy one. It would take a whole novel to describe." She smirked. "You have kids?"

"I do. Three of them. We're all good."

Now she looked away as though suddenly at a loss for words.

"I mean, I *think* we're all good."

Without raising her eyes to meet mine, she said, "I can't imagine you're not."

"They're about your age, I'd guess."

Now she did look at me. "How old do you think I am?"

"What, twenty-two? Twenty-three?"

"Good guess."

"Do you have kids? Is that an indelicate question?"

The waitress hurried down the steps, maneuvered around the pool players, and came to our table in the corner. "These are from Anton," she said, taking the empties as she set the drinks down. "He'll be back in a little bit."

Kristi opened her purse and took out a ten-dollar bill and handed it to the waitress, who folded the bill and put it in her bra.

We clinked glasses and each took a sip before she said, "It's not an indelicate question. I don't have any kids."

"Someday, maybe?"

For the first time since we'd begun talking, her expression changed. Her confidence and savvy faded, her gaze retreated. When she spoke, her voice was barely audible above the noise in the bar. "I'm getting too old to have kids."

"At twenty-two?"

"I'm thirty-five."

"No you're not. You said . . ."

"I just let people guess. I never tell them the truth. Not here."

"Why tell me the truth?"

"For the same reason I told you my real name."

"What reason's that?"

"I don't know."

I was embarrassed and flattered and feeling, suddenly, suspicious. Like I was in the middle of a game that was way beyond my ken. Like, maybe, Anton was toying with me, using one of his dancers to make a fool of me. I took my drink and leaned against the wall.

"I get nosy," I said. "Professional hazard, I guess. Don't mind me."

Kristi leaned forward and sipped her drink, which was still sitting on the table. "You're not nosy, and I don't mind. I like talking to you. I haven't talked to anyone in a long time." She stirred a splash of water into her whiskey glass and took another sip. "Last summer I had an abortion. The baby would have been born around now. I think it was probably my last chance."

I'm sure my eyes widened. Certainly, I felt a wave of tenderness for her.

"Now, whenever I think about wanting a baby, I feel like it would be a betrayal to the one I *didn't* have."

If I didn't reach across the table to hold her hand it was only because of the thousand ways such a gesture might have been misunderstood. So instead I simply said I was sorry.

She nodded, and a few minutes later took her empty drink glass with her when she stood. "I'm gonna go smoke. Want to come?"

"No," I said. "I think I'll wait here for my brother."

She buttoned the fur of her collar and took a cigarette from her bag and slung the bag over her shoulder. "It was my choice, you know? I made it for so many good reasons. But . . ."

I nodded.

"I can barely take care of me and my mom. What would I do with a baby?"

I wanted to tell her that it wasn't her job to take care of her mother, but what did I know? An image of Bett jumped through my mind, and I thought of how earnestly I'd abandoned her. But I also thought of how much she'd hurt me, and with that I was struggling in the brackish memories I hated so much. "I'm sure I couldn't understand," I said, as much to Kristi as to myself.

"I bet you could," she said, and blew her bangs up off her face and shrugged. She then turned and went out the red door.

*

"Look, Jon," Ingrid says.

The Gininwabiko lighthouse rises from sea smoke and Big Rock cliff across the bay. Ingrid's pulling into the overlook and bringing the car to a stop. She leaves it in gear, but takes her hands from the wheel and puts one of them on the same shoulder she shook to wake me.

"It looks majestic, doesn't it?" she says.

"It looks forlorn."

"That's not you talking."

Of course I'm talking, but the sound of my voice is not convincing. *I'm* forlorn, not the lighthouse. I'm also still climbing from the fog of those half-decade-old memories.

"You always loved to drive by here," she says, putting the car into park now.

"I still do."

She leans her back against the door and looks at me instead of the lighthouse. "You made up the tragedy of this place. None of what you wrote in *A Lesser Light* actually *happened*." She glances at the lighthouse again, but only for a moment. "It's a tourist stop, not a gothic fortress." Her voice is almost scolding.

"You try living there for two years with those unhappy people, and then let me know if any of it actually happened."

I can see her contemplating the very swift turn this conversation has taken. I can see her wondering if what I'm saying is dream-struck

Jon, someone she's very much learned to live with over the past thirty-five years, or if it has something to do with my disease. This is a look I'll have to get used to.

She shifts back so she's sitting properly in the driver's seat.

"Gothic fortress. That's about right. Or maybe *haunted* fortress."

"Honestly, Jon."

Yes, I think. *Honestly.*

She puts the car back into gear, checks her blind spot, and pulls back onto the highway. She's perturbed, and once she's up to speed she turns the stereo on. I reach up and turn it off just as quickly.

"I thought of those grounds as I imagined Shakespeare thought of Elsinore."

"Elsinore?"

"The castle in *Hamlet.* My favorite line in all his plays is uttered there. 'Conscience does make cowards of us all,' " I say.

"Sometimes," she says as we pass by another clear view of the lighthouse, "life is just before us. It doesn't always require the powers of your imagination. It doesn't always require a reference to Shakespeare. Or some other story. Sometimes," and now she taps the steering wheel three times, "it's just plain as day."

The lighthouse disappears behind a stand of birch trees, all extra white in the snowy woods. "And sometimes," I say, "it's camouflaged and hidden, and we have to conjure it up in our minds if we want to see it."

"You're so clever."

I'm feeling very much like I did that night at Boff's, which is to say I'm ready for a fight. "Sometimes it's easier to imagine other lives than your own. Sometimes it's inevitable," I say, and turn the stereo back on. We've passed the lighthouse, but the fog that rose from the waters beneath it has found its way up to the highway, which is now shrouded.

*

When my older daughter, Annika, was a sophomore in college, Ingrid went to visit her in Northfield. They billed it a mother/daughter weekend that would include a trip to the Twin Cities to see a production of *Hamlet* at the Guthrie Theater. Ingrid arranged outings like this all the time, and I of course thought nothing of it. I took advantage of those days and weekends when I was left alone with Clara and Ben to work around the house, and on this occasion I remember that I turned and planted the garden while Ben fished the St. Louis River all weekend and Clara sat on the couch reading a Louise Erdrich novel and sulking about the fact she hadn't been included in the trip to the cities.

Cucumbers. That's what I planted that weekend. For several years I cultivated them, always with the notion that I'd turn my crop into pickles. But each year (and there must have been a decade of them) we ended up with hundreds of cucumbers—and never one in a jar. That weekend, I turned the soil and planted the seedlings and watered them in the warm May sunlight.

At the time we might usually have been sitting down for dinner all together, I instead ordered a pizza for myself, opened a can of beer, and went into my office. I pulled from the top of the third shelf my copy of *Hamlet* and read through the soliloquies while I waited for the pizza to arrive. I remember sitting back in my desk chair after pondering them and there arising in me the thrilling, static energy that augured a new story. I never tried to divine its source, only welcomed it and was thankful and ever humble, lest it decide to abandon me. On that evening I waited for pizza, I reached into the desk drawer and took from it one of my unblemished notebooks and wrote down some hunches about *A Lesser Light*. The first thing I knew about that book is that it would be set against the Gininwabiko light.

That night, after pizza, after I drank a couple beers and walked the dog and went up to bed, I called Ingrid to say goodnight. I remember how she whispered, telling me Annika had fallen asleep almost as soon as they got back to the hotel. I remember when I asked about the play, she said it was fine, and that she was tired, too. She said they'd had dinner before the show and walked around Lake of the Isles afterward, and that the lilacs were in bloom and the entire city smelled of them. She said it was a lovely time. She asked me to tell her about my day. So I did: I told her about the fish Ben caught and the book Clara was reading and about the pizza I ate alone, Clara by then having gone out with a couple of her friends. And I told her about pulling my old exam copy of *Hamlet* from the shelf and reading the soliloquies, and how they inspired in me some jumbled thoughts about the book I'd write next. I told her I missed her. I told her I loved her. I told her goodnight.

If my recall on all these particular details seems strange, I assure you it's not. Because what happened next is that Ingrid perjured herself against the vows of our marriage, to say nothing of our shared parenthood. I turned out the bedside lamp. I patted the dog's head and pulled the blanket up against the late spring chill in the air. And I heard my phone alert me to a text message from Ingrid that read: *She's fine, I think. Maybe a little stunned and certainly a little achy, but she'll be okay. She knows what's happened, that's the main thing.*

When I texted her back to ask what she meant, Ingrid said it was a message meant for her sister, who'd asked about their cousin, who'd just left her husband. She texted back, *Sorry about that. Goodnight, my love.*

My suspicion fueled a mostly sleepless night. In fact, there were plenty of those in the week that followed, when I vacillated between wanting to confront Ingrid about what seemed unlikely or untrue, and my equally strong compulsion to trust that whatever had happened in Minneapolis—or wherever they might have been—was between mother and daughter, and my exclusion was for a good reason. And for all the years since I've sat on what I would soon learn was the truth: Annika and Ingrid never saw *Hamlet*, at least not that spring at the old Guthrie Theater. They didn't have an early dinner at Sidney's or take a walk around the lake after the show. They didn't drive back to Northfield on Sunday after brunch. What they did instead was check in to the Marquette Hotel in downtown Minneapolis on Friday morning, drove next to the Planned Parenthood on Lake Street, saw Annika into the clinic where she had an abortion, then went back to the hotel and hunkered down for the next two days until it was time to bring our daughter back to St. Olaf College for the final two weeks of the semester.

I turn off the car stereo and look at Ingrid, who keeps her eyes peeled on the highway. When I don't say anything for a beat too long, she glances back and says, "Honestly, Jon. If you expect me to track all your divergent thoughts, please know I can't."

"I've kept something from you for a long time now," I say, almost before I realize the words are out of my mouth. "I know about Annika."

"What do you know about her?"

"When you took her to the Cities to see *Hamlet*."

She adjusts her grip on the wheel.

"I'm not telling you this because I'm angry or feel betrayed. In fact, in most ways I believe I'm the one who screwed up."

"Tell me what you know about your daughter."

"I'm talking about *us*. I'm talking about what we've kept from each other. Annika is long past her choice, and I respect that she made it, and didn't feel the need to tell me."

"And you wanted me to betray her confidence?"

"Absolutely not."

"What do you want? An apology?"

"I'm the one apologizing, Ingrid. I'm telling you this because my keeping it a secret has made me less of a husband."

She's right to be suspicious. This sort of self-awareness hasn't always been my strong suit. The slant of her head now resembles how it hung in Doctor Zheng's office yesterday.

"What are you doing? Why are you talking like this?"

"I guess I'm trying to clear bandwidth. So that when I get to the dark side of this disease, I might still be able to locate some of my considerable happiness."

Now she glances at me. "I'm not sure that's how it works, Jon."

She'll say more soon, that much I know. I can tell by the expression on her face, which is somewhere between relieved and curious, but also because this particular transgression of mine is easy to forgive.

"I've wanted to tell you for a long time. I knew something wasn't right when you sent a text intended for your sister to me instead. Do you remember?"

"I do."

"But I want you to know I didn't go snooping or anything like that. I didn't mount some secret investigation."

"How'd you find out?"

"Annika and Clara were talking. Right after she got home from school that summer."

Her eyes arch. "I didn't know they talked about it. I thought I was the only one who knew."

"I imagine that was some load to bear."

"Nothing like the one Annika herself has borne."

"Does she ever talk about it anymore?"

Now her look tells me not to trespass, so I sit back in my seat and fix my eyes on the lane markers ticking by as fast as I can count them. I talked about it, often, with myself, in the particular way of mine. In fact, the burden of my wisdom was a regular conversation starter for me while I wrote *A Lesser Light*. It was also a part of the conversation I had with myself on my evening constitutionals with the dog all that summer. I like to believe that obsessing about it as I did was my way of worrying about Annika, and certainly that's partly true. But it's also true that it kindled in me some long repressed—or anyway *secreted*—part of my childhood, one that had smoldered and smoldered and found, after some twenty years, the oxygen it needed in the choice my daughter made.

"I believe I tried to capitalize on what she must have suffered," I say. The admission is sudden and profound.

"In your book?" Ingrid asks.

"Yes."

"I'd be surprised if that's true. But if worrying about your daughter led you to realizations about your characters—good, fair realizations—I suspect even Annika would forgive you for that."

"She'll never need to know about it. This is just between us."

"I've always thought our conversations were sacrosanct. I've always known I can trust you. I've always known that whatever you lifted from our real lives to include in your books has been considered and disguised, and that it's only ever in the service of the work, and not some reflection on all of us."

"Why are you telling me this now?"

"So you understand you have my permission."

"Your permission?"

"To write one more book, Jon. To finish *The Ski Jumpers*."

"That's another thing I want to talk about."

"You have time. That's what Doctor Zheng said."

"It's not a question of time, sweetheart. And I know I have your permission, and that you'd like me to do it. But there are plenty of reasons I can't. Or *won't*."

She looks out her window, at the cliffs rising up to a ridge of snow-covered pines. It's beautiful, this landscape and shimmering lake and my own brilliant wife, taking time with me. I know as well as she does what she'll say next, and when she doesn't utter it, I answer her anyway. "It's different because if I've needed to hide, there's always been the fortress of fiction to get behind. There'd be no place to hide if I wrote *The Ski Jumpers*, and I'd end up hurting too many people. Myself most of all. I don't want to do that. Not with what time I have left."

With what time I have left. These words leave her breathless just as her eyes well with tears. I reach over and take her hand. We're pulling into the little town of Otter Bay, halfway now to Misquah and Noah's place, and she signals a turn for the gas station. She pulls into one of three parking spots and turns the car off and reaches for the door handle with her free hand. I'm still holding fast to her right.

"I need to use the ladies' room."

"Ingrid, look at me?"

It takes her a few long seconds to turn.

"I promise I'm not being coy, or spineless, or anything but practical and what I hope is kind."

She feigns a smile, squeezes my hand back, and slides out the door. The cold air that blows into the car might as well be her exhalation. If this is how she's received news of my crimeless admission, and my inability to stalk and trail one more book, how will she take my real and profounder confession?

I look down at my hands and imagine I hold in them the instrument of my despair, that cursed bowling pin. Should I open the door and toss it in the garbage dumpster sitting behind this gas station? Should I bury it in the snowbank plowed against the fence? Is it selfishness or foolishness to foist these stories on my unsuspecting wife? Is my memory true and right? Even when I had the full capacity of my wandering mind, I sometimes had trouble making heads or tails of my past. Now it's like staring dizzily at the clear night sky, and trying not only to measure the distance among stars but also the godlike force of goodness I've always imagined existing in the space between my eyes and them. What I've always imagined to be something like heaven.

Am I too unwell already?

Am I a coward?

Just Because You Don't
Believe in God

T HE ACCIDENT OF BETT BEING MY MOTHER was not some unkindness of fate but rather the very real consequences of a decision made by my father and his first love, Lena Lyng, our infamous,
lily-voiced aunt. It was not long after they all arrived in Minneapolis that Lena put the five hundred dollars Andrus Patollo gave her to
good use, first by meeting a taxi on Glenwood Avenue and taking it
to an abortionist at a farmhouse thirty miles away in Anoka, then by
booking a bus ticket back to Chicago and disappearing without so
much as a word to Pops or Bett.

I learned Bett's version of this scandal when we were all reunited
after her stay at the state hospital and after Pops did his time. Unlike most momentous conversations in our family, this one found
us sitting in a booth at Vescio's instead of around our kitchen table.
Pops wore a chambray shirt and a newsboy cap that became ubiquitous in the following years, and I can still see the glint in his eyes as
he shifted them around the table, looking at his family, all together
again for the first time in three years. He tapped the salt shaker into
his mug of beer and shook his head and was at first speechless. I

was speechless myself, but from peevishness and pique, not happiness. Was it really the case that we would patch everything up over plates of lasagna? Was I really supposed to wander back into our family life as if we'd been on separate vacations, and this a natural and ordinary homecoming? I'd spent the better part of three years taking care of my brother, one of them fatefully without my father *or* mother. In their absence, I'd had to do things I still can't believe. And I did it all for Anton. No one said thanks. No one said good job. Most damningly, no one acknowledged the vulgarity and sickness that accompanied our different routes to that table or how much we'd compromised the trust between us.

What Pops *did* say, after the waitress cleared our dinner plates, was "Johannes, don't be sullen. We're all together again, that's what matters."

I remember the conversation that followed dinner with perfect clarity, and in retrospect I see it as the hour of my life when I became an adult. Not even rescuing my brother, and escaping with him, and taking care of him for that season, had yet qualified me. Nor had my own crimes, considerable as they were, or the secrets I'd been asked to keep from my brother and the whole world. It took that clash in the booth at Vescio's to mark the change. If I was sullen, I had reason to be. "You guys left us alone," I said.

"Come on, Jon." This was Pops, protecting Bett.

I fixed my furious eyes on her. "*You* left us alone."

"Your tone, Jon," Pops said, shaking sugar into his coffee. He'd ordered spumoni for each of us.

I looked at him. "It's bad enough you were gone, but then she had to leave, too?" I pointed at Anton across the booth. "He's a kid."

"Your mother didn't leave you alone."

"Of course she did."

"She needed help, Jon. We were all bowled over."

His incriminating look was almost too much to bear, but I wouldn't be deterred. "*She* needed help? What about me and Anton?"

"Your mother knew she could rely on you."

"I'm a teenager."

Pops stirred more sugar into his coffee and took a sip as the waitress delivered ice cream. "And did you take care of him? Did you step up?" He nodded proudly, and the pleasure of his expression at our weathering what we did had a gallant hue. It's true he sacrificed as much as any of us. "It seems to me you did," he continued. "I mean, look at us all." Now he reached across the table and took Anton's hand for a second. "You helped your mother when she needed it. There's terrific nobility in that."

Before I could stop myself, I said, "She's not my mother."

She didn't wince. I noticed that much before I felt the smack on the side of my head, Pops's quick right hand.

I might have kept quiet. Maybe our whole lives after would've been different if I had. But I didn't. I pressed on instead. "I hate you," I said to her. And as simply as that, it was true.

"You don't hate me," she said. "It's just that you should have been my sister's child." And again, something was spoken that should not have been.

"Bett," Pops said. "We've discussed this. We have rules about this."

Of course, we knew about aunt Lena. We knew she was Pops's first love, and that he chalked it up to the stars aligning that he ended up not with her but with Bett, whom he loved and adored and was perfectly suited to be with. What we didn't know—or rather what my little brother didn't know and was supposed to be protected from—was that when they all left Chicago together in 1954, Lena was pregnant.

"He should know," Bett said.

"Know what?" Already I could feel the lies and secrets like snakes coiling around my ankles. But I could also sense a validation for the distance I'd always felt between us.

Pops looked at me again and gave a subtle nod that was meant to remind me of the bond we'd made. Just as quickly, he looked at Bett, imploring her to stop. He must have had the intuition that what she was about to say, wrong as it was and surely as I knew the whole truth, would be the end of us—of she and me—and this on the night of our reunion, no less. But he was helpless to stop her. He knew that, too.

"Tell me," I said.

"My sister, your aunt Lena, she was pregnant when we came here."

I beseeched Pops with a wide-eyed stare, one that begged of him some guidance. But he only closed his eyes and shook his head.

"Yes, by him. But your aunt didn't have the baby. She went to a country farmhouse in Anoka. She killed the baby."

"Bett, that's enough."

"I should've been aunt Lena's son, then? That's what you mean?"

"That's ridiculous," Pops said. He was reprimanding both of us, but his attention was squarely on me.

"She wasn't a very strong person, Jon. But she was sweet and naïve. Like you. You're like her in a lot of ways."

"Goddamnit, Bett," Pops said. "Knock it off."

"How else am I like her?"

Bett took a bite of spumoni. "You need attention. You don't deal very well with the ordinary facts of life. You tell yourself stories that make you feel better about life. You're selfish."

"*I'm* selfish?"

"Bett, please," Pops said, his voice hopelessly resigned now.

"Let her finish."

"You think your life is more important than everyone else's.

154

Because you're sly—she was sly, too—you think you know everything."

My thoughts stumbled over each other, working to explain that I was the opposite of selfish, and that my taking care of Anton while she went away was the only proof required of this fact. But none of my thoughts found voice.

"Maybe you would have loved *her*," she said.

Those words, they invited me to imagine a different life, one I spent years—decades, even—conjuring. But on that night, I knew, I'd been given still another chance to save us all. I could simply reach across the table and touch her hand and tell her I *did* love her, and everything would have been on a course back to normal. It would've been a lie, to tell her that, but it would've saved us decades of estrangement and sadness. I could just as easily have destroyed our family, or what was left of it from where my brother sat, by telling the actual story with its whole, rotten truths.

Instead of saying anything, I pushed my untouched ice cream away and listened to Bett tell her side of the fiction. She painted Lena as a simpleton, as disbelieving in God, as starving for the spotlight. Bett said the only person her sister ever loved was herself. Then she corrected herself and said it wasn't love she felt for herself, but *idolization*. I remember that word perfectly. Lena thought she was destined for stardom, a notion Bett found ridiculous. The only credit she gave her was for her beautiful singing voice, but when she mimicked her—she sang the first words of "Changing Partners," Lena's favorite song—it was clear that Bett meant to demonstrate her own mezzo-soprano. She finished her spumoni and her version of things at the same time, and asked me if I wanted to know anything else.

In answer, I sat there silently for a long time. Was she ignorant? Or provoking me? We were supposed to be back together and happy now, but instead the cancer of our infinite mis- and half-truths infected us, and I couldn't parse honesty from lie or anger from sadness. None of the stories I believed right then made any sense. Everything was a fiction. One with plot holes and unreliable narrators. But I was as guilty as Bett. My own secrets and ignorance were as deadly as hers. I see that now, but couldn't back then. And because I couldn't make the least sense of our lying and cleverness, I stood and took my wallet from my back pocket and placed a five-dollar bill on the table. I asked Anton to stand up. When he did, I hugged him fiercely and whispered that he could come with me if he wanted. I whispered that I wanted him to. He looked at me with an expression I'd learned well during our foundling days—one that told me he was spooked—and instead of folding into my embrace, he stepped back, and sat beside Bett, who put her arm around him like I so often had.

"I'll pray for you, Jon," Bett said.

"Don't bother," I seethed. "I don't believe in you, and I don't believe in God."

She ruffled Anton's hair before looking at me with perfect disdain. "Just because you don't believe in God doesn't mean he doesn't exist. And as sure as you're standing there like some big strong young man, *I'm* sitting here, too. In the flesh. Your *mother*." The word sounded like an obscenity on her lips.

I was dumbstruck, naturally. What sort of liar would liken herself to God, and then chasten her son in her next dishonest breath? Even for all the rottenness still to come, that moment was the zenith of my hatred. Everything she'd just described in me might have been true, but that only made her observations more repugnant. Wasn't it her job to set those character flaws right? Wasn't it her job to reach across the table and take my hand? Shouldn't she have known that her absence, as mad as I was about it, had left an unfillable hole in me? Shouldn't a mother simply love a child, and tell them the truth? Even taking into account the tensions hovering above that booth, shouldn't a mother, given the benefits of a few hours or days, been able to see the error in her critique? Shouldn't she have been able to take some accounting of her own fallibility and outright lies? Well, Bett didn't do any of that. What's worse, she let me walk around with my confusion and duplicity for years, which made my own role in the tangle of our familial ruse all the more baffling.

I gave Pops one more chance to set things right, and when he didn't I told him I'd see him at the ski jump, and I walked out onto Fourteenth Avenue.

All this happened in April 1978. I'd just turned eighteen. I had sixty dollars in my wallet, a thousand more in the bank, and a job at an Uptown pizzeria that paid three and a half dollars an hour. My ten-year-old Ford Bronco had new tires and a full tank of gas and I'd use it to drive to Duluth in the fall, after I graduated from North High and spent the rest of that summer saving my paychecks, where I'd go to college and forget all about Bett and Pops and the wickedness that had sullied us.

Well, not quite all of us. Anton was still young enough on that warm Minneapolis night that his innocence remained intact. Or at least I believed he was young enough—and ignorant enough of our villainy—to have maintained some hope of that. Couple that hope with my own sudden and spiraling prospects, all of which required action, and I can forgive myself for leaving Vescio's that night, for walking out onto Fourteenth Avenue and expecting that he would be all right.

Of course, what kid in his shoes would have been? Bett had had her stay in the state hospital, she'd had her doses and cures and rest. And Pops? He'd had the full backing and forgiveness of his parole board. Me? I had my whole life in front of me, and a thousand dollars to get there. Anton? He had a suicidal mother just out of the hospital, a felonious father who'd done three years for manslaughter, and a brother who'd just forsaken them all, with plans to head north and disappear. But two things happened in the summer of 1978 that put my great escape on hold, both of which changed not only the course of that season but my life altogether.

That night I walked out of Vescio's I turned down Fourteenth away from the university and into the residential area of Dinkytown. I'd parked my Bronco on Sixth Street, and when I reached it I looked at the house there on the corner and saw in the window a sign that read ROOM FOR RENT. As I jotted down the phone number, a man came out and asked if I was interested. I said I was, and ten minutes later, after he showed me the room—it was up in the attic, and not more than two hundred feet square—and the tidy bathroom his boarders shared, I was signing a month-to-month lease. I went home, gathered some clothes and my stereo and a duffel full of books. I made a couple trips to the car, and then went and took the mattress from my twin bed in the attic, along with a pillow and blanket, and brought that to my truck. As I packed it in, Pops and Bett and Anton returned. Bett steered Anton inside, and Pops came over to talk to me on the curb.

"You don't have to go," he said. "Lord knows I don't want you to."

I regarded him and the house and my packed Bronco in turn. "It's for the best."

He used the toothpick between his lips to work his molars for a long second, then spit on the boulevard and nodded and said, "Where're you going, anyway?"

"I rented a room over by the U."

"When did you do that?"

"Just now. When I left the restaurant."

"A man of action," he said, trying to make light.

"You could've said something."

"Like what?"

"You could've told her about Helene." It felt devilish to mention her name. "Does she even know about Patollo?"

"For fucksakes, when was I supposed to do that? I went straight

158

from the bingo hall to jail to the courtroom to Stillwater. I haven't been out for twelve hours yet."

"She visited you every week."

"And I was supposed to talk about what happened with all those guards listening? It was for you that I didn't, son." He shook his head and put a hand on my shoulder. "I don't say that to make you feel guilty or anything, I promise. It's all just so goddamned knotted-up tight."

"Which is why I'm gonna get out of here."

Now he tossed the toothpick under my truck and put his other hand on my shoulder so we were standing like a pair of barroom dancers. "I hope you know I'll get to the bottom of all this with your mom. But our secret's safe. My word and love are my bond."

"Okay, Pops."

"Can I at least help you get yourself moved in?"

"I got it."

"Please?"

So he drove behind me, back over to Dinkytown, and helped me lug the mattress and bags up three flights of stairs. Before he left, he sat down on a built-in window bench and took a good long look around the room. I could as much as see the wheels of his memory turning, and might even have predicted what he'd say next if he hadn't spoken so soon. "Twenty-five years and four hundred miles ago, I lived in a place a damn lot like this. Except my room was on the garden level." He looked around again. "You put your skis and jumpsuit up in the corner, and it's practically the same place."

"You feeling nostalgic?"

"What I'm feeling is hopeful."

"It's a strange time for that."

He let out a little laugh. "It may seem like it, but that ain't so. Why I'm hopeful is just you, Jon. Look at you. And anyway, the hard days are behind us now. We did our time."

It was a peculiar choice of phrase, but I left it alone.

"I'm gonna let you get settled in," he said, standing to go. "Come home for dinner anytime you want. Call whenever you need something." He gave me an enormous hug, one I can still feel if I imagine hard enough, and he turned to go. But before he went down the stairs, he took his wallet from his back pocket, and counted out five hundred-dollar bills and handed them to me.

I don't believe I'd ever seen a single hundred-dollar bill, let alone one in my father's hand, never mind five of them. "I don't need that, Pops. I'm all set."

He gestured to the empty room. "You're gonna want a TV to watch the Twins games. And a chair to sit in. Use it for that."

I took the money and shoved it into the pocket of my jeans.

He pointed at it, sitting there in my hand. "I think you know to keep this between us."

I felt uneasy about that, but nodded anyway.

"You've been through a hell of a lot."

I nodded again.

"I'm sorry, Jon."

"I know you are."

"And I know apologizing doesn't make things square, but I want you to hear it all the same."

He walked to the door. "I mean it when I say come home anytime. Your mother's had a hard time like the rest of us, but she loves you."

"She should try telling me," I said.

"She should."

We walked back down to his car. "Don't forget about your brother, huh?" He opened his car door and looked up at the tree-lined boulevard. "And don't get fat on burgers and beer, you still have a lot of jumps left in you." He smiled, and gave me a hug, and got in his car and turned onto Sixth Street and was gone.

Rather than going back to my room, I strolled Dinkytown instead. I stopped in the Book House and bought a couple paperbacks. I got a cup of coffee and drank it at a café table on the sidewalk next to the bookstore, then walked down the block to the drugstore. In one of the back aisles, there were a few electronics, including a small selection of black-and-white TVs. I looked at them and thought about sitting in my room alone watching baseball, getting fat, as Pops warned against, drinking warm beer, and instead of buying a television, I moved on to the next row of goods, a series of electric typewriters. I'd never once thought of owning one, but my compulsion was simple and unavoidable and I bought the cheapest machine—it cost just more than a hundred dollars—and a ream of paper and that first Saturday night in my own place, I plugged it into the only outlet in my rented room and neglected my schoolwork while I sat on the floor and wrote my first story. When I finished, I felt empty and bereft, whether because of sadness in the story or my own life, I wasn't sure. But that feeling I'd experience often over the years.

Eventually, back then, I bought a wooden table and chair at a yard sale, an electric coffee maker, a file cabinet, and a dictionary and thesaurus, and what time I didn't spend slinging dough at the pizzeria or taking jogs along the river road after my unceremonious high school graduation, I spent in my attic chamber, becoming a writer. And even as I sit here watching the lake unfurl on one side of me, and the ghostly woods on the other, I can still summon the thrill of those words clapping out of that machine. It's a sensation that hasn't changed much over the many years since.

What can I say about those stories but that they were exercises in mimicry. The Book House had a bottomless inventory of heady novels, and I must have bought and read thirty of them that summer. Dostoevsky and Hamsun, Jewett and Cather, Baldwin and Undset, and contemporary writers like Toni Morrison and Margaret Atwood. Each morning, I'd write like the author I was reading the night before, and though those stories I composed were dreadful, they were also the first place I could safely put my sadness and anger and confessions and for that reason alone keep a sacred place in my memory. But writing those stories also gave me a chance to exonerate my father, and exalt my brother, and spend what time I was physically missing with them in some semblance of their company all the same.

*

But I mentioned there were two things happening in 1978 that postponed my leaving for good.

There was no phone for the boarders at that house where I rented my room, so the few times Pops got ahold of me that summer, he did so either by calling Enzo's Pizzeria, where I worked, or stopping by at my hermitage. If he saw my truck parked outside, he'd scamper up the stairs in that lightfooted way of his and knock on my door. He'd always bring something—a pint of raspberries he picked from his patch in the backyard, chow mein from the Chinese restaurant across the street from Vescio's, a twelve-pack of Pabst—and offer it like whatever he held in his hand was his reason for showing up. I know now, of course, that he wasn't ready to give up raising his eldest son, and these visits were a chance to make sure I was all right.

Sometime a week or two before the fourth of July, he came knocking. On that particular day, he brought with him a window air conditioner, which he informed me he'd just refurbished. Of all his gifts that season, that one was best, as the room I let was insufferably hot, even on the still sometimes cool June evenings. He helped me wedge it into the window and he cranked it on, and while I plopped down on my mattress, he sat at my desk and took a gander at the burgeoning stories piling up there.

"This is what you're doing with your free time?" He picked up one of the paper-clipped stories and looked through his reading glasses, which were always perched on his nose.

" 'Falling, Falling'? This about that digger you took over in St. Paul I heard so much about?"

"Thought I broke my arm. But that," I pointed at the story he held in his hand, "isn't about ski jumping."

"What *is* it about?"

I had to think for a minute. "It's about a guy who falls for the wrong girl."

"You got a girlfriend?"

"Nah."

"Even living over here on campus? With all these kids your age?"

"I work almost every night."

He always took inventory of my squalor, but he never offered me the chance to come home, which I understood to mean that Bett had forbidden it. "That's what you're gonna do, make pizzas for a living?"

"Just for now. I've got plans."

"I believe you do."

"How's Anton?"

He nodded his head slowly. "He misses you, Jon. We all do."

"You all do."

"That's why I stopped by."

"To tell me you miss me?"

"Smart ass. No, to see if you want to join your brother and me on a little road trip."

"Where to?"

"Madison."

"What the hell's in Madison."

"A big ass ski jump is what's in Madison."

I went over to the wall by the door and made a show of looking at the calendar, flipping the pages ahead to November and December and then counting them back out loud: October, September, August, July. "We're four or five months away from the right season for that."

He came over to the calendar and turned it to July, and pointed at the fourth, then counted back three days to the Saturday before it. "These hills down in Madison have a plastic matting on them that allows you to jump on them in summer. Selmer tells me they're gonna have a big competition over the Fourth. All the guys on the ski team will be there. As many as fifty jumpers."

"Plastic matting? What's that?"

"Selmer describes it as spaghetti noodles laid down like shingles on a roof. It covers the inrun and landing hill and as far as he's concerned, it's just like jumping on snow."

"How big's the hill?"

"I guess you can go two hundred feet or more on a good jump."

"You think Anton's ready for a jump that size?"

"Maybe. Way he tells it, you had him going off the Torrs' jump up in the woods. That's halfway between the jump at Wirth and the one in Madison. He gets his wings back on the smaller jump, he looks steady, and maybe he can do it. You sure as shit can."

Until then, the extent of our ski jumping universe had been limited to just a few venues. Wirth Park, of course, and the other Minneapolis Ski Club jumps out at Bush Lake and the Jump at Carver Park in St. Paul. Olaf Torr, those fatherless winters, had introduced us to the jump at Chester Bowl in Duluth and the Pine Valley jump in Cloquet. And of course we knew well his own jump on Lake Forsone. By then we were fully disciples of the sport, even if only recreationally. For myself, as much as I relished it, and as much as it had infiltrated my consciousness, I hadn't yet thought of it as something to master or excel at, though I knew other kids who did. The way I'd understood it is there were people who went to the seminary and there were people who just went to church on Sunday, and I was of the latter category.

Madison would change all that.

"When are we going?" I said.

Pops's smile, there in my Dinkytown cloister, was the first unguarded expression I'd seen on his face since the day I met Helene in the bingo hall. And it was the first time since he confessed to the police officers as I stood in his shadow in that same bingo hall that I believed we'd be all right.

*

We left for Madison very early. Anton was already sleeping again in the back seat of Pops's station wagon when he picked me up. Our skis and the rest of my gear were in the back, laid out like vestments, and I threw my duffel in with it. Pops had a thermos of coffee and he whispered which cup was mine. I filled his cup and poured mine and before he pulled away from the curb he withdrew his smokes and offered me one. I declined, and he lit his and unrolled the window. Before we reached the St. Croix River we'd finished the thermos of coffee and there were five or six butts in the ashtray, the sunrise yet to come.

Eventually Pops put an eight-track into the player and Anton woke up. I remember he reached over my seat and put his hand on my shoulder. I remember turning, and the dopey look on his face, and the big yawn he had to release before he could say, "Hi, Jon," like we were both old men sitting down for coffee and eggs at Al's Diner. Anton didn't smile, but I could see he was at once glad and relieved that we were together.

We stopped for gas and Anton and I got out to piss and stretch our legs. When Pops came out of the station he had a box of chocolate donuts, a pack of Winstons, two paper cups of coffee, and a new eight-track, the Eagles' *Hotel California*, which he plugged into the player as soon as he handed me the coffees and Anton the donuts. And though I was more of a Stones guy, we crossed the rest of Wisconsin with Don Henley's voice on the swirling air inside the car and I don't know that I was ever as happy. It wasn't yet ten o'clock when we turned off some county road and drove up the dirt track to the ski jumps outside Madison.

I noticed the jump first, of course. An enormous steel scaffold with a wooden deck and railings and start at the top with an American flag beating flat with the wind. The top of the jump disappeared from view as we drove closer, so by the time we parked in its shadow all I could see was the transition and take off, which must have been fifteen feet off the ground. I could also see an old timer in shorts and a T-shirt leaning against the railing with a hose in his hands, water spraying onto the inrun. The mist haloing the man's head caught the sun in a quivering rainbow.

"I'll go off that," Anton said, chocolate still clinging to the corners of his mouth.

Pops looked at me and grinned and then turned to Anton and said, "We'll see about that, boyo." He nudged me on the arm and pointed out my window. "There's your competition."

Behind the ski jump, in a field of mown grass, about twenty guys were playing a game of soccer. To a man, they were wiry and fast and there was something sober about their play. I remember thinking how glad I was that I'd taken so many runs along the river road earlier that summer. I must have watched them for a long time, because when I turned back to Pops and Anton they were standing at our tailgate, Anton already practicing his telemark like Selmer had taught him.

"Where'd all those guys come from?" I asked Pops.

"All over. That's the bulk of the United States ski team, as I understand it."

"Where are the other guys from our club?" No sooner did I ask than the Minneapolis jumpers came running up the same dirt road we'd just driven. Derick and Jason and Tony and Tim. They were all better than I was, and all seminarians, but none of them were welcome on the soccer field. If I wasn't exactly friends with them yet, we were chummy, and as they stretched and did plyometrics, I walked over and joined them in loosening up. The air, aside from being oppressively hot and humid, was also businesslike and serious, and I knew instinctively that I wasn't there to play. I accepted that, and I think now that the ease with which I did is what separated me from so many of the other guys I jumped against during the next three years.

"Blue ribbon boys," Pops said as we stood at the tailgate.

I was putting my suit on. "This is fucking weird," I said. "Why does it feel like we're at a funeral?"

He gestured to the guys walking in from the soccer field. "The only difference between you and them is the places they've been. But up there"—he pointed at the jump—"and up here"—he put one index finger on each of his temples—"well, it ain't fair to them other boys what you got."

Only then did it occur to me that we'd come to Madison to see how I stacked up against the best. Pops was showcasing me. "How do you know what I got in either place?" I said. The fact was, it had been three years since he'd seen me jump. As for what I had between the ears, well, an awful lot had changed since he went away.

"On both accounts, I have it on good authority," he said. "And anyway, all I mean to say is you ought to give this a shot. I can't think of a better way to take a break from all the hurt feelings than a little hang time."

By now Anton was all geared up. He'd been listening to us without comment, and if truth be told I hadn't paid much attention to him minus a few over-the-shoulder smiles during the drive. We'd learned to share each other's company without need for conversation, though, and I took his silence for ordinary business.

"So the idea's I'm here to jump with the big boys?"

"I guess the idea's you and me and your little brother get a little time together on the road. We get out on a ski jump on a beautiful summer weekend. Anything else that happens after that is gravy."

"Goddamn," I said, sitting on the back of the station wagon hatch to lace up my boots. "That's about the sweetest speech I ever heard."

He came and sat beside me on the hatch. "What can I say? A few years in the pokey'll make any old asshole a rock solid bullshitter."

I looked up at him while tying my boot. "We all learned how to bullshit some, eh?"

He sighed and apologized without saying a word. I believed his apology. And I understood what he thought might happen that weekend in Madison. Neither of us, though, could have guessed how it'd get started.

Pops clapped me on the knee and stood up and cracked his back. Jumpers were already ascending the scaffold. Coaches were climbing the platform adjacent the take off. "All right, then," Pops said.

I got up and kicked my heels into the ground and tied the arms of my suit around my waist like a discarded sweatshirt. I pulled my skis from the back of the station wagon and slammed it shut and was ready to hike up. It was then I looked around. "Where's Anton?" I said.

Pops looked around, too. He checked the back seat of the car. "He must've headed over to the small jumps. I'll go find him." He pointed up at the looming scaffold. "Get after it, Johannes."

I looked where he pointed. Then I looked again. "Pops?"

He had already turned to go to the smaller jumps, which I gathered by a line of tykes headed in that direction were down a path through some woods, but he stopped. He looked where I pointed, at the train of skiers heading up the jump. There were eight or ten of them, the lead already near the top, and third in line was my little brother. He glanced over the railing and saw us looking up. Could I have seen that far up, I'd surely have noticed the look in his eyes that said *Fuck yeah and fuck you.*

"That little shit," I said.

Pops raised his hand, shielding the sun, and though this shaded his eyes, the smile on his lips was lit as if by the heavens' great gaze.

"Should he be up there?" I said. "This is a big damn jump."

"Did you wanna try to stop him? Anyway, you should be up there with him."

"Yeah," I said, and hurried toward the stairs.

But I wasn't halfway up the inrun before he was in the starting gate, his bare face the picture of aged wisdom.

"Clear?" he hollered.

From behind me, some voice on the coaches' platform shouted "Yup" and with that he pulled himself into the worn tracks of the plastic matting. I turned and watched him ski past me, as if in slow motion. I watched him ride through the transition, cocked like a loaded pistol, and then launch with all the audacity of a bullet out of the barrel. He came by it naturally, there was never any question about that.

What I understood, as my brother flew through that summer morning, both of his ski tips over his right shoulder, his hands already ruddering him like goddamn wings, his chin willing him ever forward, ever farther, was that Anton had lost the most, and he'd do anything to win it back. And I don't mean that I figured it out years later, but that I knew it on the side of that jump, watching his gorgeous and effortless flight.

The guy behind me on the stairs had been watching, too, and when he turned back up the inrun said, "Who's that little fucker?"

"He's my brother. His name's Anton Bargaard."

"He looks like he's eight years old."

"He's twelve."

"He's got sack," he said.

"He sure does."

"That was a nice jump."

"He's got a million more where that came from."

*

That week changed everything. For three days, we all trained to-gether. Ten or fifteen jumps in the morning, and ten or fifteen more in the afternoon. On Sunday afternoon, while his team played yet another game of soccer in the field beyond the jump—they played soccer almost as much as they ski jumped—the coach of the U.S. Ski Team found Pops outside the warming hut. Anton and I were chang-ing out of our gear at the back of the station wagon, drinking Cokes and eating apples. They kept looking over at us, Pops and the man I'd learned was from Finland, until finally they walked over.

He had an accent that made everything he said sound scolding, even as his face expressed nothing but kindness. To Anton he said, "You jump with angry. I like it very much."

Of course, Anton didn't say anything, only blushed.

"And you land like world champion. Perfect telemark every time."

"Selmer taught me that," he said, the pride in his voice unmis-takable.

"You are twelve?"

"I am."

"And you go off jump without this man's permission yesterday?" He threw his thumb at Pops.

"He didn't tell me I couldn't go off it."

"You are not afraid?"

"I was scared."

"But you sneak up there."

"Pops always says be brave."

"Be brave! Yes!" he tousled Anton's hair. "Be brave for sure!"

Anton couldn't help smiling.

"And this boy is big brother?"

"That's Jon," Anton said.

"You think someday you jump farther than him?"

Anton wouldn't jibe me, not yet, and answered the coach by saying, "He's the best ski jumper I ever knew."

The coach shook his head. "Someday you jump farther. You chase and chase. Keep going." Then he turned to me. "Watch out this one. How do you say, he is like dog biting feet?"

Pops grabbed another can of Coke from the cooler and handed it to Anton and said to me, "We're gonna go see the little kids jump" and without waiting for my reply left me standing there with the coach.

We watched them disappear into the woods between jumps before he turned to me and said, "I am Matti Rantannen. You know me?"

"I think I do."

"Your little brother has *very* high thought of you."

"He's loyal, I'll give him that."

"You are coached by my friend Steve Brag, yes?"

I nodded. "He coaches all the juniors from Minneapolis. Well, the juniors and seniors both. I guess he's the club coach."

"He is good friend. We jump together for many years."

"Was he a good jumper?"

"He was very good at drinking beer and skipping curfew and chasing girls." He winked. "But yes, even better at ski jumping. Very strong. Like you Bargaards." He gripped the front of his thighs. "I saw your father jump too. In Chicago at the Soldier Field. I remember it yes."

"He's told us about that a hundred times."

"He was very best that day."

He gestured at the jump, and started walking toward the staircase up to the take off. I didn't know if I was supposed to follow him or not, but he paused and waved me along. Together we climbed the flight of stairs that led to the scaffold and stood on the platform there.

Matti pointed to the top of the transition and said, "You get shy here. Your weight shifts to the heels yes? You are not afraid, but it looks like you are."

I knew exactly what he was talking about, but couldn't make the correction as much as I tried. It was a subtle mistake, but like so many things in that sport it was the difference between going the farthest and going the tenth farthest. Or twentieth. "Yep. I can feel that. And I want to be committed. I'm trying. But I swear to god I think it's the vibration from the mats. They're weird. I feel like I'm skiing down a gravel road."

"But all these other jumpers here"—he waved his hand in the direction of the soccer field, to imply his team—"they are forward and they are on same gravel road yes." He didn't wait for me to answer. "Stand on track now. Show me inrun."

I stepped on the mats and set my feet apart and lowered into my inrun position: knees out front of my feet, thighs parallel to the scaffold, stomach and chest laid against my thighs, my shoulders stretched beyond my knees, my arms straight back, my forearms resting on the back of my hips, my head leading the way, eyes intent, from thirty feet away, on the take off. I remember the sensation of being coiled, and eager, even after a full day of jumping, to rocket into the air.

"This is perfect position," Matti said. He'd gone in front of me so I could see him from his feet to his armpits, but not his face. "From here you can jump like kangaroo yes. But"—and now he stepped to me and put one finger on each shoulder and pushed me back two inches. "From here you jump like a little old man."

It was true. From that position, I could hardly stay balanced on my feet, let alone leap forward at the take off.

"And still you are outjumping half of my team. Do you know how?"

"My timing's good. I pile the hell on 'em."

"You think you just make it so yes."

The truth was, I didn't know how I was jumping so far. I had no idea what I was doing in the air that compensated for my mistake on the take off. In answer to his question, I shrugged.

He smiled, and nodded, and put his hands on his hips. "We never see you before, Johannes. How come no?"

"We mostly just jump at home. At Wirth Park in Minneapolis and out in Bloomington on Big Bush."

"You do not wish to go on bigger jumps? Against better jumpers?"

"I've never thought much about it, to be honest. I just love doing it. With Pops and Anton."

Now he squinted at me. Probing. After a moment, he said, "You fix this here, and you will beat all my guys. Then we will talk again yes."

Halfway down the stairs he stopped and turned and put a hand on my chest. "You wait here," he said, then hurried down the remaining five or six steps. There was a concrete slab at the bottom, and he stepped off to the side of it and said, "You jump from there. Land in telemark down here." He pointed at the concrete.

It was a hell of a ways. "Why?" I said.

"Because I say to yes. From inrun position you jump."

I got into my inrun.

"Wait," he shouted. "You feel that? You feel your knees yes."

"Yes."

"You feel those mudderfucking knees. Those shins yes."

"Yes."

173

"Then jump."

I did, up and out and at the mercy of this strange man. I no sooner could have landed in a telemark from that height than I could have jumped back up to the eighth stair, but I was able to keep my balance and stayed on my feet, albeit in a squat. When I stood up straight I looked over at him.

"It is okay there is no telemark."

"Why did you ask me to do that?"

"I want to be careful! So I know you can land at bottom of hill. You get your shin hairs on the plastic yes. The knees out front. Then you will see. I will have fun watching."

"All right, man."

"One thing more: what size are your boots?"

"I'm a size twelve."

"That is some forty-five or forty-six European?"

"I don't know what that means."

"It is okay. I am knowing. Remember: tomorrow, knees." He demonstrated with his own short legs.

*

The next morning, as we pulled into our parking spot beneath the jump, Matti was there with a big box under his arm. When I got out, he handed it to me.

"What's this?" I said.

"It is right boots."

"I can't afford these," I said.

"Your father, he buys them."

I tried to hand them back, but he put a stiff hand up. "You need all the same as team guys. So it is fair. I give Jake a good deal."

By now Pops was out of the car. "Take the boots, Jon," he said.

"Thanks," I said, not sure if I was talking to Pops or Matti, or if I should be embarrassed or flattered or something else.

For the first time, I watched Matti smile. He punched me on the shoulder and said "Knees."

A pair of red Adidas high back boots rested in the box. Brand new. The same boots all the ski team guys wore. We adjusted my bindings and I got ready and to this day I can still remember the sensation of putting those boots on for the first time and walking as though I couldn't get off my tiptoes. As though I might fall on my face with every step. It was alarming to think of jumping in them, but since all the best guys wore them, I figured I could, too.

And I did. It took the morning to acclimate, but by the afternoon session I was doing everything Matti had told me to, and the results spoke for themselves. I was jumping twenty or twenty-five feet farther than the two days previous, putting me right in the thick of things. It was strange and exciting to be there, and to give a damn about my performance. But I took to it, and by the time the Fourth of July competition came around, Pops had me convinced I could pull off a Soldier Field–style upset.

The morning of the competition it stormed; sheets of rain blew across the valley and up the landing hill in front of the strong winds that moved it. The trees shook and lightning quivered and for a while it looked like the competition would be canceled, but before noon the weather passed and all the jumpers worked on clearing the landing hill of leaves and small branches and right at one o'clock, as scheduled, the competition commenced. We tied our canvas bib numbers on and ascended the jump. Being a junior skier, and an unknown one at that, I was number four to Anton's three, so we as much as led the charge.

I remember Anton's first competition jump, and the way my stomach lurched after him as he took his first ride, his seemingly weightless flight, the way he disappeared from view still high in the air and didn't return until he was skiing across the grass on the outrun. I remember the voice over the PA system announcing his distance, fifty-one meters, and the audible hush of the other skiers at the top of the jump who couldn't believe that distance from the tyke who'd just gone. I could hardly believe it myself.

I remember how worried I was that I'd not match him, even though my training rides had been ten or twelve meters beyond his distance.

I remember how I thought, at the top of the jump, as I squatted to fasten my bindings, sliding the cable up over the heels of my boots and latching down the front throws, that all I had to do was what Matti had encouraged me to, and drive my mudderfucking knees forward through the transition.

I remember almost forgetting to strap my helmet on before I pulled out onto the inrun.

I remember one of the other guys from the Minneapolis club telling me to have a good one as I gripped the railing at the start, and the way I focused all of my concentration on my knees as I gained speed.

And I remember a feeling of cockiness as I sped toward the take-off: *I'd done what the esteemed coach told me to do, I had stayed in that ready position, I had kept my knees out front, I was loaded for goddamn bear,* as Pops would later recount.

So lost was I in those thoughts that I almost *forgot* to jump, but I did, and quick and effortlessly, so that I was in my flight position even faster than usual, and I remember the very specific feeling of *lift.* And for the first time in my life the sensation of the pause that would become for me the best indicator of a good jump. It happened at the height of my flight, and if I'd not heard so often about it I might have bailed on the jump right there. But because I had, I let it ride, and pulled with my whole body. It felt like someone had a hand on my suit and was lifting me from above.

Of course, I had to land. Every jump must. And for me, on that day, that jump, I alighted at sixty-four meters. A telemark at that distance was impossible, but I managed not to drag my hands behind me on the plastic mats as I squatted in my landing.

I remember Anton's second jump measured fifty-two meters.

I remember my second jump was only sixty-one meters, but it scored the same because I was able to land in a telemark, and my style marks were higher. Good enough to win the junior class and take fourth place overall. Anton was fifth place among the juniors.

I remember all that perfectly. *Perfectly.* And I remember, later, driving home across Wisconsin in the dark, passing through towns with firework shows lighting up the night, the three of us singing Eagles' songs together and recounting the weekend like we were wizened old men already and had had the time of our lives.

Somewhere in the dark of that night, on a stretch between towns, I remember craning my head out the station wagon window and looking at the starlit sky, and wondering—only for a moment, one I quickly reprimanded myself for—if maybe Bett was right, at that fateful dinner at Vescio's, about God.

The Meat Market

I SOMETIMES THINK ABOUT THE WATER in the deepest trenches of Lake Superior. As I understand it, some of that water is residual of the Laurentide Ice Sheet, whose retreat more than ten thousand years ago cut much of the landscape I consider home. I think of it as the old water, and it's to those inky depths I retreat when the bedlam of my thoughts engulf me. It occurs to me now that the image that always surfaces in me—of a darkness beyond ken, but whorled with the moonlight from millennia past, like the black granite knuckled with ice so dominant on the Highway 61 roadside now—is what likely awaits my consciousness on the other side of this illness. It's a familiar place, that imaginary underwater world, one that's always brought peace and quiet, and if I try hard enough, I can even get comfortable with the idea of spending my last months and years swimming down there.

I mention all this because it was to those depths I'd gone after Kristi went out to smoke again. I sat alone, in the corner of the pool room, listening to the cracking billiard balls and the rising music but hearing only my own self-admonishments. How had I let my brother out of my life? All those years were gone forever, and the weight of them was as heavy as the melted ice at the bottom of the lake. I drank a beer and let myself sink into the comfort of my old water oblivion.

At some point Ingrid texted to say goodnight. Clara and Delia would stay the night. They'd just started a movie. It was nice to have the company. Tempted as I was to call her then, to say goodnight, of course, but also to find some equilibrium, I only texted, and said goodnight and told her I loved her. I waited for Anton to reappear and when, after as long as it took to finish my beer, neither he nor Kristi did, I got up and ambled past the bikers still shooting pool to enter the main barroom.

One group of determined young men still sat in a row along the stage, tossing dollar bills at the dancer and raising shot glasses and rousing bawdy toasts into the otherwise subdued space. But most of the remaining crowd, and there were plenty of low-slung shoulders hunched around the room, were as old as me. Men not there for the dancers or the drugs, but only to see if there was still a reflection in their glasses of bar-rail whiskey. The lights seemed dimmer, the music louder but also mellower. So mellow I could hear an old timer getting a private dance at a table near the pull-tabs tell his companion that this snowy night was the anniversary of his wife's death. I couldn't help but watch him for a moment. His lachrymose eyes—as red as the woman's fingernails combing through his mostly gone hair—conveyed a grief as ancient and of the moment as the wind still blowing outside.

The phone behind the bar rang. One of the swains elbows-up at the stage stood and staggered toward the table still manned by Phil Johnson. The guy wore a Timberwolves jersey over a hooded sweatshirt and a flat-brimmed baseball cap cocked at an angle above his sunglasses. He leaned in close to Phil, bought a cut of meat and pocketed something else, then headed to the men's room, hollering for one of his partners to join him.

Anton, whom I hadn't seen in what seemed a long time, rounded the corner just as the guy in the jersey and sunglasses did, and grabbed him by the hood and said something into his ear and as fast as it all happened, the bouncer, a big guy I'd originally mistook for one of the bikers, was up at the stage with Anton, clearing the whole crew out of the bar. They stumbled by, saving their complaints until the bouncer had shoved the last of them, and then they turned in a kind of disorganized unison and started shouting obscenities at my brother and his muscle. When Anton came back into the barroom, he headed straight for Phil. I followed.

"So many assholes," he said to me, then to Phil, "How's business?"

"What's with the vegetables?" I said.

Phil grabbed two red onions and held them up like he was cupping breasts. "It's all part of the ruse." He put the onions in a canvas shopping bag, then put the peppers and tomatoes in, too. "Business is good. The meat market's closed."

Anton nodded. "Thank fucking god. Put those in the walk-in downstairs? I'll get them later." He nodded at the dozen or so cuts of meat still sitting on either side of the table.

"Sure thing, boss."

He moved slowly, stacking the meat two packs at a time in a separate shopping bag.

Anton turned to me. "We can get down to it now, brother."

"Get down to what?"

He arched an eyebrow. "Catching up. Having a proper drink." He waved at the bar. "The great goat fuck should mellow now. Come on."

We walked to the other end of the bar and took two stools. He surveyed the remaining lonely hearts and drunkards. A new dancer was standing at the jukebox, punching numbers onto the pad. She stood obliquely, her head resting on her shoulder, long black hair raining down her shoulder and back. She was still there when the woman on stage descended the staircase and headed straight for the dressing room, pausing only long enough to kiss Anton on the cheek.

As soon as she was gone he hailed the bartender. "Hey, Barb, you met my big brother yet?"

She held the microphone to her throat. "The spitting image," she said through her voice box.

"He's way better looking than me," Anton said.

"Some of the girls think so, too," she said, and winked at us.

"You got a bottle of my reserve down there?"

She reached into a cabinet under the cash register and pulled out a bottle of small-batch Four Roses. She poured us each a couple fingers and set the glasses down and Anton said, "Pour yourself one, Barbie."

She put a single finger in another glass, added a splash of water, and raised it in our direction before quaffing it all at once. She wiped her lips on a bar napkin and put her microphone to her throat. "That one was for your dad."

"Hear, hear," Anton said, tipping his glass at Barb and then clinking it on mine.

"To Pops," I said.

Barb washed her glass in the trio of sinks under the bar and set it on a rack to dry, then filled a paper bowl with pretzels and placed it in front of us. "Shout loud when you need more," she said. "I'm your girl."

"You'll always be my girl," Anton said.

He took a deep breath and seemed finally ready to settle in for an uninterrupted drink, looking around the place as though seeing it for the first time all night. "Every day it's something different in this goddamn place," he said. "Assholes and fights and fucking drug addicts and dancers. But right there"—he pointed the lip of his glass at Barb—"is the calm in the eye of the storm. She's been pouring 'em here for twenty-two years. Can you believe that?"

"That's a lot of nights on her feet," I said.

"She had cancer whenever it was, maybe five years ago. Hence the robot voice."

"Yeah, one of the women from over at the barge office told me."

"Kristi," he said.

"Missy," I said.

"Maybe Sheb was right after all."

"About what?"

"Nothing. I'm giving you shit. She's salt of the earth, that one."

"Barb or Missy?"

"Well, both of 'em, but I meant Missy. She takes care of her mom."

"She told me that, too."

Now he looked me square in the eye. "Do I need to call Ingrid? Tell her old Jonny Boy's off his leash?"

"She knows I'm here."

"I'm sure she does." He took a tight-lipped sip of his drink. "But seriously, here's to seeing you, Jon."

"Yeah. And you." Now I took a sip. "That's good stuff," I said.

"It helps me get through the night." He leaned forward on the bar, spread his elbows, twirled his drink.

"It's not all a party?"

"It's almost never a party." He looked over his shoulder at me and smiled. "Tonight's an exception."

I held up my glass. "I haven't had this much to drink in the past ten years."

"I drink too much. I know I do. But how could I not?"

"You don't have another coping mechanism? A way to calm yourself down that's not fortified with ninety-five percent alcohol and lines of white powder?"

"I don't know. I'm stressed out all the time. I never calm down."

"You seem calm now."

"Do I?"

"Yeah, I think so."

He appeared to take some satisfaction in my observation. His shoulders relaxed, his grip on the glass loosened. He couldn't resist taking another gander around the bar, but when his eyes circled back to me, he just nodded. "What about you? What's your coping mechanism?"

"It sounds ridiculous, but when I can't think straight anymore, I imagine the water at the bottom of Lake Superior."

"I don't know which is more ridiculous: that you think of that, or that you believe you have problems."

"Oh, I have problems."

"Paper cuts? Which type of salmon to buy at the co-op? Pinot grigio, or pinot noir?"

"My last book bombed. I can't figure out how to write the next one. Teaching's a grind and even just losing these couple of days for the funeral is going to set me back a week, workwise."

"I don't know anyone except Sheb who doesn't have to grind. Give me some real concerns."

I didn't have to ponder this either. "My father just died, I can't stand my mother—I can hardly even say the word *mother*—and my brother thinks I'm an asshole. How's that?"

"More like it!" He patted me on the leg. "But I can put your mind at ease on one of those worries: I don't think you're an asshole."

"That's the booze talking."

He took another sip, smiled at me, and then looked up into the stage lights and after a dramatic pause said, "The water at the bottom of Lake Superior?"

"The quiet, the darkness, the absence of life, the weight and pressure."

"Sounds like you're describing Boff's at midnight."

"Is it midnight?"

He looked at his phone. "Not even close. The night's young."

"You keep saying that."

"I'm trying to convince you."

As though in answer, I yawned. Big and long and deep. Anton did, too, and we laughed for a second before falling into a short silence. Even in the few minutes since we'd sat down at the bar, the rest of the place had cleared so that only half a dozen battered men remained. The widower was still sitting against the back wall, alone now, awaiting what, I couldn't imagine. Another man sat at a table playing pull-tabs, the basket in front of him heaped with losing cards. Phil Johnson was gone. The sound of pool balls still came sharply from the other side of the bar, but there was no banter among the players. It was warm, the air dry and sharp and smelling now like burnt coffee and the begonias wafting from the dancer on stage.

"Ski jumping," Anton said out of nowhere. "I guess I think about ski jumping when I'm trying to clear my mind."

"Solid."

"Not about flying, though, which seems counterintuitive, I know. But flying, shit, I hardly remember any of it. Occasionally my body twitches and I have some muscle memory of being up there, but mostly that part's just a blank. What I think about is landing. Of pulling the rip cord and getting back to earth."

"You were good enough to need that rip cord. I wasn't."

"Bullshit."

"When I was driving down here today, I kept thinking back to that trip to Madison we took in the summer of '78. You remember that?"

A cocksure look came over him and he nodded his head slowly. "Hell yes I remember."

"Still one of the ballsiest things you ever did, sneaking up there."

"I was so fucking scared."

"That surprises me."

"I was *twelve*."

"Pops about shit himself."

"I had to get his attention somehow."

"What do you mean?"

"Nothing."

The hardest part about striking out on my own that summer was leaving Anton behind, and though it's true I worried about him all the time, mostly I just missed him and in those couple of years before I set off for good, I didn't do enough to brother him. In the years after *that*, even until now, I'd never given proper consideration to how my leaving must have affected him, and not only because he'd have missed me, too, but because the turmoil my striking out roused in Pops would have cost Anton plenty. I might've said something about that in Boff's, but I didn't want to risk inciting his resentments.

Instead I said, "I can still picture you taking off. And the way your tips came up over your right shoulder as you got on 'em. I was stunned. And *so* goddamn impressed."

"That's what I was after."

"I think you were after the whole world."

The last of his whiskey was down his throat as quick as he lifted the glass to his lips, and after he set the glass back down he put his arm around me and leaned in. "Your admiration *was* the world, Jon."

He rested his forehead on my shoulder and squeezed me in an awkward hug. "But it's way too early in the night to start talking about ski jumping."

"I don't mind talking about it," I said.

He let go of me, righted himself, and said, "That water down at the bottom of Lake Superior, do you imagine being *in it,* or do you merely imagine what it's *like?*"

"I guess I use it to suit my purposes. I think about it as abstraction, but I also like to wonder what it's like. And how old that water is. That's one of my favorites."

"How old is it?"

"Ten thousand years, give or take. I think of it symbolically."

"Symbolic of what?"

"I take comfort in all the ways it's bendable. I can be philosophical about it in one moment, then turn around and think about it geologically. Or poetically. Anyway, it calms me down." I chanced a glance at him. "Doesn't make much sense, I know."

"In order to chill the fuck out, you *think* more?"

"Sometimes. But I can also just sink down there and take comfort in the quiet. I guess when I'm stressed, that's where I go. That's what I use it for."

"It makes me fucking stressed just to hear about it!"

"Welcome to a minute in my mind."

He lifted his hand to summon Barb from the other end of the bar and when he had her attention, he raised two fingers. "I'm gonna need another drink to hang out up there." He pointed at my head.

"If I have another drink I'm going to fall off this barstool."

"You'll fit right in."

The dancer on stage left in the middle of a song. Her floral sweetness walked right past us and into the dressing room and because he was the boss Anton looked at a board just off the stage and saw that the woman stage-named Chastity was next up. He scanned the bar and shook his head and said, "If I know Chastity, she's been to visit Phil and now she's nose deep in his product."

"Your product," I said.

He shrugged, then said, "Technically Sheb's product."

But she wasn't. Instead she came out of the dressing room wearing sweatpants and a parka and with a bag slung over her forearm.

"Hey Chastity, what's up?" Anton said.

"I got one of the girls to take the rest of my sets. My daughter's sick and driving the babysitter nuts. I gotta pick her up." She stopped at Anton's side.

"Who's taking your sets?"

One song ended, and another began, and as sure as I lived that weekend in Madison in 1978, the Eagles' "Life in the Fast Lane" filled the room. Anton shook his head and smirked. He kissed Chastity on the hand and said, "I hope your girl's all right," then he swiveled toward me and said, "I guess you don't have a choice in the matter."

"What matter?" I said.

He threw his thumb over his shoulder and when I looked behind him, Chloe and Kristi, née Britt and Missy, had locked onto each other and in a tangle of bustiers and negligees, garter belts, fishnet stockings, and platform boots, they ascended the stage in a phantasmagoria of red and black silk.

He leaned in and said, "This is why I can't get serious with Chloe."

"Because she's a dancer?"

He sat back. "How the fuck could I judge her for that?"

"Was she, in the barge office . . ." I stammered.

"Ready to get paid?" he finished my thought.

"I mean, is that something she does?"

"Not that I know about. I think she's just playing games."

"What is it, then? The reason the two of you can't get serious?"

He looked up at her and grinned fiercely and spoke without taking his eyes off her. "It's because she thinks everything's a joke. It's because she still fucks around like this"—he lifted his chin toward the stage—"and because she's cunning as Sheb." Barb dropped another pair of Four Roses in front of us.

"Thanks," I said.

Anton was still smiling at her. "How fucked up is it that half the time I look at her, I think of an aunt I never knew?"

"You're talking about Lena?"

Now he looked at me. "We got a bunch of other relatives I don't know about?" He stood, took the wad of cash from his pocket, peeled off a twenty for Barb and a fistful for me, and picked up his drink and added, "Can you imagine what Angel would think of her? Don't answer that. Come on."

"What's this for?" I asked, fanning the cash between us.

"It's for your girlfriend."

"I'll stay right here. I'm good," I said.

Anton nodded and said, "Suit yourself" and staggered up to the stage.

From ten stools away, I could see the drunkenness in his eyes and knew mine must look similar. But he also appeared almost boyish, and charmed, and very much like he knew he was the king of the castle. He put a twenty-dollar bill on the stage and sat back with his drink folded in his hands and waited for "Life in the Fast Lane" to finish before the two women came parading over and sat down on either side of him, their legs hanging off the stage.

For fifteen minutes, they took turns dancing and playing coy. When Chloe descended, he leaned back and sipped his drink. When Kristi flitted over, he leaned in and whispered in her ear. Chloe seemed pouty in those moments and gave her attention to a pair of the guys in biker jackets at the other end of the bar, peering constantly back at Anton and Kristi. Kristi's attention was fully on my brother, though. Talking. Listening. Smiling. Her smile was as rhythmic and easy as her sway. And even though she wasn't dancing like Chloe—she'd not shed any of her clothes, and she made no pretense of a routine or any furtiveness—I felt a pang of guilt watching her so attentively and with such pleasure.

Maybe it was the loneliness of that place that made my ogling seem harmless. Maybe it was the too many drinks. Maybe it was the surreality of being back in my brother's company, or Pops's ghost already haunting me. Whatever the case, I watched their dissimilar performances through the last song with some feeling between excitement and uneasiness, liking myself less with each note of music, until I looked at my own hands in front of me and saw nothing. When I looked back up around the bar, I had the sensation of looking on a page of my own writing. Which is to say they were apocryphal—everyone was—even for all their flesh and blood. They were figments of my sordid imagination. Even my brother, finishing his drink and swiveling around to set it on the bar behind him, looked like someone I invented.

Before another song started I got up and went to the men's room. I took a leak and checked my phone and even thought of calling Ingrid, just to feel like I was back in the world. But instead I splashed water on my face and dried it with a paper hand towel and resolved to end that night as soon as possible. I wanted to be alone with Anton. To talk with him without the commotion and women and more booze. I wanted to get to know him again.

But I no sooner stepped out of the men's room and faltered back to my seat at the bar than Anton rejoined me.

"Goddamn," he said, like there was nothing more he might possibly add.

"This place is a dreamscape," I said.

"A nightmare, you mean."

"That did *not* look like a nightmare. Not from where I was sitting."

"Creeper." He winked.

"I am out of my depth, brother, and I don't know what the hell's gotten into me. I don't ogle exotic dancers. I don't drink to excess."

"I'm a good influence, is what you're saying?"

"All I need now is to waste a hundred dollars on pull-tabs and my night of debauchery will be complete."

"If pull-tabs are your version of debauchery, we see things even more differently than I thought!" His expression changed suddenly and, like a character who won't do what I expect them to, he added, "What in the world am I gonna do?"

I didn't know what he was talking about, and said as much.

As if talking now only to himself, he added, "Probably it's just this fucking night. Pops. And now you," he snapped out of it, looked at me, hit me on the shoulder, "sitting here like we never missed a beat. Why would I choose tonight of all nights to have this epiphany?"

"What are you talking about?" I said.

As though in answer to his question, Chloe came splashing across the stage, her cocktail spilling from the glass she carried in a loose grip. She set her drink on the edge of the stage, navigated the narrow staircase down, and instead of picking up her drink again put both of her hands into the air and flipped Anton off with her middle fingers. Then she turned her hands and pointed those middle fingers at me and said, "I'm gonna find you in just a minute." She disappeared into the dressing room in ten long strides.

"What'd I do?" I said.

"You showed up." He reached down under the bar counter and pulled a bottle of water out of the ice and added, "Promise, this is my last detour. I'll head her off at the pass."

With that, he followed her into the dressing room and I was left alone again at the bar.

*

But not for long. Almost as soon as Anton disappeared behind the jukebox, Kristi emerged from his shadow. She was dressed now in jeans and a hoodie and her hair was pulled into a ponytail. She sat beside me without prompting and said, "What's up with your brother?"

"Maybe you can tell me. I feel like I'm in the middle of story without a plot."

"I love stories without plots."

"Maybe more like I'm in the middle of a story where none of the characters is doing what I want them to."

"What do you want Anton to do?"

I thought about it for a beat. "I haven't known the answer to that question in about thirty years."

"What is it with you two, anyway? I can't figure it out."

"This is the second time you've brought it up."

"Anton's never once given me the time of day, and now, tonight, all of a sudden, he's curious. It's because you're here."

"My being here is weird, trust me. For Anton especially." I imagined him only a few moments earlier, sitting attentively at Kristi's feet. "And the truth is I don't know him very well these days, but it hardly seems complicated that you'd be more fun to talk to than Chloe."

Now Anton appeared from behind the jukebox again, Chloe beside him still dressed to dance. They sat down across the bar from us, and my brother nodded and arched his eyebrows, a look that said *Might as well enjoy the ride?* Then he put his arm around Chloe and they turned to the new dancer on the stage.

191

Kristi leaned over and said, "I don't think Anton would say he doesn't know you well."

"I just mean we're not exactly close. We haven't been since we were kids." I cocked my head and studied him, to see if there was any vestige of the boy he used to be. As if reading my mind, he turned and balled his hand and cocked his arm and then ran his fist toward me, his fingers exploding in what I knew was a gesture meant to resemble a ski jumper taking off. I nodded and couldn't help smile and turned back to Kristi. "That was a long time ago."

"You're either full of shit or blind. I can't tell which."

She called Barb and ordered a shot of tequila. Only after she put salt on her thumb and downed the Cuervo and sucked the lime and wiped her lips with the napkin did she turn and ask if I wanted one.

"I think I'm done drinking for the night."

"A wise man," she said. "No way am I driving home tonight." She wiped the inside of the shot glass, and kissed the residual booze from her fingertip. "What are you two doing now?"

"It looks like Anton has closing time in mind," I said.

"That means you do, too?"

"I guess so."

As though he were part of our conversation, Anton turned and again balled his fist and sent his hand flying, his face dopey and drunk. I might've returned the gesture but as soon as I thought to, the office door burst open, followed by the blotted shine of the fluorescent lights in there. Sheb, in all his enormity and with a wide-brimmed hat of some sort topping him off, filled the doorway. For a half-moment, we stared at each other uncertainly. But as quickly as he'd entered, so too arose on his face an unkind recognition, and he sneered at me.

Making his way to the bar, he bellowed, "You're still awake, Johannes." Then standing above me, he lifted his reading glasses up his nose and peered at me through the sparkling lenses. "Ah, but your eyes say not for long!"

"Probably not for long, no."

Chloe hurried under his arm, and he leaned into her and reached around and held her breast in a gloved hand. "This wonderful lass." He winked at me as he gave Chloe another squeeze and kissed her on the cheek. "And you," he said to Kristi. "You are—what's the word—toothsome? Have I got that right, my author friend? Or is your mind too addled to think straight?"

"Toothsome is a good word, Sheb. So is degenerate."

"You think I'm a simple, vulgar man. But tonight, you're keeping the same company as I am." He let go of Chloe and sat on the stool on the other side of Kristi. "But who's keeping score?" He raised a hand in Barb's direction and nodded when he caught her attention. She went to the same cupboard that held Anton's Four Roses and this time brought out a bottle of aquavit. He peeled off his gloves and ran his hands across his head and looked over at me, still sitting there. "The past is the past, right? And every moment we start again, always with better hopes? That's how I've always lived. It's as close to a code as I have. Best not to look back for too long, to dwell on what's already happened. Don't you think that's the best course?"

I didn't answer, even as I felt my arms and shoulders flex against his words.

Barb set five shot glasses on the edge of the bar and poured each full of the aquavit.

"And one for yourself, my lovely," Sheb said, passing the glasses around and leaving two on the bar.

Barb poured herself half a shot and topped it with water again. She held it aloft and waited while the rest of us raised our glasses.

Sheb cleared his throat and lifted his chin before beginning his toast. "Jake was my cousin and my confidant, and I never loved anyone more. I already miss him like hell." He looked to Anton, who took the mantle, "I never quite got over the mess he made, but not a minute has gone by in the past week I haven't wished he was here. I expect another several years of that." He looked to me, and all I had left to say was "I expect the same, little brother. Here's to Pops."

We clinked our glasses and quaffed the aquavit and from that moment on the evening took the shape of fantastic hallucination.

The Greatest Depth

I MET INGRID ON A NOVEMBER NIGHT, in 1980, in the Lemon Drop Restaurant in Duluth's east end. It had been snowing for three days solid, and I can still see the heavy condensation on the plate windows overlooking the parking lot. I'd eaten meatloaf and mashed potatoes and mushy peas and was drinking a cup of coffee with my scoop of ice cream when she came up and sat across the table from me.

"You look like how I imagine the eavesdropper in that Dickens story would."

"What?"

"'To Be Read at Dusk,' you know? I'm in Victorian lit with you."

My expression must have betrayed my confusion.

"Professor Benken's class?"

Her confidence was startling, and beautiful, and before I'd said one meaningful word I already felt lifted up by her. "Of course," I said.

"Have you finished *David Copperfield* yet?"

"I read it a couple years ago."

"Are you not going to read it again? Haven't you forgotten just about the whole thing?"

"I probably have. And probably should."

"Of course you should!" She reached across the table and grabbed the bowl of ice cream and took a bite, then slid it back.

"Would you like one?" I said.

"No thanks." She pulled a napkin from the dispenser and wiped her lip and smiled at me. "I'm Ingrid. You're Jon. Mr. Serious Jon."

I smiled back. "Not so serious. Just surprised to suddenly be having a conversation. I've been sitting alone here for an hour."

She settled back in her seat. "What does someone think about for an hour sitting in this place?"

"Mostly I've been thinking about how winter'll be different from now on."

"Why's that? Looks and feels like regular winter to me."

"That part's true, but it's usually about this time of year I start getting geared up."

"For what?"

"I used to be a ski jumper."

"Used to be? Like back in the old days? You look a little young to have a past."

"I don't mean it like that. I had a bad crash earlier this year. Busted my leg pretty good."

"Ouch!" she said.

"Compound fractures. Tibia and fibula. Those are the bones down in your shin."

"I know what bones they are," she said, a little defensive. "I'm a biology major. A good one."

"I didn't mean to insult you. Sorry," I said.

She dismissed my apology with a wave of her hand. "Did you ever take the jump up at Chester Bowl?"

"I did. Many times. I love that hill."

"I grew up right by it. We used to go and watch the tournaments. I bet I've seen you."

"I bet you're right."

"Compound fractures," she said, taking another bite of my ice cream. "That's serious. And the reason you quit ski jumping?"

"I quit to come here."

"To the Lemon Drop?"

"Very funny. To college. It was time to move on."

Now she ran the spoon around the bottom of the bowl, sipped the slurry of melted ice cream and chocolate sauce from the spoon, and said, "Wait a minute. It was time? So you're older?"

"I'm thirty years old, the oldest freshman at UMD."

She sat back with a blank look on her face.

"Too old?"

A smile appeared slowly. "I get it," she said. "How old are you really?"

"Twenty," I said. "*Going* on thirty."

She seemed relieved, and suddenly even more in control. She lifted a menu from behind the napkin dispenser and pretended to look it over.

"I'll miss my Pops and brother this winter, that's why I'm glum."

This led us into another half-hour conversation. About families and friends and what we wanted from life. She had much better answers than I did, and was unabashed about them, too. Randomly she said, "Do you have a car?"

I nodded. I would've driven her anywhere.

"Does it do all right in the snow?"

"Heck yeah it does."

"Waitress!" she hollered across the restaurant. "Please bring us the check."

"What are you doing?"

"I want to go somewhere with you."

I remember how already, in the first hour of knowing her, she'd stirred something more than plain desire in me. She was smart and confident and playful and, taken altogether, these qualities made her beautiful. A beauty that got lovelier out in the flurries.

We hopped in my Bronco and drove up the shore, past the mansions along London Road blanketed under the bounteous snow, more of which fell even as we made our way over Amity Creek and into the parking lot at Brighton Beach. She turned the radio on and asked me to turn the headlights off and she nestled into her seat.

"I can't even believe I asked you to take me here. Please don't get the wrong idea. Please don't be a creep."

"I'm not a creep. And I don't have any ideas." I looked out across the snowswept and rocky beach, the waves rising and settling like the curls of her hair.

"You know what we call this, right?"

"Call what?"

"The waves, the storms?"

"The gales of November."

"Pretty good for a Minneapolis boy."

"I'm not from here, but one of my best friends grew up on High Street. His dad worked on the ore boats. In fact, he survived the wreck of the *Ragnarøk*."

"Seriously?"

"His name's Noah Torr. Maybe you went to school with him?"

"I don't know him, even if I've heard the name. Olaf was the dad, right?"

"He's like an uncle to me."

"No wonder you know about the gales of November."

We watched the waves crash on the boulders and listened to the spray haze the windshield as the radio played. For hours we sat there, the conversation turning from families to school to books we'd read and loved and hated. She told me about her friends and life in the dorms and her majors, which were education and biology, and her favorite perch in the library, where she went almost every day to study.

Eventually, our talk turned back to the lake and the storm, which still sent my Bronco shuddering with each gust of wind. She described for me how the water in the lake resided there—some of it—for hundreds of years, and that all the molecules splashing into the darkness, borne by the gale, were the equivalent of but a paper-thin layer of the whole body, and that the oldest of the water in the inland sea must surely be left over from the ice that retreated to leave the basin for the lake in the first place. As I sat there, my body heavy in the seat of my truck, I believed I could feel something beyond the combers, something more like that old water howling up from the depths, godlike, to announce the seriousness of what was happening between us.

"Can you feel that?" she asked.

I swear she spoke those words just as I imagined the depths. I swear I could see through the darkness—out the windows, across the space between us on the bench seat—that her eyes and that night confirmed a trusting confluence that's rarely been broken since. I swear.

"Imagine all the water out there," she continued, "a thousand feet deep, more than that, even. Imagine how heavy it is. How permanent. How cold. How dark." Another wave came ashore, leaving another scattering of water across the windshield.

"That makes me feel really calm," I said. "Calmer than I've been in a long time."

I could see the silhouette of her lips turn up. I can still remember the way she shifted toward me and tucked her feet up beneath her on the seat and rested her head on the headrest.

"It makes me feel restless beyond words to think of it."

"Imagine how quiet it would be."

"Do you like being alone?"

"I spend a lot of time alone. I don't know how much I like it. I don't mind it, I can say that much."

"I hate being alone," she said.

What I thought, as still another cold mist washed over the car, was that she didn't have to worry about being alone anymore. Not if she didn't want to be. Not if she liked me as much as I was obviously going to like her.

*

"Does the bottom of the lake still make you feel restless, Ingrid?" I say now.

She holds the steering wheel with both hands and glances over at me and gives a knowing shake of her head. "You're playing some of our classic hits?"

"You have no idea how many times I've gone myself to those depths."

She lifts a finger and points at the lake. The horizon has folded seamlessly under the low-slung clouds so it's indistinguishable from the lake below. All of it mirrors Ingrid's doubting eyes. "It still troubles me. Even more than it used to. Especially on a day like this."

"What kind of day's this?"

"Like the lake's where we're headed."

"I'm sorry, love."

"Me too."

We pass over the Wood-of-the-Soul River with its steep cascades crusted by terraced ice and its main chute seething a fine vapor.

"Back at the lighthouse, what you told me about Annika, that's what you needed to get off your chest?" she says.

"Maybe call it the beginning?"

"The beginning of what? Airing your dirty laundry?" She shoots a cold stare, and the car swerves. She jerks the steering wheel to center it on the road again, overcompensating and hitting the rumble strips before righting it altogether. "I wish you'd just talk to me. You haven't said anything for thirty minutes, and all of a sudden you're talking about a conversation we had forty years ago."

"I don't mean to be obtuse."

"It's like following a falling snowflake, Jon. I just can't do it. If you want to tell me what's on your mind, just say it."

"You remember the night of Pops's funeral. The snow and getting stuck down in Minneapolis for the night. My spending the night with Anton."

"All night you caroused at that disgusting bar he runs. Yes, I remember."

"Something happened that night that I never told you about."

Her face flushes with anger and she grips the wheel fiercely. "Do you mean to tell me—"

"You've asked to hear," I interrupt, "so let me tell."

She casts a doubtful gaze at me but drives on resolutely.

"Anton told me about Bett that night. He said that when Pops went to prison, after he'd been away a couple months, Bett tried to commit suicide."

"What?" Her voice now is changed.

"She took a bottle of sleeping pills. Almost died. Anton found her, and called Sheb, who came and took her to the hospital. She spent four days on a respirator before she recovered and went away."

"How did you never know this?"

"No one ever told me."

"Where were you? Why weren't you at home?"

"I was at Noah's when it happened. She sent me up here. For the long Thanksgiving weekend. To jump at Chester Bowl. When I got back, all Sheb told me was that she'd gone to the state hospital in St. Peter because she wasn't well. That's when he brought Anton and me to his school."

"And even Anton never told you?"

"Not until the night of Pops's funeral."

"He would have been such a little boy then. When Bett did that. Was he keeping it a secret from you?"

"Anton kept pretty much everything a secret back then. That year he basically didn't speak. I mean truly didn't speak. He communicated by writing things down in a little notebook he kept."

She drives in silence for a couple miles. "*This* is what you wanted to tell me?"

"His telling me set in motion a series of, what, confessions? Admissions?"

"Between you and your brother?"

"Yes."

We pass over the Prudence River and the vacant campground on the lake side of the road. She slows for a curve and turns to me, tentatively, like she's afraid to hear more but knows she must. She doesn't speak.

"I was upset after he told me about Bett."

"Because of what she'd done, or because he hadn't told you before then?"

"Both, I think. But if I'm being honest, I was angrier that he'd never told me."

"I'm not surprised. You never had any compassion for her. You never forgave her anything."

I don't respond. There's no argument.

"Well, what happened after he told you?"

"We drank. We hung out at Boff's."

"With those women you told me about?" There's a shift in her tone. Slight, but it's there.

"Yes."

"You got drunk with those women?"

I stare into the trees blurring past on the side of the road, willing the particulars of that night to come out of the forest of memory yet also stay back among the darkness of the pines.

"You're awfully quiet," she says.

"You know I was drinking with those women. They were with us for most of the night."

Now it's her turn to stare ahead.

"I wanted to get even with him. Something like that."

"With Anton?"

"Because he had that secret. About Bett."

"You divorced yourself from all of them. Such a long time ago you did."

"I know that's true. But I was devastated. About Pops. And it was like Anton had stretched the rupture between us even further."

"I'm sure that's not true. I'm sure he told you in order to bring you closer together."

She's right. He was only doing what I hoped to accomplish myself. Clear the debris between us. I can see that now. "I think you're right," I say. "But that night, it felt like he wanted to push me farther away. And I was mad at myself, too. Then and now. That I'd let us grow so far apart. That I'd pushed them all from my life."

"That part's well-traveled ground, Jon."

"So's this highway, and still, here we are." I don't mean to sound defensive. And I'm not stalling. I should apologize.

"Would you just tell me whatever's on your mind? So we can get on to the business of enjoying this day."

"That's fair." I shift in the seat so my back's against the car door and I'm looking at her profile. "You remember that Anton's girlfriend was one of the women at the bar?"

She only glances at me, warily.

"Well, she had a friend. Missy was her name. And for a while that night, while Anton was tending the shop, I spent time talking with her."

"Talking?"

"Yes, talking."

"What else did you do with her?"

I'm in motion now. I don't want to stop. "She told me about taking care of her mother and what she was studying in college—"

"Sounds like the two of you were bosom friends."

"Ingrid, please."

She's driving now as if she were behind the wheel of a big rig, her hands up high on the wheel and her chin thrust forward. She looks, I just realize, like she's ready to take a punch.

"Well?" she says.

"Missy, she told me about an abortion she had—"

"Why in the world would you be having this intimate a conversation with another woman?"

"That's a fair question, but it's not the point I'm getting at." I shift back so I'm facing forward again. "It was right on the heels of Anton telling me about Bett taking the sleeping pills. My thoughts were corkscrewing, Ingrid. I was thinking about Annika and her abortion. But I was also thinking about Lena Lyng."

"Bett's sister? What about her?"

"When I was a kid, whenever she came up, Bett was quick to excoriate her. I mean, she hated her with *gusto*. Lena wasn't even a topic we were allowed to talk about. We knew how Pops started out with her, and that she left him there in Minneapolis soon after they arrived, but mostly we were left to believe she was as good as dead." I clench my eyes to the kaleidoscope of memories, of the stories true and untrue. "We discussed this as a family only once, when we went out for dinner the day Pops got out of prison.

"Lena left, Bett told us, because she was selfish and weak. Good riddance, that was the message. Bett also told us that Lena was pregnant when they left Chicago, and that she had an abortion before leaving Minneapolis. An elaborate story about taking a taxi to a farmhouse out in Anoka for the procedure, then going straight downtown to the Greyhound station and catching a bus back to Chicago."

"I feel like I've heard this before," Ingrid says, some of the edge off her voice.

"Probably you have. Probably I've mumbled through this story before. But it's never been right. Never true."

"I still don't understand, Jon. What are you telling me?"

"It was all horseshit. Bett's story was. I knew it. Pops knew it. Bett must have known it."

"About Lena Lyng?"

"The only part of it that was true is that she took a bus back to Chicago."

"How do you know this?"

"I know because some years later I met my half-sister. Her name was Helene. She showed up in Minneapolis with Andrus Patollo, and my whole life came undone."

"You have a sister?"

"A half-sister."

"How have I known you for almost forty years and never learned this?"

"Like I said at the beginning, I've made mistakes."

I can as much as see her calculations and she starts to say something, twice, then stops and finally mutters, "Why would she lie about it? Did your father know?"

"Pops met her once. Or once that I know about, anyway."

She shakes her head and sighs and I notice she's driving eighty miles per hour.

"Slow down, honey?"

"I feel like you've hit me with a hammer," she says. The temper in her voice is one of anger and frustration. She doesn't employ it often. "And you're just standing above me poised to whack me again."

"No, love. No no no. I'm right here, and without a hammer. I'm doing my best."

She's going even faster now, the town of Misquah coming at us with alarming speed. We rip past the pole barn of a hardware store and its passing seems to draw her back into consciousness. She glances at the speedometer and flinches and stands on the brakes. We both slam against our seatbelts and the car nearly skids into the parking lot of The Landing. She pulls into a parking spot and turns off the ignition and steps outside. I step out, too, and fold my arms on the roof as she walks in a circle.

After a moment, she stops and assumes my same position above the driver's side door. She takes off her sunglasses and closes her eyes. "Jon, did you sleep with that woman?"

"Did I sleep with a woman?"

"The night of your father's funeral?"

"Of course not."

Her eyes flash open, but they bring no relief to her uneasiness.

"Is that what you think I'm talking about? Is that what you think I have to tell you?" The fact that this has only just now occurred to me tells me all I need to know about how selfish I've been. I hurry around the car. "Oh, Jesus," I say, turning her in my arms. "I promise you, no. Never."

She buries her forehead in the collar of my coat.

"I'm so sorry. That you had to think that even for one minute." I push her away, just far enough so that I can see her face, which is covered in tears. I wipe them away with my chapped thumbs. I hold her chin. "You are my great and only love, Ingrid. You are my whole stupid life."

This elicits more tears, and she drops her head back on my shoulder.

"I have so much more to tell you. So much about that night and about my life. But I'll only tell you if you want to hear. Okay?"

We stand here in the dirt parking lot of this gas station, a couple of old companions and lovers surprised by the resolve of time and its endless surprises. I can't tell if she's angry or merely stunned, and I can't imagine the questions she's forming in the very particular way of hers. But rather than asking any of them, she only says, "I want to hear everything, Jon. And I appreciate how hard it must have been to carry that around with you for all these years. I don't understand why you never told me, or what it means that you didn't, but I suppose you can get to that eventually." She leans back so she can look at my face. "And I don't know what else you have to say. But whatever it is, I'll listen. I want to know. But right this second let's go in The Landing and buy up their supply of bear claws to bring Noah, and let's go have that visit before you tell me more about Helene. Can we do that?"

She lets go of me and walks past the pair of gas pumps and into The Landing. A few minutes later she comes out with a pastry box and two bottles of water. We get back in the car and head for Noah's place.

*

If the highway slinking along the shore of the big water is the main artery of my life, the county road that slinks into the hills above Misquah is the vena cava to an epoch in it more enduring than any other. This was the road that delivered Anton and me from the school for boys and the most fiendish, corrupt chapter of Sheb's life. It delivered us to a season of peace, and a season of a thousand jumps. More than anything, it delivered us to our brotherhood, one I thought incapable of splintering.

This morning, it's merely delivering me back to us. To Ingrid and me. As we ascend the five-mile hill, lined now with ever deepening snow, the trees infringing on the asphalt shoulder, slick with ice and unplowed snow, Ingrid seems to be loosening with the knowledge that my admission was of a half-sister, and not a lover. I can see fewer of the crow's feet around her eyes, her shoulders and hands are lax, her voice, when she points to a red fox bounding across the road ahead of us and says "Look, Jon," is settled. It takes fifteen minutes of wending through the woods before we turn off on Lake Forsone Road, and those are the only words either of us utters.

The pavement is pocked and still half-covered with patches of snow and ice. It ascends sharply, and I wonder twice if the car is up for the job, but before long we've reached the plateau and drive along easily for another ten minutes. The trees above are so dense it's as if we've entered another tunnel.

"Turn right here," I remind her.

"I always forget." She slows, signals her turn, and we're now on a dirt road that's completely covered by packed snow. The woods are all pine, and except for when we cross over a culvert near the public access, it's like the car is cocooned.

"Slow down, love," I say. Even though I've been here a hundred times, it's not always easy to see the mailbox that announces Noah's home. He's redone it since the last time we visited. A new box that looks big enough to be a little free library stilted on cedar posts with a red metal flag of the old-fashioned kind to announce a pick-up. I take it as a good sign, given how down he's been the past few months. Maybe this modest improvement is indication that he's up and running again.

This notion finds some validation as Ingrid steers down the slope to his cabin. It's better plowed than the county roads, and the canopy above is trimmed high and wide. The plowed snow on either side of us rises above my line of sight.

"It's like driving down winter's gullet," I say.

"Imagine how deep the snow is in the woods."

"And Noah all by himself up here to keep himself shoveled out. That's no small job. I know."

"It's still strange for you? Coming back here?"

"It feels less like arriving at a place than in a dream. It always does. Until I see Noah, then it feels like a homecoming."

She slows for the last big downhill curve. "Jon, did your sister—your half-sister—have anything to do with the winter you lived here?"

The cabin comes into view through the gaunt trees. There's smoke rising from the chimney, and a garage built where the shed used to be. Ingrid parks beside it and turns the ignition off. Before we get out I take her hand and say, "She has everything to do with it."

*

Noah's helloing from the middle of the yard, his thumbs tucked under the suspenders he wears now like a kind of uniform. The isolate woodsman. Ingrid beats me to him, carrying the box of pastries in one arm and throwing the other around his waist. He's wearing a pair of wool pants and only a handsome flannel shirt under his suspenders, and he untucks his thumbs to return her embrace. Noah's a good six inches taller than I am, so a foot taller than Ingrid, and she appears a child in his long arms. He's shaved his beard, so his sweet smile—even with all its inherent sadness—is larger than usual.

"At least one of you is excited to see me!" His voice is booming and kind and just to hear it brings me a relief that nothing else could. He's been my best friend since we were teenagers, and he's never once let me down.

"If you think I'm gonna come fawn all over you like that, forget about it," I say.

He grabs Ingrid's arm and hurries her to the door, opens it and makes a show of pushing her inside, then says, "I'll lock you out here, old man. Your pretty wife and I will feast on whatever's in this box." He makes a show of shutting the screen door and shouts, "You better believe we will."

It's been many months since I visited Noah, and though not much has changed there is a tidiness to the place in winter that I admire. The yard is cut with paths through the snow. One from the house to the garage. Another to the woodpiles that sit beneath a lean-to in a new clearing beyond the drive. They're damn near works of art, the woodpiles. Six feet tall and cylindrical, all of it birch. Two of them. It must be twenty cords. His old man had a thing for firewood, too. Some bone in the Torr body, I guess.

I crane my neck and look down to the lake. There's a path through the snow in that direction, too, and under the deck that surrounds two sides of the cabin all his ice fishing gear is stored on a toboggan. If he's still the same man I've always known, that sled gets pulled down to and across the lake just about every day.

One of his garage doors is open, and I can see his other life's work sitting up on blocks. His father's Suburban. Ever since he moved back here, Noah's been at work on the restoration. He once admitted being thirty grand into it, and nowhere near completion. From the looks of things, he's still not close.

I stare at the boughs high on the towering pines, some of them still holding snow, and so like spirited clouds with dark underbellies. This is one of my favorite places. And one of my most haunted.

Inside, Noah's already putting the bear claws on a platter. He'll eat two or three, to go with his uninterrupted coffee, and even at our late ages he's lean enough to strap on a pair of jumping skis and take a ride on the family jump just down the lakeshore.

"Coffee's brewing, Jon," he says. "Sit down."

"Where?" I say.

"It's not that bad. Here . . ." He comes out from behind the counter and fills his arms with newspapers and magazines that were covering half the couch. He stuffs them into the tinderbox beside the pinging hot stove.

"It's like you've discovered your own personal interior decorating style. Shambolic chic."

He's already back behind the counter, pairing napkins and plates, but he pauses at my dig. He looks at Ingrid, who's leaning against the other side of the counter, and says, "He moves like a goddamned tortoise, but his tongue's as sharp as a hatchet blade." Now he turns to me. "Shambolic, we're supposed to know what that means?"

"It means your place is a mess. You're a hoarder now?"

Again he turns to Ingrid. "No hello, no how are you, no it's good to see you. Is he really this old and batshit? Has he really forgotten all the rules of civilized society?"

"Society?" I say. "You're a hermit."

He puts the percolator on the stovetop and sparks a match to light the burner. Much has changed in here since I was a kid, and despite my ribbing it's the sort of place that might appear in the Sunday Homes section of a newspaper. In the years after his father passed away, I spent many summer afternoons helping him shore up the place. We replaced the roof. We installed a bathroom and the small kitchen. We rebuilt the deck that surrounds two sides of the house. And we built a new dock.

He brings the platter of bear claws to the coffee table and he hugs me like he knows my fate. When he lets go, he holds my face in his hands and says, "It's good to see you, you cranky bastard."

"And you."

"Sit down. Really," he says. "The reason the place is such a mess is because I was going through some old files." He picks up a stack of papers from beside the pastries and flips through them. What he's looking for isn't there, and when he sets them back down he pauses and says, "For you! Hold on." And as quickly as that, he's disappeared into what I know he calls the port bedroom. His bedroom. And his father's before him.

There are two bedrooms. Doors on either side of the stove, neither much bigger than the beds that command them. When Anton and I hid out here, we slept on the floor in front of the stove, the bedrooms being impossibly cold back then, even with a stoked woodstove. Now there's a plush rug in the center of the room, the walls closer all the way around than I remember, and I'm reminded of the mixed feelings that long-ago season inspired in me: that the possibilities for Anton and me seemed at once enormous and confined in this space. Or to the Torrs' twenty acres on Lake Forsone.

"He seems well," Ingrid says when finally I settle my eyes on her. "And he's very happy to see you."

"I *am* happy to see him," Noah says, reemerging from the bedroom. "And you, too, sweetheart." He sits on the couch and summons us over to sit on either side of him. He's got a file folder half an inch thick and he opens it like it protects a last will and testament.

"So much ceremony," I say. "What the hell is it."

In answer, he only hands me a photograph. It's of Anton and me, in the jumpsuits Olaf gave us that winter, our skis leaning against our outside shoulders, my left arm resting on his helmeted head. The jump is in the background, rising up with the lakeside trees.

"That's you and your brother," Ingrid says.

"There's a whole host of things in here." Noah taps the file. "I thought it might help you with the book you're writing." He pushes himself up from the couch and bolts into the kitchen to check on the coffee. "Speaking of which, I expect a starring role. You've gone long enough without writing the real heroes in your life."

"Maybe you can talk some sense into him, Noah." This is Ingrid again, turning to Noah, who is ready to fill three coffee cups.

"What sense?" he asks.

"Jon's decided he's done writing books."

Noah sets the percolator down. "Is that true?" They're the first sincere words he's spoken since we arrived, and they settle on me like his father's voice used to—all somber and serious.

"It is."

"Tell him how foolish that is," Ingrid says. "He needs to do something, the doctor said so—" A dread silence overcomes her. She's let slip what I asked her not to, and though I'm certain it was an accident, it catches me off guard and I take a deep breath.

Noah looks between us. "What doctor?"

"Just a checkup," I say. "You know, gotta keep the tip of the spear sharp." I tap my noggin.

Noah pours the coffees but keeps glancing at me. He delivers a cup to Ingrid, and one to me, and sits in the chair across from us now. "So, why stop writing?"

"I guess I should say I'm not going to write the ski jumping book." I take a sip of coffee and then raise my glass to him. "You always made the best cup."

He deflects the compliment with a wave of his hand. "Why?"

I turn the picture of me and Anton around and say, "Because I'd rather remember these boys than the ones that book would force on me."

"As if you're capable of letting the past lay," Noah says. "Or is it lie?"

"Let me guess, no pun intended?"

"I didn't even know I made a pun."

Ingrid says, "I wish you'd be serious even for just a minute."

Noah straightens, like he's been reprimanded. The scars from his father are deep. As are those from his marriage, which is now ten years finished. "What should we be serious about, Ingrid?" He's earnest now, and she and I both know it.

"About Jon, that's what. About his writing this book. About his taking care of himself."

I take a bear claw from the plate, dunk it in my coffee, and take a bite. "I'm sick, Noah," I say. It's out before I can doubt myself. Practically of its own will.

"What kind of sick?"

I look at Ingrid, whose eyes are glassy and lips pursed, and then back at my friend. "I've got younger-onset Alzheimer's. I found out yesterday."

He sits back in his chair like he's been stunned. To Ingrid he says, "Is this true?"

"Of course it's true," I say. "You think I'd joke?"

"It's true," Ingrid confirms.

He sets his coffee on the arm of his chair and leans forward, elbows on knees. "Tell me what this means?"

"It means I'm going to start losing my memory. It means I'm going to get even crankier. It means life is going to be hell for Ingrid."

"You found out yesterday? How do you know it's not a bad diagnosis? Does it make sense to get a second opinion?"

"It's been months getting to the diagnosis. I don't think it's wrong. And it explains a lot about how I've been."

"What do you mean, how you've been?"

I look down at the floor, ashamed.

Ingrid answers for me. "He's been having a hard time with memory function. Even simple things. I don't think the diagnosis is wrong either."

Now Noah looks down at the floor, too. "Jesus Christ, I'm sorry," he whispers.

"I'm going to retire after the sabbatical. We're going to get all our affairs in order so that things go as easily for Ingrid as they possibly can. You're going to be seeing more of me in the next little while."

"More of you?"

"Ingrid kicked me out. I'm moving back in."

There's a flash of pleasure on his face before he recognizes I'm joking. "I'm going to spend time with the people I love. While I can. In the flesh." I take Ingrid's hand and hold it and look her in the eye. "That sounds better to me than dredging up the past."

When I look at Noah, he's tearing up.

"He wasn't going to tell you," Ingrid says. "He hasn't even told the kids yet."

"I hope it's okay," I say, "that I did?"

"Goddamnit, Jon." He pushes himself up and comes over to me and as much as lifts me from the couch. The hug he wraps me in reminds me of Pops, and if there weren't so many tears already streaming, I'd let loose myself.

Instead I say, "What do you have in that folder?"

III

Palimpsests

Patollo's death occurred the same night I met Helene, my half-sister, for the first and only time. In the days between that fateful, chthonian hour and the morning Anton and I were set free on the Torrs' family ski jump, I imagined a hundred versions of the child I might have been if I'd been Lena's son instead of Bett's.

He took many forms, this boy, this young man. Sometimes he appeared as a sort of prince, moving among the Chicago gentry with aloofness and the carte blanche a famous mother bestows. She, of course, would have doted on him at every turn. Other times he was a gangster's stepson, a pistol-packing wise guy who walked around with hundred-dollar brogues and a fedora cocked at an angle over his slicked-back hair. Some days, he was a gambler, and others a bank robber. Several instances found him a movie actor, or a singer like his mother, or a Wall Street broker. Anything felt possible, given how beautiful and enigmatic Helene seemed in the hour I knew her.

But for all the allure these would-be boys and young men possessed, none of them ever took root, and not only because I didn't know how to trudge a path toward them but because they always

meant a life that excluded my brother. And despite the many reasons I wished my life were otherwise, without Anton it would have
had no meaning.

In the years after my rupture with Bett, Anton and Pops and I soldiered on in a new and abbreviated way. That trip to Madison was
the first of many others, and our tooling around to the small Mid-
western towns with ski jumps for competitions became the only real
connection I had with my father and brother. Our adventures, which
culminated with the Olympic trials in Lake Placid, New York, in
1980, were our reward for the hard times. But before the three of us
got there, Anton and I had a ski season unlike any other—one that,
when I look back honestly, and kindly, I see as the defining months
not only of my ski jumping legacy but of my entire life.

When Noah was eight or nine years old, his father planted half
a dozen telephone poles in concrete footings. He built a scaffold
around the poles that led into a natural dip in the hillside, after
which they built the takeoff. On the slope beneath, they cleared the
trees and shrubs and reshaped the hill where it met the lakeshore
into a long and gradual transition so that after the lake froze and
covered with snow it would serve as the outrun for a jump on which
leaps of 130 or 140 feet were possible. All of this was made for Noah,
but given the months Anton and I spent hiding out there, we probably had more jumps on that hill than the boy it was intended for.

From the top of the scaffold, off to the right and down through
the treetops, we could see the cabin and the persistent wisps of
woodsmoke. We used the smoke to measure the speed of the wind
and to see from which direction it came, and if (as was most often
the case) it streamed away from the lake, we knew the fates were
being kind. We knew a headwind would soon greet our flights. And
because the top of the jump was above the trees, looking down the
inrun was like staring into a tunnel, the boughs of the pines reaching

over the railings to shade the track even on the sunniest days. It was a narrow inrun, too, which made everything seem faster, steeper, and that narrowness encouraged us to be compact and alert. I can still feel the eagerness even before I pulled into the track. The sense the wilderness would engulf me for as long as it took to ski down the inrun. I can still remember the way it seemed I was kneeling in a bush as I squatted to put my bindings on. The way my body contracted, and not just physically but almost as if I'd be better served if I imploded.

Then I'd stand again, and slide my skis back and forth, and look out over the treetops to the lake that spread before me in a dazzling, blinding whiteness, one framed by the winding shore and the greenness of the trees that held it. Such strangeness it was to mark that spot fifty or sixty yards out on the water as my destination. The lake, in winter, was made of ice several feet thick. I knew this, and knew how safe it was, but still it gave me pause. From up on top, we twice saw the neighborhood wolf pack traipsing through a new snowfall, emerging from the shadows beneath the palisade on the north shore of the lake and heading for the creek, where they no doubt hoped to find open water. We'd watch them from the safety of the top of the jump, certain the wolves knew we were there and that they'd let us have our fun, but recognizing that here, in this wilderness, we were the visitors. More than once I told my brother—my little brother, who'd hardly speak at all—that if he didn't get his shins forward, or flatten his back in the inrun, or cock his ankles in flight, or get some other element of his jump right, that I'd sic the wolves on him. If he smiled in response to this, I didn't see it, and after the wolves retreated into the woods, at the mouth of the creek that in summer spilled into Lake Forsone in a fine rushing cascade, I'd jump first, because I knew my brother was nervous about the wolves, even from a mile away.

I taught him many things that season, and mastered as much. Technique, yes, but also mindset. It was a hell of a time for that. And what did those jumps look like? Those leaps my little brother took with his audience of one, standing down on the lake, watching his performance as though to see it would make everything all right. And it did. Those mornings. From the top of the slide, up over the trees, he'd wave his mittened hand, asking permission to go. As though there were something or someone to get in the way of his jump. I'd wave him on, and the minute my hand dropped, out there on the lake, he'd pull onto the inrun and disappear in the tunnel of trees, emerging only at the end of the transition, in his inrun position, his arms back and resting on his hips instead of flung out in front of him. That was one of our great discoveries, that that arms-back position allowed for so much more precision and quickness and smoothness on the take off, where every jump was decreed. For Anton those jumps became better one after the next, almost without exception, from New Year's Day until the last of them in March.

Where I was powerful, he was quick. Rabbit quick, and just as springy, and I could see that he had an instinct for flight. He found it so fast, his position in the air, his short, little body commanding so much from itself, his skis stick straight and practically touching, the taped tips coming up over his right shoulder. Willful. That's what he was. And light. And elated, no doubt. His shadow would fall from him as he came over the knoll and then lead him in flight down the hill until it met his feet in landing. An effortless telemark every time.

Twenty jumps in the morning. Twenty more in the afternoon. Hardly a day missed because what else was there to do in our exile? They were our clock and our schoolroom and our psychiatrist's office, those jumps were. They were our church and our prison and our hospital room. And of course, they were our playground, and our window to normal, and not even the fact of two boys living alone in the woods, orphaned and on the lam, could corrupt the simple pleasure of those thousand-and-more jumps. Or the thousand-and-more walks back up the hill. Or the thousand-and-more utterances between us to *Have a good one.*

Those scant words, by the way, were often the only thing he'd say all day. Unless he was talking in his sleep, which he often did.

So it was we lived ten seconds at a time. Pull out of the start and into the track for one two three seconds down the inrun, our bodies, as strong and lean as they'd ever be, still tensed and ready, like a hot engine waiting for the clutch to be disengaged. I felt for three things as I sped toward the take off: that my shins were pressed as far forward as I could make them; that my forearms were relaxed and resting in straight lines along my flanks and hips and that they culminated in straight fingers pointing back up the jump; and that my bottom rib pressed against the meat of my thigh. If all those things aligned I was in the right position, and once I finished the inventory—in the first and second seconds of the inrun—I could shift my focus to the take off, which I'd see only in the half second before it was time to leap. By then, I was going thirty-five or forty miles per hour and the difference between jumps of 100 feet and 130 feet was just a matter of timing. A quarter second too early or too late and I'd be on the short side. But if I hit it just right, if my legs pistoned me from the ball of muscle and bone into the wing of flight at precisely the moment my feet hit the end of the inrun, well, then the lift I felt was immediate, and the results preordained. It became, during those perfectly timed jumps, only a question of the finer points of flight, and because this jump was relatively small those nuances were less important. But still, I might add a few feet by will alone, and once I was flying over the knoll, the thrust of my chin, the cocking of ankles, the ruddering of hands, the determination to wait for the right gust of wind coming up under my skis—any of these things might add feet to my distance. But any of these things had to be done with a subconscious mind.

This is one of the things we disagreed on, and one of the reasons he was so much better than I was. I accounted for those machinations of flight only in memory, but he could manipulate them while he was up there. He was conscious in every moment, even at the sprightly age of ten or twelve or fourteen, so that by the time he was fifteen, and I was twenty, he'd already be on the verge of besting me.

I understood he could control himself in a way I couldn't. I could see it from out on the frozen lake. His adjustments, how he'd inventory his position and account for it. How he could coax from flight consciously what I could only hope for. It was being witness to genius. It was like watching the anointed.

Because ski jumping is a sport that demands the inward gaze, because its yield is so individualized, and because so many factors out of the jumpers' control affect their safety and performance, it's not a sport that lends itself to vicarious experience, not even for ski jumpers themselves. But standing out among the wolf tracks, watching my brother's angelic flights, it was impossible not to wonder what it was like to be chosen.

I can still see the look on his face, the humble, deferential modesty. The simple happiness. The clear focus. How could a boy in his spot possess all that, jump after jump, day after day, week after week? If ever I was inspired in this life, it was on those days. They dazzled. So did he.

With each jump came the need to climb back up the hill, wearing footholds into the compacted snow like a game trail. The snow by midwinter was shoulder deep on Anton, so that if he got far enough ahead or behind me, he appeared to be little more than a hatted head bobbing among the hummocks of snow. When fresh snow fell, and it often did, the two of us would sidestep the landing hill, packing the new snow down. Out on the lake, we'd shovel the heavier snow-falls off to the side so there was a kind of horseshoe-shaped berm of snow and on very fast days, instead of skidding to a stop, we'd crouch down as we got onto the lake in order to carry as much speed as possible to the end of the outrun, then ride up the berm and launch for a second flight into the cold air.

When we finished, in the short light of the winter afternoons, we'd climb the hill one last time and where the ground met the scaffold, instead of taking the two-by-fours pounded into the wood deck of the jump up to the top, we'd veer left, with our skis on our shoulders, and march to the cabin, where we'd lean those skis under the eavestrough and go inside and unlace our boots and put them under the woodstove to dry. We'd hang our jumpsuits behind the stovepipe and lay our mittens next to the boots, and while Anton spread out on the couch to doze, I'd put on a pan of beans and franks and make a pot of coffee and stand at the window in my long johns staring into the wilderness, hoping nothing would ever find us.

Unlike the hundreds of other days we spent jumping, that time north of Misquah was singular. They did not—they *do* not—beget other memories of other jumps in other places. Maybe it was the fact of our being alone. Maybe it was the fact I felt as much a father as a brother. Maybe it's because those days were standing in for real life, when real life attended every other ski jumping memory.

It could have been any of these things, but it's also true there was an aspect of my brother's flights that was as unmistakable as the perplexity he wore on his lonesome face. And it was that aspect I'd spend the rest of my ski jumping days chasing. Hell, even after that season, and the winters that followed, and in the almost forty years after, I kept searching. Or some part of me did. I searched for it in my friendships, in my love for my own children and my darling wife. I even searched for it in the books I wrote, through the characters I filled with longings and imperfections.

And though it's true we became strangers, though whole years passed without so much as a phone call between Anton and me, never mind an evening spent with a couple of beers and burgers, it struck me always as unconscionable that I never got a chance to tell him that.

*

"Grace. Godly grace, that's what it was," I say, the sound of my voice surprising on the cold expanse of the snow-covered lake. For a moment, I'm startled to be here and to discover it's Noah I'm talking to. We've snowshoed down to the shore and then up it. Now we stand at the spot where the landing hill used to be.

"What the hell are you talking about, old man?"

"Grace," I say, as though I were some sort of Christian thinker. "I'm talking about Anton."

Noah puts his hand on my shoulder and says, "You weren't talking about anything."

I hold his arm where it lay. "I know. I'm not gone yet." With my free hand, I point up into the woods. "Walking down the hill, I was remembering our winter here. His and mine."

"The best use ever of this place." He takes his hand from my shoulder and turns toward the palisade across the lake. He doesn't have to tell me what he's thinking about. And I know there's nothing to say about the long look in his eyes. After he settles that moment's account, he turns back to me.

"Do you actually believe in God?" he says.

"Most of my adult life I've wished I did."

"So, you don't?"

I shake my head. "The closest I ever came was that winter."

Noah glances again across the lake.

"Do you?" I ask.

"There's a Lutheran church in Misquah and I spent a few winter

Sundays there after Nat and I split. But I haven't been in what, five years?"

"Which I guess is a way of not answering the question."

"I've tried. How about that?"

I nod.

"This diagnosis," he says, his voice trilling on the *s*.

"I'm pretty scared, Noah. Especially for Ingrid. I wasn't going to tell you."

"I'm glad you did."

"I haven't even told the kids yet."

He bites his lower lip, and looks at me from up in his rare air. "How's it going to go? What can I do to help?"

"Slowly or quickly, I'll lose all my memories. I'll become impossible to live with. I'll need assistance. Might be five years, might be more, but the memories and some of my faculties are already starting to fade. The absentminded professor is now truly absent minded."

"What about work?"

"I've taught my last course. I'll retire."

"I mean the books, Jon."

"I had only one more I wanted to write anyway. If five years of trying couldn't get it done, there's no point now. And like I said, I'm happy to hold on to the good memories rather than dredge up the bad."

"That's bullshit. You're standing here like what you see up there is your salvation. They aren't bad memories. They're the best you have."

"They might be some of the most important, but they're not the best." I look through the trees, to the woodsmoke rising again from the cabin's chimney. "The best I have is sitting up in your cabin. She's studying that map you drew, waiting for us to finish our ramble along the shore."

"Fair enough."

"What about you?" I ask.

"Me?"

"What do you see when you look up there?"

He gazes up the hill, which is overgrown. There's no sign that a ski jump resides on that slope save for the six telephone poles lingering among the treetops. "My dad. The prick."

"He was no prick."

"Not to you, he wasn't."

Now I turn and stare in the direction he's spent so much of his time out here looking at. "Must be awfully damn weird, having him out there."

Noah turns and looks, too. "I can't even fish over there anymore. Some of the best trout waters in all the goddamn state, and I'm afraid I'll hook his anchor."

Twenty-odd years ago, Noah was summoned from Boston by his father, Olaf, who was dying of cancer then. They were almost perfectly estranged, but Noah came anyway. If he was searching for some kind of reconciliation with his father, he found a whole lot more than that, including a request that he bury Olaf in the lake. Dutifully, Noah did. But it cost him. All these years later, I think there's still a part of Noah that can't forgive his father in the same way I can't forgive Bett. Maybe our resentments are the reason we've stayed so close.

"Does he ever, you know, visit?"

"Like a ghost or something?" Noah says.

I shrug.

"First you ask about God, then you ask about ghosts?"

"When you put it like that . . ."

"Aw, hell. No. He doesn't visit me. But I talk to him all the damn time. It's embarrassing."

"What do you talk about?"

"Mostly I scold him for being such an asshole. And blame him for making me one."

"I remember your old man as one of the most generous people I ever knew."

"You didn't see how he treated my mom. Or what it was like when he got into the cups. Couple of Irish whiskeys never changed anyone so much as Olaf Torr."

"Does he talk back?"

"You mean am I nuts?" Noah asks, and smiles at me. "No. But I sure have gotten good at putting words in his mouth. He's found some zillion ways to apologize."

"That's something, at least," I say.

He shrugs, then points up the hill. "If we came at it from around back, I could show you the half of the deck still clinging to the railings up there."

"Naw, it's better from down here. Easier to imagine with the fuller view."

He turns his face into the cold breeze from across the lake. "Feel that?" he says.

"That's the stuff dreams are made of," I say.

"Anton isn't the only one had his days here."

"We did all right."

"Yes we did."

Noah turns his snowshoes back up the shore. I follow, and we make a fresh set of tracks alongside the ones we laid a half-hour ago. It's a hundred or so yards to the path up the hill, and before we ascend Noah stops. "You talked to Ingrid yet? About Patollo and all that?"

"I've been working up to it."

"Probably it's just a matter of spilling, eh?"

"Probably."

"You know she's going to understand completely, right? And love you more? If that's even possible."

"We'll see."

"I don't know what you're up against, and of course I'll not tell you how to live your life. But Ingrid will do anything for you." He touches my shoulder again, this time with the icy wind filling his eyes. "And so will I. You got that?"

"Yeah," I say. "I got it."

✳

Back in the cabin, Ingrid's standing at the drawing desk before the window overlooking the lake. A pair of lamps are clipped to the edge of it, along with a plastic basket that holds dozens of pencils and paintbrushes. An aluminum T-square rests on a ledge at the bottom of the desk, and another on top, so the two rulers intersect at the bottom. I've heard about this project but was unprepared for the scope of it.

Noah described it as a reckoning with the shore, but from where I stand, the draft taped on the desk looks more like a chart. It makes sense, given that for years Noah owned a shop out in Boston that peddled antiquarian maps and lithographs from all over the world. Like everything else, he lost his business in the divorce. But unlike most people I know who have been through that ringer, he doesn't dwell on it. Natalie, his ex, still lives in Boston. Their son, an aspiring political consultant, lives in D.C. and visits each year for the fishing opener.

Aside from the unmistakable curve of the shoreline itself, the drawing is silhouetted by a grid of latitudinal and longitudinal lines, a legend noting towns and rivers and other landmarks. On this one, there's also a border that serves as checkerboarded scale. Each half-inch equals one mile.

"How's it a reckoning?" I say.

He's at the counter, pouring still more coffee into our cups. "You think you're the only one with an imagination?" He brings the cups over, hands me mine.

"I think it's beautiful, Noah. I love that the compass rose only points north," Ingrid says.

I put my readers on and pull the stool out from under the desk and sit down.

"I'm still drafting," Noah says, pointing at a banker's box on the floor filled with rolled papers. "I began thinking I'd be pretty straightforward about it. An actual representation of the topography of the shore, with a few flourishes." He points at a series of marks just off the shore. "Like the locations of shipwrecks. I wish I were a better artist, so I could in a way animate them. But since I can't—since basically I can only draw lines—I've come up with another plan." He takes one of the scrolls from the box and unbinds it and spreads it on the table. It's essentially the same map as the one underneath, but this one is titled "Polaris." A series of perhaps a hundred lines seem almost to emanate from above the page and converge in a single spot off the shore near the Gininwabiko lighthouse, which is casting its own pencil-drawn light out to sea.

"What is this?" Ingrid says. She leans in for a closer look. "It's like beams from the sky."

"That's exactly what it's supposed to be. These particular beams are meant to be shining down from Polaris, and they culminate on the wreck of the *Lisbon*."

"What's it for?" I say.

"What's what for?"

"The maps, the stars?"

"I told you, a reckoning."

"I think I understand," Ingrid says. "Do you have one of these for the *Rag*?"

Noah drops to one knee and flips through more of the rolled

maps. The one he selects is titled "Andromeda," and the pencil rays of starlight shine on an area just west of the northernmost slice of Isle Royale, at the edge of the map. Something about this one feels three-dimensional, like the perspective of the shoreline has been flipped up to a water-level view. The effect is almost like an M. C. Escher etching.

There's of course no need to look to see which wreck it indicates, but if there were any confusion, the serious look on Noah's face would tell me all: it's as steely as the pencil lead on the parchment beneath my hands.

"So each wreck is illuminated by a different star?" I ask.

"A different galaxy, technically. And the number of lines emanating from the galaxy is a reflection of the number of major stars."

"How do you know all this?"

"You can find just about anything in books," he says.

"Noah, this is really something," Ingrid says. "What a beautiful idea."

"His old man used to brag about his celestial navigation skills," I tell her. "The way he talked about it, I can still hear him."

"He didn't talk much, but on the subject of the stars he wouldn't shut up," Noah adds. He shrugs a shoulder and takes a sip of his coffee and says, "But enough about all this. You're not here for these drawings of mine. Or they're not what I really want to show you, leastways. Let's finish these bear claws and have a look at all this."

We walk over to the couch and chair and take our seats around the coffee table and Noah says, "Even if you're not going to write that book, there's still plenty to interest you here."

He pauses to look at the picture of Anton and me before going back into the file folder. The next thing he brings out is an old mimeographed copy of ski jumping results from the Snowflake Ski Club in Westby, Wisconsin. The date on the header is 1953, and two names leap immediately to the fore. In third place, Olaf Torr. And in fifth place, Jakob Bargaard. Only three points separated them.

I look up to Noah's wide grin. "Incredible, isn't it?"

"Holy cow," I say.

"You think that's something, look at this."

Now he unfolds and hands me a facsimile of a newspaper page. *The Minneapolis Tidende*, the banner reads. The print is smudged and miniscule, but he points to a column on the bottom left of the page, and again I see his name: Torr, this time preceded by Eivind. "My great-granddad," he says. "1900. Best I can remember, that was from a competition in Hammerfest, Norway. Something called the Jannebakken."

"Well, god*damn*," I say.

"I don't know, Jon," Ingrid says, her voice unsure, like she knows what she's about to say is going to put me on edge, "it sounds like a pretty good place to start a novel."

Now Noah comes sailing to her defense. "Your wife is right: you ought to give it a whirl. You're making excuses and for what?"

"Thank you, Noah," Ingrid says. "You've always been able to talk sense into him."

I take the last bite of my bear claw, the glaze sticky on my fingers. Another thought occurs to me as I wipe my hands on the napkin Noah provided: that though he and I are old ski jumpers ourselves, and though so much of our memories and subconscious energy is spent remembering it, and though we talk about it almost every time we get together, our fixation is on a sport no one knows or cares about, and this strikes me as another reason not to pursue the book they keep telling me to write.

I set the plate and napkin on the coffee table. "No one wants to read a novel about ski jumpers," I say. "On top of all the other very sensible reasons I've given the both of you, there's that simple fact as well."

Noah looks at me like he's offended. Like what I've just said is about the stupidest thing to ever come out of my mouth. He sets his own plate down and says, "Dummy, it's not just about ski jumping, but about everything that happened with your mom and dad and brother. Even I, drawer of lines and not much else, know that."

"What do you mean everything that happened?" Ingrid says.

I can see it happening. The familiar, intimate, easy way Noah and I have always talked, the confidences we've shared. In at least this one respect, it's not the same with Ingrid, and the thing I've been struggling all morning to tell her he's about to lay bare.

"The murder," I say quickly, before he can finish exposing me.

"You mean with Pops, and all that?"

"My father never killed anyone," I say.

"What do you mean?" Her stare is cold. Probably colder than she means it to be. But how could it be anything less? "I just don't understand." But then she does. All at once.

She puts her coffee cup on the table and says to me, "I think we better get going." She stands and folds her hands and speaks next to Noah. "My husband can be forgiven for not being himself today. And I hate to leave early. But Jon and I need to talk. I hope you understand."

While Ingrid puts on her coat and hugs Noah goodbye, I sit immovable on this chair. It's the same old furniture that's inhabited this place from the time I first knew it. And this brings me some comfort. I've sat through more than a few difficult moments right here.

I watch Ingrid coax Noah up. I watch her pull his face down to hers and kiss his ruddy cheek. I hear her thank him for the visit, and apologize again, and then turn to me and say, "I'll wait in the car." And then I watch her remember her purse, and grab it from the counter on her way out the door.

When the screen door slams shut outside, Noah finally looks at me and shakes his head and says, "I'm not even sure what just happened."

"You know, outside of Pops and Sheb and Helene Lyng, you're the only person who knows the truth of that whole rotten mess."

He's still standing where Ingrid left him, hovering above me and the coffee table with the empty plate and file folder half-strewn about. I can see plainly how bad he feels, and it makes me miserable in turn. So I wrangle myself up, step around the table, and gather all the old archives and return them to the file folder. "Can I take this? I'll make sure you get it back."

"Of course."

We're only an arm's length apart and if sympathy has an aura, Noah is radiating one. "We've been friends for damn near fifty years. Can you imagine that?"

"Couple of old ski jumpers, we are."

"Listen, practically for as long as I've known Ingrid I've also known she should have the story you do. That she doesn't, well, put that in the column of marks against me." I hug him. "I should never have saddled you with the truth of that goddamn day. But, well, I guess I can't undo that."

"You don't need to worry about undoing anything." He raises a finger. "I almost forgot. Take this, too." He steps over and opens the freezer and removes a box of fish.

"I predicted this. Not eight hours ago I did."

"I'd be hard pressed to surprise anyone these days," he says, then puts his big old hand on my shoulder.

"One other thing, Noah, before the hay is in the barn. I want you to know you've been as much a brother to me as Anton. More even."

He nods. And if he's not crying again, his eyes are as glazed as the bear claws.

"I'm gonna go out there and talk to her."

As I turn to leave, he grabs my arm. "Jon, you know that what happened, with that gangster and you and your dad, none of that was your fault. So put that in the ledger while you're at it. It's a mark to your credit."

"We'll see about that."

We walk across this rickety floor, all polished and worn and still holding the palimpsests of my worried pacing from that long-ago winter.

"What do you think the statute of limitations is on something like this?" I say.

"That crime was confessed to. The time was served."

"I'm talking about not telling Ingrid."

"She's only going to love you more," he says.

"Like I said, we'll see."

He follows me out to the car, which Ingrid has already turned around, and heads over to the driver's side and taps on her window. I'm putting the file and the fish in the backseat as Ingrid rolls down her window.

"Anything you ever need, call, okay?"

"I will. Thank you, Noah."

Then he stands up and looks at me over the roof of the car. "And you," he says, "stay sharp. Do what your wife tells you to. Got it?"

"Got it." I slide into the passenger seat.

"Thanks for breakfast, you two," he says through her still open window, then taps the car roof before Ingrid veers up the hill.

*

We're not even off his private road when Ingrid pulls over and puts the car in park. Even bare, the trees encroach like some infinite army of skeleton sentries. I watch them for just one moment, then turn to my wife.

236

"One of the reasons Anton and I ended up here that winter is because I believed I had to get away. I believed I'd be found out, and they'd free Pops and put me in prison instead."

"Why?"

"Why?" I echo. "Because I was guilty."

The Bingo Hall

THE MINNEAPOLIS SKI CLUB used to run a bingo hall up on Broadway between Bryant and Colfax Avenues North. A bunch of folding tables and chairs lined the creaky floor and surrounded a raised platform where the caller sat behind the brass hopper on game nights. Above the stage an electronic board kept the game's tally. On all the surrounding walls, photographs of the great club jumpers of the past lined the hall like a gallery of presidents. Pops was up there, his mouth pressed into a howling O, his skis so close together they might have been confused as a single board were it not for the pair of tips that came up to his left shoulder. He wore the number 16 in that photograph, and I never once saw him glance at it.

I looked forward to the monthly club meetings with unbridled excitement, even into my teenaged years. It was an extra opportunity for the club jumpers to get together and talk shop and revel in our shared exuberance. And revel we did. Whatever else was on the agenda, we took advantage of those nights to anticipate and replay the season as it came or went.

It was also true that after the junior jumpers had covered our agenda items, the men of the club set us loose in the basement while they tended to more legitimate topics, foremost among them fund-raising and budgets.

The basement. It had once been a bowling alley but like the rest of the building had fallen into ill repair, and for us it was mainly a place to store skis, which lined the entire length of the lane farthest from the door. There was also a sort of makeshift office down there. Like any good racketeer Sheb kept a bevy of hideouts, and since he had helped set up the bingo hall for the ski club—obtaining the gaming license through a connection at city hall—his reward was yet another place to conduct his sordid business. But already I'm ahead of myself.

When it was time for the club leadership to discuss their monthly accountings of bingo hall proceeds, we boys were sent downstairs to goof around. Not only were the dark recesses of that basement excellent grounds for scaring the hell out of each other, they were also ideal spots for secreting away to ogle the dirty magazines Sheb kept in his desk. We'd pilfer them one at a time and squirrel away with flashlights in corners and closets and behind the old service counter. A couple of the guys would sneak packs of cigarettes, too, and we'd light them up and pretend to be our dads.

And because Pops was the club president during most of my childhood, and because when we weren't down there at club meetings we were down there meeting Sheb for one reason or another, I considered the subterranean corridors of that hall to be like my own backyard. Anton and I had even fashioned our own fort in the aisle behind the pinsetters. From there, we could spy on whatever business Sheb and Pops were engaged in at the desk on the other end of the lanes. And there was no shortage of business down there. We saw lots of handshake deals between Sheb and men in suits and ties. There were plenty of young men, too, guys I recognize now must have been apprentice or aspiring drug dealers. Sometimes Sheb was just having a drink and a laugh with a friend. It was not uncommon for uniformed police officers to walk down those stairs and sit with Sheb for an hour over cigars and bottles of beer. What all those meetings had in common is that the tone of them, regardless of who sat across the desk from Sheb, always seemed affable, no matter what angle we snooped from. He was a well-spoken and serious negotiator, and if he couldn't find agreement with a would-be colleague, he'd laugh it off and move on to the next meeting. No harm, no foul. I often heard him announce that the secret to success was not to keep your enemies at bay, but to not have any in the first place, a lesson he must have learned from Andrus Patollo. Not that he ever would've given him credit.

Unless the meeting had to do with ski club business (and Sheb helped manipulate the park board and city council members, usually with simple arm-twisting but sometimes with bribes or more), Pops was not a party to these meetings. We understood Sheb was family, and I admit that back then I often thought fondly of him and even relished his visits to the house and marveled at his easy way with people from every walk of life. He showed up at Christmas, and our birthdays, and for summer barbecues at the pit in our backyard. But we also understood that his business dealings were profane and illegal and we weren't even allowed to talk about them in private.

All of this made that day in 1975 so much more beguiling. It was mid-March. A string of warm days and rain had brought the ski jumping season to an end, and Pops offered to help Selmer move all the skis from the clubhouse at Wirth Park to the bingo hall basement. He of course brought me along to assist. Anton would have come, too, but he had an ear infection and was laid up in bed.

Our first stop was the chalet at Wirth Park. Pops pulled up at the rear entry where in summer the golf course maintenance vehicles and mowers were parked. We went back and forth between the station wagon and the clubhouse locker room with armfuls of the skis

that Selmer fitted out to kids who came on Saturdays to try ski jumping. Next were the boxes of boots, several of which had to sit on my
lap as we drove. Then we parked on Broadway and shuttled the gear
into the basement and lined it all against the bowling lane wall.

I reminisced about the different skis I'd used over the years, some
of which still had my name magic-markered on the tips, and I felt
the sense of completion at the end of a winter. Pops was jocular and
teasing and we went through the highlight reel of the previous few
months. We talked about Anton and his strides and it was an afternoon so perfectly father and son that what would happen next seems
almost impossible to believe.

He'd bought me a Coke and we were sitting on either side of
Sheb's desk when the phone rang, that loud shrillness suddenly in-
terrupting our gabbing. He looked at me with a goofy expression
and said, "Who in the hell'd be calling here? Should I answer it?"

Before I could muster a reply, he took the receiver up and said,
"Hulloh?" A second later he covered the mouthpiece with his hand
and whispered, "It's Sheb," lifting his shoulders in a questioning
way.

For the next few minutes he sat back and listened to whatever
Sheb said, Pops's only response an occasional raised eyebrow or
"Huh." And then Sheb said something that altered my father's expression to one I'd never seen. His face contorted and blanched
ghostly white and he didn't say another word until, a moment later,
he said, "Five minutes? Okay."

When he hung up the phone he stared at the receiver on the desk
for some time before he looked up, startled to see me sitting there
with him.

I said, "Is everything all right? What did Sheb want?"

He stood, looked around frantically, and finally settled on the
end of the bowling lanes. "Why don't you take that Coke back to
your hiding spot?" He gestured into the darkness. "Here." He went

to the wall behind the counter and turned the lights on along the wall opposite the lined-up skis, which was also the aisle back to the fort.

"Why?" I said, taking the bottle as he handed it to me.

He only put a hand on my shoulder to steer me away, walking with me halfway down the aisle before saying, "Just stay back here, okay? Whatever happens, don't make a sound. Don't come out."

How to describe the fear and agitation? My father, who had never once appeared scared, never mind terrified, was suddenly wraithlike and mute and sitting in the chair opposite Sheb's desk as I so recently had. Worse than his pallor and silence was his sequestering me, back among the cobwebs and old wooden bowling pins. I pressed myself into the darkness awaiting what I couldn't begin to imagine, but I was terrified, too.

And so it was strange, even almost a relief, when Sheb showed up with two others in tow: a man almost equal his size dressed in a long coat and matching black homburg hat and a woman a hundred times more elegant and dignified than had ever descended those steps before. Pops stood when the three of them reached Sheb's desk and shook the tall man's hand. Standing beside him, Pops appeared half the other man's size and for once was not only diminutive in stature but also plainly daunted.

The woman was introduced next, and when Pops shook her hand he held both it and her gaze for a long time. From where I sat behind the lanes, I couldn't hear much more than the occasional exclamation, but it was clear from that dark distance this meeting was living up to my father's sudden dread of it. Even Sheb, who was by then as brash as he'd ever be, seemed diminished in the presence of this other man. Sheb shrank. His gaze turned downward. The assertive way he spoke with his hands vanished after the first sharp word from the man in the hat, and he holstered his hands in his trouser pockets instead.

This man paced from Sheb's desk to the ball returns, gesticulating calmly, pointing to the woman as though she were the evidence and he the prosecuting attorney. His coolness was as evident in his gait as it was in his dress, and for a moment I was lost in his swagger. He did most of the talking, and as much as Sheb was clearly listening, Pops was not. His attention went entirely to the woman, who stood with one foot firmly planted on the ground and the other raised and resting on her ankle.

She wore a knee-length dress—the front half was white, the back half black—and black shoes not right for the slurry of melting snow and rain outside. Between the buckles on those shoes and the hem of her dress, black stockings shone even in that dim light and from as far away as I hid. A fur stole slung across her shoulders blended up into hair so blonde it appeared almost as white as the front of her dress. She could have been my age, or she could have been thirty, but in any case her prettiness was as profound as the tension in that group.

Twice Pops took his eyes from her, both times peering across the bowling lanes and into the darkness he must have imagined I occupied. But in neither instance did his expression betray his feelings. Nor did they offer much in the way of suggestion, those looks. So I just sat there, frozen, scared, and intrigued by what possible alignment of fates led my unsuspecting father to this meeting of wolves. He looked, I realize now, like the raven who alights beside the pack.

Having been relinquished to that dark nook, I worked as fast imagining the purpose of that assembly as I did taking inventory of the players. And for all the powers of my young imagination, I could not fathom either. Not properly.

Not then, and not ever.

My confusion increased along with my fear. The man in the hat seemed to be getting more agitated with each passing word, most of which came violently from his own shouting mouth as that behemoth moved among the three of them, scolding and unrelenting. He paid special attention to Pops. Or anyway he seemed to, brandishing a special blend of mockery and abhorrence, describing him, finally, as someone who deserved a bullet to the back of the head.

What boy who ever loved his father so much could sit in that dark spot, alone, hoping the storm of that gigantic man would not land on his Pops? What boy wouldn't have scooted out from behind the lanes and slithered up the aisle under the half-wall parallel to the lanes? What boy wouldn't have found himself close enough to that unwilling party to see the scintillating mother-of-pearl handle of the pistol in the man with the hat's holster? What boy wouldn't have gasped, and shuddered, when that same man in the hat told his Pops to shut the hell up and take his goddamn medicine?

Pops pulled an old metal desk chair from the shadows and sat as though the man in the hat had whipped him in the gut with the butt of that pistol. Pops put his elbows on his knees and studied the floor as though the answer to all this strangeness might be written in the dust and debris.

At some point, I'd set down the Coke and picked up two bowling pins instead. I can remember discovering they were in my hands and being both surprised and emboldened. I knew from our hiding out down there that even where I stood—not twenty feet from them now—I was invisible behind the half-wall. I set the pins down as quietly as I could and raised myself up so only the top of my head and my eyes peeked above the concrete.

I could see the woman looking back in the direction of my shadow. As though she'd sensed a ghost. No sooner did I notice the cigarette in her hand—and the way she held it loosely beside her painted lips, and the way she tipped the ash with metronomic flicks of her thumb—than the man in the hat said to my father: "She's your daughter, you moron."

His daughter. Pops's daughter? My *sister*?

For a brief moment, I expected Pops to rise and tell the ox that was impossible. That he must surely have been mistaken. But as soon as I thought it, she looked at me again, and all I saw was myself looking back.

"Helene?" my father said, softly, but loud enough for me to hear.

"I already told you her goddamned name. I told you three times."

Pops watched her for a moment, and if she couldn't look back, who could blame her. What must she have known about meeting her father for the first time, at her age, which I could see was closer to mine than I had originally thought.

Pops spoke now to the young woman named Helene. "What happened to your mother? What happened to Lena?"

The man in the hat let this question stand. In fact, he seemed to relish how uncomfortable it made her. When she didn't answer after a moment, he said, "Well, girl? Tell him."

Her voice sounded just like Bett's when she spoke. "There was an accident on the L."

"An accident!" the man in the hat exclaimed.

"It *was* an accident, Andy," she said.

She might as well have summoned the devil, uttering that name. It was Andrus Patollo. Of course. It had to be.

As if to prove me right, he removed his hat and set it on the edge of Sheb's desk, then ran his enormous hands over his perfectly bald head. He turned to Pops and said, "She jumped in front of a goddamn train."

"When did this happen?" Pops put that question between the two of them.

Patollo answered. "Last Saturday."

"I'm sorry," he said to Helene. "I'm so sorry. And I'm sorry this is how you're meeting me. I never knew. I promise that's true."

"If it is," Patollo boomed, "then your shrew wife is not only the craziest thing I've ever met, but also the best con."

"Hey," Pops said, sitting up in his chair.

"That's right," Patollo said. "She's known. Bett was down to visit a long time ago." Now he picked up his hat and leaned against the desk.

To Helene Pops said, "Is it true you met your aunt?"

She nodded.

"She never told me about you," Pops said.

Again, Helene nodded, with perhaps even less conviction or understanding than she had a moment before. I realized she was as frightened as I was.

"She never told you because she's a scheming bitch. Just like her sister. And you"—he pointed at Helene—"are every bit as bad as either of them." His expression was not one of annoyance or anger even, but of something almost like pleasure. He looked at them in turn, like a scolding parent to his three knuckleheaded children, landing finally on Sheb. "Which is why I'm handing her back to you all, who should've been responsible from the start."

Pops, ignoring Patollo's bluster, spoke again to Helene. "You're what, twenty years old now?"

Helene started to answer, but Patollo's voice boomed over hers. "I don't care if she's ten or twenty or thirty years old, she's a leech, just like her mother and aunt, and I'll not be responsible for her."

I could see Pops's anger rising, and could also sense that Patollo would not abide much pushback. He seemed like Sheb in this way, but Sheb, for all his normal bluster and posturing, was strangely neutered in Patollo's company.

"Why don't you give me a chance to talk to Helene," Pops said. His voice was level. Eerily so, given the tension in the room. He stood, and took the girl's arm and brought her to the chair he'd just occupied and helped her to sit as though she were feeble. "Everything'll be all right, okay?" he said. "Give me just a second here." Now he turned to Patollo. "Let me talk to her without all your ranting."

He glanced over his shoulder and down the lane, as though to remind himself of me. I can still see the sideways tilt of his head, like he could tell I wasn't where I was supposed to be. But that can't have been true. Maybe it was merely a shrug of apology. Or of confusion. Or a message that he hadn't forgotten about me since his daughter suddenly walked into his life.

In any case, I wasn't down there to receive his questioning look. And for all my own confusion, I was now intrigued as well as befuddled. What would he say to that scared young woman? How would he handle that belligerent oaf? How was my life going to be different from this day on? How would his?

He went and knelt by her side. He put a hand on the arm of the chair and screwed up the courage to look at her, to lift her chin to look back at him. "I'm sorry about your mom. It's a goddamn terrible thing. Whatever happened."

She slid herself free, and looked in my direction.

"What do you do down there in Chicago? You go to college?"

"Of course she doesn't go to college," Patollo grumbled. "She's dumb as a goddamn potato."

"Just shut the hell up," Pops said.

"There's the vinegar I remember!" Patollo boomed, assuming a position like a prize fighter and punching the air left–right–left.

"Sheb, tell him to give me a fucking break, would you?"

Sheb didn't say anything. He didn't even look up from his hands, which met at the fingertips as though sewn together. Patollo's reaction to this was to stand taller, to reach into the pocket of his jacket a hair's breadth from the pistol, and take out a cigar. He made a great show of clipping it and lighting it and puffing on it. I remember the smoke filled the room in no time at all.

Oblivious to all of this, Pops kept his attention on Helene, who now seemed almost trembling with fear and humiliation. "What do you do in Chicago?"

She mumbled her response.

"With your mother?" Pops said.

She shook her head.

"Well you won't miss that, will you?"

A look of unabashed relief washed over her face, and I knew it was not so much the words he'd spoken as the way he'd said them. His voice, when he wanted it to be, was unmistakably soothing, and I could well imagine how she felt receiving those words.

He leaned in closer to her, so close he nearly blocked her from my view. She nodded and shook her head and sighed, but with each minute that passed he was winning her trust, and when he finally stood and dusted his hands, he turned to Patollo and said, "What is it with you, treating women like auction items?"

Patollo flicked an ash from the arm of his jacket and took another puff of his stinking cigar. "Have I not raised your daughter? Have I not provided for her in every way? Did I not let you walk away not only with your life, twenty years ago, but with my *truck*? Do you think it would've been any trouble at all for me to have had someone come and retrieve it? And you?"

"We're not talking about back then. And if you didn't send someone after me, that's a choice you made yourself. I don't give a damn about it. As for *raising* my daughter, well, I suspect you and I have different ideas about how that goes. But still and all, I'm happy you brought her to me. Grateful, even."

"Then you should say thank you," Patollo said.

For the first time since they had arrived, Sheb spoke. "He doesn't need to say shit to you, you dried-up old sod." He planted his palms on his desk and pushed himself up as Patollo stuffed the cigar in his mouth and rolled his shoulders back and put his thumbs in the belt loops on his pants.

"Look at *this*," Patollo said, pausing dramatically between each word. "Finally decided not to let the runt over here do all the talking?"

"He'll talk for himself." Sheb came out from around the desk so the two giants were standing square. "I'm just good and tired of you thinking you have some jurisdiction here. We're not in your den of thieves—"

"We're certainly not!" Patollo nearly exploded. "This rat-infested crypt is more like the bottom of the sewer pipes in my mansion." He puffed three times on his cigar. "You've amounted to exactly what I thought you would, Magnus."

Sheb collected himself. He found yet more resolve, and kept going. "You've always mistaken your name in the paper for meaning something, you know that? You've kept that fat head shaved bald so the light shines there. All you understand is the grand gesture. It would be sad if it weren't so pathetic." Now he took a step away from Patollo and wandered the stage they inhabited like a thespian. "Me? I'm diversified, Andy. You may see a shit hole, but it's only a part of a larger enterprise."

"Larger enterprise my ass. We stopped at that dump just down the street. I thought I'd show Helene some of her future. It even made me sad."

"Why? Because there's no fountain? Because real people work and go there? And this girl," he looked at Helene, who still sat mortified at Pops's side, "if she *did* work there, she would do so of her own free will. And she'd be treated with respect and dignity."

"By the Saturday morning drunks swilling down there? I doubt it."

"The guys belly-up now, most of them, they work the third shift in the train yards or recycling plant. They're good family guys. Union guys. Boff's is where they go to warm up. It's their happy hour. And it's called service." He walked back to the chair behind his desk and sat heavily. I could feel the floor shudder. "And do you know what they've made me, Andrus Fucking Patollo?"

Patollo only glowered at him.

"I'll give you a hint: it's something you're not."

Patollo appeared puzzled, and his bluster paused while he contemplated Sheb's riddling. It was plain to me that this was an unfamiliar position, his being on the end of something that might be described as a lesson.

When, after a few seconds, Patollo hadn't responded, Sheb said, "They've made me a millionaire, Andy. For all your conniving, you never got there, did you? I know you're not there now. You're as bankrupt in accounts as you are in spirit." He wrapped his hands behind his head and sat back, flung his feet up on the desk. "You've brought Helene here because you can't afford to take care of her anymore. And ain't that something."

Patollo finally removed the cigar from his lips and held it in his left hand. His expression was unreadable, but he looked from Helene back to Sheb, and I could as much as hear the machinations in his mind. When he spoke, it was with half his previous conviction. "You've heard the story about the father and the son, Magnus?"

"Yeah, yeah. And the holy ghost and fuck you."

"The father raises the son. He teaches him to be fierce and wise. How to work hard and take pleasure in life. How to provide. And the son, the thankless nit, he comes of age. He grows big and strong. Bigger and stronger even than the father. He develops a sense of himself that's all out of proportion. He thinks he's a man and in the eyes of many he'd be mistaken for one. *Except* when he's with the father. The father, despite his growing older and losing strength, still eclipses the son. And the son, thinking this truth must be corrected, confronts the father, tells him that he'll be in charge now, that he'll duel the father if he must. And the father, because he loves his son, and because he raised him to be fierce and wise, advises him to withdraw his challenge. He tells him, *because he loves him,* that he does not want to duel, that it would be an unfair fight." He paused in his ridiculous speech and stared again at Sheb, some of his confidence restored by all the gabbing. "Do you understand, Magnus? That the father is protecting the son? That the son can never best the father *because he is the son?*"

Patollo removed his jacket and laid it over the ball return so that he was looking straight at the place I crouched. I was huddled beneath the half-wall, afraid to glance back, and only when he spoke again, his voice carrying away from me and toward Pops and Sheb and Helene, did I dare risk another peek.

His hands had transformed into two post mauls swinging at his side. His shoulders twitched. His suspenders and the leather strap of the holster crisscrossing his back made him even more imposing in his shirt sleeves than he'd been in his hat and coat, and his obvious ease in this stance—now with his knuckles planted on the desk, not far from Sheb's black boots—made me fear for the man we called uncle.

But if Sheb were scared, he didn't show it. He didn't so much as flinch. Instead, with his hands still behind his head, he said, "The main problem with your story is that you're not my father, and I'm damn sure not your son."

Sheb lowered his legs. He stood up. And he mocked Patollo with an insincere smile.

All this time, neither Pops nor Helene had said a word. I'd almost forgotten they were there, given all the pontificating going on between the two thugs. They must have forgotten, too, because when Pops's voice came tinkling through the air—"Why don't you just go ahead and leave"—Patollo took a boxer's step back, and, in the same motion, withdrew his pistol and pointed it at Pops.

How many moments of tragic significance were borne into the rest of my life with those next few minutes? How much of my future was damned by that old man's impotent rage? By his clinging to his younger self, the one who built an empire on toughness and cunning and no small amount of legerdemain, if Pops and Sheb had been accurate in the stories they'd long told about him. In those stories,

Patollo always ended up the butt of their joke. A cranky cur bested by a couple of first-time dealmakers and swindlers.

It was almost as if he'd felt their mockery and scorn, and come to settle accounts. I couldn't move, much less protest the gun still pointed at my father. None of us moved. None of us spoke. Not for a moment or two. Not until Helene's voice filled the bowling alley in what I might best describe as a howl.

"Don't you dare hurt him, Andy," she said, pleading for a father she'd known all of ten minutes, rejecting at the same time the man who had stood in as that figurehead all her life. "Just do like he said and go away."

Her voice stirred in Patollo more rage. "For fucksakes, shut up! Both of you!" He waved the pistol back and forth between Pops and Helene, his face contorted in confusion and wrath and I was certain he was going to kill my father.

Summoning some depth of courage I'd never even suspected before, I slid back down the half-wall, silently picked one of the bowling pins off the floor, and duck-walked the remaining length of the lane. Now instead of rising to glance above the wall, I peered around the end of it, my eyes at knee-height. Patollo stood only ten or fifteen paces from me.

No one had moved or spoken in the few seconds I spent moving, and yet it was somehow obvious tempers had worsened.

The next voice I heard was Sheb's. "Your argument's with me, Andy. All Jake over there did was win a bet, one he shouldn't've had to make in the first place. Don't make this more than it has to be."

Now Patollo swung the gun in Sheb's direction. "You'd stand there in your Sears and Roebuck suit and tell me how to do my business?"

"What I'm saying is, none of this is reason to wave a gun around."

Pops spoke next, after he stood and slowly faced Patollo. "Almost twenty years has passed since the last time we stood next to each other. I was nobody then, I'm nobody now. You've done for me something so kind I can't quite muster up thanks, but I want you to know how much I appreciate your bringing Helene home. I sincerely do. This angel has landed, that's all I care about. Anything else, well, I apologize for the way we left town a couple decades ago. Whatever that truck cost, we'll make right for you. But please calm down. This is my child here."

When he gestured at Helene, the most profound jealousy I'd ever experienced welled up in me. It's a jealousy that's not been matched since, and I can't help but think it jolted me into a kind of subconscious rage that allowed for what happened next.

Patollo lowered the pistol, just enough that if he'd pulled the trigger it would have shot out Sheb's knee. He'd been listening to Pops attentively, and I'm convinced even to this day that if Sheb had left well enough alone things would have ended right then and there. But he didn't—of course he didn't.

"I just figured it out: this is the last desperate act of a washed-up goon," he said, as if he was thinking out loud. To Pops he said, "Don't grovel at this has-been. We ought to be kicking his ass six different ways." Now his voice grew into a tumult. "What son-of-a-bitch thinks he can raise another man's daughter? Or thinks he should be thanked for bringing her home? Just get the hell out of here."

"All around me, fucking children." Patollo anointed Sheb then Pops then Helene with a tip of the pistol barrel.

"Please—" Pops began.

That final plea must have been one too many, because as soon as Pops spoke that word, Patollo bayed, and he raised the gun again, pointed it at Pops, and started to walk slowly toward him, moaning as he did so that I thought the ceiling might collapse on us.

I moved with every bit of quickness and instinct I possessed, closing the distance that separated Patollo's massive back and shoulders with catlike steps, the last of which was more a leap, with the bowling pin cocked like a baseball bat. At first I doubted I'd even be able to reach the top of him, but I jumped, and I swung the pin with all my momentum behind me and clubbed him over the left ear. His keening stopped as soon as I hit him, and I heard the rattle of the pistol across the wooden floor before I did the thump of Patollo's head landing on a piece of sharp and boomerang-shaped chrome trim peeling from one of the broken-down ball returns, which pierced his head behind his right ear.

I don't know which was most abysmal—the silence that echoed from my throbbing head into the hollow of that bingo hall basement, or the slow spilling of words from my father's mouth saying, "Oh my God, Jon, what have you done?"

What had I done? The blood pooling around Andrus Patollo's skewered head, the spasming of his hulking, lumpish body suspended between the ball return and the dirty floor, the cry coming from my new half-sister, Sheb's bated breath, all of it told me what was already unmistakable: I had killed a man.

I had killed a man because I feared for my own father's life.

And now my father feared for mine.

"Son," he said, the tone of his utterance enough to bowl me over with dread and terror. He stepped right around the splash of Patollo's blood, and swept me back a few paces before he took me in his arms like I was a toddler again. "What have I done?" he whispered over and over again. *"What have I done?"*

*

When I turn to face Ingrid, all I can see is the reflection of my bottomless shame drowning in the tears in her eyes. For a long time she only sits here sobbing, and I start to wonder if I'd told some fictional version of my dreaded story. Maybe one that absolves me. Or maybe I haven't even spoken at all. But finally she takes a shuddering breath and wipes her eyes on the sleeves of her coat and says, "How can this have happened?"

It's still two hours before sunset, but already the woods are gathering darkness. How long have we sat parked here in the middle of Noah's woods? How long before my wife tells me I'm forgiven?

"Who else knows about this, Jon?" she says after another long pause.

"Knows that I killed Patollo?"

She winces when I say it, appears shocked. But then nods.

"Only Noah," I say. "I'm sorry he knew and not you. I thought—I always thought—if I could somehow silence the fact of it into oblivion, I'd be all right. The opposite has proven true, though. And now . . ." All I can do is stir the space between us with my hands, acknowledging the mess I've made.

She grabs my hands, settles them, holds them. "You understand that this all happened *forty-five* years ago? A whole lifetime has passed since then. Pops and Sheb, they're not even alive anymore."

It's startling to hear, and if ever time felt dubious, it's now.

"You don't have to look back there ever again," she continues. "And all this talk about being faithless and keeping secrets? Well, weren't you only afraid?"

As simply as that I feel absolved. I *have* been afraid. For a single moment, I revel in my unburdening, but the way she holds my hand reminds me of the new fears unleashed only yesterday, in Doctor Zheng's office.

There will never be a way to confess *those* into forgiveness. Not for me, and not for Ingrid.

Closing Time

AFTER THE LAST STRAGGLERS LEFT, stumble drunk and one at a time, after Barb wiped the bar and washed the glasses and made a fresh pot of coffee, and after Anton pulled the chain on the neon OPEN sign and it flickered off, and walked the last dancer and Barb out to their cars, and brushed them free of the foot of snow, he came in and punched several numbers into the jukebox and dimmed the lights and manned the bar while The Rolling Stones' "Dead Flowers" twanged into the air.

He took our orders and poured our drinks (I had a cup of that hot coffee) and the five of us—Sheb and Anton, Kristi and Chloe and myself—sat on our assorted bar stools and sipped our drinks. Sheb lit a cigar and offered them around but found no takers. Anton and the women lit cigarettes and it wasn't long before our end of the bar clouded with sweet-smelling smoke.

"Hard to imagine the two of you together," Sheb said, without any of the bitterness or recrimination that usually accompanied his speech. "Jake would be happy as hell about this."

Anton and I exchanged glances and nods and I said, "I'm happy, too. Despite the occasion."

Anton only sipped his drink.

"Your old man always said he wished he could get the three of you together again. Father and sons. He didn't have many regrets in life, but that was one of them." Sheb looked at me. "That you'd gone so far away."

"I'm just up the road, Sheb."

To the women he said, "You two would've loved Jake. Just a sweetheart. A perfect gentleman. I never knew a harder working guy. Relished the simple things."

"He was too scrawny for my taste," Chloe said, then turned to Anton and added, "I like a little meat on *my* man."

"Sweetheart," Sheb said, "there's only about ten pounds difference between Anton and you, and you're a goddamn waif."

"He's got it where it counts," she said.

Everyone laughed while Anton blushed. We quieted into a momentary lull. They smoked and we drank and some very particular half-light in the bar filtered my thoughts. Finally, I said, "About Pops there's one thing we can say for sure: without him, none of us would be here."

"I'd be here," Chloe said.

"He means me and Sheb," Anton said. "And he's right. And he's not just talking about Pops's *meat*."

Even Sheb smiled at this, staring into his aquavit through the haze of his cigar smoke. "He wanted a certain life, and he took it." He swirled the glass and put it to his lips and then swirled it again. "I wouldn't be me without him. I'm not too proud to say." He finally had a sip of his drink. "I can't believe that little fucker's gone."

Pops's passing was a loss for Sheb just like it was for us. Whatever I thought of him, Sheb was Pops's cousin and best friend. And

Pops was probably the only real friend Sheb had, and for as much as Sheb strutted and cocked, he must have known that. Must've known that the only person who truly tethered him to the Earth was now above it.

"Tell us something we don't know about him, Sheb?" The words were out of my mouth before I realized I'd spoken, and the look on Sheb's face suggested he was as surprised as I was.

"Well," he said, "let me think about that for a minute." He seriously considered the question, and I thought I could see him skipping over several things he might say. After a while, he continued, "He was in love with your mother—with Bett—from the first time he saw her. Lena, and all *that*"—he glanced at me and nodded in some way I understood to be furtive, suggestive of the secret kept between us—"well, he didn't know what to do. He was on the wrong side of Lyng Street and couldn't get across."

Anton looked at me. "The wrong side of Lyng Street?"

"How to get across?" I said.

"You know what I mean," Sheb said, sitting back and puffing on his cigar. "I remember the day he met her—the day Lena introduced them. After he visited their apartment for the first time, we met for a beer down at Marge's Still. He walked in like he was running from the cops, all flustered and suspect. And goddamn if he didn't say then and there he had a problem. A big one. I guess you could say a tall and gangly one." He smiled at his own cleverness, but the sincerity was pouring off him. Sheb never seemed less himself. "'I know I'm stuck,' he told me, 'and I'll be good to Lena, but I'm in a world of confusion, brother. And if Lena's sister is gonna live with us forever, you might as well hang me out to dry now.'"

"The way Pops always told that story, she was like a strange, tall shadow from the start. Didn't talk much," I said, recalling the many times we'd heard about how they had met in that apartment on Halsted. "He described her as ghostlike. More than once he did."

"She was. According to him. I believe he said it was almost like she was invisible. But—and this describes Jake to a T—he also thought there was something mysterious about her. Later in life, and I mean way later in life, he admitted that Lena was nothing but a pretty face, and he knew he was nothing more to her than a taste of normal life. But he felt something with Bett. And he wasn't goddamn wrong, was he? The two of them were damn happy together."

"Ma's about to be a ghost again," Anton said, his voice a whisper barely heard over the music. Like the smoke floating all around. "I keep trying not to think about what this is gonna do to her."

"We'll take care of Bett," Sheb said. "She's like a sister to me, and she's got you, too." This he said to Anton, who appeared genuinely lost in the prospect of her grief.

"The last time I talked to Pops was just last Thursday," Anton said. "The day before he passed." He grew paler with each word and for the first time all night I felt like he was finally in the moment, with all its unyielding weight. He pressed a thumb to each eye before he spoke again. "He was going on and on about his snow blower, and what a piece of shit it was, and how if he'd only followed through on one or two of his damn dreams, he might've invented a new and better snow blower, then all the chumps like him wouldn't have to grapple with them all winter long. They could just go out and start it like their car. It'd be as easy as that. He must've talked at me for a half-hour about it." He smiled, but also stifled a sob. "Then he changed the topic as if he'd just shut the fucking garage door. 'How's Angel?' " Again his breath caught and again he thumbed his eyes. "He asked about her every single time I saw him. Every single time." He repeated those three words slowly, almost as if he couldn't believe them.

"He was fond of that girl," Sheb said. There was more he could have said—about my own children and how Pops barely knew them, about my own absence from the rest of my family, about how I barely knew Angel—but didn't. I might even have given him a knowing glance. A look of thanks.

"You guys are all so serious," Chloe said, her words slurred. "Who picked this sad music?"

Now "Moonlight Mile" was mingling with the smoke. Even though Chloe was right, the sadness of the music made everything somehow more bearable.

"Hey, Britt, it's a blue night." Anton's voice came gently from behind the bar, and the way he looked at her suggested a feeling more complicated than he let on.

She answered him by hopping on the bar, swinging her legs over, and landing in his arms. "I'm sorry, baby. Let's dance to this blue song, then."

They swayed together for a moment before she turned her face up and kissed him. Kristi watched, tapping her ash onto the floor. If the scene inspired anything in her, it wasn't plain to see. But I watched her watching them all the same until she said, "Hey, Sheb, tell us about your dad."

It sounded almost like a taunt, coming from her sweet voice—like she wanted him to suffer the memory. But Sheb turned solemn in the way Anton had, and he opened up without any prodding. "He was a butcher, down in Chicago. Worked at a shop off Logan Square owned by the most cantankerous son of a bitch I ever knew. My old man wasn't far behind him. He drank too much. He beat the hell out of my mom. He had untold girlfriends and except for the occasional Sunday evening supper, he wasn't around much. That was fine with me." I could see him calling up memories long dormant. He studied his own hand through the cigar smoke rising between his fingers. "He had these motherfucking hands. You couldn't believe them. Each finger like a number-eight hex bolt. His nails were always long." He pushed the sleeve of his shirt up. "And his forearms—Jesus Christ. They were like the slabs of pork loin. All muscle. I remember that about him." He rolled his sleeve back into place and puffed his cigar. "He had tinnitus, and after long days at the shop he'd sometimes have to sit in a dark room until the ringing stopped. Those days were the worst. His temper was goddamn volcanic, and you better not catch him when the ringing was bad, or he'd beat you silly. He once hit me so hard I had ringing in my own ears for days after."

He looked up at us as though startled by his memory. Balling his fists, considering them, he added, "You can see why I left. Fifteen years old and out on my own. Got a job bussing tables at The Valhalla. Never looked back." He nodded. "The only thing that stayed the same for all these years was Jake."

Everyone nodded in silent agreement while the song ended and another began. "Sway" this time.

Sheb shrugged his shoulders. "Another sad song, Chloe . . ." Whether he meant his story or the music, who could say?

Before anyone spoke again, the office door swung open and a woman walked in. I startled, but no one else did. She walked right up to the bar and sat next to Sheb and said, "This must be Jake's other son?"

"The one and only," Sheb said. "Jon, this is Norma."

"Hey," I said. "Nice to meet you."

She wore a Patagonia parka, the shoulders dusted with snow; she unzipped it and hung it on the back of her chair. The black Western shirt underneath, with roses embroidered above the pockets, was skin tight and revealed a slender, slight physique. Anton poured her an aquavit without her requesting one, and as soon as she had it Norma raised the glass and said, "To Jake. Sorry I couldn't be at the funeral."

Anton raised his glass and nodded and said not to sweat it.

"I suppose I missed the party?" Norma said, then turned to Chloe. "Look at you, you sexy bitch. You have a line for Auntie Norma?"

Chloe flipped open her purse and took her vile of coke out, then cut a line on the mirror of her compact. Norma snorted it and her eyes fluttered and she wiped her nose and said, "Thank you, you dirty whore. Now come give me a kiss."

Chloe extended her cheek and Norma kissed her and then turned to Sheb and kissed him, too. "Now I'm ready for another drink. How's my Mag?" She twirled into Sheb's lap.

"We're telling stories about our fathers," Sheb said.

"My daddy liked dick," Norma said, feigning embarrassment. "It's a wonder I'm here at all!"

"Thank god you are," Chloe said. "Who else would take care of Sheb?"

Sheb smiled up at Norma's face, which was ageless and free of wrinkles. "Who takes care of who?" Sheb asked.

"Daddy, you take care of us *all*." Norma slid from Sheb's lap and danced over to the jukebox. Over her shoulder she said, "I know who picked this music, and it ain't any of you bitches sitting over there." She put reading glasses on and started flipping through the selections.

Sheb watched her for a moment, then turned to me. "She's the same as any of us. Orphans all around."

"The sins of our fathers, right, Sheb?" I said, meaning nothing.

But he considered it thoughtfully for a long moment before he winked at me. "More like the sins of the sons."

"What's this all about?" Anton said.

"The Bitch Is Back" replaced the Stones, and before Sheb or I could fake an answer, Norma high-stepped up to the stage, gripped the brass pole, and spun around with as much flair as any of the women had throughout the evening. She sang along as she preened and teased and locked her eyes on Sheb, who chuckled and pretended to look away.

Chloe, in a move I might already have predicted, ran up on the stage with Norma and peacocked around with her.

Anton looked at me and shrugged. "What can I tell you?" he said.

"Is this Sheb's steady?"

Kristi, who had seemed bored and ready to call it a night, perked up. "He's as likely to offer me a thousand dollars for a blow job as he is to take one for free from her."

Again Anton shrugged.

"Don't they live together?" she asked.

"Not many people know that," he said. "Sheb keeps this part of his life pretty quiet. And Norma?" He nodded at her on the stage, now waltzing with Chloe and cachinnating at some shared secret. "She's the perfect foil to his bachelorhood, which he pretends is his defining feature. She owns one of the salvage yards over here. If she came in during the day she'd be wearing a reflective vest and a hard hat like the men she employs. She'd be ordering High Lifes and pizzas and acting like she didn't know Sheb from the governor. She was probably babysitting her grandson tonight. Her daughter works at one of the clubs downtown."

I studied Norma again. She was holding hands with Chloe as they sat, their backs against the red velvet curtains. Sheb was talking and they were both listening intently and I was glad not to be able to hear.

"When can we get out of here?" I asked Anton.

Anton looked at his watch and winced and then reached under the counter and turned the music down. "Hey, Sheb, it's closing time."

"Talk about a party pooper!" Chloe yelled.

Sheb turned around, his face raised in a questioning look.

"The cleaners will be here soon," Anton said. "And it's two o'clock in the morning."

"Don't you bitches know it's never closing time when Norma's around?" Norma said. But even her voice was subdued. She pointed at Anton. "Unless you want to let me take your girlfriend home tonight."

"Please do," Anton said.

"I'll go," she said.

Anton shrugged, then said to me, "That coffee gonna keep you up all night?"

"Probably," I said, and yawned big. "But I'd be asleep on this bar right now without it."

"Hey, Norma," he called across the bar. "Is it still snowing out?"

"If only all that snow was blow," she answered.

Again, my brother looked at me. "Cool with you if Britt and Missy crash at my place? I can't send them out in this."

"Of course," I said, then looked at Missy, who had laid her head on the bar facing away from us. Her hair shimmered in the bar light. As soon as I observed it, the lights went up. Fluorescent and static and matching the snow on the security monitor under the bar. The footage showed the parking lot and four cars still in it, three of them submerged beneath dollops of blown and fallen snow.

Anton put the dirty glasses next to the sink and wiped the bar where we sat. When he got to Missy, he leaned down and said, "Hey, sleepyhead."

She rolled her head without lifting it and smiled at him as if she'd just been dreaming of his face. "Hey."

"You really were sleeping," he said. "Why don't you and Britt crash at my place? Jon and I will sleep on the couch."

"Is it still snowing?"

He nodded. Time would prove that what I suspected happening

in those moments was true: their looks passed tender and fond between them. For the first time. Right then. I was drunk and it made me happy, and when Anton nudged her with the rag and said "Come on" and then wiped where her face had just been, he gave her a questioning look that said as much in its simplicity as all the night's chaos had said in its confusion.

Norma buttoned her shirt and left the stage, Chloe following and finally showing some signs of slowing down. She even covered her mouth with the back of her hand and stifled a yawn. Sheb followed the two of them back to their chairs at the bar and helped Norma with her puffy coat and Chloe with her faux fur. We stood there in a stupor while Anton checked that the doors were locked, turned off the lights, and finally killed the music. Then the six of us passed through the office, where Anton checked the safe under the desk, unbolted the deadlock, and let us out in the driveway between his apartment building and the back of Boff's.

The snow had let up but still fell, grabbing light from the parking lot lamps thirty feet up. Sheb said goodnight to the women, then Anton gave Britt the key to his apartment and told her we'd be right up. Britt and Missy trudged through the snow in those ridiculous boots, disappeared behind the wall separating the buildings, then reappeared on the staircase heading to the back of Anton's place.

It was then that Sheb turned to me. He seemed to be regarding me honestly and without malice for the first time all night. "I've been giving you hell, Jon, but with all guard down, I want to tell you I'm sorry about Pops."

"I know you are. And I'm sorry for you, too."

He nodded and removed his glove and offered his hand and we shook. "Take care."

"Yeah, you take care, too, Sheb."

We stood there for a minute, my brother and I, watching Magnus Skjebne and his girlfriend walk over to his truck. He opened the door and started it and emerged with a brush to clear the windows. After he'd worked his way around it, he waved once more and backed out of the parking spot, idling past us and onto Washington Avenue. The snow reflected his taillights even after the truck had disappeared around the bar.

"I'll probably never see him again," I said, a prognostication that came true.

"What a fucking relief."

"I should feel that way."

"But you don't?"

"I'm not sure what I feel, but it's not relief."

Anton looked at me and smiled and shook his head. "It's always some goddamn drama with you."

"I'm cursed that way."

He checked the door, switched a key for a second deadbolt and levered it locked, then set an alarm system with an electric fob.

As we crossed the alley he said, "Almost every night I close this place down. And almost every night I swear I'm going to quit. Tonight, I don't feel like that."

"Maybe I'm more fun than you thought."

He looked over his shoulder and smiled as we passed through the wall and climbed the staircase. Inside his apartment, Missy and Britt had collapsed on his couch, each on one end, their feet meeting in the middle. In the kitchen, Anton dropped his keys in a bowl and dimmed the lights and poured glasses of water. He handed one to me and brought them to Britt and Missy.

"Anyone want something to eat? I've got leftover Chinese food or frozen waffles or cereal."

"Why don't you take me to bed, baby?" Britt said.

"You and Missy go get changed. Come out and say goodnight?"

"Let's go," Missy said. "I'm so tired."

They rose from the couch in unison, all limp and liquefactive, like a waterfall in reverse, and went into the bedroom. Anton watched them as they passed and shook his head when they disappeared into his room. Without saying anything he turned on the oven and opened the freezer and removed a pint of ice cream and a frozen pizza.

"How do you stay so skinny?" I asked.

"I snort a fucking eight-ball every day."

"Do you really?"

"Not every day." He risked a glance, no doubt expecting my disapproval, but it was too late for that. "Plus I hardly ever eat. That sandwich at Ma's is the only thing I put in my stomach all day." He cut the wrapper off the pizza and set it on a cutting board. "Well, that and a few drinks." He cracked the seal on the pint of ice cream and dug a spoon in. "You want some?" he said.

"Nah."

"Are you as tired as you look?"

"I probably shouldn't have drunk that coffee. I won't be able to sleep despite how tired I am."

"Hey," he said, changing the subject without warning. "What was all that shit about the sins of fathers and sons?"

It wasn't the first time I deflected the topic, but it was the first time I paused, and wanted to tell him the truth, but still didn't. Instead I merely shrugged and said, "Who knows what Sheb was talking about."

"You're full of shit." He jumped to sit on the counter and took another bite of ice cream. "But if you've got secrets, please keep them. I've finally found my balance and I'd like to keep upright."

"I'm not full of shit. And I'm glad you feel that way. I wish I did."

"It's there for the taking, man." He scooped another bite. "I gotta say, this whole night"—he spread his arms as though to encompass everything—"it's been good. Really good, even as sad as I am."

"Are you flirting with me?" I said.

"Fuck you. I'm being serious. It's good to see you."

I sat on the counter opposite him. "I agree. It's better than good."

A round of laughter came from the bedroom, and we both looked toward the closed door. Anton kept his gaze there longer than I did, and when he finally turned back he said, "I've got trouble on my hands."

"I saw that."

"What did you see?"

"When you woke Missy up. Missy? Kristi?"

He shook his head and bit his lip, glanced at the bedroom door again. "I wasn't making that shit up? Whatever that was?"

"If you're talking about the look you two exchanged, I don't think there's much to be confused about."

"Why, why, why? Why does it happen with these women, one right after the next?"

"I have a pretty good idea."

"I'm sure you do," he said, but without the passive aggressive resentment that would usually have accompanied such a dig.

"She's cool, if you want my two cents."

He leaned forward and lowered his voice. "Good luck to me breaking things off with Chloe. I can't even imagine."

"I guess you don't have to have that conversation tonight?"

"I certainly do not."

As though our gossiping had a summonsing power, Missy walked out of the bedroom in a pair of Anton's sweatpants and a T-shirt with the Captain Morgan pirate spread across the front. She came into the kitchen, telling Anton that Britt wanted to talk to him.

"I'm sorry," he said to her, then hopped off the counter and went into his bedroom, closing the door behind him.

"He's gonna break things off with her," I said.

"Look at you, gossiping like a schoolgirl."

"I just thought you might like to know."

"Why would I like to know?" She filled her glass with water and traipsed over to the couch. "Come over here."

I obeyed, not unlike a schoolboy myself. When I sat down, she pointed at the projector and said, "What's up with this? Some vintage porn?"

"Something like that," I said. "It's an old movie of our dad ski jumping."

"Very cool," she said, putting her head back and yawning. Without looking at me she said, "You got a good taste of your brother's life tonight."

"Yes, I did."

Now she lifted her head. "He's a really good guy." She finished her water and set the empty glass on the table and looked toward the bedroom door. "It's like prom night when you and your date are only friends."

"I never went to prom," I said.

"Seriously? How's that possible? I guarantee you girls in your high school wanted to go to prom with you."

"By the time senior year came around, I was living in a boarding-house by the U. It's a long story, but basically my mom and I didn't get along. We still don't."

"Moms," she said, leaning her head back and closing her eyes. "I never went to prom either."

"No way."

"I was like the goth girl. Fuck the man, that kind of thing. I was drunk for half of senior year. It's a miracle I graduated."

There was laughter from the bedroom—Britt's—and we both glanced at the door.

"I bet Britt went to prom," I said.

"She probably went to six of them."

"A boy in every port," I said.

"Or at least every school. Do you know she went to college? A good college, too."

"Really?"

"Tulane. She was a psych major."

"That explains the mind games."

"She's diabolical. She's also just crazy." As if to prove Missy right, another shriek of Britt's laughter peeled from the bedroom. "Was she fucking with you?"

"I think she was trying to get Anton's attention."

"She's got it now." I thought I detected a note of envy in her voice. As I sat there in the unlit apartment, watching the snow taper outside, drunk and sobering, edgy from two cups of coffee, sitting beside that bewitching woman, listening also to the intermittent laughter staccato from the bedroom, I felt I was on the precipice of two states I couldn't name. Somewhere between dream and longing and sadness and hope.

"Can I ask you something?" Missy said, her voice barely rising above the ones in my imagination.

"Of course."

"I'm sure I'll sound like an idiot, but I really want to know."

"Okay."

She sat up, tucked her legs under her, and pulled her hair back. "Do you think it's possible your books are ever *meant* for someone? I mean someone in particular."

"I don't understand the question."

"I guess I felt like *A Lesser Light* could have been written for me. Not like I'm a muse or something. Obviously. Just, holy shit, it's like I *was* her." She covered her face with her arm and laughed at herself. "Never mind. I'm drunk and rambling."

I was flattered, of course, and curious. But I was also mystified, truly and simply, that this woman I'd not known six hours earlier could have felt the connection she was trying to describe.

"How in the world did you come across that book in the first place?"

"Anton. He saw me reading another book one day before my shift and asked me about it. Then he told me about you, and about your new book. I went out and got it the next day."

"What'd he say about me?"

She nudged me with her bare foot. "Look at you, fishing around for compliments."

"It's not that. I just can't believe that he ever paid attention. Even as little as we talk, he's never so much as mentioned my books. It seems strange he'd be telling people to read them."

"He told me it was weirdly sexy. In a corset and bonnet sort of way."

"He used those words? Really?"

"I remember exactly."

"I wish I could've had that blurb on the jacket. That's perfect."

"But you didn't answer my question."

"I don't know the answer. I'm flattered you felt that way, but the truth is I hardly knew what was happening when I was writing that book. Those characters just kind of sailed off on a sea of their own language. Their lives came to me altogether and completely and I hardly had to do anything more than sit around and listen to them. The lighthouse keeper—Theodulf is his name—I saw a lot of Anton in him. And Willa, his wife, the one you called a bad ass, well, I don't even know what to say about her."

"I fucking loved her."

"I can see that."

"Are you kidding?" She wedged herself up and leaned on her elbow. "Maybe if you're like me, you're always searching for people you wish you could be. I wish I could've been Willa. I especially wish I could've lived that long ago." She lay back down and put her arm up over her eyes again. "I wish I got fucked like that."

This was not an invitation. I knew that surely. But still I blushed, even while she shielded her face.

"I wish *they'd* finish fucking so I could go to bed," she said, then rolled on her side.

I got up and took a blanket draped over a chair by the window and spread it across her. She didn't say anything, only nestled into the soft leather of the couch and sighed.

I walked over and looked again at the picture of Anton in flight on the ski flying hill in Harrachov. I stood there staring at it, wondering at my memory of him and the conversations we'd shared earlier that night. And though in the days and weeks after, I'd come to realize we spent the night of Pops's funeral becoming friends and confidants again, in that surreal hour while the snow stopped falling outside, while Missy fell asleep on the couch and Anton finished his business in the bedroom, I regarded that picture of him as though he were a character like the lighthouse keeper in *A Lesser Light*. Like I knew him better than anyone in the world, but also that I could never know him as well as I wanted to. I'd lost that opportunity in our childhood, even as much as I'd loved him.

I don't know how long I was standing there, caught in the eddy of my emotions, before he came up behind me and said, "Sorry about that."

I startled, like someone had jumped out from a shadow, but then smiled at the sight of him. "Sorry about what?" I asked.

He pointed his thumb at the bedroom door. "About Britt. She's blind drunk and in a mood to fight."

"You don't have to babysit me. Just throw me a pillow and I'll sleep on the floor."

"No way. I'm not going to go fight with her some more. Want to eat that pizza?"

"Sure."

We went to the kitchen and he put the pizza in the oven.

"I see you put Missy to sleep. Did you sing her lullabies or just bore her with college professor shit?"

"It's two-thirty in the morning. Everyone's supposed to be asleep."

He turned the oven light on and sat on the counter. "I won't be asleep before five. Never am. It's fucking awful."

"I get up every morning at five."

"I guess there's always a Bargaard on watch."

"I guess there is."

"What the hell do you get up at five for?"

"It's when I write. Started when the kids were little—when there was no other time for it—but I'm so habituated that it happens now even without an alarm clock."

"That's some old man shit."

"Tell me about it."

"You were getting after it tonight, though."

"Following your lead, brother."

"About damn time," he said, but then seemed to sober all at once. He looked over his shoulder at Missy sleeping on the couch. Watched her a few moments. When he spoke, he did so in her direction. "I have to find someone outside the business. This is just"—he searched his conscience for a beat—"obscene. Dating these women twenty years younger than me just because we get drunk in the same bar every weekend."

"Missy is thirty-five years old."

"How do you know that?"

"She told me. We talked about all kinds of life."

"You filthy dog."

"Not even," I said. "And besides, she's got designs on the boss man."

He glanced at her once more, then shook his head and changed the subject again. "Sorry to drop that bomb about Ma on you. I guess it's been a hell of a reunion."

"I'm glad you told me about Bett. It's good that I know." My thinking sped up again, caught in the whirlwind of all the secrets I still kept from him. Secrets, no doubt, that would have helped him in his own way. And I *wanted* to tell him. About Pops and Patollo and how that all went down. The time and mood were right for it. But as I took a deep breath and imagined the rest of the night and the next morning, I saw the easiness that was on offer, and thought, for the moment, that that would be better than more truth saying. It had been almost forty years since Anton and I passed an evening together, and I wanted it to stay that way, our spending time together. To *finish* that way. I convinced myself I could tell him another time. Any time, really, now that we were mending our bond.

"I'm glad you're glad," he said. "And I'm not going to tell you how to feel about Ma. But I hope you give her a break. She's an old lady. And though she's tough as an ax handle, she's not gonna be around forever."

I conjured her then, from only hours before, standing in her kitchen making sandwiches. She no more resembled the woman who raised me than I did the boy who had once called her Ma. Nor did she know me very well. Certainly, I knew her even less, considering how Pops had kept her in the loop on me and my family's lives without telling me much about her in return. That was our agreement, and if he tried from time to time to coax me back to her, he also knew that doing so risked pushing me further away from him, and so whenever he sensed my temperature rising, he'd change the subject. For all my adult life, I harbored those feelings for her. And for all those years, they'd been predicated on a false assumption.

And yet, I still wasn't ready to forgive her. Or accept her. Or do anything more than have a sandwich in her company.

All I could say to my brother was "You're right, she's tough."

A couple minutes later he removed the pizza from the oven and sliced it into triangles. We sat at his dining room table wolfing it down. To my surprise, Anton brought up the winter we spent at the Torrs' place on Lake Forsone.

"Someday you'll have to tell me about it," he said.

"You don't remember?"

"Not really." He shoved half a piece of pizza into his mouth and washed it down with a drink of ice water. It was the easiest he'd seemed all night. As though he'd been through another gauntlet and could finally rest on a subject we both loved.

"Seriously?" I said. "We were there three months."

"I know we were there, just not much else." He took another bite. "I guess I remember being scared."

"You don't remember ski jumping? We must've taken a thousand jumps that winter."

"I remember we jumped."

"That's the winter you got good. You were only eleven."

Anton took another bite of pizza and smiled and said, "Brother, I was good before then."

We stifled our laughter and wiped pizza grease from our fingertips. "Okay, but that was the winter you got fearless."

"I was fearless only on that jump. In the rest of life, I was terrified."

"We both were."

He wiped his fingers again and then deliberately set the napkin down without looking at me. "I don't remember you being scared."

"You don't remember much about the ski jumping either,

275

though." I gave him a little kick under the table. "I only did what I thought best. And I'd do it again now, if everything was the same." He hadn't looked up, so I nudged him a second time. "We've been through a lot. More than most. And if we fucked up—if *I* fucked up—I'm sorry." Now he did look up. "But what I've chosen to remember is the fun we had jumping. And watching you get good. Like, way beyond your years good."

"You don't need to apologize, Jon. It was so long ago."

"What are you talking about? It was only five minutes ago."

He got up and brought the plates to the kitchen. Instead of returning to the table, he wandered over to the living room window. He looked up and down Washington Avenue and then checked his wristwatch. Like he was making some very earnest calculation. He tilted his head at Missy asleep on his couch, then tilted it at me. As he came back to the table he said, "I have a great idea."

The School for Boys

OF ALL SHEB'S MASTER SCHEMES, none eclipsed St. Balder's School for Boys, a place we were unlucky enough to call home for one impoverished month. Who can say from what abysmal hole in his soul Sheb welled that institution, but it was as unrighteous as any place that ever had an address in Minneapolis. Looking back on it now—on those barred windows, the rat-infested basement, the teachers who whipped the worst of us, and Sheb presiding over it all, the depraved headmaster—I see everything wrong with this world.

How did we end up there? Before the night of Pops's funeral, the answer to that question was as clear as a fever dream in a fictional language. One day I was camped out at the Torrs' house in Duluth, getting ready for an early-season day on the jumps at Chester Bowl, and the next I was in a Greyhound bus, ticket paid by Sheb. He met me at the station in downtown Minneapolis and brought me home with hardly a word between us. When we got there, he spoke to me in a way he never had before. As though he were a cult leader, and this my initiation.

"Your mother's gone to a hospital. She's very sick."

Our house was cold and dark. It smelled like bacon. It felt empty of my brother. It was. "What's wrong with her?"

He studied me with the gaze of a wild animal looking on its prey. I'd never been afraid of Sheb (even when I had reason to be) but sitting in the living room under those eyes I felt an urge to run. To hide. He seemed an altogether different man from the one we thought our uncle. "She's touched," he said finally. I had no idea what that meant, though it sounded like witchcraft.

"When will she be home? Where's Anton?"

"Your brother's at my house. And your mother won't be home for a while. Months, they say."

"Who're they?"

"The doctors at the hospital."

"What hospital?"

He sat down in the wicker-backed chair opposite the sofa, his huge frame filling it out like a Rottweiler in a picnic basket. "Jon, she's at a state-run hospital in a town south of here called St. Peter."

"I want to go see her."

"She can't have visitors. It'll be a little while before that's allowed."

"What does that even mean, touched?"

"She's had a hard time since your Pops went away." He looked at me as though he had to stare through the secret we shared in order to see me. "She had a breakdown, Jon. She doesn't know how to live without Jake."

That was the most obvious thing in the world. None of us knew how to live without Pops. But didn't she *have to*? Wasn't that a mother's *duty*? To take care of her children? Especially if she's all they have?

"You're going to have to come with me for a while," he said.

A lesser prospect had never been offered. "Why?" I said. "At your house?"

"I'm going to have you stay at the school."

He spoke with a kind of authority new to me. As though he'd been granted—not just taken—power over us.

"St. Balder's?"

Now his voice turned terse. "It's the only school I oversee, Jon."

Of course we had heard about his school for boys, a con unparalleled even in Sheb's quiver of scams. While he was contriving the place—wheedling it through city administrators and the state welfare offices—he spoke openly with Pops about how easy it all was, how brilliant. How there was no shortage of delinquents, and what better use of the young thugs could there be than to gather them together and get the state to pay Sheb for each one. So much better than a prison, he'd convinced the powers that be. And money in his pocket.

The building, a converted hotel and office building on Second Street downtown near the river, was donated by the city on the eve of its being condemned, with the understanding that repairs and improvements would be made. Sheb fixed up an administrative floor, including a fine office for himself, and renovated the rest only enough to pass the muster of uninterested inspectors.

"So we're going to be like the other kids who live there?"

I had heard him talk about what a rough bunch they were: petty thieves, runaways, arsonists, drug dealers, fighters. All under the age of eighteen, most of them what would have been classified as foster kids. The prospect of living among them was as instantly grim as the halls were rumored to be.

"Of course."

"And we'll still go to our old schools?"

"You'll go to school at St. Balder's, like everyone else there." He looked at me for a moment. "You can't expect me to drive you all over the city each day."

"But it's hardly a school. That's what you told Pops. You said you were basically getting free work out of the boys. You said something about cars and vacuums?" Sheb had told Pops that he had the kids working to restore cars and other durable goods, which he then turned around and sold at a profit. He called their labor educational, and the people he hired as teachers were as much shop managers as instructors. I couldn't imagine not going to my regular classes at North High. I couldn't imagine Anton mucking it in the repair shops of that disgraced old building.

"Anton can't do that. He has to go to school like a regular kid. He'll be miserable. He'll get the shit beat out of him by those guys."

Sheb considered me long and hard, then took a deep breath and said, "I guess it'll be up to you to protect him. And besides, he could use some toughening up."

"He's *ten*."

"When I was ten—"

"Your parents weren't in jail and a hospital." I got up and paced the living room. Up and down, up and down. When I sat again, I said, "We'll just stay here. I'll take him to school in the morning, and then go myself. I'll take care of him."

That hideous smile. I knew what he'd say before he said it, so when he shook his head and spoke I was already abandoning my convictions.

"Johannes, this isn't something you're ready for. Your brother can't count on you. He's too young. So are you, for that matter." If his words were meant to console me, they didn't.

"No," I said, though what I protested that moment I'm not quite sure. My father's imprisonment, Bett's ill health, my own culpability in the whole fucking mess, all of it.

"Anton has his kit, you grab yours. Tonight you'll stay at my place. Tomorrow we'll get you enrolled."

I don't remember much of the rest of that night, but Anton and I were reunited at Sheb's. Back then, he lived in the upper half of a duplex on Twenty-fifth and Irving. His landlord was a Finnish woman who lived downstairs and still spoke with an accent and hosted a Bible study that offended her tenant enough that he'd sometimes sneak outside while they were gathered around Leviticus and piss on their tires.

When I arrived at his house that day, she was ready with lemon bars. Anton, who had been left in her charge, came barreling out into the foyer to wrap his arms around me while he cried and cried. Mrs. Huomppa, that was her name. She told Sheb what the day with her young charge had been like, reporting that he'd not spoken a word. Silence would become the defining feature of my brother that winter. In fact, it was the reason we ended up at the Torrs' place.

*

After four weeks at the School for Boys, I had heard and seen more skullduggery than I'd ever known existed. Not only did the boys impounded there fight and gamble and cajole and generally fuck around, but they formed alliances like I'd later learn prison gangs did, walloping on the isolated new kids until they made allegiances. As nephews of the headmaster (a term Sheb used to describe himself, preposterously) things were simultaneously better and worse for us. On the one hand, the boys feared Sheb with a vengeance, so we were regarded as possibly possessing some of the same degeneracy by virtue of our blood ties. But we were also the runts. Wispy and wiry like Pops, and fine haired and soft spoken to boot. To see us as a threat would have required a powerful imagination. And since most of the boys at St. Balder's were already engaging their powers of imagination to invent fiendish new ways to torment each other, they quickly figured out we were nothing, even with Sheb as a supposed ally.

Because the age groups were sequestered on different floors of the dormitory, most days I did not see Anton until dinnertime in the main floor cafeteria, the only meal we gathered for collectively.

I'd seek him out and sit beside him, a risk for him, given the especial meanness of the younger boys and their belief that a big brother was a marker of cowardice. Their behavior toward my brother bordered on diabolical, and by the time Christmas rolled around he had all but stopped talking and as often as not came to the cafeteria with a new bruise on his tender face. Over the gruel that passed as dinner— watery meatloaf and instant mashed potatoes, fried chicken and canned peas, bologna sandwiches on days-old Taystee outlet bread, and countless other variations on what I imagined Pops also suffered at the prison cantina—I'd try to coax from Anton some good news about his days. Of course, such news no sooner existed than happiness, and the only response I ever got from him came in grunts and tears.

My own experience was the loneliest of my life, but because incidents of violence were somehow less frequent among the older boys I managed a calmer existence than he did. Days we spent learning how to disassemble carburetors and change brake pads, or how to work and operate a backhoe or drive a tractor trailer. The simplest minded among us were relegated to vacuum cleaner repair classes or something I thought of as a course in janitorial science but was really an excuse not to pay a service to clean the halls and lavatories. In other words, we were being groomed for the low-wage jobs that would keep our kind in poverty. We were the riff raff. We were throwaway boys.

They kept us on a strict, military-style schedule. Reveille (a cacophonous bell that rang through the building, probably an old fire alarm) yanked us from bed each morning at six o'clock. We met as a full student body in the hallways for calisthenics, led by a resident assistant. Sit-ups and push-ups and deep knee bends, a hundred of each, before breakfast in shifts, usually just cold cereal and canned fruit and coffee, starting with the older boys, who would then head to their assignments for eight hours, with a brown bag packed with mealy apples and soggy sandwiches for lunch. Six or seven hours we would toil under the hoods of cars or in the dusty bags of vacuum cleaners, all of which were donated and all of which, once refurbished, were sold. The idea, of course, was that proceeds would be funneled back into St. Balder's, but my suspicion is that Sheb took those funds and parlayed them into his next racket.

After classes, we were free to roam the city or hang out in the common area and watch TV. Like bands of mismatched soldiers, most kids scampered out the door for their misadventures. They walked around downtown and over to Dinkytown and some even caught buses for Uptown, all of them in search of trouble in one form or another. They didn't have much money and their clothes were usually grease-stained or torn or both, and to envision them as anything but hellions was to give them credit where it wasn't due. Mostly I stayed in the commons and watched TV with Anton. *All in the Family, The Jeffersons, Wild Kingdom.*

Only once did I venture out with a group of guys from my floor. We walked up Hennepin, past the Masonic Temple and the theaters and the gay bars, past the topless joints and the fast food restaurants and beauty schools and markets, until we found the last blighted blocks of the main drag. Half of the mob went into the arcade to drop quarters into pinball machines, while the others ducked into Fantasy Gifts to drop quarters into the video booths. I looked in the window at Moby Dick's, was heckled by the daytime drunks, and then went to Shinders to poke around the magazines and book racks. Eventually, we all convened again, stopped for sodas at McDonald's, and returned the same way we'd come, drunk on our freedom if not on cheap beers. That foray began and ended my tours of the city, but the rest of the kids made a ritual of it, despite the bitter December weather.

Several times each week, the police would show up with a couple of St. Balder's boys who had been caught spray painting a bridge underpass or pinching records from Music City. In my memory, they remain not only unapologetic but something more like perplexed. How else should they live? How else should they get their hands on the new Led Zeppelin album? How else should they express themselves? Their eyes wanted to be alive, and their sentence at St. Balder's didn't much allow for that. With their transgressions, those sentences would get worse, as they elicited a special meeting with Sheb, the sum of which would later become the stuff of bedtime legend.

Those late, insomniac nights, rumors spread that Sheb was all manner of unspeakable horrors. A pederast who wouldn't take no for an answer. A pervert with a penchant for animals, especially woolly lambs, and for making the deviants watch. A murderer, even, which explained why some of the misfits were summoned from their quarters and never heard of again. In point of fact—as much as I ever knew—he was little more than a rapacious prick hell-bent on terrifying the boys left to flounder in his charge. The list of crimes I witnessed measured no more than an occasional whipping administered to the most flagrant of our criminal lot. To execute these whoppings, he employed a billy club, the square edge of which made direct contact with the bare hamstrings of the unfortunates. He kept that paddle polished, and it shone in the hallway lamplight on the nights he made rounds at curfew.

I wish I could say I had some special access to him in that place, but he treated Anton and me like he treated everyone else. Which is to say, if it's not already clear, he was a grade-A sonofabitch to us. And he seemed to save for me a special and warning glance, one that said *I know you, you murdering reprobate.*

Of course, he was right, which might partly explain why I suffered that place as long as I did. My shame—not only for doing what I'd done to Patollo but for letting my father take the fall—was immovable. I pilloried myself to it and might never have shaken myself free if Sheb hadn't tried to halve my brother and me.

*

It happened on the day after Christmas. A Friday. The boys at St. Balder's who had family to visit were gone, leaving about half of us there. Miserable. Sad. Watching football on the TV in the commons, a pathetic fake tree hardly decorated in the corner. I'd asked Sheb to take us to visit Pops in Stillwater, but he said he couldn't. Said he had other Christmas plans. This made no sense to me then, Sheb having spent every holiday with us, at our house on Russell Avenue, in all the years preceding. I couldn't fathom whom he might celebrate with instead, but sure enough he was nowhere to be found on Christmas Day. Or the day after, not until the late afternoon.

He found us in the commons and told us to meet him in his office. I expected, or at least briefly entertained the notion, that he'd asked us there to give us a belated Christmas gift of some sort. Hanging from the transom above his door, a wreath, already going brown, dropped needles on us as we entered. It occurred to me how like his desk in the basement of the bingo hall this headmaster's desk was: unkempt, clandestine, a place for shady business. If I'd not known before then that Sheb was a bona fide crook and conman, I'd be certain soon.

"How's your time here so far, boys?" he asked, settling into the squeaky chair.

When I didn't answer, Sheb took a cigarette from his shirt pocket and lit it and pushed the pack an inch toward me in offering. To accept was unthinkable: I would have been allying myself with him, and given his treatment of us since Bett went away I couldn't cotton to that, not even as much as I wanted to appear his equal. The smoke of his cigarette smelled aromatic and fine and heady. "I don't smoke around him," I finally said.

He loosened his collar. The only adornments on his desk were a lamp and a stack of papers that gave the impression of a busy man. He sat back, drew on his cigarette, and then regarded the glowing embers of it with a curious gaze. The smoke seemed to dissolve within him, dulling his flesh, blurring his sunken blue eyes, which still studied the cigarette tip. In my memory, he never exhaled.

When he finally extracted his attention from the smoldering tip, he looked at me but addressed Anton. "You haven't said a word since you got here, son."

"He's not your son," I said, remembering his invective against Patollo. All the reasons I had to be furious rose in me without distinction, without discrimination. Like a meteor shower in reverse.

Sheb only smiled. Then he did look at Anton. "I have reports from all the teachers that you're completely mute. And that the other boys around here—older and younger alike—are having a goddamn heyday with you."

This was news to me—not that Anton wasn't speaking but that other kids were marking him. "Is that true?" I asked Anton. "What are those fuckers doing?"

He hid his face behind his hands, tried turning himself inside out.

"Let's just say we're lucky the ten-year-olds can't inflict too much harm," Sheb said. "And anyway, that's not the real problem."

"The real problem is that you have us here in the first place."

"Is that right?" He smirked, and flicked ash on the floor. "Or, if it weren't for me *having you here*, you'd be in the state's custody. You wouldn't get the benefit of this personalized treatment." He as much as stabbed me with his glaring look. "Let's not forget how we got here in the first place."

Because you hang out with gangsters and pimps? I thought. *Because you were going to let someone shoot my father?*

"You oughta know I had to report this to the state. With both parents—what, *indisposed?*—and in state custody, they were going to set you up in foster care, Jon. With some old pervert and his disciplinarian wife who'd as much as beat you blind. That's not happening here, is it? You don't have a mark on you."

"That's some way to measure success," I said, but for that brief moment my energy flagged. If Sheb was right about anything it was that no good could come of our situation, and likely this was better than the alternatives. At least we were together. I put a hand on Anton's shoulder and shook him a little, got him to peek out from under his folded arms.

"We're not here to talk about your complaints, anyway." Sheb folded his hands behind his head, his cigarette still clutched between his fingers, so it looked like his ear was a chimney. "Given the peculiarities of Anton's not talking, I've decided it's best if we get him some help."

"What kind of help?"

"From a place that specializes in this sort of thing."

"Where?"

"Down in Faribault. The School for Imbeciles."

"For imbeciles? What are you talking about?"

"We're incapable as an institution to provide for him."

"What the fuck kind of providing are you doing for any of us?"

He brought his hand down and took a puff and then put it back behind him. He shook his head slowly. "Every one of these boys would be in foster care or on the streets if it wasn't for this school, you thankless little prick."

"I don't give a shit about the assholes you got cooped up here, but you sure as hell aren't about to send Anton away. Especially to some school for imbeciles."

"And now you're what? Your brother's keeper?"

"There's nothing wrong with him but that he's scared as shit."

"He hasn't spoken in more than a *month*."

"He talks to me," I said, though I wasn't sure that was true. "And anyway, what's he had to say?"

"He might've started with *thank you*. Same as you." Now Sheb leaned his arms forward and folded them over the desk so the smoke clouded his face. "I'll bring him down there on Monday. The good folks in Faribault are ready to help. They'll do that, and then we'll see about bringing him back here."

"There's just no goddamn way I'm letting him go," I said, whispering or screaming, I can't remember which. Baffled as I'd been by Sheb's unwillingness to let Anton simply stay at home with me while Bett was gone, the idea that he would shuttle my brother off to a place like he described was more than I could stand.

Sheb must have seen the anger in me. Must have read my thoughts about wanting to kill him, because he very casually set his cigarette in an ashtray, removed a white cotton cloth and a can of furniture oil from a drawer in his desk, and then, from farther back, his club. He held it before him, dotted it with polish, and began to rub the oil into the fine-grained oak with the cloth. "Sit back, Jon. You pissant. You thankless, brooding shit." He stroked the cudgel like he was jerking it off. "This isn't a negotiation. He'll be moved Monday morning. Why don't the two of you spend the weekend together. Play a game of cribbage. Go see a movie"—here he set down the billy club and removed a ten-dollar bill from his wallet and slid it across his desk—"and grab a cheeseburger. Monday morning you can ride with me down to Faribault. It's a couple hours away." He ceremoniously put the furniture polish and the cloth back in the drawer and lifted his club again. He held it up to the light and then pointed it in my direction and looked down its smooth edge as though it were a telescope lens.

"Come on, Anton," I said, giving Sheb a livid glance as I took my brother by the arm. "Let's go."

"One more thing, Johannes," Sheb said, his voice almost sultry with the pleasure of humiliating me. Or what he imagined was humiliation. "There're some Christmas cookies left in the freezer down in the galley. Help yourself."

*

I walked with Anton back to his room. When we got there, it was empty, and I sat on his bunk. He just stood there in front of me, wretched, I could tell, but nothing more.

"Is it true you've not spoken?"

He shrugged.

"Christ. Fuckall." I balled my hands into fists and punched my knees in unison. Like a two-cylinder engine. "Goddamnit."

Anton sat on the floor in front of me and held on to my shins.

"Sheb's going to send you away. Just like that. Can't you *say* something?"

Tears streaked his face. I could practically feel the heat emanating from his little body.

"Hey, now. Come sit here." I patted a space next to me on the bunk. I had no idea what I might tell him, no plan yet to stop his banishment to the home for imbeciles, and certainly no way to stop him from crying. Hell, I was almost crying myself. But when he wiggled his way up on the bunk and nestled into me, a thought occurred to me: we could just get out of there.

I looked at the top of his head under my arm. I felt the shuddering of his breath as he gained control, and when his breathing leveled off altogether I said, "How about we go get a couple of those cookies?"

We went down the hall to the galley and sure enough, there in the refrigerator, a Tupperware box full of butter cookies still sat on the rack. I checked that we were alone, filled our pockets, and slid the container back in the fridge. We returned to Anton's room and closed his door and sat on his bunk and stuffed our mouths. I promised him everything would be all right and that all he had to do was listen to me. And though it's true I had no plan to put into action, I knew I'd come up with one.

Later, in the quiet of the middle of the night—a night I remember as well as the one I met Ingrid, as well as I remember the one of our wedding—while I stood at a window overlooking the street below, obsessively counting the hours until Monday, watching the intermittent traffic, wondering how in the world I'd save my brother from Sheb's contemptible plan, cursing my parents (and cursing myself), I felt much how I imagined Pops must have been feeling over in the penitentiary. It was woeful, to be sure, and a feeling that hammered at me for a long time. I kept thinking ahead to Monday, and the inevitability that I'd be entirely alone. Entirely without family. And even though I saved my special scorn for Bett, I didn't relinquish Pops of his responsibility in all this, too. That he'd put me in a room with a man like Andrus Patollo. That he'd leave himself so defenseless as to require salvation from his son—well, wasn't it naturally, even *ordained to be*, the other way around? Hadn't it always *been* the other way around? For all he'd taught me, how to grapple with circumstances like the one I now struggled with while standing at that window had never come up. Never anything like it.

I recognized I'd have to shuck the limits of the wisdom he'd passed on to me and untangle this mess on my own. I stuttered at first, getting Anton and me out the front door but then finding us just standing on the street cold and hungry and without a place in the world to go. If I took him home, Sheb would be there by six-thirty the next morning, when roll was taken after reveille. We both had friends, of course, but none so close we might reasonably ask them to shelter and feed us and keep our whereabouts secret until our mother could reclaim us after her stint in the funhouse. Right? I flipped through the people I knew. Friends from North High. Selmer Dahlson. Families from the ski club. I adored many of these folks and had been given much by no few of them. But we might as well have been visitors in a strange city for the options that presented themselves to me while I stood there.

I shifted my view and turned to look north up Second Street. It seemed darker in that direction, the wide street narrowing into the warehouse district past Hennepin Avenue. I closed my eyes and imagined what would happen if we just walked into that darkness, my brother and I. Where would we end up? I don't know how long I kept my eyes closed, but before I opened them I was in Duluth, on the doorstep of my best friend's house. The only bosom friend I truly had. And though I had no idea what would happen once I got there, I'd already decided we would go. We would leave the next night. Not out the front door, past the security guard who sat sentinel behind his cage, but out the back. We'd get to Duluth, and we'd ask Olaf Torr if he'd take us in. If he'd give us shelter.

Back then, before we made our escape, I knew Mr. Torr to be a charmless, not unkind man whose stoicism and uprightness were his defining features. At least those were his morning qualities. Afternoons found him in the cups, his Irish whiskey as ubiquitous as his toque and choppers. His drinking made him more taciturn, but not mean. At least not that I ever saw. And what in the morning might have passed for a statuesque posture, the afternoons found tilting. Most of my memories about him are colored by this duplicity. He was six and a half feet tall before noon, not quite six-two by the time dinner rolled around.

He had survived one of the most famous Great Lakes shipwrecks in modern times, an experience that led to his Irish whiskey habit and the dissection of Noah's childhood. And though it would take until Noah's adulthood and the eve of Olaf's death for the two of them to reconcile, I always understood their relationship through the reflection in Noah's eyes. From the first time I met him, at a tournament in Duluth at Chester Bowl when we were eleven or twelve years old, I understood he was the sort of kid who had to walk lightly around his father. Olaf wasn't mean or demanding or anything like it, but you could tell from the slope of his shoulders and the weary dullness of his eyes that he bore his tragedy every minute. Even now I can see him crossing the parking lot, a fresh nip taken at the trunk, and his gait had in it some remnant of the waves he'd survived. Noah saw it himself, I know. We've talked about it enough over the years, but in those days of our youth—before I landed on the front steps of their house asking for help—Noah had something like a shield against his father's vices, the kind that announced he'd suffered, too, and because I saw this, and believed I understood it, I recognized in Noah my opposite, and so admired him immediately and profoundly.

And though we'd never once talked about our friendship, not yet, not back then, I trusted it would be enough. It turned out to be.

In the middle of that Saturday night after Christmas, with only the clothes on my back and the key to our house in my pocket, I snuck down three flights of stairs to the main floor of St. Balder's School for Boys and went to Anton's room, careful not to wake his roommate. I remember the way he looked at me, coming up out of sleep, and how I mistook his parted lips as being on the verge of speech. "No talking," I whispered, then winked at him. I remember the way he clutched his sheets, the way he tried to scratch his way back into the safety of his dreams.

"Adventure time," I tried, whispering again, attempting to take hold of him.

Now he kicked back to the head of his bunk and looked at me in a way I still remember as imploring. I knew every word I said, every minute we waited, was a waste of time we couldn't afford.

And I knew, too, that for every second he was awake, his misgivings would become more uncompromising. So I did the only thing I could think of. I lied.

"Sheb just woke me up. He said Ma was back at home. He said he'd take us himself, but since he's the supervisor here tonight, to just come get you and take a cab. I already called one."

He looked around then. At the darkness of the night outside his window, at his sleeping roommates, at me in my coat and jeans. I saw him wavering still.

"Let's not wake your roommates? Here . . ." I stood up and went to his footlocker and removed his jeans and coat and for a reason I'll never know he decided to trust me. Or at least to come with me on this midnight run home.

*

I did call a cab, from the phone at the end of the hallway on the main floor. I asked the dispatcher to have the driver pick us up in the alley behind the building, and not five minutes later, through the window beside the door, I saw it pull up. When I opened the window instead of the door—which had an alarm that would sound if we pushed it open—and when I muscled Anton through the window first and then came tumbling out behind him, he must have known he'd been duped. But he got in the cab anyway, and soon enough we were turning left onto Hennepin Avenue and driving past all the emptying bars. In the months to come I'd think often of the way the neon lights played with the dark, the way the lonelyhearts slunk into the night, their coat collars turned up. I imagined the cab and bus rides they'd soon take, to empty apartments and hotels and boardinghouse rooms, and I couldn't divert my eyes quickly enough, knowing what awaited Anton and me back at our house. It would be quiet and it would be cold and I just hoped everything I needed, or at least thought I needed, would be there for the taking. As the taxi turned on Eleventh Street and crossed the railyards and then found the wide-open blacktop of Olson Memorial Highway, I made a list. I can't imagine how faulty and incomplete it must have been, given the absence of any plan more than this.

But when we got to our house, after I paid the taxi driver with the ten bucks Sheb had given me the day before and fished the key out of my pocket, when I unlocked the door and let my brother into the dark chill of the kitchen, the smell of rotten garbage coming from under the sink, any instinct I might have possessed abandoned me altogether. Anton started crying, great soundless sobs that collapsed him right on the entryway rug.

I didn't even try to console him this time, just hurried from room to room fetching our provisions. I went first to the coffee can buried deep in Pops's closet. It was where he kept a roll of cash and his loose change, and in order for any of this to work I needed a stash of considerable money to have remained in there. It wasn't my habit to raid the family coffers, but I didn't see any other option. I pried the plastic lid off and found, to my great relief, a roll of bills. This money was probably the bulk of our family savings, and as I peeled it back and counted it off a not small part of me felt a wash of guilt. Three hundred dollars later, and I might as well have been bankrupting my parents. But still I took it.

In Anton's bedroom, I stuffed socks and underclothes into a pillowcase. I took jeans and shirts and a sweater and folded that in, too. I grabbed from his bookcase a handful of comics I knew he cherished, and from his bed, which was made according to Bett's exacting standards, I took a stuffed animal—a dog (because he'd always wanted and never got a real one) he'd slept with for several years and brought it to him, still sitting on the entryway rug. As soon as I handed it to him, he seemed to dissolve a little. Seemed to find his bearings.

"You want to know the plan, or you just want to come along for the ride?" I said.

He only rubbed the dog's muzzle with the underside of his chin, his breath coming more and more easily with each pass of the soft snout.

"I've gotta get a few more things. We'll be ready to go soon."

Even now I can't imagine what thoughts might have raced through his young mind. I suppose confusion and fear were at the forefront. Between my lying to him about Bett being there and the obviousness of my getting us packed, he was likely mad at me, too. *Asshole. Lying sack of shit.* These are the names he might have been calling me in the echoing chamber of his head. But at that moment I couldn't concern myself with what he was thinking. Except that I needed him to cooperate, to come along, to do so in a hurry. And despite the fact that saving him—that's what I thought I was doing— was the entire purpose of my half-baked plan, I had thoughts and feelings of my own.

Anger and fear were among them, but the most pressing, even as I hurried through our house—a place, I might add, that already seemed as foreign and estranged from me as my childhood—was a desire to be free of them all. A feeling as strong as vengeance. It's a horrible thing to admit to myself. And no doubt it helps explain why Anton's memory of that episode in our lives is hazier than mine.

From my own attic bedroom, I took only clothes and a few novels and, for a reason that seems clear now but was baffling then, a new spiral notebook. From the kitchen pantry, I filled a couple paper bags with canned goods and an unopened package of spaghetti noodles and all the cereal. And then I walked past Anton three times carrying things out to the car and loading them into the trunk. When I slammed it shut, I looked up and saw our skis there, Anton's and mine, and packed those inside the car the way we always did, with the tips on the dash and the tails against the rear window. Inside, I grabbed our boots and goggles, and threw those into the trunk as well.

The last thing I had to load was my brother, who after all of this still sat crumpled with his stuffed dog, no doubt howling within. I sat on the floor beside him. I didn't look at him so much as at the toy dog on his lap. I didn't expect to mollify him or explain things. Hell, I didn't know what I was doing myself. The only thing I knew with any certainty was my motivation.

I said, "I'm just not gonna let Sheb send you away. Our folks have already gone. You and me are all that's left, and no way am I going to let you go. I just won't do it."

He still didn't look up. Still nuzzled the pet dog.

"We're gonna get in the car. I'm gonna drive. Okay?"

Finally, he pushed himself up off the floor. He carried the stuffed dog over to the counter and to the notepad Bett kept beneath the phone for taking messages. He brought the notepad and a pen back to the floor and sat down and wrote: WHAT ABOUT MOM?

Have sadder words ever been penned? How could I answer him, knowing, then, nothing about what had happened to her, feeling unrestrained in my anger toward her? So I replied in the only way I knew how: I wept, there on the floor of our entryway, and when I was done crying I said, "Fuck her."

*

Somehow, over the course of those tumultuous months between Patollo's death and our stint at the School for Boys, I'd tested for my driver's permit. And though four months separated me and my sixteenth birthday, and though I hadn't driven for a month, I had it in me to back our old Ford out of the garage and steer it north. We had a road map in the glovebox and when I stopped outside Minneapolis to gas up, I studied it, and told Anton he had to navigate. Even back then you could nigh sleep between Minneapolis and Cloquet for the straight highway connecting them, so we passed through the middle of that night in stupors.

Anton slept while I tuned the radio from one frequency to the next, trying to maintain a signal. In Hinckley, we stopped for donuts and coffee at the twenty-four-hour café. Anton sat up when I put the long john under his nose, and for the last hour to Duluth he stayed awake with me. To his credit, there were no tears. I guess in fairness there were none for me either.

It was still dark—deep dark, the starless sky bearing down on the car like we were hurtling not up Highway 35 but down the road to hell—when we crested the hill on the west end of Duluth. As we did, the city and harbor lights blossomed below. I remember Anton sitting up. Like he was surprised. Like maybe he thought I'd got us lost, but here we were.

"This is Duluth," I told him, and turned the radio off as we coasted down the hill into town. That weightless feeling? That feeling not unlike flight? It gave me the impression I could be someone else in that city. That the distance behind us could stay there. I suppose landing there provoked in me the notion that I someday wanted to live in that city on the water. That I simply *would* make the distance between Minneapolis and Duluth permanent. I willed at least that much of my life to come true.

"We'll find some place to have breakfast and when it gets light we'll head over to the Torrs' house. You remember Noah, right?"

He pushed himself against the door and eyed me suspiciously.

"What?" I said.

He shook his head.

We found a diner that opened at five and sat at a booth. After the all-night adventure of getting out of town—and a month of eating mostly gruel at the School for Boys—I found myself famished, and I ordered a breakfast that could have fed me for two days. Eggs and pancakes, sausage and biscuits and juice and coffee and another pastry, this one a pecan roll as big as my face slathered in whipped butter. Anton pointed at the oatmeal when the waitress asked him what he wanted. "And some orange juice," I said, like I was his dad, keeping him in vitamins and good health.

After we ate—or, I should say, after *I* ate, Anton settling into his recalcitrance like a headstrong dog—I got up and went to the phone booth and thumbed through the white pages, looking for the Torrs' address. They lived on High Street, and when I asked the waitress how to get there, she directed me up past Skyline Drive. I thanked her. We sat in the booth sipping coffee and tearing to pieces the paper placemats. When the sun finally broke over the buildings across the street, I said, "Let's rumble."

A waitress passed by our table, and Anton reached out a hand and made a gesture like he was writing something down. "You want a pen, hon?" she said, and when he nodded she pulled a Bic from her apron pocket, tousled his head, and said, "Leave that on the table?"

Anton looked at me for a long time before he gathered his thoughts or his courage and pulled a napkin from the dispenser. He cupped his hand around the napkin and lowered his head and scribbled his message. Finished, he slid it across the table and looked down into his folded hands.

Before I read the note, I said, "Why aren't you talking?"

He didn't look up.

"You can't go around writing your thoughts on napkins. You're gonna drive me nuts."

But I read his missive anyway. DOES MOM NO WE LEFT?

I glanced across the table. He was peeking at me. Horrified, no doubt, of the answer to this question.

"I lied about her being home. But I had to." I risked another look at him. "Anton, what the hell was I supposed to do? Let Sheb send you off to a place for *imbeciles*? You don't belong there any sooner than Pops belongs in prison."

He bristled and shook his head in a short, vehement little burst, then grabbed another napkin and wrote: FUCK POPS.

"What the hell's this?" I said. "Pops is up to his ass in it. And here you are, sitting in a fancy restaurant on a vacation."

Vacation was, of course, the wrong word. We were no more on one than Bett or Pops. But still, why would he berate our father like that? Why was he mad at *him*?

He crumpled the two notes he had already written and took a third napkin from the dispenser. HE IS IN JAIL FUCK HIM. He glowered at me, furious. Like he could see the truth of the situation. Then he grabbed the napkin back, and scribbled: TAKE ME HOME

I looked around the almost empty diner, then leaned across the table and whispered my rebuke. "We can't go home, shit-for-brains. Sheb'll be there, and he'll load you off for that place." I tore his note in half and dropped it in my water glass. "Come on."

I paid the bill and we went out to the car and found our way up to Skyline Drive and then High Street. I matched the address from the torn-out white pages to the number on the house and pulled our car to the curb. I turned off the ignition and looked at their house. It reminded me of ours, and feelings of loneliness and abandonment came rushing out as I peered into the big window facing the street, the curtains still drawn against the early hour. I'd willed us there, with hardly a thought to the wisdom of the idea. All night I'd been pushing my doubts back, focusing only on what we had to do. But now that we were faced with the mirror likeness of our own left-behind home, I started to sob. I couldn't help it. I closed my eyes and lowered my head to the steering wheel and I wept and wept and I foundered in my tears like a boy lost at sea. I didn't notice Olaf coming out the front door, didn't see him walking down the pathway shoveled clear of snow from the front stoop, didn't even hear him tapping on my window, not until Anton reached over the skis between us and nudged my shoulder.

When I looked up he was standing there, jackknifed at the waist and squinting into the car. He made a motion like I should roll down the window, and when I did he merely said, "I'll be good and goddamned, if I'd known the Bargaard boys were coming, I'd've had the fixings for flapjacks ready to pour on the griddle." He smiled like we were the punchline to a joke he'd been telling himself all morning. "Get your skinny asses out of the car and into my house."

As we followed him up the sidewalk he turned and spoke over his shoulder. "I guess I should say thanks straightaway. You boys showing up gives me another reason not to go to church this Sunday morning." He opened the door and again looked over his shoulder, this time putting his finger to his lips. "The kids are still sleeping." Once inside the vestibule, he closed the door behind us and whispered, "Take your boots off, eh boys? No sense making a mess on the carpet. Hang your coats on this here"—he notched a long finger over one of the hooks on a coat tree—"and come on in. I was just about to start the coffee when I saw you pull up. Want a cup?"

"Yes, sir," I said. They were the first words I'd spoken since he knocked on the car window, and with them he lurched through an archway into the kitchen.

Anton and I removed our boots and hung our coats and stepped into the living room. We sat next to each other, close enough we could have held hands, and waited without so much as looking at each other. The Torrs' house smelled like crackers and jam; the furniture was tidy and appeared too small for a man Olaf's size. The piano in the corner had been Mrs. Torr's, who passed away when Noah was younger. Maybe it hadn't been played since. Remembering her put a new light on their house, and how it seemed so much like ours: even for all the finishing, there remained an air of the absent mother. Like it wanted tenderness or affection but didn't get much.

I hadn't even noticed that Anton was sleeping. He'd put his head down on the arm of the couch, and when Mr. Torr brought the coffee in, he raised one cup at my brother. Now his voice turned impossibly soft. "Tired boy," he said. "If you're anything like Noah, you want some sleep yourself."

"Yes, sir," I said.

He handed me the coffee and sat across the room. He took a sip. "You don't need to be so formal with me." He looked at his watch. "You drove through the night?" How could such a gentle voice come out of such a big man? Instead of pressing me, he sat back in the chair and crossed his long legs and drank from his steaming cup. After a minute, he said, "Yes sir, young Anton's gone down like a puppy."

Anton had folded into himself, his feet nearly up under him, and I could tell he slept soundly. I hoped dreamlessly, too.

"Does your mother know you came up here? I imagine she's worried."

"She's not home."

"Not home, you say? Where is she?"

"She had a breakdown. She's in some hospital."

If this news alarmed him, he didn't let on. Olaf only turned to look out the window. "You came here because you didn't have anywhere else to go?"

"We were staying at this school our uncle Sheb runs. But he was going to send Anton off to a place for imbeciles."

He nodded. "Well, all right then."

"I just didn't know where else to go, Mr. Torr. I felt like I had to get away. Sheb's a real piece of shit, and he'd come looking for us. He'd find us. You guys are the only friends we've got who don't live in Minneapolis."

"I'm glad you trust me, Jon."

"We don't want to be a bother, I'll tell you that. Which is why I thought maybe you'd let us go stay at that lake place Noah's always talking about. We could just camp there for now."

"You want to go stay at the cabin on Lake Forsone?" His brow furrowed. "You know that's way up by Misquah. You know there's no running water? No heat but what that old potbelly stove puts out?"

"Noah's told me about it. And there's a ski jump, right?"

A smile came over his face. Knowingly. "You can ski jump right here in Duluth. You know that. But I have to ask you, Jon, how long are you thinking of staying? What about school? When's your mom going to be home?"

"To be honest, I haven't given school much thought. And I don't know about Bett. I don't know what happened to her. I don't care, either."

He scratched the back of his neck and sighed. "That's a strong position."

I checked to make sure Anton was still sleeping. Leaning forward, I said, "She abandoned us. And since, well, Pops, you know . . ." I collected my thoughts. "Since Pops is away, I have to take care of Anton. I know your place up north is rustic, but like I said, I don't want to be a bother. And no one would find us there, that's for sure." I hesitated, but pressed on. "It's been an awful year. Just awful. I don't know how we've made it."

He took another long drink of his coffee and another deep breath. "Someday you'll survive much worse than this, Jon."

Maybe his own tragic past endeared us to him. Maybe he had a soft spot for my adventurous spirit, or my brotherly affection. Maybe he admired my moxie. Or maybe, since Noah's mother had passed away years earlier, there was just no one around to prevail with better judgment. Whatever the reason, Olaf agreed to usher us up to the cabin on Lake Forsone, and later that Sunday afternoon—after

Noah and his sister woke, after we all shared eggs and bacon and more coffee, after I napped for a couple hours, after Solveig found a friend to spend the evening with—Anton and I followed Olaf and Noah Torr in their big old Suburban along the North Shore to Misquah. Before we drove to their cabin, we pulled into The Landing and Olaf bought us fifty dollars of groceries.

I bought Anton a pocket-sized notebook and a pack of pencils. And before the sun set, we drove down the freshly plowed road to the cabin on Lake Forsone. It was our first night there. The first of a hundred.

Just a Wolf

A COUPLE OF MILES THIS SIDE OF GUNFLINT, Ingrid pulls the car into the False Harbor Bay overlook. Even from fifty feet up on a mound of ancient granite, I can feel the lake pounding the cliff face. The wind is straight out of the east, rising, hurrying the gloaming and bringing the water in quickening waves each more furious than the last. In the distance, up the snowbound shoreline, following the gray fringe of the trees between the water's edge and the highway, I can see the silhouette of town against the coming evening. The streetlights hum amber. The village buildings draw their shapes against the darkness of the hills above. I look at my watch. Sunset's not for another half-hour, but the weather's bringing the gloom like it's a duststorm.

Ingrid has not said one word since we pulled out of Noah's drive. Under normal circumstances, I'd be able to divine her mood. This, of course, is one of the benefits—if not also a hazard—of spending so many years together. That we don't always need to tell each other what's on our mind has spared us many disagreements and led to just as many moments of intimacy.

Her gaze is off in the distance now, willing, I imagine, the wind to deliver her something to say. But what more is there? My mind is clearer than it's been in as long as I can remember, and if Ingrid's is less so then I merely have to wait for her questions. In the meantime, I'll listen to my own silent calm. It's been a long time since I heard it.

After some minutes—enough that a bank of lowering clouds let loose its snow a mile out to sea—she turns to me and says, "This girl, your half-sister . . ."

"Helene."

"Yes, Helene, what became of her?"

"I don't know."

"How's that possible?"

Her incredulity is warranted. Over the many years since our first and only meeting, I've often found myself casting a quizzical look off into a distance just like this one, not quite thinking of anything, and after a while I'll realize it's Helene on my mind. I tell this to Ingrid, who seems as unsatisfied as I usually am after such reflection.

"How's it possible you never knew before that day? Did your father?"

"Bett knew, but Pops didn't. Not before that moment. He never heard from her again. Or so he claimed."

"I just don't understand, Jon. How could Bett know, but not your father?"

"Bett stayed in some contact with her sister. I guess it was their secret."

"That's incomprehensible to me. That's *reprehensible.*"

"To me, too. But then again, we're talking about Bett. The way Pops described it, for as much as he loved her—Bett, I mean—he always felt, even until the end, that he didn't quite know all of her. He said it was like she'd locked the cellar door, and he'd never gotten down there."

"I can't imagine."

I reach for her hand and hold it. "I'm sure I've told you they spent some months apart after he got out of prison? Separated, I guess. The first night of that separation, which was soon after I moved into that room in Dinkytown, he actually came to stay with me. I thought it was cool, having him there for a night. Like our own private camp." I think back to that singular night, and our weird joviality, but the memory is as fleeting as the night itself was. "Later he spent a month living at Sheb's place."

Ingrid smiles, but I can tell her mood is shifting. From cloudy-minded to something entirely more focused. The look of sadness creeping up on her is as unmistakable as the weather's purpose in the coming dark. I'd say something to quell it, but I know she prefers to sort it out on her own, and so we settle into another spell of quiet.

This is the sort of situation that makes me wish I *were* writing *The Ski Jumpers*. I've always been most intrigued by the moments on which life hinges. This is true in fact and in fiction, and though anyone passing by us on the highway, if they glanced into our car, would see a couple of folks watching the lake churn, I know what's happening between us is something much closer to a great reckoning than it is a simple pause. In an hour or tomorrow morning or in a week, Ingrid will know it, too. But for now, she's overcome. I see it as plainly as I do the galloping waves. We're still holding hands, and I lift hers with mine and kiss it softly.

She starts to cry. Soft and slow-moving tears from the corner of each of her beautiful eyes. I only kiss her hand again.

"What will I do, Jon? What will we do?" She speaks softly, but there's no mistaking the urgency in her voice.

"You'll love me. You'll help me until you can't. Which is just exactly what I'd do for you."

"And after that?" She's holding my hand so tightly now it almost hurts.

"After that we'll do what we've always done, or what you've always done: figure it out."

She pulls her hand away. "That's not what I'm talking about. I know I'll figure out how to take care of you. I'll figure out how to take care of myself, too. I can do all that." She turns to look at me, reaches up and brushes my wispy hair over my ear. "What I don't know how to do is live without your love, Jon. You'll be alive on this earth and unable to give it to me."

"That's not true, sweetheart."

"You don't get to choose. You can't just will it so. Your mind— your sweet, tender mind—will do whatever it wants."

Of all the worries yesterday's diagnosis put into motion, none have snowballed like my concern for Ingrid. My love and devotion for her, like hers for me, is the wellspring of our lives. Our years of marriage are proof. And if it had been her diagnosis yesterday, the most unsettling prospect to come of it would be my fear of losing her love. It's been as much a part of my life as the blood coursing through my body.

When I say "You'll have to do the loving for both of us, Ingrid," I wish I could take it back as soon as I've said it. I don't mean to lay another burden on her. How could she possibly bear twice the weight?

She closes her eyes against the view. "I'm so scared. I'm afraid of being alone. I'm afraid of how lonely I'll be."

Since yesterday morning, I've seen her loneliness a hundred times. It looks like a cold cup of coffee, lost to a morning taking care of me; or a long night wiping piss off my legs; or Ingrid cutting up a peach like she used to for the kids and spooning it into my slack mouth; it looks like wanting a kiss goodnight, or to make love in the morning, eyes too tired to open; it looks like wanting to dance after a glass of Friday night wine. All of which is to say that it doesn't look good. Not for her and not for me. We both know this.

Of course, I don't tell Ingrid about these thoughts. Instead I start humming a favorite song by Jason Isbell.

"How many nights did we sit over our cribbage board listening to that sweet man sing?" she says.

"We were singing, too, love."

I can as much as see her think *That's another thing we won't be doing anymore.* But she doesn't say anything. Only forces a half-smile before she stretches across the distance between us and kisses me like we're nineteen years old again.

I'm so surprised that I forget to breathe, and after half a minute I have to sit back to take in a lungful of air. It's like I'm breathing in the wind off the surging lake. Ingrid takes a deep breath, too, and looks out at that same lake. She sighs. "We've been married for more than half my life, Jon. And all that time you kept today's news from me."

I understand she's asking for an explanation, and not about Helene. We've said all there is to say about her.

"I don't know why I never told you before. I was a coward—"

"I can well imagine why you never told me, Jon. It doesn't even seem that mysterious. Who wouldn't want to keep it a secret?" She's terse. Maybe even angry. She shakes her head and grips the steering wheel so I can see her knuckles whiten.

"What is it?"

"I can also imagine believing everything would be better if I knew what you did to that horrible man." Now she swivels to face me. "But I don't know if that's why you told me. I don't know if you've done this to appease your own guilty conscience or if you believe it's better for us if I know. Maybe"—she pauses for a moment—"you're thinking only of yourself. And giving me another load to bear."

"No," I say, but in answer to what I'm not even sure.

"This man I've loved for so long, now you tell me he's a killer?"

"I told you because—"

"Oh, I know why you *think* you've told me. I do, Jon. But I'm not sure how it makes my life better. I don't think it does."

I feel—momentarily, and no doubt because that episode has just come back to life for me—something like I did all those years ago, standing above the dead body of Andrus Patollo in the basement of the bingo hall. Back then I had Pops to step in and not only clean up my mess but absolve me of my actions. There's no one to help me now, and I feel a panic rising in me.

"I'm sorry, Ingrid," I say, my voice now faint. "I'm so sorry."

She doesn't answer me. Only touches up her hair in the rearview mirror and says, "Let's go see our daughters."

I'm out of words—finally—and helpless as the child I was back then.

But before she starts to drive, she says, "I'm not going to think about this again until I can make sense of it. I'm going to try to enjoy our evening and think you should, too." She puts the car in gear. "But I'm also going to say that I think you should have just written your last book, Jon. I really do. You could've put today's admission in it and spared me the onus." She's exhausted. That much I can tell. But she's also forgiving, and when she adds, "Let your daughter surprise you," I understand she's already moving on.

*

We're driving past the ranger station and the edge-of-town campgrounds and cottages and then down the long hill into Gunflint, the lights below pulling us along like an undertow. I have that feeling I sometimes get after failing a morning at my desk. Like my story has lost its equilibrium. Except now it's not some fiction, but my life. As if by telling Ingrid about Patollo I've made it true again—or for the first time—and now I'll need to finally face my own trial.

Of course, the only jury I'll ever have to endure is driving our car right now. Someday she'll ask me more about it. But not now, and that's fine. If we were back home in Duluth, now's the time I'd kiss her on her forehead and shuffle into my office and open one of my notebooks and make believe I live in another world, one where the puzzlement and melancholy weren't my own.

Instead I reach across the space between us and tuck a loose strand of hair behind Ingrid's ear. "I'm sorry."

"Later," she says, glancing at me for a heartbeat.

"I don't mean about what I just told you, though I'm sorry for that, too."

Now she reaches over to me. She grabs hold of my hand. "I'd rather not, Jon. Not now."

"Okay."

How unlucky I am, to never have believed in God. To have instead put my faith in the lies Pops told me over that old kitchen table, or over the telephone late at night? To have instead written my faith in the novels I've penned? How much easier would it have been to simply pray? To send into the universe wailing orisons and wait for their reply?

Ingrid turns into the parking lot of Hivernants Brewing. The lot's full of big pickups and snowmobiles, but she manages a spot in front of the thrift store next door and turns the car off.

"I'm going to get a growler for the weekend. Do you want to come in?" she says.

I take my seatbelt off and open the door and together we walk across the parking lot, which is like a blistered minefield of potholes and ice. But inside the bustle and warmth are delicious, as is the yeasty smell of the beer tanks in a room behind the bar. That room is also flooded with people, and I can see a woman whose face I recognize standing behind a music stand with a microphone, addressing her audience.

The taproom is crowded. Skiers and snowmobilers up from the

Twin Cities or down from Thunder Bay. A band is setting up on a small stage, a standup bass and three-piece drum kit and acoustic guitar. The musicians stand next to their instruments and wipe their brows with back-pocket handkerchiefs. There's a roaring fire in the enormous hearth and, taken all together, it feels like a perfect place to be.

At the bar, Ingrid gets the attention of the keep and asks for a growler of the Devil's Maw IPA. Then she remembers I don't like those hoppy beers, and she orders a half-growler of the Burnt Wood Lager, too.

As she pays, I ask the bartender what's happening in the room behind him. He glances over his shoulder like he's surprised to see a hundred people sitting on folding chairs. "That's Greta Eide," he says. "She's an author. Some sort of celebration for a book she wrote."

I thank him and drift over to the double glass doors that separate the fermentation vessels and the brewhouse from the taproom. The usher at the door opens it a crack to ask me if I'd like to come in. I shake my head, and watch Greta through the glass.

I actually know her. When *A Lesser Light* came out, Greta interviewed me for a feature that ran in the *Strib*. She wrote a kind and thorough article, talking not only to my editor in New York but also to several of my students. She looks different now. Older and younger at the same time. I watch her for a few minutes before she glances in my direction. A wave of recognition crosses her face, and she smiles. I smile back, and tap on the glass and ask the usher if I can buy a book from the pile stacked on the table. It's called *Water Sky,* and the cover is a photograph of ice-choked water with the sun shining above.

"After the reading," she whispers, and lets the door close the inch it was open.

Ingrid comes up behind me and peeks over my shoulder. "What's this?" she asks, and before I can answer she adds, "I read a review of this in last Sunday's paper. You know her."

"Well, I've met her."

"Let's get a copy."

"After the reading, that's what I was told."

As though she has not heard, Ingrid hands me the jugs of beer and opens the door just enough to slide through. She steps to the table and takes two copies from the stack and removes her wallet and then her credit card and offers it to another woman sitting behind the table. The transaction takes less than thirty seconds, and as Ingrid returns to the taproom Greta Eide looks over and smiles again.

I raise a pitiful hand and smile back, resolving to track down her email and send a note of congratulations.

"Two copies?" I ask as we thread our way through the still-gathering crowd.

"One for us, and one for Clara and Delia."

"You are the bearer of gifts, it seems."

"Shouldn't we bring our daughter things?" She opens her car door and turns to put the books in the backseat. I set the beer beside them.

"You're right," I say.

We turn on Third and head up the hill through town, past the Art Colony and the First Congregational Church, then another block west and back north again. This is the street that connects with the Burnt Wood Trail, which makes a looping curve before the two mile straightaway up the hill. The darkness assembling in the trees is gorgeous and haunting and before we turn on the Old Toboggan Road it's spilling onto the trail, too.

"I'm glad we beat the dark," Ingrid says. "Remember at Christmas? That deer you hit right about here?"

"I think about that poor buck limping through these woods."

312

"The look he gave you."

"I bet he hasn't lasted the winter. Not on three legs. Not with all the wolves gallivanting about."

"Always the wolves," she says, as though these are the first words to some song we're wont to break into.

"Always the wolves," I echo back, as though I'm late with my harmony.

*

The driveway into Clara and Delia's place is well groomed. They bought a plow they can easily attach to the front of their pickup and which they keep in an outbuilding during the half of the year it's not needed. Like their thousand-square-foot garden and the solar panels on the roof of their house, the plow is a righteous nod to their independence and self-sufficiency, to say nothing of their almost remarkable capabilities. There's more evidence of this in the woodpiles, which, like Noah's, are readied for Armageddon.

Ingrid parks under the quavering light above their studio, and for the last time today we step out of our car. It's not been ten minutes since we walked out of the brewery, but the looming woods make it seem a hundred miles ago. I reach into the back of the Honda and grab the books and beer and our suitcase, and we head across the gravel to their front door, which is framed by elaborate scrollwork hand-carved by Delia from a white pine that toppled in the wind a few years ago. Before we even have a chance to knock, the door swings open and here's my daughter, her sweater buttoned up, her dog at heel and ready and regal. There's not a creature in these woods that would challenge Dolly, named for the country music singer both Clara and Delia love—and that includes the aforementioned wolves.

But never mind the wolves. What's better medicine than a daughter's voice?

"Hi, Daddy," she says, sweeter than any prayer ever muttered. And better than any story.

"Hello, Clara Belle," I say.

Ingrid merely hugs her greeting.

"How was the drive?" Delia asks, stepping around the corner with a dishrag in her hand and an apron slung over her shoulders and tied at her belly.

Dolly barks and wedges herself between the four of us so the rest of the hugs need wait until we get out of the entry.

"It was lovely," I say when it's my turn to kiss Delia's cheek. "Ingrid always steers a straight course."

"No one talks like that anymore, Dad," Clara says, as though I've just spoken in Old English.

"Maybe not where you're from," I say.

Delia makes a sweeping gesture with her hands, inviting us in and taking our coats as we slide them off. "We're making moose stew and boule bread for dinner, hope that sounds good?"

"If it tastes half as good as it smells, we'll be in culinary heaven," Ingrid says. "And we brought this." She offers the beer.

"And this," I say, stepping back to the entryway and the books I set down while I took off my coat. "The author of this book lives right down in town. On the cove."

"Of course," Clara says. "She comes to the brewery all the time. Delia sees her at the restaurant, too." She lowers her voice so Delia can't hear from the kitchen, where she's gone to pour glasses of beer. "Her husband's gorgeous!"

"I heard that!" Delia teases.

Clara shrugs and winks at Ingrid.

"She wrote a story about your father when his last book came out," Ingrid says.

"I remember that," Clara says in her expressive way. Like the memory of that *Strib* feature is something she ponders with some regularity.

"Well, I don't," I say. "Let's talk about *anything* else. Maybe even Greta Eide's book?" I hand one to Clara.

"Thanks, Dad."

"It was your mother's idea."

"Thanks, Mom," she says in the direction of the kitchen, where Ingrid has gone to help with the beers. She soon brings a pint glass capped with foamy head to me in the great room, then says, on her way back to the kitchen, "It's been such a long time since I read a book that I loved. Maybe this will be it."

"It's supposed to be good. And sexy. Did you see the review last weekend? I heard her on WTIP earlier this week, too. She seems like a smart woman."

"I always say be careful of those assumptions," I say, and risk a look at Ingrid standing beside our daughter-in-law over a Dutch oven full of aromatic stew. She returns my glance but doesn't offer any retort.

"What's up with that?" Clara whispers.

"With what?"

"That look you just gave Mom."

I look at her again, standing at the big cast iron range with Delia, and remember the trying day we've had. Instead of replaying it for our daughter, I only admit that her mother wants me to write another book and that I'm not up to it.

"Are you all right, Dad?" she asks.

"I'm fine," I say, then turn back to Clara and finally relax. There's nothing to do for the rest of the weekend but be happy and content. "How are *you*? What's the report from Gunflint?"

She sits back in the cushy couch and tucks her legs beneath her, settling in for what will surely be the first of many happy conversations this weekend. "We're so good, Dad." She takes a long look across the great room. "And so happy you're here." Across the room Delia turns toward the refrigerator, and Clara takes the opportunity to lean forward and whisper, "You have to tell her you like the stew no matter what. She's been working on this recipe since she got the moose last fall."

"Did I hear about that?"

"Out in Wyoming? With her dad and brother?"

"Of course," I say, shaking my head like an agreeable old man. But the fact is I don't remember Delia going moose hunting in Wyoming. Or anywhere else. I *do* recall she's an avid outdoorswoman, and that she and Clara love to fish the lakes and rivers up here. Especially the steelhead run on the Burnt Wood River in springtime.

"Anyway," Clara says, sitting back again but still speaking softly, "you should compliment her."

"I'm sure I'll have good reason to."

And it does smell delicious. Meaty and like cardamom and onion. Their home is lovelier than ever. From where I sit, I can see the mass of Lake Superior beyond the lights of town. It meets the horizon in the uneasy darkness.

"The lake's been tumultuous lately," she says. "There's no ice at all. Too much wave action."

"Same thing down our way," I say, and recognize as I do that I sound, perhaps for the first time, like a doddering old man.

"Are you okay, Dad?"

"Why do you ask?"

She cocks her head and gives me a good once-over, her expression a duplicate of her mother. "You seem sad."

"I'm the opposite of that, kiddo. I couldn't be happier."

She settles even further into the couch. Wraps an afghan around her shoulders.

"Tell me about sabbatical?" she says.

Ingrid and Delia stroll in, each carrying a pint of beer. Delia raises her glass and says "Skol!" I raise mine in return.

"Your father's going to retire after sabbatical," Ingrid says.

"Really? That's wonderful! Think of all the time you'll have to write."

Ingrid and I exchange glances. I know she's asking me if now's the time to tell her, and before I send my own answering glance, Clara says, "What's going on with you two? You're acting weird. Is everything all right?"

"It is," I say. "We just haven't talked much about what we'll do. It's a new development."

"I heard some pretty big stories on the way up here," Ingrid says, looking past me and on to Clara. "But nothing's going on. Your father has a lot on his mind."

"Starting with wondering how you two are doing," I say. "Delia, Clara was just telling me about your trip to Wyoming last fall."

Delia looks at me, then quickly at Clara and Ingrid. With those glances, it's clear to me I've just embarrassed myself. Ingrid as much as announces my plight by getting up and coming to sit beside me, putting her hand on my hair and brushing it behind my ear.

Delia's voice softens and she says, "We were up in the Bighorns. My dad and my brother and me. My dad's business partner has a place just outside Sheridan, and they've been hunting there since I was a girl. Last year they let me come along, and what do you know? I bagged a big old bull."

"We've still got a hundred pounds of moose meat in the deep freeze. And that's after eating it every day since she got back," Clara says.

"Not *every* day," Delia says. "But you've made your point. Tomorrow night we'll order pizza." She takes a long gulp of her beer and adds, "I'm sure it's ready. Should we go ahead and eat?"

Some dread has come over us, and we move to the kitchen to

scoop our bowls of stew like a band of pilgrims moving not toward a feast but rather into the famine of a long winter. I'm the pox. I know this. And as they grab their bowls and spoons and as Clara ladles, her eyes misty through the steam rising from the Dutch oven, I say, "Rather than moping and dodging, I'm just going to tell you what's going on."

I sit on one of the bar stools under the countertop, set my glass of beer in front of me, and speak without looking up from it. I tell Clara and Delia about yesterday's diagnosis. I tell them about sitting in Doctor Zheng's office and how I've been getting more forgetful and irritable. I tell them I'm all right, really, and that I was going to wait until Annika got here tomorrow, but I didn't want to ruin our evening.

"Ruin our evening?" Clara says.

I look up from my beer. She's leaning on the counter, searching for the punchline that's not coming.

"I wish you wouldn't have told them yet, Jon."

I turn to Ingrid.

"You said you were going to wait."

The pall I've cast over the room is as rich as the stew's aroma, and I don't know how I've caused it. "I told you because I didn't want everyone wondering what was wrong. I wanted us to enjoy our dinner and play a few games of euchre and be *happy*. That wasn't going to happen with all the suspicion in the air." If my voice sounds half as pleading as it feels, I've never been so pathetic. Judging by the wounded look on my daughter's face, I'm mistaken about everything. Both Ingrid and Delia are silent now, staring at their bowls as I, only moments ago, stared at my beer.

Clara sighs. Twice, three times, then starts to cry. She wipes her cheeks as she walks down the hallway to her bedroom. I look at Ingrid, who finally looks back, but only for a moment before she sets her stew on the table. She comes over and gets my bowl and brings it across the room, too. She motions for me to come sit by her, and when Clara returns, the three of us are seated at their sturdy table.

She's holding what appears to be a frame. Hugging it, really, with arms folded around it and to her chest. Her tears are steady now, but she's not weeping. These are the stoic tears she made famous as a teenager, those days that suddenly seem a lifetime ago. I know enough to wait, which I do for as long as it takes her to gather herself. She moves her hands to the opposite edges of the frame and holds it out in front of her and studies whatever's there for a long time. In the silence of the room I hear the bubble of the stew ten feet away on the stovetop.

By the time Clara turns the frame around so I can see what's inside it, her tears have stopped. "This is the surprise we wanted to give *you*," she says, taking a couple steps toward me.

I take my glasses out of my shirt pocket and hurry them on and look at what's before me: a portrait of Clara sitting in the leather chair in their living room, the dog lying at her feet, her legs crossed and her hands folded over the little paunch of her belly.

"This is your work, Del?" I say.

She nods.

There's a warmth to the painting, which is not in Delia's usual monochromatic and almost menacing style but rather is full of light and something like *hope*. I study it a long time, smiling at the way all the light—from the window, from the sconce on the wall, from the dog's upturned eyes, from her own eyes—seems to gather on her lap.

"It's beautiful," I say. "Both the subject and the painting itself."

Clara hands it to me. "It's for you."

"It's too beautiful for me."

"Don't you get it, Dad?"

I glance at Ingrid, who's crying now, too. "I don't."

Clara leans over and touches my cheek like a parent might her child, then lowers her hand to her belly in the painting. She takes my hand and stands tall and puts my fingers on her real-life belly.

Again, I glance at Ingrid, who's now smiling through her tears. To Clara I say, "You mean?"

She nods and I set the painting on the table and stand and hold her.

"My goodness," I whisper into her ear. "My goodness." What I don't say, for all the obvious reasons, is that where one life ends, another begins. But the thought of her news gives me enormous courage. So much that I begin to laugh. I laugh until I start hiccupping and when I finally get ahold of myself everyone else is laughing, too. Laughing and crying and talking and listening and hugging and holding hands around the table.

By the time I learn it's a little boy, and that he'll be born in August, and that his name is already Erik Johannes, we've finished our moose stew and the loaf of homemade bread, and our beer's been replaced with coffee, and the homemade toffee Delia usually makes at Christmastime is only crumbs on the dessert platter.

All's forgiven. All's right again.

*

Clara was the only one of my own children who took to ski jumping, and only for three winters. We spent those seasons at Chester Bowl, she and I, jumping on the bunny and rabbit ears with a group of five or ten other kids, and though she had fun she was as likely to build snowmen or play along the creek's edge as she was to take a morning of jumping seriously, and at the age of nine she decided to try cross country skiing instead. Her senior year of high school she was a state high school champ.

She had scholarship offers to go to college at places like New Hampshire and Middlebury and Northern Michigan, but she decided to stay in Duluth and go to St. Scholastica. Her reasons, as I remember them, were mostly vague and unconvincing. But what father wouldn't want his daughter so close by? She lived with us until she was twenty years old, when she met Delia and got an apartment downtown. Moving up here to Gunflint is the most daring thing she's ever done. At least that's how she describes it.

We're walking along the Old Toboggan Road, Clara and I, with her dog heeling beside her on the dirt road. This track is mostly cocooned by the forest around it, but occasionally it opens to the long view, down the hill, and you can see across the lake to the horizon. I reckon from up here it's a fifty-mile view. For all the day's bluster, the clouds are scuttling toward that horizon now, leaving a palette of star-speckled sky so bright even the brilliant moon can't dim it.

"Are you scared, Dad?" So far, excepting a few pleasantries about the moose stew and the cold night, we've walked mostly in silence, something we've always been good at. "Because I am. For you and me both."

"You don't have anything to be afraid of, sweetheart. You're healthy and strong and as happy as I've seen you."

"Well, you're not."

"I'm okay."

"You're the worst liar I've ever met."

"Actually, I'm one of the best." I mean to sound teasing, but instead it comes out like a threat, and she takes a sideways step across the road. The dog moves in lockstep with her.

After another minute of silence, she says, "What's it mean?"

"My sickness? Well, likely it'll come on slowly. It'll take a while before I'm debilitated. But I'm already forgetful. You saw that earlier."

"But you've always been forgetful."

"Not like I'll become. In fact, hold on a minute." I take her by the shoulders and frame her in the break in the trees, with the lake and sky behind her. I step backward halfway across the road and ask her to look up at the moon, which she does. I notice the dog looks where she does.

"This is weird, Dad."

"Shush," I say, and to keep it not weird I resist the temptation to kneel on the spot. "Just let me look at the woman you've become. Let this be the memory I take with me."

I haven't intended to be so melodramatic, but the fact is seeing my girl, and learning she's pregnant, has made me especially nostalgic, and I want desperately to hold this night in some reserve.

The dog turns her snout over her other shoulder. She moves to face the direction we've just walked from, the road behind us curving into a dense thicket of aspen and pine.

"What is it, girl?" Clara asks.

Now the moon makes shadows of them both on the road. The dog growls, but barely, and somewhere up on the hillside a choir of wolves lets loose their baleful howls. The dog cocks her head and her ears flip forward.

"How close are they?" I whisper.

"If I were guessing, I'd say they're on the Burnt Wood. Up on one of the ridgelines. So, a half-mile away?"

Then, as suddenly as the first chorus came, there is an answer from down the hill. A lone voice. The dog jumps and faces that direction. She takes a couple steps backward so her rump is right on Clara's leg. She has pinned her ears back now and sharpened her eyes and her shadow has fallen into Clara's.

"Good girl," Clara says, and we stand for a moment in the silent moonlight.

And then we hear it—so very near—the snapping of twigs and the whooshing of snow before the unmistakable skitter of stones on the dirt road, two leaping steps, and again the wolf enters the woods. It's so close that I swear I can feel the breeze of its passing. When I look back from the darkness, Clara is smiling broadly and the dog is ready to launch. But my daughter squats and rests her hand on Dolly's hackles. She leans over and kisses her. Or whispers in her ear. And pacified, the dog sits, her ears thrust forward again.

"Good girl," she says again. Then in a normal voice she says to me, "What a bonus."

This morning—a lifetime ago—has met its other end. And her smile almost tricks me into believing that what leapt across the road was just a wolf.

IV

Lake Placid

I ONLY EVER LOST A SKI IN FLIGHT ONCE. When I remember it now—and usually the thought comes unbidden—I have the phantom sensation of my tibia and fibula breaking again through opposite sides of my leg. Which is what happened in real life, in the first days of 1980, in Lake Placid, New York, on the last jump I ever took.

We left Minneapolis two days after Christmas. Pops picked me up in Dinkytown at midnight, Anton already spread out under a sleeping bag with a pillow scrunched against the door in the backseat, asleep like a cat on a couch. Which left Pops and me in the front, able to catch up. We talked about my plans for the summer, which included finally moving to Duluth. In the year since Madison, I'd given myself over seriously to ski jumping, and though I knew we were headed to New York for the Olympic trials, I also believed I had no chance and that we were likely playing out a fantasy of Pops's that he never had the opportunity to fulfill himself. Certainly, I saw it as my swan song, that long trip to New York.

Somewhere in Wisconsin I finally dozed off, and I didn't wake until we were on the outskirts of Chicago before the sun came up. Our reason for leaving in the middle of the night had been to miss rush hour in that city, but whether because of the freezing rain or commuters or some other reason altogether we didn't, and found ourselves in crushing traffic. What should have taken an hour took three, and by the time we had the windy city in our rearview, Pops had regaled us again with a retelling of the Great Chicago Heist. But it was a different rendition than the one we were used to. He was subdued and melancholic. Like the story had bended and now, instead of being an exciting thriller, it was a sad tragedy.

I was driving by then, over the Skyway bridge and into Indiana. We stopped at a McDonald's in Gary, and Anton came up to the passenger side while Pops slept until Detroit, when he took over again, driving us through customs in Windsor and on to the Trans-Canada Highway. We passed through London and Preston and then to the Western Toronto suburbs and through the city itself. Four hours later, and in the dark of night again, we crossed back into the States at Ogdensburg, New York, where we had dinner in a roadside pub and watched, on the grainy television behind the bar, a period of the Red Army hockey team playing the Rangers at Madison Square Garden. We still had a couple hours to go, so Pops ordered four cups of coffee for the road and emptied them into his thermos once we were back in the car.

In the years since, I've imbued our arrival in the mountain village soon to host the Olympics with a magnificent purpose and no small amount of revelation. But if I'm honest, and strip away the mawkishness, I can only conjure up the dark and quiet highways and the specter of the mountains shrouding the night with a low-hanging halo of extra darkness. Well, that and the prospect and promise of what I was sure would be my humbling in the week of tournaments ahead.

For all that remains dubious, two prolonged details emerge. One, of course, was the ski jumping, which proved not only cataclysmic but was also, unmistakably, the best performance of my life. But even above those many jumps, those storied competitions, there was the fact of Anton. The resolute jumper. The fierce competitor. The taker of names. The unhappy brother.

*

We checked into a motel outside town, unloaded our skis and gear in the foggy and too-warm night, and settled into our home for the next week. Pops rearranged the furniture, shoving the bed against one wall and putting the TV in the closet so we could wax our skis on the dresser. Anton did his first, melting the wax on the base of a hot iron so it dripped across the base of his skis, then using the same iron to melt it into the grooves. His seriousness was something new. Something fierce and final and the quality I still associate most with him.

When he finished, he took his skis outside and leaned them against the window. While I melted the wax onto the base of my own skis, I could see his silhouette out in the fog, the tip of a cigarette flaring with each puff like an SOS signal.

"What's up with Anton?" I asked Pops, who was lying on the bed reading a brochure advertising the new Olympic village.

"What do you mean?" He didn't look up, or out at him.

"He's hardly said a word since we left Minneapolis."

"Not everyone has the gift of gab you do, Jonny Boy."

"I'm not talking about any gift of gab. He's miserable."

Now he did look up from his brochure. "What do you think's wrong with him? His brother's squatting in a goddamn flophouse. He can't hardly learn anything at school. His mother's more or less quit talking to *anyone*. She spends half her life in bed, the other half imitating a goddamned ghost. Even his red-headed girlfriend just broke things off. All he's got is this." He meant us. He meant Lake Placid and ski jumping and the hot wax on our skis. "He's focused, something you might want to get a little more of."

"You want me to get more focused? On *what*? I don't even know why we're here."

He sat up and lit a cigarette of his own. "We're here because you're a good goddamned ski jumper. There's no reason you can't jump with anyone out there tomorrow."

"And what about Anton?"

"I just told you about Anton." He took a long drag on his cigarette. "You'd have me leave him at home with your mother?"

"I mean can he jump with anyone out there? Have you considered the possibility that he's going to be humiliated?"

"He's fifteen years old. That's too young to be humiliated."

I didn't dare point out what happened to me when I was fifteen. Instead, I checked the wax on my skis.

"And anyway, he's damn good himself. Watch out he doesn't kick your ass."

"I hope he does," I said, and brought my skis outside.

Anton was smoking another cigarette, exhaling a series of smoke rings.

"Looks like you about got the valley full of smoke," I said, gesturing at the fog, which hung lower and heavier than when we'd arrived. "Since when do you smoke? Does Pops know?"

"Fuck Pops. I don't care if he knows."

"Fuck Pops? Not this again."

He flipped the butt out into the parking lot. "You bring the scraper out?" he said.

I had it in my back pocket, and offered it to him. He started scraping the wax from the bottom of his skis. It came off in parchment-like curls the same color as the fog.

"Why are you so pissed off?"

"I'm not," Anton said.

"Why aren't you talking to me?"

He looked up from where he squatted. "I don't hardly know you anymore, Jon. I haven't seen you since last summer."

"I was just over for Christmas."

"Yeah," he said, "long enough to eat all the krumkake and then leave again."

A bench sat beside the door, and I plopped down on it. "That's fair."

He stopped scraping his skis and looked up at me. "Why do you hate us?"

"I don't hate you, Anton. How could you even say that?"

"Whatever," he said. "It doesn't matter."

"Of course it matters."

He got back at his skis, using the rounded corner of the scraper on the grooves.

The night settled so still and so quiet I could hear the rasp of the wax as it curled out of the grooves. I could hear Anton's spit land on the pebbled walkway before the motel. I could hear the faint ring of a telephone somewhere inside. I could hear the ice melting on the roof, and its patter as it fell into the gutter. After he finished one ski, he started on the other, going from tip to tail in a single motion. I could practically see the subject change in his mind before he said, "What've you heard about these jumps?"

"That they're perfect."

He nodded and took another pass at his ski. "Is it stupid that I'm here?"

"What do you mean?"

"I mean, how bad am I gonna get my ass kicked?"

"You're not gonna get your ass kicked. You just won't let that happen. In fact, I bet you a hundred dollars you finish inside the top twenty."

"I'll take that bet," he said and then started a third pass, but paused. "You could win."

"That's ridiculous."

"The three best jumpers are all over in Europe now. They've already made the team. That leaves only ten or twelve guys who stand a chance. You're one of them."

His confidence staggered me, and for a moment—a kind of perfect moment—I believed him. But then I cleared the thought. "I can think of twenty guys who are better than me. I've had only fifty jumps this winter. And those on a forty-meter. We'll get only a few training rides before we have to make 'em count tomorrow. I don't like my chances."

He nodded his head like he was agreeing with me. "You're a goddamned crybaby. Grow a pair."

He went back to work on his ski. I peeled an inch from the base of mine with a fingernail. "How do you know about the guys in Europe?"

"I heard Pops talking to Ma. It'll be a miracle if she's still at home when we get back, for all the fighting they've been doing."

A semi truck passed. A door opened down the row, and someone came out and walked to the office with an ice bucket in his hand. A minute later, he came back, cradling it like a baby.

"Who are the guys in Europe?"

"Jim, John, Chris."

I couldn't help doing the math. Counting the guys who were left. I'd understood, when Pops called to ask me if I wanted to go, that there were four spots to be had. The three jumpers Anton had just named were shoo-ins. They were the best. I thought the rest of the competition was for one spot. I was mistaken.

"Look at you," he said. "You want me to get you a piece of paper and a pencil? Better yet, I could just tell you who's left to beat. I seem to know fuckall more than you."

"You're a goddamned Rhodes Scholar, I guess."

"When it comes to ski jumping, you bet your ass I am."

"All right then, tell me this: how are *you* gonna do? You've got it all figured out for me, how about holding up a mirror?"

"I got just one goal."

I waited for him without asking what.

"I wanna go a hundred meters on that big bastard. That's it. That's all I want."

*

That night Pops slept on the floor while Anton and I shared the queen bed. I can still see him lying on the floor, an ashtray on his thin, bare chest, smoking cigarettes one after the next.

I hardly slept myself, wracked as I was by sudden expectations. Where they came from, beyond Anton's cajoling, I can't imagine. My record over the previous year, since Matti Rantannen had singled me out in Madison, had been steady if not remarkable. During the winter of 1978–79, I won a few competitions in the Midwest on smaller hills and had jumped well on the titans—in Iron Mountain and Ishpeming, Michigan, and Westby and Eau Claire, Wisconsin— but not so as I might have realistically expected to compete for a spot on the national Olympic team. Many, if not most, of those trips I took with Noah and his father.

Curiously, as my results improved, my passion for the sport ebbed. So much of the pleasure of those winter mornings had been tied to being in my father's and brother's company, and my ascendant performances came with their absence. Perhaps that's how it had to be. Perhaps the long shadow Pops's own ski jumping career cast over our family was always going to eclipse my own accomplishments, and so in order to excel, in order to reach my potential, I had to be out from under that shadow. Who knows? Whatever incited my improvement, it had come without Pops's watchful gaze. And without Anton's cheer. And so had little meaning.

Even with all of Anton's animus, being together again in Lake Placid that first night brought me back to the simplicity of it all, if not the joy. This was true even before we took our first jumps. Hell, it was true before we *saw* the jumps, which happened the morning following that night of lost sleep.

The fog hadn't yielded overnight, and we drove out the valley road to the jumping arena called Intervale. Not until we had parked right up under them did we see the towering scaffolds, so dense was the fog. I remember marveling at the audacity and modernness of the complex. The jumps we grew up on were rickety things, seemingly made of matchsticks, each as old as the folks who helped keep them upright—folks with names like Selmer and Olaf and Jakob. The jumps in Lake Placid, though, were made of concrete and steel and glass, like they descended from the Chicago skyline Pops viewed the last time he stood with purpose atop the inrun at Soldier Field.

"Goddamn, they look like spaceships," Pops said, stepping out of the Ford and twisting his face up. "And there's no snow anywhere," he added, looking at the ground and into the trees. Even at that late hour of the morning, the forest surrounding the jumps and certainly the mountains in the distance lay blanketed in that still stubborn fog, but I could tell he was right. The ground was wet and steaming.

"Are we gonna be able to jump?" Anton asked, taking his skis from the rack atop the car.

Pops shrugged and lit a cigarette and pointed ahead, to the smaller jump, where a parade of jumpers in red and blue jumpsuits hiked up the inrun. "Looks like it," Pops said.

Anton had put his gear on at the motel, so he headed straight over to the queue, shouting over his shoulder that I should get my ass in motion. Pops looked at me and tilted his head and said, "I guess he's right."

I grabbed my duffel from the trunk and my skis from the rack intent on doing just that. But before I could head to the locker room, Pops said, "Jon, do you know why we came out here?"

"I believe so."

"Well, what do you think?"

I looked up at the ninety-meter jump, under which we still stood. "I think this is a big damn jump."

"No bigger than Pine Mountain. Not even as big, in fact. It just looks like it." He tapped me on the shoulder. "And that's not what I'm talking about anyway. You know that."

"I know why you brought us out here," I said. "I'll give it my best shot."

"That's all I've ever wanted you to do, bud. And if you were asking for my opinion of things, I'd say you're as good as the best guy here. Show your brother how it's done?"

"Sure, Pops. I'll try."

"I believe it. Now go on and get ready. I'll find the coaches' stand. Look for me when you get up there."

But by the time I got to the top of the jump, I couldn't find him. The fog had lowered, revealing the distant mountaintops but not the bottom of the inrun. These were the first peaks I'd ever laid eyes on, and I breathed them in. A new kind of oxygen filled my lungs. When I looked back down, the green light on the inrun sidewall flicked for a new jumper, and away he went. Then another and another. One after the next. When it was finally my turn, I narrowed my focus on the tracks in front of me, how they disappeared just fifty feet below. By that point in my young life, I'd stood in the starting gate of various jumps many thousands of times. I'd been afraid and excited, nonplussed and unmoved. But I'd not often felt what I did in that moment at Lake Placid, which was not fear or excitement or anything else, but only *resignation*. It was welcoming, and I grabbed hold of the wooden gate and pulled myself into the track. Just one of more than seventy jumpers vying for those four spots.

Only it wasn't *my* ambition, one of those spots. It never had been. What I'd always wanted from ski jumping—the thrill of the speed, the ecstasy of flight, my father's respect, my brother's admiration— those things had disappeared. The simplicity of that realization, the sadness that came with it: together those things inspired a calmness in me I'd not much felt since Pops had been sent away for my crime. And that calmness carried into the flights of that week. Maybe even that first one, in the fog on the morning of the first day of the trials. I'd almost call what attended me grace. It was a flawless jump. Past the K-point. A leap that, paired with another like it, would have won me a medal in the very Olympics I was competing to be a part of. The most perfect jump of my life, and one almost no one glimpsed. Even Pops, when I got back to the top of the landing hill and despite his having been right on the coaches' stand, said, "Looked good from the bump?"

"It was all right," I said, and started heading up for another training jump.

But they were already halting practice. Between the fog and the imminence of the first competition, they cut us off. I went back into the locker room and got a cup of coffee and found Anton sitting in the corner.

"What do you think?" I said, taking a seat on the bench next to him.

"Jump's amazing."

"How many rides did you take?"

"Three," he said. "You?"

"Just one."

"I guess you better be ready."

"I guess so," I said, and sat back with my coffee, took a long, tight-lipped sip. "I'm ready," I added.

He let a little smirk come across his face. "Yeah, I saw your jump. You bottle that, and we'll be coming back here in February."

It had been a long time since Anton said a kind thing, never mind a very flattering one. "How about your jumps?" I asked.

"That fog is freaky, huh? You can't even see the take off from the start. You can barely see the landing from the air."

"From where I was flying, I couldn't see the landing hill at all."

"Now you're King Kong? Well, good. Here . . ." He reached into his duffel and tossed me a bib. Number nineteen.

"What number are you?"

He unzipped his warmup to show the bib already across his chest. "Number one. Good luck."

"Follow my lead," he said.

There would be four tournaments, one that day on the seventy-meter, another on the same hill the next afternoon, then two on the big hill the following Friday and Saturday. We had only an hour before the first tournament got under way, so we just sat in the locker room sipping coffee and watching the anxious faces of our competitors. I knew plenty of the guys but had never seen just as many. They'd come from as far away as Steamboat Springs and Winter Park, Colorado, they'd come from any of a dozen towns in the Midwest, the guys I knew, and they'd come from places like Dartmouth College, the University of Wyoming, and Northern Michigan University, places that I'd never heard of before I saw their team jackets. And to a man they were focused and fierce-eyed and as they did their plyos in the parking lot outside, I noticed their hops. Guys not taller than five foot eight who could have dunked a basketball.

Probably I should have shrunk beside so much competition. Or under my brother's teasing. Or under Pops's steady and disarming gaze. But what I felt instead transcended expectations. Mine or anyone else's. I could only replay my jump of that morning. The effortlessness. The lightness. And because I'd executed it with hardly a conscious thought, I felt ready to duplicate it. I'd just close my eyes and feel the same thing.

Fifteen minutes before the competition began, a call went out for jumpers to start heading up the hill and for the judges to take their places. Anton and I laced up our boots and buffed our goggles with the hem of our turtlenecks and checked our chinstraps and gloves and, without much more to do than that, followed directions to the tower of the jump, where a hidden staircase switchbacked inside the concrete support tower. When we reached the top, we stepped into the many-windowed enclosure and awaited the call to get to the starting gate. The fog in the valley had lifted or blown away and all that stood around us were the glinting Adirondacks.

Before Anton left, he came over and put his hand on my shoulder and made sure no one else was listening. "I'm going to go seventy-five meters, Jon. You go eighty."

I remember looking at him like he was some sort of savant. "If you go seventy-five, I'll go eighty-five," I said, not sure where this braggart had been my whole life.

"What if I go eighty myself?"

"Then I'll give you my Bronco when we get home," I said.

"Including a full tank of gas?" Then he added "Vroom, vroom" and was out the door. I followed a few minutes later and stood in the starting gate below him as the announcer called his name and alerted the crowd—there must have been a couple thousand spectators in the stadium below—that the first jumper in the day's competition was also its youngest.

He took a long, steadying breath, Anton did, and reached for the two-by-fours staked on the edge of the starting gate. He gripped one with each hand and closed his eyes for as long as he'd breathed.

338

When he opened them again, he looked at me and winked and pulled into the tracks without lowering his goggles.

Turning into the track, he settled his inrun position. Being as short and slight as he was, he appeared almost to fold himself inside out. Every part of him aligned with the perfectly straight tracks. His shoulders and arms and hands, his knees, it was as though his limbs were rulers. As he neared the take off, I thought I could see an even bolder move forward. A line of light appeared between his heels and the blocks on his skis. His ten fingers curved inward. And just when it looked like he'd not move from that position, he discharged. In the time it took me to blink away my disbelief, he was in his flight position and rising. He was so light and easy, like a kite on a hard wind. As he sailed from view, the jumper standing next to me, someone I'd never seen before, said, "That little shit's got *balls*."

A few seconds later he emerged on the outrun. Just a speck now in his blue jumpsuit, slowing to a stop out by the stadium seats. I could barely hear the announcer say, "What a whale of a start for fifteen-year-old Anton Bargaard, here all the way from Minneapolis. The jury's going to have a tough decision to make after that. It looked to be almost all the way down to the critical point." There was a pause, the static of the starter's walkie-talkie.

Then the announcer's voice on the PA: "Seventy-nine and one-half meters for Anton Bargaard. A tremendous jump. No one saw that coming!"

I felt charged and inspired by Anton. And like I'd better damn well keep up. Regarding the keeping up, it was the first time I'd ever felt *that* particular fire, and as I climbed the last section of stairs to the start gate, and awaited my turn while the jumpers between us went, I resolved on a very specific focus. I didn't picture my own jump, as was my practice, but rather Anton's. The quickness with which he launched, the lightness in flight, the rising where he should have descended. I'd imitate him.

339

And so, dreamlike, I put my boots in my bindings. I slid the cables up behind my heels and threw down the front throws and put my goggles down over my helmet and took my own deep breath while closing my eyes to the blue skies above. *Shins*, I thought, meaning I wanted to feel pressure from the tongue of my boot hard upon them in my inrun position. *Eyes*, I thought, meaning I wanted them focused and looking about twenty feet beyond the tips of my skis. *Ribs*, meaning I wanted as many of them as possible resting across the flat of my thighs. *Stay low low low low, arms on your ass.* I thought it for as long as it would take me to get down the inrun, five or six seconds. Then I slid forward and reached for the two-by-fours and shook my head clear of the sensation of my own discharge from that crouched inrun position. I trusted the memories in my muscles. I trusted my instincts.

I suppose one of the things traveling down that inrun with me was a sense of needing to best Anton, not just imitate him. Certainly, from this vantage and all the years between then and now, it seems impossible that it would have been otherwise. I was as inspired by him as I was worried I *wouldn't* match him, which I didn't. Not on that first jump. I went seventy-nine meters, and by the time I climbed back up the landing hill, I was already sitting in third place after only thirty jumpers, with most of the best yet to come.

When I saw Pops, he stood outside the locker room with his hand on Anton's shoulder. They both wore shit-eating grins and my brother was nodding his head like it was attached to a metronome.

"Nice jump," I said to Anton.

"You too," he said.

"What'd you feel, Jon?" Pops asked.

"Like my blood was sand."

"My blood was ice water," Anton said.

*

Before the second round began, I went and sat in the car and closed
my eyes and tried to clear my mind. It'd been as heavy as my blood,
my mind had, and sitting there with the eight-track playing, I took
the cap off and let some of the pressure out. I might even have dozed
for as tired as I was, but sure enough I climbed the tower in time for
my second-round jump.

I looked down at Pops, standing on the coaches' stand with his
hand raised. When he dropped it, I imagined his happy smile and absorbed it as I steered into the tracks. I remember the inventory of my
body, and feeling the calm in it, of getting lost in it to such an extent
that I almost forgot to jump. Which turned out to be a good thing,
when paired with my determination not to leap too late, because it
incited an explosiveness I wouldn't otherwise have mustered. I immediately found myself in full flight, high above the knoll, rocketing
and like a paper airplane at once. The landing hill blurred far below
me, not coming into focus until I spread my arms, wing-like, and
landed in a deep telemark.

Eighty-five meters. Longer than any jump in the first round, and
good enough, by the end of the competition, for third place. Anton
finished tenth.

The Bargaards were the talk of the first day. We were whispered
about and pointed at by the jumpers changing into the college and
national team warmups. We were approached by the reporter from
the *New York Times* who wanted to know if we'd been sandbagging
back in the Midwest for the past year, if that was all part of our plan.

As if we had a plan. I just told that reporter that our coach was
our dad, and he was a ski jumper, too.

That night, at a restaurant in the village, not far from the ice rink
that would, some weeks later, be host to the most momentous sporting event in United States history, as we raised glasses of Coke and
cut our steaks, Pops sat back like he had just been crowned the king
of Norway. When the waiter asked why we were in town, Pops told

him we were just stamping our passports to come back in February, when we'd parade with our countrymen in the opening ceremonies not two blocks from where we then sat. This elicited a free dessert, courtesy of the restaurant manager, who hailed from Eau Claire, Wisconsin, where he'd ski jumped as a boy.

It all seemed right and wonderful and the next evening, after the second round of competition, in which I'd again taken third place, we returned to the same spot and ordered the exact same meal from the same waiter even though it was considerably more expensive than our usual fare.

Later that night, after Anton and I hit the sack, Pops dragged the phone over to the window and called Bett. He whispered into the receiver, looking over his shoulder and through the moonlight to check he hadn't woken us. Because I was so curious, I feigned sleeping, rolling on my back so I could hear with both ears. He spoke like a drunkard, giddy and silly and incredulous at how we were both doing. He told her about the first two competitions and the beauty of the mountains and Olympic Village and the fine steaks we were feasting on each night. The most telling part of their conversation came after he mentioned talking to Matti Rantannen—the head coach of the U.S. Ski Team, he reminded her—and how Matti reported hearing about my results the previous winter, and that though he hadn't expected me to come here and beat the boys on his team, he wasn't surprised either. He said that if I kept it up, I'd be leaving Lake Placid with the rest of the team for a few weeks in Europe.

You might think, given the unexpectedness of those developments, that Bett's return questions might have come around to me. But I don't think they did. After Pops described my jumps with an excitement he could barely contain, in a voice he could hardly keep a whisper, he waited while Bett spoke on the other end of the line. I could see his head nodding against the light through the window, could see him tap a cigarette from his pack on the table and light it

up, and could hear, as he exhaled that first draw, a kind of acquiescence in his voice when he responded, "Well, he's doing fine, too,"
and proceeded to fill her in on her younger son. They talked until I
fell asleep.

*

The next five days were allotted for training on the big hill. Each
morning we drove to Intervale and took our turns. And if at first
glance on that foggy morning of our arrival the jumps looked like
skyscrapers, well, the elevator with the 180-degree views shooting
up the concrete column that supported the jump only reinforced the
notion. It was futuristic. It was sensational.

Anton had never jumped a ninety-meter hill before, and his light
quickness on that high-flying mammoth made him a natural. He
got up over the knoll like he had a hang glider's wings affixed to his
back. And though he possessed every natural instinct a flyer might,
and though he was fearless, he couldn't quite catch up to the top-
rung jumpers.

I was in that rung myself. We drifted toward each other like mi-
gratory birds, jumping in succession at the end of each practice
round. The coaches, especially Matti, studied and analyzed our
jumps, a clipboard always under his arm like he was some sort of
professor. Often, after a jump, he'd give me a free word of advice.
Being the boss, he could do what he wanted, but each time he gestured for me to come over and then explained some finer point, the
boys actually *on* his team would scoff and scowl and stomp off like
jilted beaus. Matti spoke of ski jumping like a physics problem, and
between his accent and the calculus of his method, his advice mainly
found my ignorance. It was then I'd step over to Pops and ask him
to translate.

If Matti was professorial, Pops was a poet, and he'd describe
for me, with startling accuracy, what he saw, which almost always

mirrored what I'd felt. Like he'd taken my jumps himself. Or at least like he once had. He knew where the glitches in the tracks were, where the headwind offered the best air, where the landing hill ice almost set me on my ass. What was even more clairvoyant, he knew how my temper was evolving. He knew that while I matched the ski team guys jump for jump, and while my nerves crescendoed late in the week, what I needed wasn't Matti's minor technological adjustments but rather to divine a fuller sensation of my entire body and spirit, or to summon the jumps of my past and of my dreams, all the best ones.

Pops was of course paying equal attention to Anton, whose demeanor resembled mine in no way at all. Though he was jumping better than he ever had before—by miles, even—he presented no threat to the top six guys. His reaction was not one of deference or acquiescence but rather to get his teeth in the tongues of our boots. This was no new posture for Anton. From the time we returned from the Torrs' place four years earlier, he'd been like that. Irascible, sneaky, even furious sometimes. All that energy went into his jumping in Lake Placid, for better and for worse. If I was saintly in my disposition, my brother was a scoundrel. And Pops managed him with all the discernment of a great prophet, feeding Anton bits of hellfire while he fed me tufts of heavenly clouds.

I suppose he did that for the rest of our lives, which helps account for where we ended up. But during that week, up until the last moment of our togetherness, when I was able to step outside the competition and the coaching and learning, I saw my father for the genius he was. And remained. He loved us equally, if differently, and understood that what motivated and inspired one of us would have inevitably failed the other. Many years after that week in upstate New York, during one of our late-night phone conversations, Pops made several admissions and one observation. He believed it was during that trip he first glimpsed the addictive tendencies that would later haunt Anton, tendencies he deemed failures of his own.

Naturally, I worried about Anton. But I've been friends with enough alcoholics over the years—I'm a writer, after all—to know that there are plenty more likely reasons for his problems, not least Bett's own predisposition to her pills. And as a kid trying, unexpectedly, to make the Olympics, Anton's manic moods in Lake Placid became a disturbance, if not something even more.

But I mentioned that Pops made an admission, too, which, when I remember it, helps me to keep these threads on the loom. It was the last time we ever spoke, at Christmastime. After the usual catching up, he poured himself an egg nog and sat at the kitchen table—I knew the sounds of that old house, even over the phone—and we started talking about ski jumping, as we so often did. Back then, I was spilling out pages of *The Ski Jumpers* at a prolific rate, each one an addition to the teeming failure of it all. Among the many things we touched on was the trip to Lake Placid. We called up the usual memories—the thrills and spills, the long drive out there, the steak dinners—but when we got to the end of that long conversation, I asked him a question I never had before.

"Why'd you take us? What in the world made you think I could compete?" I asked. To which he replied, "I didn't. I thought Anton might be able to someday, though, and I wanted to give him a taste."

I don't think he intended to offend me, but I also never could have imagined that truth. When I said "Really?" even I could hear the defensiveness in my voice.

Pops hurried the conversation ahead, reminding me, as he did so many times over the years, of my triumphs that week, and how he was sure it was his fault as much as mine, having carried with him out to New York the same curse that followed him everywhere. He complimented me on my outstanding performance, as though

I were still that nineteen-year-old kid in need of his father's praise, and not older on that night than he'd been in Lake Placid. And he reminded me that if it hadn't been for that damned toe clip, I would have spent the Olympic fortnight back on the jumps in Lake Placid, and not laid up in bed. "Calamitous," he always used to say. "And not only because it cost you what it did."

I never was sure what he meant by *not only*.

*

On the morning of the third competition, as we left the now-familiar confines of our crowded motel room, the warm, damp weather we'd met upon arriving had been replaced with a sharp cold. The wind was sudden and scary and I noticed it straightaway, but Anton's attention had turned inward. He didn't speak a word that morning, not even when we got to the jump and learned the competition, originally scheduled for eleven, had been postponed. He just got a cup of coffee and took a walk back down the road, smoking a cigarette and sipping his joe.

Most of us kicked a soccer ball around under the big jump, the shadow of which the morning sun stretched twice as long as the height of the tower. We paused when we saw the jury gather outside the locker room at noon, those old timers and former Olympians whose job it was to call the shots, and we speculated about what they'd decree. One of the jumpers, an asshole from some town in New Hampshire, came up to me, the soccer ball under his arm. "They hold this competition, and your brother's gonna end up on Whiteface." He pointed across the valley at the mountain famed for its downhill ski area.

"What's that supposed to mean?"

"He's light as a fucking sparrow is what it means. He gets caught in that headwind . . ." He raised his hand as though a jumper in flight, and rolled it over before exploding his fingers. "That's his arms and legs, scattered all over the place."

"Or," I said, lifting my own hand, "he gets on one, and floats to the screw hole down there." I pointed to the landing hill. "And wins the whole shebang."

"Is that what happens out there on the plains? Some little fucker gets wind and goes?"

"What happens out there? We don't have mountains. That's true. But what we've got is courage. Anton above most."

He dropped the soccer ball onto his foot and juggled it for a few seconds. Then he kicked it high into the air, where the wind blew it fifty feet behind us. "I hope he *does* have courage. I want to see him go in that." Here he traced the trajectory of the ball just a moment before.

"Don't worry. He will." I turned to leave, but paused. "You ever fly Pine Mountain?"

"Nope."

"But you've heard about it? You know how windy it gets up there in Michigan? Michigan being on the plains, as you'd have it. You've heard about the ice? You've heard about how high it flies?"

"You know, this jump has eaten plenty of sad sacks, too. We got wind and ice here just like you."

"I don't know," I said. "If it was blowing like this in northern Michigan—and it usually is—they'd've sent us home the minute the jury finished their circle jerk. That we're even thinking about jumping tells me something."

"I get it," he said. "You're tough guys. I guess we'll see."

"I guess we will."

And we did, of course. Just after New Hampshire jogged off to fetch his windblown ball, the chief of competition called all the coaches and jumpers into the locker room. Five minutes later we were told the competition would begin at two o'clock.

We picked lunch from the Coleman cooler Pops dragged around in the back of the station wagon all week. Ham sandwiches and mealy apples and potato chips. In the hour between lunch and the commencement of the competition, Pops kept himself in Styrofoam cups of coffee from a machine outside the locker room, and Anton slept in the front seat of the car. I took a short jog along the road that ran from the top of the landing hill to the bottom, and from the stadium below paused to look up at those jumps from the vantage of the spectators.

That sport was just plain foolishness. It always seemed so from the bottom of the hill. By the time a jumper reached the end of the inrun, we'd be traveling sixty miles per hour. The take off, which rose fifteen feet above the knoll, which was itself a three-story building, would launch us some twenty or more feet into the air, where we'd glide on our long skis like it was the most natural thing. Our nemeses were wind and icy landing hills, and both were in full effect that day. The flags of forty nations flailed in those gusts around the outrun, which even on the bottom of the hill poured steadily uphill. The landing hill, I remember, was as hard as the concrete road I'd just jogged down.

I was glad to be alone. Glad to have had that conversation with New Hampshire so I might feel the bolster of my confidence. No matter what happened, no matter what call the jury made, I'd be ready to go if for no other reason than I'd talked myself into a corner. And the truth is, the pressure that thought put on me sharpened my mind. Almost as much as the wind and ice. I breathed it in, and jogged back up to the locker room, where I got ready without speaking to anyone.

*

In the opening round of that windblown competition, the first two jumpers fell. The second of them had to be driven away in an ambulance, and we'd later learn he had a broken leg and a torn rotator cuff. When the third jumper also fell, another guy from New Hampshire, I'd learn, the jury met again to consider canceling the event. But they didn't and over the course of the next couple hours, the coaches lined the landing hill with walkie-talkies to keep measure of the headwind and report to the flagman when it was time to send the jumpers. Anton had the longest jump of anyone heading into the last six skiers, of which I was first to go. I remember before I took the elevator up, Pops told me to watch for his hand to drop from the coaches' tower, not the flagman. He promised me good, steady air.

And he delivered. I can still recall the feeling of it, the wild pressure of it, the sensation of being blown away, of being hollow, and howling, and using the strength in my neck and shoulders to pile on my skis out over that landing hill. I'd never before experienced any of that, and I had the longest jump of my life. 110 meters I went, into the lead by far. Anton trailed me at ninety-eight meters. The five jumpers who followed me, including New Hampshire, all came in arears. I watched it from the spot in the stadium I'd earlier jogged to.

When I got back to the locker room, Pops only smiled and nodded and whispered in my ear as he held my arm. "Good air, eh?"

After another short postponement during which the jury convened again, and again decided to push on, the second round commenced. There were a few more crashes and some near misses, but no more ambulances, and after another jump of 110 meters, I won the day. After three competitions, I stood in third place overall, a virtual shoo-in for the team. Anton, after a second-round jump of one hundred meters, was eighth on the day and in the triple-digit club with me. We celebrated that night with our last steak meal, and even my brother, for all his surliness, found a little joy.

I wish I could say that's how it ended in New York, with Anton and Pops and me out for our celebratory steaks. I wish I could say we finished that dinner and went ahead and won the next day, too, and after that we made the long drive home together, the stories of the week already becoming myths with the Eagles playing on the eight-track behind our rollicking laughter. I wish I could say those stories lived on, that we told them over and over through the years. But we didn't, and that's not how it ended. I didn't even drive home with them. We never sat down the three of us again, in a restaurant or in the family car or anywhere else. We never laughed together again, either. Not once.

The next morning brought a calm coldness, a day opposite the one before. The jury never had to consider whether to hold the competition. There were no delays. At eleven o'clock the trial round began, at noon the first competition round, and again I found myself leading after it was done. I felt a sizzling in me, like my blood had been replaced with electrical currents and my bones were conduits. The locker room quieted when I walked through it. Even New Hampshire nodded congratulations.

Of course, if I've learned one thing over the years it's that the story's not over until it is, and in Lake Placid on that cold early January afternoon, as I rode the elevator up to finish what I started, *it* would finish me.

I was last to go. I imagined the judges in the tower had already given me my marks and put their pencils down. I imagined they wanted the uninterrupted pleasure of watching me. I imagined Pops on the receiving end of countless congratulations. I imagined my brother, the laughter of the night before still rumbling in his taut belly, watching from my perch in the stadium below, his hand up to block the magnificent sun, so he might see my triumph and revel in it with me.

What I didn't see were the visualizations I practiced before every jump, the ones ingrained in me by Pops and Olaf Torr and Selmer Dahlson, all the way back at Wirth Park. I didn't close my eyes to see

350

myself soaring through the air, or rub my thighs to feel the twitch in them. I merely put my skis on, and lowered my goggles, and gripped the railing to pull myself into the track. Six seconds later, going as fast as interstate traffic, I jumped for the last time.

I both felt it and saw it, the true weightlessness of my right leg as the tip of that ski vanished from sight. For the first time in my life, I remember a conscious thought in flight. It said: *you're screwed.* Then I rolled upside down and from twenty feet high crashed into the concrete-hard snow. I can't say that I landed like a piece of shattering glass so much as a piece of shattering *body*. And like I've already said, my tibia broke through the skin on one side of my leg, and my fibula through the skin on the other. Same leg, I should make clear. I can still feel the bones in there now, when the barometer lowers or my heart rate rises. But for all the damage done, it was my bloodied face that worried me most when I came to a stop after sliding four hundred feet down the landing hill. For a minute, I thought my nose had been altogether dislodged, same with my right ear, which was made mincemeat after my helmet popped off. The ringing in my head resounded like a full orchestra, until I tried to stand and put the weight of my body on my left foot, to which my other ski was still attached, despite the tip being broken off.

It was then I collapsed. The pain enough to knock me unconscious. A consciousness I didn't regain until I was in that Burlington hospital room some hours later, and even then it was only long enough to see Pops's face before they lowered the gas mask to my nose and mouth.

Night of Nights

MY BODY FELT LIKE THE SNOW above me looked, as alive to the happiness of my brother's company as the flakes were to the breeze in the streetlights. I felt like the dust of a shattered star. Fine and faint and aglow and drifting. The flesh on my calf burned the way it did whenever I exert myself. And only three blocks into our ski and despite the bitter cold, I was sweating like I'd just taken a sauna.

Anton's great idea, at three o'clock in the morning, with Missy and Britt sleeping in his apartment, was to pillage his storage room for cross country skis and boots and poles and then trek across the northside. He wanted to go to Wirth, back to our old stomping grounds, and because I was potted and flying on the coffee I'd drunk—and because after the night we'd had I'd have done anything he asked—we clipped into those bindings and started poling across the Broadway interstate bridge and toward the neighborhood of my childhood. The fast food places and bars and liquor stores and drugstores were deserted but lit up like the Vegas strip. The snow was everywhere blown into gentle waves, some of them four or five feet tall and crashing into bus stop shelters and parked cars. As for cars driving east or west, there were none. We had the city all to ourselves.

We started singing old songs as we pushed through the intersection at Lyndale Avenue, my breath heaving between lyrics. Anton was making a point, one I understood and could even appreciate, and so a block later I made a heroic effort to get a couple ski lengths in front of him and then dropped into a telemark and came to a powdery stop in front of him.

"You win," I said.

"My head grew heavy and my sight grew dim . . ." he sang, a childlike grin on his face.

"If you push that pace, I won't make it to Penn, let alone the parkway, never mind the jump."

"I had to stop for the night!" he finished. "I can't help it. It's been this way since I was fucking six years old. Always trying to keep up with you."

"I don't have to stop for the night. Just slow down. You passed me a long time ago, brother. A long, long time ago."

"All right, we'll slow down. You ready?"

"I'm ready."

But we went only another block before we stopped again. This time on the corner of Bryant Avenue. My senses were twisting and on those uncanny streets, with unfamiliar buildings and stores all around me, I couldn't be sure of the source of my uneasiness.

"Your premonition's right," Anton said.

I looked at him, confused. "The bingo hall?"

"Used to be right here."

I skied from the middle of the street over to the sidewalk and stopped under a Burger King sign. I could as much as see Patollo's ghost rising from the parking lot. The sight of him matched one from a hundred nightmares in the years since I'd killed him. I slid toward him, but he vanished in a whorl of blowing snow.

"Jesus Christ, Jon. There's no historical marker for your murderous old man here. It's a goddamn Burger King. That's all." His voice carried like static between us.

"Is that really how you're going to remember him?"

"Well, he killed him." His voice was sharper, and I could see the exhaustion on his face even from where I stood.

I started to close the ground between us. "His funeral was just tonight, Anton. Our father's funeral was tonight. You gave him a *eulogy*. A goddamn lovely one, I might add . . ." My voice trailed on the snow. I as much as watched it blow off into the night. After a minute I said, "I owe you an explanation. The real story doesn't resemble the one you think you know."

He knocked his ski poles together. "This thing where you get all philosophical? It's exhausting. It's a known fact Pops killed Patollo. That makes him a murderer. It doesn't have to be dressed up in layers of mystery and make believe." He shook his head and buried the tips of his poles again. "Just . . . *why?*"

"It's not that simple. I promise you."

"He *confessed*, Jon. Without so much as a word in his own defense. He let that prosecutor shove a thousand goddamn words down his throat. He could easily have gotten away with a self-defense argument, but he wouldn't even pursue that. It's like he *wanted* to go away." He was almost shouting and in the wild and otherwise empty night his voice sounded just like it did when he used to have tantrums as a little kid, only four notes deeper.

He knocked his ski poles together again. Harder this time, to emphasize his anger. "You blame Ma for everything, but don't you see it's *Jake* who shit the bed? He's the one who fucking tossed us all to the wolves." He closed his eyes and shook his head and looked up into the streetlights and yelled, "Fuck!" Then he pointed a ski pole at me and poked me in the chest with it. "And you, you fucking deserter. You fucking kidnapper."

I nodded. *Go on*, I thought. *Get it all out.*

"You walked out on us and were gone for forty years. For my whole fucking life. Now you think you can come back here and visit your demons? It's bullshit, Jon. You fucking traded out."

I collapsed, snow pouring down the back of my pants and up into the cuffs of my coat, one borrowed from Anton. I tried to shake it out, but shifting around only allowed more to go down my pants.

I might have sat there all night if a city bus hadn't come plowing down Broadway. I hopped up and brushed the snow off and this time did get some of it out of the arms of the coat. The bus drove past, the faces of a pair of third-shifters sitting behind windows running fast with melted snow. It left a huge plume of snow in its wake, and parallel tracks that we'd eventually follow to Golden Valley Road.

But before we resumed our all-night ski, I confessed to my brother what I should have decades earlier. "I'm going to tell you something. You can kill me if you want to."

"Fuck you and your melodrama." He turned to start skiing back to his place.

"We're not going back there. Not until I tell you this. Will you listen?"

He unzipped his coat and pulled out his flask. He unscrewed the cap and took a long, tight-throated drink. He screwed the cap back on without offering me any. "Say it, Jon. Then we can go back to my place and wait for morning. You can get out of here. You can be free again."

I thought of all the ways I could deny wanting to be free of him. Freedom had never been my reason for running away, after all. It was true then as it is now that I loved my brother fiercely, and everything I did for us I did in the name of that love. But he didn't want to hear about all that any more than he wanted to sober up, so I forged ahead on another course instead. On the one that mattered. In a voice as flat as the drone of the now disappearing bus I said, "Pops didn't kill Andrus Patollo."

"Fuck you," he said. "I suppose you think Sheb did."

"Sheb didn't do it." I kept my eyes steady on him.

He finally looked across the sidewalk, knowledge of what I was saying creeping up on him. "No," he said. "I don't believe it."

"There was nothing else to do. Patollo had a gun drawn on them. He was furious. He was going to shoot someone."

Anton only stood there shaking his head.

"Sheb was taunting him. Boasting about having more money and more class. And there was Pops, with all the history between them. Patollo felt like he owed him a lesson, I guess. He was pointing the gun at Pops."

Now Anton wasn't even shaking his head, only staring at the falling snow as if its persistence might yield still other unspoken truths.

"I'm telling you, if I hadn't clubbed him, he would've killed Pops."

I knew I was pleading. To Anton. To the past and the fates and to Pops, who I suddenly imagined was with us in the bright blowing snow. But what else could I do? How could I convince my brother that it wasn't Pops's fault that we all ended up where we did? How could I convince him to forgive our father? How could I ask for forgiveness myself, after so many years of lies? This last question spurred me on to the rest of our confession.

"That's not everything," I said.

He mumbled, and when I asked him what he said he looked up and spoke clearly. "Next you'll tell me you poisoned Ma."

It wasn't a question. More an accusation—which, in its way, wasn't altogether untrue. If that bowling pin to the back of Patollo's skull was the first blow in a chain reaction, Bett's swallowing a bottle of sleeping pills was about the third or fourth echo of Patollo's fat head piking that piece of sharp chrome. With this logic, he was right. I had poisoned her. Or at least set into motion the reason she would eventually do so herself.

He finally looked at me. "Well? What else did you fuck up?"

I thought of Helene, our half-sister, sitting there at the head of the bowling lane, as perplexed and terrified, no doubt, as I was myself. I thought of how much she looked like me, and how, in the half-hour we had to ourselves, she revealed herself to sound like me and even smile like me. And though it wasn't my fault that Pops had fathered this other child—it wasn't even *his* fault, for all he knew about it—I should have told Anton of our sister a long time ago.

I grimaced as I told him on that snowy street.

"A sister? You're full of shit."

"It's why Patollo was here. He was getting rid of her, after Lena Lyng died. She killed herself, too. Or at least that's what Patollo said."

I waited for Anton to say something, but he didn't. I heard a plow clearing Lyndale and looked back in time to see the red and blue safety lights flashing like a cop car. I don't remember how long we stood there in silence, but Anton broke it.

"What was her name?" he asked.

"Helene."

"Helene," he repeated. "How old was she? Or is she? Are you still in touch with her?"

"I'm not. I never heard from her again. But I bet Sheb has."

"You're probably right. Fucking Sheb." Now he looked at me kindly. "Tell me about her? You didn't say how old she was."

"She was twenty back then. Five years older than I was."

"What did you say her name was? Helen?"

"Helene." Then I said, "She looked just like me. Like the female version. Right down to the same button nose. And her voice . . ." I got lost for a moment on the trail back to hearing her speak for the first time. "She talked just like Bett."

"What do you mean she talked like Bett?"

"Just the sound of her voice. And the way she drew her vowels out. It was like they'd grown up in the same house or something."

"And you never saw her again? Why not?"

"I mean, before the cops showed up here"—I pointed at the ground, at the Burger King parking lot—"she and I were left alone while Pops and Sheb came up with a plan. I remember they made us sit with our backs to Patollo, who was just pinned there." I closed my eyes to bring it all back. "That's when we talked, she and I. When she asked me about Pops and you and Bett. When she told me about her mom—about Lena—and when she said she was scared. She didn't know what she was going to do now that Patollo was, well, now that Patollo was gone. She said she just wanted to go back to Chicago. That she hated it here."

"What'd you say?"

"I had no idea what to say."

Anton had a look I'd seen before. Like on the night we left Minneapolis for Duluth and the Torrs' lake place. Or like the night I walked out of Vescio's. Or when he left the hospital room in Vermont with Pops. Something like panic was on his face. Something like misery. Like the entire world was on the verge of swallowing him whole, and maybe I could give him a hand. But then he remembered the countless times I'd failed him, and he steadied his gaze on the snow.

"So she went back to Chicago? Sheb set her up?"

"That'd be my guess."

"Did Ma know about her?"

"She did. But until that day in the basement of the bingo hall, Pops didn't. At least that's what he said."

"And here I thought Pops was always the truth teller."

"What do you mean?"

"I mean he never lied. That was his thing, right? And yet, all these years and he never told me about this half-sister, this other child of his."

"In fairness, neither did Bett."

"I mean, we fucking ate dinner together every Sunday night. Like, for *forty years*."

"Seems like it might've slipped, I agree."

He moved closer to me and spoke beneath the wind. "And *you* killed him? Holy shit."

"I'm sorry I never told you. You could've forgiven Pops a long time ago."

"How did you live with it?"

"I don't know," I admitted. "We all had to find ways to carry on. With our secrets and our lies and all the shit we never told each other."

"I guess you felt like you owed me a shock? After I told you about Ma earlier?"

"I definitely owed you this, but not like you're saying. I should've told you years ago. Decades." I paused, and wondered if what I was about to say was honest. I believed it was. "I thought by not telling you, I'd spare you hating me on top of them. I thought by not telling you I had a chance to win you back."

"Win me back?"

"Your opinion has always mattered to me. I've been miserable not knowing you. I regret it so much."

He looked stunned, and for a moment just stood there. But then he took a chance and said, "What about Mom and Dad?"

"Do I regret not knowing them?"

He nodded.

"I knew Pops."

"And Ma?"

I looked away and shook my head.

"Jesus, there's just no end to this thorny shit, is there?" Again, this wasn't a question to be answered. "I suppose you told him to keep that secret?"

I merely shook my head again.

"Jesus Fuck have I been angry with you."

"This isn't news."

He kicked the snow from the tips of his skis and took a long look into the darkness. He didn't look at me when he said "I guess this explains why Ma always blamed you."

It wasn't a shock to hear it. And after all we'd confessed that night, the truth is I didn't have the will—then or ever, come to think of it—to muster much more than a shrug. "I didn't know that."

He shrugged, too, and looked at his watch and said, "It's almost four. You want to keep going?"

"I do."

"Tell me more about our sister?" He knocked his poles together one more time.

"I will if you take it easy on me," I said, gesturing up Broadway, unrolling before us in one long snow-covered bridge to our past. "And if you'll indulge me in some memories of jumping at Wirth. We haven't talked about it in how long?"

"About jumping? Since 1980. That's thirty-five long years, big brother."

"That sounds like a long damn time."

"It's more than half our life ago."

"We won't get it back in one night, but we've made a good start," I said.

He looked at me with that cocksure glimmer back in his eye. "That's the truth. But before we go down our favorite rabbit hole, tell me more about Helene and that day?"

And so we pushed off again, each of us in a track left by the bus, and I told him more about the half-hour I spent with our onetime sister.

*

The shock of that dead man hung like a hawser from one of us to the next—me to Pops to Sheb to Helene and back to me again. Blood pooled beneath his head and filled the air with a metallic tang. I started to cry and Helene took a step closer to a man she clearly loathed, even cocked at the waist to inspect his lifeless body.

"Don't touch him," Sheb said, his voice calm. Almost sweet. "Don't go closer."

"Jon," Pops said, grabbing my arm, "and you . . . child. Come with me." Later he admitted that in the shock of the moment he couldn't remember his own daughter's name.

She looked up at him and said, "What?" As though that one word could encapsulate the infinite questions needing answers.

"I'm taking you upstairs," Pops said.

"No," Sheb said. "Not yet. No sense putting them up where any-one passing by could see them."

It occurs to me Sheb was made for a moment like that. His whole conniving life, all his misdeeds—they lent him a grotesque confidence.

"Johannes, Helene," he said, signaling us with a wagging finger. "Come sit." He pulled two folding chairs into the shadows. "Over here while we figure out what to do."

He went back to his desk and summoned Pops, whose neck he took in his big hand and whose forehead he rested on his own. I couldn't hear what they whispered, even as much as I strained to do so. I did see their heads shaking yes and no, I saw their shoulders shrug. I saw Pops nearly eat his own balled fist.

While I watched them—and absorbed the fact that I'd killed a man, a famous family nemesis, no less—Helene watched me. I could feel her eyes on me as surely as I could the weight of my deed. When it became too much, I returned her gaze.

She didn't look away or even blink. Instead she was like a vain child studying her reflection in a mirror. Eventually she spoke. "Is he a nice man?"

Speaking softened her face, and she seemed suddenly fearful. "Pops?" I said. "Or Sheb?"

"Jakob Bargaard."

"He's real nice."

She looked over her shoulder at him, then back at me. "He seems like it. He's calm."

"I don't think he's calm now."

"Well, you just killed Andy, so probably he's a little worried about that."

Killed. She might as well have hit *me* over the head with a bowling pin for the weight of that word on my conscience. I started to cry, burying my face in my hands and picturing the prison I'd soon occupy.

"I'm sure it's scary," she said, sweet-voiced and gentle, "but I have a feeling you'll be all right."

"All right? I'm gonna go to *jail.*"

She shook her head and glanced across the bowling lanes. "I'm happy he's dead. You have no idea how terrible he was." Now she touched my knee in a motherly way. "You did the world a favor. Or at least you did me one."

I looked up at her through my wailing eyes.

"He used to beat her, you know? Mom. She had a black eye half her life."

"Lena?" I said.

She looked at me like I was a child. "Yes, that's my mom's name. That was her name."

"Why'd he beat her?" Of course I knew that some men hit their wives, but I'd never seen it. Pops never even raised his voice at Bett, much less a hand.

"He gets mad about everything. His club is going bankrupt. He owes a lot of people a lot of money. Mom wasn't drawing them in anymore."

"She was still singing?"

"What else would she do? He moved her to Wednesday nights. Jazz nights, he called them."

"She sang jazz?"

"She sang everything." She clenched her eyes shut. "*Everything.* Sometimes she still sang me to sleep." Her eyes fluttered open, almost as if she were just waking.

Bett had never once sang me to sleep. Not that I remembered. "Did she die by accident?"

"I think she probably didn't. But who knows?"

"Aren't you sad? About her dying?"

"What a stupid question."

"I'm sorry." I felt the shame of my ignorance. But for an instant it spared me the seriousness of the situation.

"It doesn't matter."

We looked at Pops and Sheb, still forehead to forehead. I can imagine now how their conversation might have gone, but on that day I was stupefied, and I asked Helene what she thought.

"Probably they're deciding if they should call the police or not."

"Should they? Maybe they shouldn't."

She shrugged. "Andy wouldn't. He'd have some creeps come and take the dead guy away. Who knows where he'd end up."

The thought that maybe we'd all just walk out of the bingo hall filled me with a sudden, galloping hope. I'd even get a sister out of it. One who seemed worldly wise and interesting. It was a hope short in lasting. My next thought was about how Pops always demanded responsibility, how he viewed it as essential for dignity. For the same reason he never missed a day of work, he wouldn't let Sheb bury Patollo without alerting the authorities. Which meant, I thought, my fate was sealed.

I started to cry again.

"Why do you keep crying?"

"Because I'm going to jail."

"How old are you?"

"Fifteen," I said, feeling every bit a child younger than that.

"They don't send kids to jail."

"What do you mean? How do you know that?"

Now she seemed exhausted. Very much like a frustrated big sister. "I bet you go to church, don't you? Every Sunday. Put on a button-up shirt, say your prayers, praise God, the whole racket."

"No."

"No what, you don't wear a button-up shirt?" She smiled and shrugged and looked again at the men. "Do you have a cigarette?"

"No," I said again. Was she turning on me? What had I done? Why did I wish to impress her? How was I thinking about anything but the dead body impaled on the bowling ball return?

"I bet you do," she said in such a way that I understood that part of the conversation was over. "Andy had to sell his house. I think he came to try to get money from that ugly man." She flicked her head at Sheb, who was now leaning against the edge of his desk. He was indeed ugly. Uglier than ever.

"Sheb wouldn't have given him anything. He keeps it all for himself."

"I respect that," she said. "God, I wish I had another cigarette. It stinks down here. What is this place, even?"

"It's the bingo hall," I answered quickly, hoping to gain back her confidence.

"It's disgusting."

I turned away but kept my eyes on her, trying to make it seem I could be as aloof. We sat there while Pops and Sheb hammered out their ruse. I retied my sneakers and glanced at her boots. I knew I'd regret not being able to devise then the questions I'd surely have later, so I let the first thought I had simply blurt out. "Why did he bring you here? What do you want?"

She studied me for a moment, even leaned forward and tilted her head like she was searching for a new angle from which to observe me. "You look different than I thought you would. So does he." She lifted her head toward Pops. "Mom always said I looked like him, but I don't. But you do, and I look like you. It's weird."

"You knew about us?"

"Of course I did. And I knew you didn't know about me. Your mom is strange. Is she crazy?"

I wasn't offended, as I probably should have been. But instead I understood her observation about Bett to be the simple articulation of a feeling I'd always had myself. As it settled on me that Bett knew about Helene but we didn't know about her, the depth of her deception revealed itself. To this day I can't fathom its machinations. I've rarely even tried. And on that day in the bingo hall basement, I gave up after the mere realization it was true, and I said what any awestruck little brother might say to his beautiful sister: "You think I look like you?"

"Duh," she said. Then a thought clearly flashed in her mind. "Wait, are you like your mom? Kind of, you know, lamebrained?"

"She's not lamebrained."

She studied my face again. "I think you are. I see it." She flipped her finger at my noggin, as though its contents spoke for themselves.

"How did you know about us? What did Lena say about me?"

"God you're spooky. Maybe you're like an idiot savant or something?" She looked at me again, her eyes as inquisitive as the policemen's surely would be soon. "Or maybe you're just freaked out right now. That makes sense, too." Then she looked away, satisfied, before leaning down and picking one of the bowling pins from the rubbish. She gripped it like a cudgel. "I have to say, you *clobbered* him." She set it down. "Does your mom sing a lot?"

"No. Do *you?*"

"Never."

"Why not?" I wanted to know her, that much was clear to me even then.

"Because songs are just pretty lies. I hate lies."

"But songs aren't singing, right? You must be a good singer?"

"I'll never know," she said without an ounce of flair. Like she'd made a choice and would abide it forever.

They were the last words she'd say to me. They might as well have been tattooed on my consciousness for the impression they made. I was spellbound by her singular conviction. By her ambivalence. By her own sense of herself. I possessed none of those things. Not then, and probably not ever.

When Pops called to us, he did so by name. "Helene," he said, his voice catching, "Jon, come over here you two."

She popped right up, crossed that dimly lit distance as if it were a walk she'd taken a thousand times before. I was slower to follow, believing, as I did, I was walking the plank to my own imminent fall.

When we stood opposite them, Pops looked at me with unvarnished conviction. "Listen to me, Jon. I'm going to say this quickly. It's not an invitation to a discussion. This is how it's going to happen. Plain and simple. We're going to call the police. We're going to tell them I clubbed Andy. He took his gun out and was threatening Sheb and I clubbed him in self-defense. You and Helene weren't even down here. You were upstairs getting a Coke from the vending machine. You have no idea what happened. Neither of you do—"

"No," I interrupted.

I don't know why I protested, but it didn't deter him in any way.

He turned to Helene and paused, his attention fully on this new daughter. For a long moment they stared at each other before Pops reached out and took her hand. "Sweetheart," he said, his voice gentle in a way it had often been with me. "Listen, we have so much to catch up on. So much to learn about each other. And we will. You can stay here as long as you like. We'll make room for you. Of course we will. But first I need some assurance that you'll do what I say." Then he addressed both of us. "The police will be here very soon"— Sheb was on the phone as Pops spoke—"and when they arrive, all you need to tell them is that you were upstairs getting Cokes. Everything else, tell the truth. But neither of you saw this, and Jon certainly didn't do it."

Already, in an instant, I had started to wonder whether I *had* done it. Clubbed Patollo, that is. Or if I'd only wanted to. Only imagined it. I might have convinced myself if I'd had more time, but Pops was ushering us upstairs and hurrying quarters out of his pocket for the vending machine.

"Over here," he said. "You both sit here. Don't go anywhere. Don't move."

And so we were left alone again, while he waited at the entrance, like a big city hotel doorman, for the police to arrive. Helene cracked open her bottle of Coke and sat back and crossed her legs. Five minutes later she removed a bottle of fingernail polish from her purse and commenced painting her nails. A red as bright as Patollo's blood.

*

"Are you sure she wasn't just fucking with you?" This was Anton, as we skied by a fried chicken place and veered left onto Golden Valley Road.

"I mean, she was definitely fucking with me."

"Do you really think she knew about us? About Pops?"

"Why not?"

367

"It sounds like she wasn't curious at all. About him or us or anything. Was she really so disinterested?"

"She thought I was a simpleton. She was curious, but she also knew she wasn't going to have anything to do with us. Pops, maybe. But not us."

"Why did she even come here?"

"Patollo made her. He wanted to wash his hands of her. That's the only thing that makes sense."

"Why would he care?"

"I gather he and Lena were a thing. Which meant Helene was a thing. One he didn't want to deal with anymore."

Anton nodded like this made all the sense in the world. "Then the police showed up?" he asked. Since we'd turned off Broadway and on Golden Valley Road, where no traffic had passed in what must have been hours, our skiing slowed. Snow came up to our shins, and we were as much as snowshoeing, shoulder to shoulder.

"About ten of them. A whole squadron."

"And you just sat there with Helene, having a Coke?"

"Yep. Until they came to question us."

To his great credit, Anton looked back cautiously. He didn't press or judge me. Or suggest I'd somehow fucked up. What I'd told him in the previous twenty minutes broadened his life in ways it would take years to traverse. I had my own discoveries to make. But in that moment, and the next couple hours, I was intent to be happy with my brother. And I think he felt the same way.

"You must've been scared."

"Never been more so."

"And Pops just stepped in front of that bus."

"He felt responsible. I mean, who knows men like Andrus Patollo?"

"I'm surrounded by them," he said, obviously too tired to revisit this particular patch of shitty ground.

"I'm a dumb ass."

"I know what you mean. I made choices a long time ago. Bad ones. Here I am."

The resignation in his voice stopped me cold. Anton stopped, too.

We both looked up at the dark, free of snow for the first time all night. The sky was as black as his eyes, which I met when I looked down.

"If you knew back then what I told you just now, would things be different?"

He shrugged. He knocked his ski poles together. "You didn't ruin my life, Jon. My life is all right. I've got Angel. I drink too much. I should quit snorting coke. I should've taken better care of Esme. But I'm happy. I work hard. My daughter's brilliant and beautiful and already ten times the person I ever was. That's something. I'll figure out the rest of it. I always have."

I started to speak, but he knocked one of his ski poles against one of mine and shook his head and smiled and he spoke instead. "Look at us. Look at all this." He lifted his arms as though to summon more snow. Or the King of Kings. "The night's almost over, brother, and we've got a couple miles to go. Let's beat the sun?"

I smiled back at him. "You think the sun's coming out of those clouds?"

"I'd bet a hundred dollars."

"You still owe me a hundred from our bet in Lake Placid."

"What bet?"

"That you wouldn't finish in the top twenty," I reminded him.

Anton scrolled his memory, smiling when he found it. "Double or nothing, then?"

"All right."

He stretched his arms and pretended to check the time and said,

"This has turned into more of a footslog than a ski, but we're up for it."

"We are."

"I know what'll fuel us on."

"Tell me," I said. "More songs?"

"I've heard about enough of your caterwauling."

"You're on a word-roll, Bargaard."

"Working to impress the judges."

"I give you a nineteen-point-five."

"That's exactly what I'm talking about," he said. "It's gonna take us a good half-hour to get there. That's plenty of time for each of us to go top five. You start?" He kicked right up next to me.

"Lake Placid, 1980, ninety-meter, first comp ride."

"You've been rehearsing this."

"Since you left me in that hospital room in Vermont thirty-five years ago, brother."

*

As the night grew its darkness like a blooming flower, we skied across the rest of that north Minneapolis road, past North Commons Park where we played Little League, past the YMCA where we took swimming lessons, past the houses of boyhood friends. We skied into the darkness of the residential stretch of that road, where not a single light shone from any window and the corner streetlights wavered as though at the mercy of the wind, which came up with the snow's passing.

This game, like the places we'd just passed, was another holdover from our childhood. Who could say which of us dreamed it up first, but we could pass hours—in cars, when we should have been sleeping, out in the summer garden picking raspberries—chronicling our five favorite or best things. Songs or pretty girls or things Pops cooked on the grill or movies or television shows. Of course, the best rounds of this game always had to do with ski jumping. But those games before 1980, the last year we played it, had been with the child Anton. And though I could have continued in our serious vein of conversation for another week, he was right that what the rest of that night called for, after all the revelations and recriminations, was a trip down happier memory lanes.

I went first because my career, such as it was, paled beside his. I took my last jump in Lake Placid at the age of nineteen. He took his in Harrachov, Czechoslovakia, at eighteen. I could curate my list from twenty or so jumps, almost all of them in Minnesota or Wisconsin or Michigan. Anton must have been off a hundred jumps in ten different countries.

The truth is, I felt giddy at the prospect of knowing this about him. Which is why I rifled through my list. I described the jump in Lake Placid, one in Iron Mountain, on the big hill at Pine Mountain. I picked a ride at Chester Bowl, in Duluth, when I beat my pal Noah Torr to win the junior class competition earlier in the year Pops went away to jail. I remembered the first jump I took off the hill we called Big Bush, the other Minneapolis Ski Club hill out in Bloomington, which even when I was jumping it in the late seventies was rickety and frankly hazardous to stand on, never mind ski down. But, oh, how I loved it. Icy and fast and with nasty headwinds. It was a jump to make us tough. The sort of hill Pops said put hair on your chest. One cold Tuesday night I went what Pops guessed was sixty-two or sixty-three meters, which would have been a hill record if it had been in competition, but since only he and I and a few other Minneapolis jumpers were there, the only record book it ever appeared in was the one I kept in my mind, for a night just like this. I could remember now as clearly as the moment after it happened the feel of lift, the pause as I went over the knoll. The certainty I would go too far. The thrill of that.

Last I described not a single jump but that season the two of us shared at the Torrs' place on Lake Forsone. And though I couldn't say this for violating the rules of the game, what I meant was that my pleasure came in watching my brother. It's just true. But I described the jumps we took as though I'd landed his. Maybe he could tell, but he only smiled and huffed as we skied on, our eyes acclimating to the dark as though we were owls winging through the drifts.

"That's already six," he said when I finished. But then he added, "I know there's still one more. Save it? We'll do number ones together?"

"Yeah," I said.

And we pushed on, past Thomas Avenue, further into the night of our lives. Further back.

Anton started as though his answer had been given a hundred times before. The easiness in his voice? I'd not heard it all night. I'd not heard it since he was ten years old.

"I had good jumps at Pine Mountain and Chester Bowl, too," he began. "And at Bush, of course. But I'm gonna go back to Lake Placid with you for number five. Not to the long jumps on the big hill, but to the jump that would have cost you your Bronco if the guys doing the marking down there had had the sense to judge *right*."

I affected the voice of a television sportscaster. "Coming in *just* shy of eighty meters, from the Minneapolis Ski Club, the youngest competitor here this week, Anton Bar*gaard*." I put the tip of my ski pole up toward his mouth, as though it were a microphone. "Tell me, young man, what's it like to miss the mark by eighteen inches?"

I could see his smile in the dark. He stopped skiing, took hold of my ski tip and brought it closer to his mouth. "I'm glad you mentioned being from Minneapolis, Howard Cosell, because anyone could see that jump went flying by the eighty-meter mark. I was short-sticked, plain and simple. And I think I know why. See, I've got a brother out here this week, and he's quaking in his high-backed boots about the shavetail coming up behind him. He *paid off* the distance markers. There'll be a full investigation, you can rest assured of that."

He dropped my ski pole and planted his own and off we went again. I believe it's true there was an energy in his stride, a second wind come up on the heels of his memory. I skied into his draft.

"Next," he said, over his shoulder and above the lifting breeze, "I'd have to go to my first competition abroad."

"Sapporo, Japan," I offered.

"That's creepy," he said, again over his shoulder. Even with all his banter he was putting a small distance between us, a ski's length already. "You're what, like my fan club?"

"I paid attention!"

He skied harder, somehow gliding in the powder. "Okurayama, Sapporo," he said. "That jump was so beautiful. You can't believe it. And huge. Practically a ski flying hill. I was seventeen. There with all the A-team guys. First jump training, I went 125 meters. It was just a perfect jump."

"Easy when you weigh a hundred pounds."

"Double that now," he said. "But I can still get around." He dropped one knee and threw his poles out wide in a powdery telemark. "I landed like that."

I believed he did. Having come from the Selmer Dahlson school at Wirth Park, Anton's landings were legend from the time he was a little boy. His skis practically one, his down-knee only an inch above the right ski, his arms ramrod straight, like he was pushing the world wider.

"Those couple of years I more or less spent living in foreign countries were a fucking blast, I'll tell you that. So many parties, so many women, so much fine foreign grass, and so little school. No wonder I fucked it all up."

I pushed hard, to catch up with him on Golden Valley Road. I wanted to spend the rest of the night happy. My whole adult life with Anton, from that day in the bingo hall, had been an exercise in regret and sadness and measured responses, and for once I wanted the old sauce again. Skiing beside him, I said, "Come on now, we're talking top five. No regrets. None of that sad sack shit."

He bit. His face relaxed and he leveled his poling and shortened his cross country stride and we went on side by side.

To put a finer point on my admiration of his success, I said, "The only reason I kept going as a writer is because I quit as a ski jumper. You inspired me that way."

He glanced at me. "You quit ski jumping because you had only one leg, right? I mean, half the time—even when you had two—you jumped like you were a wing short, but that's another story."

"Let me ask you something, smart guy: did you ever once beat me? Mano a mano?"

"I was five years younger than you!" He feigned outrage, then, as a faux consolation for me, added, "I still am."

"Youth is wasted on the young, I guess." We took a few more strides. "I'm serious," I continued. "I mean it. You were so god-damned good. If I hadn't quit ski jumping and watched you kick ass, I never would've stuck with trying to write books. The rejection was unrelenting. Any normal person would have walked away. But I thought about how you soldiered on and how I didn't. And so I kept writing."

I could tell he was embarrassed. Rather than give one of his snarky replies, he only looked dead ahead into the darkness.

"Five: Placid. Four: Sapporo. Three?" I pushed.

"The Holmenkollen, same year. I sucked, but it was a holy experience."

"I visited the Holmenkollen a few years ago. Ingrid and I did, when we traveled to Norway. It's different now—looks like a spaceship—but I can picture the old Holmenkollen. The one with the troll's hut on top?"

"That's the one. The knoll was actually a building. Like the big hill in Lake Placid. There were a hundred-something jumpers. The first fifty of them Norwegians—every one kicked my rube ass."

"You know, Pops would mail newspaper articles to me up in Duluth. Things he'd clip out of the sports section. He was so proud."

"And every time I was home, we'd grab a bottle of beer and sit at the kitchen table after Ma went to bed, and he'd tell me all about you and college. Like you were some kind of Rhodes Scholar. The Dean's lists and the academic awards. Grad school, later on."

"I barely finished grad school," I said.

"Well, I barely finished high school, so I guess we have that in common."

"We've got plenty in common," I said. "Harrachov must be on your list?"

"Number two," he said.

"That's one Pops sent the clipping for."

"I kept it myself. I don't have much of that stuff. Wish I had more."

"You've got the big posters."

"Is that sad?" he asked. "Leaving those things up there." He was talking about the pictures in his dining room, the triptych of images.

"Here's the thing: I think I have about five pictures of me ski jumping. The only good shot is from Lake Placid, but it's all blurry. And despite that, and despite the fact it's been more than thirty-five years since I crashed and burned, I still think about it almost every day. I've made a huge liar out of myself, remembering how good I thought I was. A picture like the ones you've got hanging would be a nice reminder. And a check, right? That was as good as you got, and there's proof."

"Why do you do that? Act like you were some sad sack of shit? If you hadn't crashed, you'd have gone to the Olympics. Straight up. Every time I ever strapped them on, I aspired to be as good as you. That was true in Sapporo, Oslo, Harrachov, you fucking name it. Don't act like you were a scrub."

I was taken aback. Though it's true I always added a few meters to my longest jumps in my memory, I also knew that some of them were damned good. My jumps. And what he said about the Olympics was a fact: I would have made it. For an American jumper, that's the pinnacle. Or it always has been. That's as good as we get. But it's also true that I would have been the last man on a team, and what Anton said about the fifty Norwegians beating him in Oslo could have been said of jumpers from Finland and Austria and Germany and Poland and Japan. They were all so much better than we were as nations of jumpers.

And yet, Anton had competed with them. As a gangly, knuckle-headed teenager, he competed with them. He took eighth place at the Junior World Championships as a sixteen-year-old. He may have stunk at the Holmenkollen, but at a tournament in Trondheim, Norway, he took twelfth place. Again, as a teenager. He competed with the very best the world had to offer. In Harrachov, as the young-est competitor in a field of sixty jumpers, he took eighteenth place. If he'd been able to keep his life on track—if he hadn't robbed the li-quor store in Czechoslovakia and been kicked off the team—he not only would have made the Olympic team in 1984 but might have done something once he got there. He was that kind of talented.

"Remember Pine Mountain?" he said.

"High flying Pine Mountain," I said. "I loved that jump."

"I did, too. Remember the feeling you had the first time you went off it? How it seemed like you'd never come down?"

"Exactly," I said. I even lifted one of the cross country ski tips and jutted my chin out like I was midflight. It's still something I think about, the height over the knoll on that jump in Michigan. It was legend.

"Well," Anton said, "double that, and you're in the neighborhood of Harrachov. Thirty-five or forty feet up. Going 120 kilometers an hour. The mountain wind just *howling* crosswise. And me, like you said, damn near a hundred pounds. A flea. Half the guys bailed on their first jump because it was just too goddamn frightening. They just wanted down. But I recall the first jump on that hill and the conscious thought, while I was up there, that I *never* wanted to come down. It felt like an option."

I looked over at him, skiing beside me, and admired him in a way I never had before. And not because of his prowess on one of the biggest ski jumps on the planet, or because of his accomplishments the world over, but because he'd somehow managed to live his entire life with an attitude similar to the one he described in that moment. Unabashed. All himself. I knew that first jump was the longest of his life. 160 meters. 500-some feet. I knew that his ski flying results that weekend constituted his best international finish. I knew that for one round in that competition he beat Matti Nykänen, widely regarded the best ski jumper in history. And I knew that he looked back on it all with something like disgust. The notion that he was so close to the summit and that he fell so spectacularly from it, well, it haunted him. Of course it did.

But I also couldn't help thinking that the memory and feel of that flight was something he got to walk around with every day. I was envious of that. I didn't have anything that compared.

"There were, like, a hundred thousand people there. Literally. And it was raining. And half the crowd had umbrellas open. And even now, when I feel myself in that flight, like, paused, I remember the umbrellas. I thought I might land on them, for fucksakes. And I remember how when I finally did land, that insane feeling of being back in the world, back *on* the world, coupled with the tremendous roar of that crowd, it left me feeling like a goddamned *king*."

"That's just—"

"The thing is, I remember just as well when the crowd quieted down. It was over. The jump was over. Their excitement was over. You were gone. Ma was a goddamned ghost. Pops, well, who knows. But it was all just so . . ."

I waited, absorbing the sadness of his words, suspecting the word he wanted was something like *fleeting* or *ephemeral* or *hollow*. I knew the sensation myself. But for Anton, whatever the realization he had at that moment in Harrachov followed him doggedly all the rest of his life. He never got past it. He was never able to accept it as merely *part* of the experience of life. It became, I think, the backdrop for everything. No doubt it's the reason he spent that night swilling Czech beer and then busting into the liquor store for more after everyone else went back to the mountainside hotel.

We were coming up on the parkway. Just another half block, which we skied in silence while he considered his thoughts. I imagine that's what he was doing, anyway. I was still up in the air with him in Harrachov.

"Happy," he finally said. "Plain and simple."

I'd almost forgotten he'd yet to finish. "Happy?" I said.

"Fuck yes. Glorious. Ecstatic. *Perfect*," he added. "Like this," he opened his arms wide to the night. "Which brings us to number one. You'll think I'm full of shit."

I suspected then we had the same answer, and that we were skiing to it even as we spoke in that bottomless night, even as we called up better, farther jumps.

"I know you're not full of shit, because it's the same for me."

"I can still see us all. Holy man, I can see it all so perfectly."

378

"Me too," I said, glad for the darkness.

"Pops there on the knoll."

"Acting nonchalant. Like it was the most natural thing in the world."

"He even told me it was as easy as putting my pants on."

"He said the same thing to me."

"The top of the jump was so deep."

"You had to just edge out over and hope your skis fell in the tracks."

"And of course it was icy as shit."

"Because it always was."

"And you were there watching."

Of course I was. We were always there together back then. And you boosted me up. Well, we boosted each other up. That's for damn sure. I can still see the treetops. And the judges' tower. And the lights barely making a dent in the darkness. The trees, they held their leaves way into winter. Were they oaks? What do I look like, a fucking arborist? I don't know what kind of trees they were. But they made a noise. Like a shushing sound. It made it all easier, somehow.

We were on Theodore Wirth Parkway now. A plow had come through, so the snow was mostly cleared, but enough of it remained that we could ski freely down the hill and over the train tracks. Anton took telemark turns in his cross country skis. I caught up to him and we skate skied across the long flat between downhills.

It's the place I go back to most, in my memory. You need better memories. Impossible! All I cared about was that you saw. That you watched. I raised my hand to ask was it clear. Yes you did. And I slid out over the edge of the start and I was in the inrun. Don't let that quick transition set you on your ass! No, sir. And then . . . we're in the air. For the first time, really in the air. Really up there. And on our way. That's the thing. It was just one jump. One little jump at that. But it's what launched us. And we were all there together. You remember the look on Pops's face when you got back up the landing hill to take another? Hell yes, I do. Never prouder. Definitely not. And never happier. Him or us. Him or us, yep.

He had about him, even those many years later, something like an essence. Like he was made to be on skis. Like, if he could have conducted his entire life on them, he'd have ended up the mayor of Minneapolis, or a nuclear physicist, or a movie star. Everything about him was right, just then.

He came to a sliding stop before the last downhill to the creek and the clubhouse. "I'm wrong. I thought this was a great idea, but it's a terrible idea. I'm wrong."

"What do you mean," I said. "I haven't had this much fun in a long time."

He looked off into the woods, which were buried in snow. Like we were in a tunnel. The streetlights were still on, but there was, between the snow and the sky, a *lightening*. We'd beat the sunrise after all. As sure as it would rise before the clouds.

"I mean I brought you here to make a point. To give you one more dose of shit before you hit the road again."

"I don't get it."

"I'm just wrong, that's all."

Now I looked in the direction he was staring. I saw only the snowy trees and cloudless sky, the first skein of light over the distant city. So I looked back at Anton. His face clearer now. He was crying.

"What's going on?" I said.

"I was being cruel. I wanted to hurt you."

"Whatever, Anton. Don't sweat it."

Now I pushed off first. I skated for ten strides until I had some speed up and then got into something like an inrun position, the long ski poles sticking straight up behind me. The downhill road sweeps gently to the right, and I steered myself into the center of it without breaking my position. My legs burned pleasantly, folded in half and with the rest of my body atop them. I strained my neck forward, intent to reach the bottom of the hill before my brother, which I did.

As I approached the little stone bridge over Bassett Creek, I rose in slow motion. Something like how I'd move on the take off of a ski jump all those years ago. When I was upright, I pushed my chest and chin out and pretended flight. I pretended I was in Harrachov, above a hundred thousand people. I pretended I was as good as my brother. And then I landed in a telemark, and turned to look across the fairway, into the waning darkness of our night of nights.

His shoulders were slumped and his head quietly shaking as he skied up beside me.

"I don't get it," I said.

"I'm sorry," he said as plainly as those words could be uttered.

I looked into the first hint of light and then back at him three or four times before I pushed onto the sidewalk and then over the hummock that bordered the fairway. I was halfway across it before I understood it wasn't a trick of the dawn. The jump was gone.

Last, I turned back to my brother. My eyes must have asked the question my mouth couldn't form. He said, "It was torn down more than twenty years ago. Condemned and then gone. A few of us tried to save it, but there was nothing to save it for. The whole program is moved out to Bush now. Has been for a long time."

I didn't respond. I couldn't. Instead I just stared up at the vacancy I imagined in the dark.

Close Your Eyes and
Dream It Back

MY PHONE CALLS WITH POPS started with his first from prison. We hadn't talked directly since that day in the bingo hall basement. He spoke with Bett first, then said hello to a sullen Anton, and saved me for last. He said he was sorry to have brought me into that mess and sorrier still for what I'd had to do. He said he'd never be able to make it up to me, a notion that seemed preposterous when he spoke it but took on a new and inevitable quality as the years slunk by. Almost three of them he spent in the state pen on that manslaughter charge, calling us every month to say hello. After he got out, and after I moved to Duluth, we talked on the phone often enough. Usually in the evening, after Bett had gone to sleep and I'd returned from work or classes. It was a habit we continued until the Christmas before he passed, when we spoke for the last time.

Occasionally, we'd speak about our fateful day, and of Patollo and Sheb and the ignoble turn our lives took. If those conversations were difficult for both of us at first, over the years they became almost nostalgic, and he'd usually praise me for overcoming the sorry conditions he had laid at my feet. He asked once or twice about the time

Anton and I spent at the Torrs' place on Lake Forsone, but I believe that topic stirred in him a depth of regret he found too hard to surface from, and so the rest of that story had to live inside me and me alone. I had to live alone with my memory of Helene, too. Only once or twice did Pops mention her, that young woman who swooped in under Patollo's vicious wings, and left as swiftly under Sheb's, never to be heard from again, his voice then trailing into a faraway tone that announced a depth beyond sadness.

I can't imagine the yearning. The looking back and only ever finding her absence. Sitting now at the dark window at Clara's, staring at the mellowing lake, I suppose the same fate is in store for me. That's what Doctor Zheng said, anyway. Time would win. That's exactly what she said, and of course she's right. I at least got to love my children. Pops could not have said the same at the end. Not about his daughter.

If he were alive, I'd call him now. I'd wait for his jolly voice. The happiness in hearing from me. It would do me good. But of course I can't call him. Five years is a long time to go without your father's voice. That's one thing I've learned.

Ingrid comes from the bathroom, switching off the light and fan as she opens the door. "Sitting in the dark, Jon?"

"To see the night," I say.

She sidles up beside me and puts her hand in my hair and sighs. "It's getting late. You must be exhausted."

I nod.

"My goodness, but it's lovely to be here with the girls and their prospects."

"Oh my," I say. It's almost more than I can bear. Certainly, it's more than I deserve.

"And Annika joining us tomorrow."

"Remind me not to be stupid around her?" I say.

"You've never been stupid."

That's not true, though I appreciate her saying as much. I lift my face to hers. "I'm sorry. For laying the burden of this disease at your feet. And for the stories I told you today. The fact I've kept them from you all these years. I don't know which is worse."

She doesn't reply.

"I always thought I could live without you knowing. Turns out I can't die that way, though. I suppose I'm being selfish. I'm sorry for that, too."

"You've had quite a day, Jon. We'll have time to talk about all that. It's not important we do it now. We have other things to think about—joyful things. Why don't you join me in bed? I need you to keep me warm."

She leans down and kisses my head and I say, "I'll be to bed in a little while."

"Don't fall into the lake out there." She crosses the room and pulls the covers back and climbs in.

"Sweet dreams, Ingrid."

"Oh, I hope so."

The rustle of the comforter behind me and the quiet night outside put me in mind of another fateful night's sleep, one I'm happy to revisit, even if I can hardly see it anymore. I close my eyes, and there's my little brother on the couch at the Torrs' cabin on Lake Forsone, not twenty miles as the crow flies from where I sit now. Olaf, after ushering us up there, had left with Noah the next day. Headed back home to Duluth with promises of checking in as often as he could, leaving Anton and me alone. I played brave, but by God I was scared. Olaf had showed us how to break the ice on the lake to get water. He'd told us which pile to pull our wood from. He'd bought us more groceries at The Landing, and he instructed the woman behind the counter that if we two boys needed anything else she should let us have it and charge it to his account. He told us that if either of us broke a leg on the jump, we should go to the hospital up in Gunflint and have them call him. Then he smiled and said, "Better not be you that breaks a leg, Jon. I don't know if our quiet friend is ready to make that drive yet."

In ordinary times, Anton would have smiled and taken the bait and assured Mr. Torr that he could damn well drive *any* car, broken leg or not. But this Anton still didn't respond. Not at all. In fact, the last thing Olaf said after he got in his Suburban and rolled down the window before returning to Duluth was, "Put some words back in that boy's mouth, eh?"

I said I'd try, and we watched him drive up the hill and away from the cabin. When his taillights disappeared in the gloaming, I said, "You don't have anything to worry about, got that? Fuck Sheb and that twisted school for boys." I looked down at Anton with what I hoped was a steadfastness like Pops's. "We're gonna camp here until I can figure things out."

He wouldn't look at me.

Back in the cabin, he sat by the woodstove and stared into the fire. I put a pan of baked beans to warm on the stove and made a pot of coffee and added sugar to his. He drank it like he was an old man, the scalding hotness unfelt. We ate the beans and Salted Nut Rolls for dinner and sipped our coffee and later I said we should go outside and take a piss before bed.

There was something alight in the dark. Layer upon layer of defiant light. First a new falling snow, then the fallen snow, then the sudden warmth of our bodies out in the yard. In the woods, the darkness had a firmer hold. But even still there were shadows. Mirages. Forms that might have been bears or wolves or antlered moose but were probably only pockets of darker evening. Were probably only the idea of Sheb haunting me.

To distract Anton, I told him to look up at the sky. It was filtered by the empty limbs of a thousand towering trees. But I said, "Imagine how many stars we'll see on nights like this."

He just zipped up and turned back for the cabin. When we got inside we pulled the lumpy mattress off the queen bed in the second bedroom and arranged it at the foot of the stove. We got pillows and afghans, one each from the chair and the sofa, and before we hit the sack Anton took his notepad out and wrote: WHAT ABOUT MA?

"I don't know," I said, hardly able to mask my vitriol. I hated her then as much as I ever would. I was scared. Even more afraid, I suspect, than Anton. "But we got groceries to last us a month and enough wood to build a fire to the moon and a ski jump in our back-yard. What's better even than that is we aren't stuck at St. Balder's anymore. We're our own men now. If Bett wants to find us, she won't have to look far. Mr. Torr is going to let Pops know where we are. He can tell Bett if she wants to know. But Sheb? That motherfucker? He could search for a year and never track us down. We're safe from him."

I doused the lantern and put another log on the fire and collapsed under the skunky afghan. Anton laid down, too, and we stared at the ceiling.

"I'm already too warm," I said, not even a minute into dream-time. "I guess Sheb and his twelve-degree dormitory can kiss our hot asses, eh little brother?" The nightsounds curled about the cabin. "Goddamn freak, wanted to send you away to a home for imbeciles, why? Because you're having a little trouble with your words? Fuck no."

Anton rolled over to look at me and took a deep breath.

"Get a toothbrush on those chiclets in the morning, eh? Your breath smells worse than one of Sheb's Sunday morning farts."

He laughed. Anton did. And then to put an exclamation point on it, he farted himself, and we laughed together. When we settled down, I could hear the wind swirl around the house, whistling in through the leaky windows above the couch. Through that window, I could see those tree limbs dancing.

"We're gonna be all right, Anton. I promise."

He took a deep breath and was asleep just like that. The way kids go. Me? I was so tired I thought I'd sleep forever, but I lay there a long time instead. Listening to the sweet ease of his slumber. Listening to the wind. Listening to what might have been wolfsong, or what might have been the start of the dream of the rest of my life.

"What are you doing over there, Jon?" Ingrid asks.

I turn to her, lying in bed. I can see her prettiness and already tousled hair in silhouette. She looks as if she's just woken from a dream herself.

"Just watching the lake, sweetheart."

"The deepest parts?" she asks.

She can't see my smile. It's one that finds me because I know I'll be okay as long as I've got her by my side.

"I was just remembering when Bett came up to the Torrs' cabin to retrieve my brother and me after we stayed there that winter."

"Was it really a whole winter?"

"A couple months."

"Can you imagine her relief laying eyes on you?" Ingrid says.

I'd never once thought of that, always reverting instead to my own admonishment. My seething anger. It's never found rest.

"She would have been mortified," Ingrid goes on. "Her boys alone in the woods for all that time while she was just holding on for dear life."

I have an instinct to disagree with her, but I don't. There's not enough time for that anymore.

"She just rolled up there? Said, 'Time to go home, boys'? Something like that?"

"Exactly like that, actually. Olaf brought her." I could see Bett standing in the doorway, looking around our bunkhouse. " 'You'll have to tidy up here before we leave,' she said, like we'd been at a friend's house for a sleepover. Olaf said no, we should just grab our things and leave, he'd take care of the cabin."

Ingrid rolls on her side and fluffs her pillow.

"We grabbed our things and went out to the car and that was it. We stopped for donuts at Tobies on the way home. We slept in our beds at home that night. We went back to our regular schools the next day. Pops got out of the hoosegow a couple years later. We went to dinner at Vescio's the night he did."

"All those years and you never patched things up. What a pity."

Outside the lake wasn't deep enough.

"I should have. You're right."

She sighs, a sound that tells me she's had enough of all this, and says, "Now you'll be a grandpa! Another chance for something new. A chance to do things better."

I don't disagree, but look out at the darkness and see something less than chance. Instead of admitting that, I say, "Indeed."

"Come to bed, sweet husband of mine."

"Will it bother you too much if I call Anton first?"

"Right now?"

I check my watch. "It's only ten o'clock. He'll be up."

"Are you going to tell him, Jon?"

"I think so. And anyway, I want to hear his voice."

Answering, she pulls the covers up to her chin and rolls to face away. Like she won't be listening. Like I can have my privacy.

"Sleep sweetly, sweet woman. I love you."

"Yes, you do," she says, and I can hear the smile in *her* voice.

*

"Well god*damn*, if it ain't my big brother," Anton says.

"I'd ask if it's too late to call, but you're probably just sitting down for lunch."

"That's not true! Though I did have some peanuts and a Coke. Do I need to pour myself a strong one?"

He's off the sauce. Has been since Boff's closed a year ago. The city wouldn't grandfather the adult entertainment zoning laws to Anton after Sheb died. But don't worry about him: he sold the property to a developer and is coasting on that.

"Where are you? Sounds like you're in a wind tunnel."

"I'm up in Gunflint. At Clara's. She and Delia are expecting. I'm going to be a grandfather, can you believe that?"

He coughs. I hear the click of a lighter and him taking the first drag off a cigarette. As he exhales he says, "Congratulations, Jon. That's something else." He takes another drag from his cigarette and says, "Sounds nice, having your girls up there. But surely you didn't call to tell me about your family gathering. What's going on?"

"It's not enough to just want to say hi?"

"Of course it is, but that's also not why you called."

I hear the squeak of a chair sliding out from under the table. "You're at the kitchen table, yeah?"

"I was playing solitaire with my late-night snack." He takes a drink of his Coke. "How'd you know that, anyway?"

"I heard the chair move. I thought it sounded like the kitchen."

"Your intuition remains a goddamn fright. It's like you're a witch or something."

Now I hear him open the fridge, then the crack of another can of Coke. "I gotta tell you, man, it's still weird living back here."

"I can't imagine."

He sits back down at the kitchen table. "Tell me why you're really calling?"

"I wanted to talk to Pops," I say, recognizing as I say it that it's true, "but, well, I guess that would just be talking to myself."

"I guess it would."

"How's Angel?"

"Asleep in her bedroom, actually. She's here for a visit. And she's going to the U next year, so she'll be living with us."

"That's spectacular."

"It is indeed."

"Missy's happy about it?"

"They're like best friends. You wouldn't believe it. The way they outfox me, it's not fair."

"I've spent plenty of time being outfoxed by my wife and daughters, I think I know what you mean." I pause, thinking about how much Ingrid has taught me over the years. And how much my daughters have taught me. And how I've had so little to offer in return. And now Bett streaks across my mind, as an absence as much as an image. "Maybe we can chalk up some of our thickheadedness in this department to Bett."

I can as much as see him nod, in that way of his that's come to be an acknowledgment of my unbreakable grudge. To his credit, he remains patient with me. He takes a drink, lets out a soft burp. "Ma was a lot of things, but great teacher of sons sure wasn't one of them."

"I do that out of habit more than anything," I say.

"Do what?"

"Make my faults and shortcomings her responsibility."

"Oh, she did a number on us," he admits and, as so often happens when we talk these days, the schism between us seems to shrink a little more.

"What do you know about her that I don't?"

"Everything," he says. "Not only did I take care of her the last years of her life, but now I spend a bunch of time sitting around listening to her ghost."

"The house is haunted, eh?"

"I'm not sure if it's the house or me."

"Did she ever tell you why?" My confidence in the question—asking it, yes, but also wanting the answer—trails off in a long, uncertain exhalation.

"Why what?"

"Why she took all those pills?"

He takes a drag from his cigarette and says, "Well, she was depressed, obviously. Angel majored in psychology, and she's coming to the U to get a master's degree in behavioral psych, so she has some authority on the subject. Her theory is Ma was schizophrenic. The obsessive-compulsive streak, the isolation, the suicidal thoughts. Of course, Ma wouldn't've ever had it diagnosed. She wouldn't even have thought about it."

"Schizophrenic? I'm not even sure what that means."

"It means she should've had help. A doctor and treatment. Drugs. Instead she had nothing. It means she looked deep into her unhappiness and swallowed all those pills because she thought it was the best solution. Of course, schizophrenia's just a hypothesis."

"I've spent a lot of time thinking about her today."

"Regrets?" he says.

"Sure. Of course. But mostly just wondering."

"Anything in particular? Beyond her mental health?"

"I guess I was wondering about what might really have happened between her and her sister and Pops. It must've been a soap opera the way that all went down."

"To hear Ma talk about it, Lena couldn't get out of here fast enough. She turned around nearly as soon as they got here. And because Ma relied on her as much as she did, because Lena was about the only thing she ever knew, Ma was wrecked."

"Not so wrecked she didn't stick around for Pops."

"I guess that's true."

"I wonder what happened, that time Bett went to see Lena in Chicago. When she met Helene."

"I can tell you what happened: she knocked on her sister's door, asked her if she could come in, and was told no."

"Ma told you this?"

"Yup. I would've turned right around myself, but Ma went back the next morning. That's when she met Helene. Sounds like they had a cup of tea together—she and Lena—before Lena told her she didn't want to see her anymore. Far as I know, Ma never reached out again."

"We're a long line of misfits," I say.

"We had our reasons, they must've had theirs."

"True enough. Thank God those days are behind us, eh?"

"No doubt," he says, and takes another drag on his smoke. "So, if you were talking to Pops, what would you say?"

It comes out of me like it was slingshot: "I'm sick, Anton."

He says, "I could've told you that" before he realizes I'm being serious. Then he adds, "Not the common cold, I take it?"

"Not by a long shot."

"Well, fuck," he says.

"I've been absentminded lately. More than that, really."

"Fuck," he says again. "Goddamnit."

"They call it younger-onset Alzheimer's. Things are going to get gray."

He's silent.

"I wanted to tell you." I realize as soon as I say this it's because I want him to understand how much he's come to mean to me again. And that I want to mean as much to him.

"What can I do? Do you want me to come up there?"

"You're welcome any time, of course. That'll always be true. But there's nothing to do."

"What does it even mean? Younger-onset?"

"Just that I'm young for Alzheimer's, which sounds ridiculous, given my old and creaking bones." I reach down to my leg and press back against the scars on either side of my calf. "I've still got some time, though. I mean, I might function for a couple more years."

"A couple years is good," he says.

"It's better than nothing."

"I'm sorry," he says. "I never know how to talk about this shit."

"No one does. You don't have to apologize."

"Is Ingrid all right?"

I look over at the bed. Her silhouette now cocooned under the comforter. The steadiness of her breathing makes me think she's sleeping, and not just pretending. That would be like her, easy to bed. I can hardly believe how much I love her.

"She's doing as well as can be expected. We just found out yesterday."

"When are you going to be home? We'll meet you."

"We're headed back the day after tomorrow. We'll be home by lunchtime."

"We'll bring something to eat, then. All three of us. Can we do that? Can we come?"

"I'd love that."

"Then we're all set."

"You know, I was at the Torrs' cabin today. On Lake Forsone."

"Really?"

"Well, Noah lives there now. He's turned into his dad, I guess. All alone in the middle of the woods."

Now it's Anton who doesn't say anything. I suppose it's traumatic, in a way, to conjure that place up.

"I was just thinking about the jump there. All those rides we took."

"Here we go!" Anton says, the tone of his voice instantly lifted. Lighter. *Flying.*

"It's too late to get on that train, but I just wanted to say I'm sorry. I don't think I've ever apologized."

"Hey." He says it like a scolding parent. Like he's going to dictate the rules and limits of this conversation. "You said all your apologies that night we skied across town."

"It was one of the best nights of my life."

"Me too," he says.

Then we sit in silence for a spell. I shift the phone from one ear to the other and turn from looking at Ingrid to looking at the lake again. The sky's broken and a line of stars is on the horizon. Their light shines on the clouds above them and on the edge of the water farthest away.

"You should see it here. The sky above the lake."

"I've seen it before," he says. Then he says, "I love you, big brother."

*

I've brushed my teeth and stripped down to my skivvies and taken my watch from my wrist and removed my notebook from the back pocket of my trousers and set it on the bedside table next to my watch. I've left the window curtains open because I want to see the rest of the sky come to light. I want to dream under it, beside Ingrid.

And so I rest my eyes. Finally. And stretch my ankles the way I always do. I lay my hands at my side and I lift my chin up to crack my neck but leave it jutted up there for a minute, pulling into sleep, hoping to catch the same dream I woke up from this morning.

Acknowledgments

I WAS BORN AND RAISED a ski jumper, and though I was never as good as Anton or Jon Bargaard, a considerable part of my personal story is tied to memories of those long-ago winter days. I started ski jumping at Theodore Wirth Park in Minneapolis when I was seven years old. By the time I quit at nineteen, I'd jumped with hundreds of competitors all over the country, many of whom have remained lifelong friends. Among these ski jumpers were Selmer Swanson, Tony Johnson, Craig Randall, Larry Robillard, Dustin Berger, Tim Moran, Dodd Ginn, Matt Laue, Larry Olsen, Mark Hammel, Aaron and Ed Karrow, Cal Bragger, Steve Haik, Bryan Sanders, Jason Posmer, Kurt Stein, Brett Bietila, Eric Hiatt, Tony Benzie, John and Karla Keck, Max Doman, and Walter Steiner. Jason Dove and Derick Krotz, you're two of the best friends I've ever had.

I owe special thanks to Jay and Jerry Martin, for sharing stories of their childhood and stellar careers. And to Greg Windsperger, for the fabulous conversations about the era of American ski jumping written about in these pages. Chris Broz, thanks for welcoming me back into the fold after a too-long hiatus. I refer to five real-life ski jumpers in this book: Erling Erlandsson, Arnfinn Bergmann, John Balfanz, Jay Martin, and Matti Nykänen.

My dad brought me to the ski jumps on hundreds of winter days. For this, and a thousand other reasons, thanks, Pops.

My brother, Tony, is not only one of the most dedicated ski jumpers I know, he's my best friend, too. We've told each other a lot of stories over the years, all of which have no doubt informed this book.

At the University of Minnesota Press, enormous thanks to Heather Skinner, Matt Smiley, Maggie Sattler, Shelby Connelly, Daniel Ochsner, Laura Westlund, Kristian Tvedten, and Zenyse Miller. To Erik Anderson, more thanks than I can muster for the shared vision, the unbridled enthusiasm, and the soulful connection.

Thanks also to Jesseca Salky, a champion. And to Rachel Altemose.

Thanks to fellow writers Chris Cander, Nick Butler, Nicole Helget, and Sarah Stonich for the community of support and friendship. And to Ben Percy, who has listened to me talk about this book for the better part of ten years.

Cormac and Augie, have a good one. Finn, Eisa, and Beckett, thanks for helping me keep my feet on the ground. I love you all.

Emily, if I had four hundred pages more, it still wouldn't be enough room to list all the reasons I'm grateful for you, and inspired by you. Thanks, love.

PETER GEYE is the author of five novels, including *The Lighthouse Road,* a World Book Night selection, and *Wintering,* winner of a Minnesota Book Award. He was born and raised in Minneapolis, where he learned to ski jump at Theodore Wirth Park and where he continues to live with his family.